MAROR

LAVIE TIDHAR was born just ten miles from Armageddon and grew up on a kibbutz in northern Israel. He has since made his home in London, where he is currently a Visiting Professor and Writer in Residence at Richmond University. He won the Jerwood Fiction Uncovered Prize for Best British Fiction, was twice longlisted for the International Dublin Literary Award and was shortlisted for the CWA Dagger Award and the Rome Prize. He co-wrote *Art and War: Poetry, Pulp and Politics in Israeli Fiction*, and is a columnist for the *Washington Post*.

MAROR

LAVIE
TIDHAR

HEAD of ZEUS

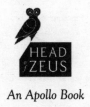

An Apollo Book

First published in the UK in 2022 by Head of Zeus Ltd,
part of Bloomsbury Publishing Plc

9 7 5 3 1 2 4 6 8

A catalogue record for this book is available from the British Library.

ISBN (HB): 9781838931353
ISBN (XTPB): 9781838931360
ISBN (E): 9781838931384

Typeset by Divaddict Publishing Solutions Ltd

Printed and bound in Great Britain by
CPI Group (UK) Ltd, Croydon CR0 4YY

MIX
Paper from responsible sources
FSC® C171272

Head of Zeus Ltd
First Floor East
5–8 Hardwick Street
London EC1R 4RG

WWW.HEADOFZEUS.COM

CONTENTS

Part One	'When the Heart Is Sick, the Body Follows'	1
Part Two	The Girl on the Beach	73
Part Three	'My Name Is Elisha Barnea'	141
Part Four	Small Time Crooks	177
Part Five	'The Watcher Is Pure in Thought and Deed'	195
Part Six	'You Won't Breathe in this Country'	211
Part Seven	Lebanon	275
Part Eight	Hava	313
Part Nine	Night Train to Cairo	341
Part Ten	Kippy	365
Part Eleven	Puerto Boyacá	403
Part Twelve	Under the Pines	439
Part Thirteen	High Rollers and Happy Pills	459
Part Fourteen	Caviar	483

CONTENTS

Part Fifteen	Arad '95	505
Part Sixteen	'Three Shots from a Very Close Range'	533
Part Seventeen	Room 816	539
Part Eighteen	Death in Cancún	545

PART ONE

'WHEN THE HEART IS SICK, THE BODY FOLLOWS'

2003, Tel Aviv

1

INFECTED MUSHROOMS

'No one knows and no one sees, and the cemeteries are full of innocent men' – Natasha

Avi was in bed with Natasha when the telephone rang.

His head still pounded with Infected Mushroom beats. The night before, at the Barbie. Strobe lights and a cloud of cigarette smoke. Ecstasy. He held a bottle of Goldstar instead of a gun. He was off duty and besides, the spare was tucked in his trousers in the back.

Figures moved through the haze, no faces. That's what made it safe for them to meet publicly like this. Not that Natasha didn't make an entrance. She always did. Came right up to him in her fur coat and gave him a kiss on the lips. She stuck her tongue in his mouth and slipped him a pill and laughed. He kissed her back, hungrily. He couldn't get enough of her.

The telephone kept ringing.

Avi fumbled for the receiver. Avi said, 'What?'

The room was in darkness but light broke in through the gaps in the Venetian blinds. He heard car horns outside, drills beating asphalt from where they were digging up the road. The voice on the other side was brief. Avi's mouth tasted like an ashtray. He kept grinding his teeth. He was bugging out.

'What is it?' Natasha said. She rolled over and pressed against him. Her skin burned hot. Avi said, 'Alright,' and replaced the receiver. He said, 'I have to go.'

Natasha pouted. She reached between his legs and smirked

when he hardened against her. She moved her hand, up and down. 'Are you sure?' she said.

Avi's teeth ground. Natasha kept stroking. Avi fumbled for the remote control. He turned on the TV.

Sirens, onlookers, a collapsed building, the metal skeleton of a burned-out car. Army and police sealing off the area. A news anchor with a microphone. Avi turned the volume up.

'Early this morning a car bomb exploded on Yehuda Halevy Street,' the news anchor said. 'As the adjacent skewer grill restaurant began to open, children walked blithely to school and tragedy struck.'

Avi's head pounded. Natasha said, 'What—?'

Her hand slackened on his prick.

'The car bomb, packed with explosives, blew up in a ball of flame,' the news anchor said. He spoke in that sort of monotonous voice with a sing-song rhythm, all the syllables spoken evenly until the last, where it rose suddenly for emphasis. *Tragedy struuck. Ball of fla-aame.* Avi's breath came ragged.

'Amidst the rubble were familiar scenes. The wounded. The dying. And the dead.' The news anchor paused.

And the deeee-aaad.

'Two children were among the casualties. Five people in total are dead, and many more were injured in the heinous attack.'

Natasha sat up, her hand covering her mouth.

'That's awful,' she said. She turned and looked at Avi. As though he could save them. He couldn't escape her eyes. They were bright and guileless. They reminded him of the Dead Sea at sunset.

He said, 'I'm mad about you, Tash.'

'Police and Red Magen David ambulances were on the spot in minutes. No terrorist organisation has yet claimed responsibility for the attack. The prime minister has spoken from Jerusalem to say no stone will be left unturned until—'

Avi pulled away with effort. He found the remote control and switched the television off. He said, 'I have to go.'

'It's not far from here,' Natasha said.

Avi grabbed his jeans off the floor. In the back pocket, inside a twist of paper. He palmed the pills and dry-swallowed. The high-pitched whine in his head turned into a buzzing of bees. He pulled on a shirt. Got dressed. Put on his gun.

'What do they need you for?' Natasha said.

'I don't know.'

He knelt down to kiss her again. She wrapped her arms around him. 'Use the back exit,' she said. 'Make sure no one sees you.'

'No one knows about this place,' Avi said.

'No one knows and no one sees,' Natasha said, 'and the cemeteries are full of innocent men.'

It sounded like something one of her brothers would say; and thinking of her brothers made the buzzing noise in Avi's head worse.

'I'll be careful,' he said.

He left her there. Took the stairs down two at a time. Stopped by the fire door exit, pulled out the black plastic film canister from his pocket and popped the lid. Tapped a small heap of the powder onto his fist and snorted it straight.

Lights brighter, sounds louder. He pushed open the doors and the sun blinded him before he put sunglasses on. The drilling from up the road dug right through his brain. No one in the alleyway. He went onto the road and saw no suspicious parked cars and nobody watching. He walked two streets over to his parked car. Got in. Popped a tape into the player and turned the volume up high, a techno remix of Beethoven's 'Für Elise' pumping out. It was by some Turkish guy, or so the pirate tape seller at the Central Bus Station told him when he got it. Avi let the beats and the piano keys swallow the noise in his head and turn it to pure music. It took him back to being, how old was he, eleven or twelve, piano lessons every Tuesday afternoon with Mrs Idelovich, who still spoke Hebrew with a thick Hungarian accent and smoked thin menthol cigarettes. She kept at him, even as he longed to be outside. It was the summer his father had the stroke, the summer Avi first met the Goldins.

He hit the gas and sped up the road, past the construction crew, the sound of the drills mixing into the electronic beat on the tape. Busy traffic along Har Ziyon Avenue. Avi hit the brakes as a taxi and an intercity Egged bus narrowly missed each other in front of him. The taxi driver leaned out of the car window, waving an angry cigarette at the bus driver.

'Watch where the fuck you're going!' he screamed.

'Who gave you a fucking license!' the bus driver shouted back furiously. 'Fucking taxis, you're like vermin in this town!'

He had the cadences of a former rabbinical student. Avi hit the horn. The two drivers glared back at him with shared hatred. Avi stuck out his badge.

'Police!' he shouted. He hit the horn again and as soon as the bus started moving Avi cut through, close enough to see the taxi driver's startled face on his right, then hit the gas again and didn't let get go until he was past Levinsky with the refugees on his right, took the corner hard and screeched onto Menachem Begin.

Trucks and taxis and courier bikes, the air hot and thick with fumes. Avi cut across traffic and took a right over a pedestrian crossing in a red light. He screamed laughter as pedestrians scattered. A right again and there was the inevitable police cordon. He screeched to a halt and staggered out of the car. The pills started to kick in.

'Yeah, yeah,' he said when a uniformed cop tried to stop him. He flashed his detective badge.

'What's going on?' Avi said.

'No idea,' the uniformed cop said. 'I'm just watching traffic.'

'Doing a good job,' Avi said. He gave him a pat on the shoulder and ambled past. He scanned the street. It was crawling with police and bomb squad and medics and journalists. Residents unhurt in the blast stuck their heads out of upper storey windows and watched the circus.

The exploded car sat on the curb. Its blackened chassis was all that was left. Glass on the floor from the exploded windows. Blood drying on asphalt. Witnesses stood talking to detectives. The car was parked in front of a money changer's. The shop's front door was blasted in and the wall collapsed but you could still make out the sign. On its left was a greengrocer and on its right a skewer restaurant, the sort of no-frills grill place that had paper napkin dispensers on the tables and you could go in and out and still get change from a fifty.

Something about this particular arrangement rang a bell in Avi's mind, and not in a good way. His head pounded and he gnashed his teeth. Ronen came over and shoved a plastic coffee cup in his hand and sniffed and said, 'You smell like a whore.'

Avi took a sip of coffee. It was hot and sweet and black. It burned on the way down. He said, 'What are we doing here, Ronen?'

'You tell me, Avi.'

'It's a car bomb,' Avi said. 'Terrorists?'

Ronen shrugged. 'Could be, could be,' he said.

'Well, what else would it be?' Something else occurred to him, something that bothered him. He said, 'How did you know where to find me?'

'I didn't,' Ronen said. 'Cohen gave me the number and said to call you in.'

'*Cohen*?' That bad feeling grew worse. And no one should have known where he was. And no one should have had that phone number. 'Shit.'

Ronen nodded to where camera crews gathered a respectful distance from the explosion, yet with the view firmly in their sight. 'He's giving a press conference any minute now.'

'What does he want with me?' Avi said. In all his time in the service he tried to stay away from Cohen.

'I'm not an oracle, Avi. Come on.' Ronen nodded to the waiting press. 'Maybe we'll both learn something.'

'Did you get me a sandwich?'

'No, I didn't get you a sandwich. Here.' He pulled out a crumpled green pack of Noblesse and tapped until a cigarette popped out. Avi took it and accepted a light. He drew smoke and sipped Turkish coffee.

'Thanks, Ronen.'

'Quiet. They're starting.'

Quiet was good. Quiet was what he needed. The pills *really* kicked in then. The electronic drum beat pounded in his head. The car still smouldering. Witnesses with bandages talking to police. Cameras flashed. He felt the journalists hush.

He followed their gaze. Saw *him*.

Tall, trim, in his late fifties maybe. Grey eyes, as cold as the sea of some distant land. Nothing like the Mediterranean. They said his eyes were cold but his blood was hot. And he was smart. Too smart, anyway, to be a policeman.

The journalists quieted down. Everything slowed and stilled. Avi froze, only his heart kept beating in tune with the music. He shook himself from the spell, took another drag on the cigarette, coughed. His hands shook holding the coffee. Cohen turned, looked at him once. *Saw* him. He nodded, then went to the media.

'Chief Inspector Cohen,' he said. 'But you know me.'

He waited. The burned car was behind him.

'A bomb attack,' Cohen said. 'Five people dead, two of them children.' He glared at the cameras. 'Just another terrorist atrocity. Just another headline in the paper.'

He shook his head at them.

'No!' he said. His voice boomed. 'What happened here today is beyond the pale. *Criminal* terrorism has taken place.'

'What?' Avi said.

'What?' Ronen said.

'The car was loaded with explosives,' Cohen said. 'It was left parked, and seemingly abandoned, in the early hours of the morning, directly outside this money changer's shop. A shop that was visited, just before the bomb went off, by businessman Aryeh Rubenstein.'

Avi went cold. The beat *pounded*. The journalists shouted questions. Cohen stood tall.

'According to eyewitnesses Rubenstein came into the shop for a period of some fifteen minutes. The bomb went off when he stepped outside. In the short delay before it exploded Rubenstein made it safely back to his car, which was parked two spaces down. He was barely hurt, and is currently being treated in hospital for minor injuries to his arm.'

'Are you saying another crime family tried to kill him?' shouted one of the reporters from Channel 2 News.

'We cannot rule anything out at this point,' Cohen said. 'But in consultation with the army and border police we are focusing on this incident as a criminal enterprise. I believe this was an assassination attempt on Mr Rubenstein's life. He was lucky – the employees of the change shop weren't. At the time the bomb went off a group of children happened to be walking to school. A boy and a girl died instantly. One more child is in hospital in a critical condition.'

Cohen's voice choked. 'Children, dead in our streets!' He waved his finger at the cameras. The reporters pulled back from his wrath. 'I assure you, the police will leave no stone unturned until the heinous assassins are brought to justice.' He paused, let his arm fall to rest, and said, 'I will now take questions.'

The reporters shouted questions. Avi turned away. He'd seen enough. He dropped the empty coffee cup on the ground and flicked away the cigarette.

'Rubenstein, eh?' Ronen said. 'That's crossing a line. A bomb in a public place like this? This is criminal terrorism.'

Avi didn't marvel how quickly Ronen picked up the new term. *Criminal terrorism*. Who came up with that one? he wondered. Probably Cohen himself.

What did Cohen want from him? What did Cohen *have* on him?

He thought of the black film canister in his pocket. He was dying for a line. Instead he followed Ronen to the witness from the grill place.

The man was an Arab, and nervous with it – as well he should be. It didn't do to be an Arab in these circumstances. Or any circumstances really.

'So?' Avi said. 'What did you see?'

'I already told this one,' the man said. He looked at Ronen pleadingly. 'What am I going to do now?' he said. 'They won't pay me if the restaurant's not open.'

'You're lucky you're not in a cell,' Ronen said.

'A cell? What do I need with a cell? I told you, I'm the dishwasher.'

Ronen sighed, pulled out the Noblesse, offered the witness one. The man took it gratefully and lit up. 'It was terrible is what it was,' he said. 'Those kids, they go past here every day that same time. Never could have imagined it. I saw the car but I just thought… Well, nothing. It was just a car.'

Avi hopped from foot to foot. Avi helped himself to Ronen's cigarettes. He said, 'Forget about the kids. Tell me about the man in the car.'

'Him?' The dishwasher looked even more nervous. 'Big guy, pot-belly, came in a black Mercedes. Came out the back seat, you know. Had a driver. The driver stayed in the car. He had another guy with him, stood outside the door the whole time he was inside.'

'How did you see all this?' Avi said.

'I was having a smoke. I get in a bit early, before the kitchen opens.'

'You recognise him?' Avi said.

'Who?'

'The man.'

'I don't know anything,' the dishwasher said.

'Yes or no?' Avi said, only a little threatening.

'Maybe, I don't know. He comes sometimes. Almost every week maybe. He goes in empty, he comes out with a bag.'

'What's in the bag?'

'How should I know?' the dishwasher said. He gestured at the ruined front. 'It's a change shop,' he said. 'What else they got in there but money?'

'What happened when the man came out?' Avi said.

'Nothing. He walked to his car and his bodyguard followed. The kids were just going past. I had my cigarette down to a stub, I was just about to go in to start cleaning. Then like two seconds later the bomb went off.' He looked at Avi with eyes like a wounded bird's. 'I'm lucky to be alive,' he said.

'Aren't we all.'

'Guess he got lucky too,' the dishwasher said.

'I guess he did,' Avi said. Someone called out his name and he turned.

Saw Cohen with a *come here* gesture.

'Thanks,' Avi said to the dishwasher.

'For what?' the man said. But Avi was no longer listening.

He went over to Cohen. Stood to attention and saluted.

'At ease,' Cohen said. 'What is this, a parade?' He extended his hand. 'Detective Avi Sagi? I'm Chief Inspector Cohen.'

'I know who you are.'

Cohen looked at him with some amusement. 'And I know who you are,' he said.

'Yes, sir.'

'I read your reports.'

Avi sweated.

'Yes, sir,' he said.

'Stop that. You can call me Cohen.'

Avi nodded.

'How come you never came to me?' Cohen said. Sounding almost wounded. 'I have a place for good people in my team. And I hear you're good people, Avi.'

Good people.

Avi ground teeth. Cohen nodded as though something had been decided.

'Come on,' he said.

'Where?' Avi said.

But he thought he already knew.

2

THORNS AND THISTLES

'If you wrong us, shall we not revenge?' – Shylock

The summer of his piano lessons with Mrs Idelovich, the summer he met the Goldin brothers for the first time, Avi's father had a stroke. He remembered the hospital from that time: the linoleum floors and that scratchy sound they made when you walked on them, an unexpected cry or a sob from a room down the corridor catching him unawares and making him jump, the light that was always too bright, men smoking in the corridors. Now the walls were the same off-white but there were new 'No Smoking' signs everywhere and outside the door to Aryeh Rubenstein's room stood two armed police officers.

Cohen met Avi at the hospital entrance. They'd driven over in separate cars, a small mercy for which Avi was grateful. He chewed on a mint on the way over and gripped the wheel hard.

'A heinous crime,' Cohen said. He looked at Avi dispassionately, like a biology teacher about to demonstrate surgery on a frog. 'It will not go unpunished. Retribution, Detective Sagi. "Vengeance is mine," said the lord. Deuteronomy 32:35. "Whoever sheds the blood of man, by man shall his blood be shed." Genesis. Do you know, I have a granddaughter the same age as those children who died?' He gripped Avi by the shoulder. Avi winced.

'If you wrong us,' Cohen said softly, 'shall we not revenge?'

'Exodus?' Avi said.

'*The Merchant of Venice*,' Cohen said. 'Shakespeare.'

'Ah.'

'I want whoever did this, Detective Sagi.'

'I understand.'

'Do you?' Cohen said. 'Do you understand me?'

Avi stared into Cohen's eyes. Saw the cold absolute that was there.

He swallowed.

He said, 'Yes.'

'Then come.' Cohen let go of Avi's shoulder.

They walked up stairs and down corridors. A room with the door half open, and behind it Avi saw a small girl lying on a bed, bandaged and surrounded by monitors. He saw her heart beat, peaks and troughs on a monitor. A nurse inside glared at him and shut the door.

That summer his father sat slack in the living room, in the armchair where he used to read the newspaper. The house was so quiet that summer, and only the sound of the piano keys as Avi haltingly tried to play 'Clair de Lune' and 'Für Elise'. The sound of the damn keys. The house was so quiet and the blinds were drawn and only his mother came and went. He was desperate to escape that house. He wanted to break things.

'At ease, gentlemen,' Cohen said. The two policemen standing guard saw him and relaxed. Cohen slipped one of them a fresh packet of Marlboros.

'Take a smoke break,' he said.

'We're not supposed to—' the other policeman said before his partner grabbed him by the arm and dragged him off.

'Thanks, Cohen.'

'Take your time,' Cohen said. He pushed the door open and Avi followed him in.

'Stay back—' A heavyset man tried to block their way. Cohen hit him in the stomach and then kneed him in the face on the way down as the man collapsed. Avi winced at the sound of the bone cracking.

'Hey, what— Oh, it's you, Cohen.'

The bodyguard groaned and stayed on the floor. Avi helped him up.

'Good thing this is a hospital,' he said.

'Go get cleaned up, Semyon,' the man on the bed said. Rubenstein. He turned a belligerent face on Cohen. 'What do you want? Who's the kid?'

'He's with me.'

The bodyguard, Semyon, left the room. Now there were just the three of them, and Avi really didn't want to be there at all. He felt things were slipping out of control. Perhaps they had been for some time.

The last time he saw Rubenstein in person, Avi was a kid and it was the night Shai Goldin got shot in the legs.

'Listen,' Rubenstein said. 'I had nothing to do with it, Cohen. Fuckers tried to kill me!'

'You make me look bad, Aryeh,' Cohen said. 'A bomb, in a residential area? Civilian casualties? You've lost control of the situation.'

Rubenstein stood up glaring. Avi saw he only had minor injuries, a scratch on his cheek and an arm in a sling. 'No one can come at me like this, Cohen. It's a declaration of war.'

'I can't have a war, Aryeh.'

Rubenstein shrugged, one-handed. 'It's not up to you and me now, Cohen,' he said. 'Now it's up to God.'

'You do nothing,' Cohen said. 'Is that clear?'

'You're ordering me?' Veins stood up in Rubenstein's face. 'You forget yourself.'

'We'll solve it clean.'

'Clean,' Rubenstein said. He sounded like he'd never heard the word and didn't like it much. 'Look,' he said, 'even if I wanted to, the boys have their blood up, don't they. They want action.'

'Then hold their leash.'

'I can give you a few days,' Rubenstein said. 'A week, maybe. Shit like this is bad for business. But I want heads.'

'Any idea who did it?' Avi said. His voice felt rusted with disuse. Rubenstein turned his attention on him.

'I'm just a businessman,' Rubenstein said. 'I have no enemies.'

'Alright,' Cohen said. 'I want you lying low for a while. Take a holiday to that place you have in Cyprus, maybe.'

'Oh, believe me, they won't get a shot at me twice,' Rubenstein said.

'Give us a minute, Avi,' Cohen said.

'Sure.'

Avi went out. He shut the door. He leaned back against the wall and took deep breaths. His hands shook. Something vibrated in his pocket. He fished out his phone, flipped it open. Two messages, one from Natasha – *Need to see you.* The other from Benny requesting a meet.

Shit, and shit. And he couldn't go anywhere *near* Natasha, not now. He followed the sign to the restrooms, checked the stalls were empty, did a line of coke, then he figured what the hell and did another one, which was all that was left at the bottom of the film canister. He stripped off his shirt and washed under his armpits with paper towels. He drank from the tap, cupping the water in his hand. He dried himself on the electric dryer.

When he got back the door was open, the bodyguard was back with a plaster and a scowl on his face, and Cohen was leaving. The two cops were still on their smoke break.

'What about my police protection?' Rubenstein said.

'I am your police protection,' Cohen said.

Avi fell into step behind him. Down the echoing corridors and past nurses and doctors and worried relatives, until they were finally out in the hot and humid air. Avi could smell gasoline, cigarettes, the sea.

'I knew your father,' Cohen said.

'You did?'

'He was a good man. Honest.'

'Yes.'

'It was too bad, what happened.' Cohen shook his head. '"Cursed is the land for you",' he said. '"In sadness shall you feed upon it all your days. And thistles and thorns it will grow for you".' He searched Avi's face. '"For dirt you are and to the dirt you shall return".'

'Genesis,' Avi said. He still remembered at least some of his Bible lessons. He had a sudden moment of déjà vu, like he'd experienced a moment much like this once, long ago.

'Yes. I want you to find the men who did this, Avi. Do it right. Do it quick. Before Rubenstein unleashes his dogs and my city goes up in flames. Can I rely on you?'

'Yes,' Avi said. He knew saying anything else would be a mistake. Thorns and thistles, he thought.

'I already spoke to your supervisor,' Cohen said. 'You're seconded to my unit at Serious Crimes until I say otherwise. But I want you flying solo on this. Keep me informed of your progress, but only me.' He passed him a phone. Avi took it numbly.

'And Avi?' Cohen said.

'Yes?'

'When you find them, if they give you trouble... You know what to do.'

The sun was already high in the sky and it erased the shadows. Avi felt the gun still tucked into the small of his back.

He said, 'Yes, Cohen.'

'You're a good man, Avi.' Cohen slapped him on the back.

Avi stared after him. His phone buzzed again.

He flipped it open.

'Yes?'

'Not on the phone,' Benny said.

Avi sighed. Avi fidgeted.

Avi said, 'I'll be there in fifteen.'

3

FRESHWATER EELS

'You don't pick a fight you can't win' – Benny

Benny Pardes sat where he always sat these days, behind the table in the old Persian restaurant that's been there longer than Avi's been alive. Celebrity pictures hung on the walls, from earlier, better days when everyone used to come to the Shiraz, faces Avi could vaguely remember from the eighties: a children's TV presenter, smiling widely with the owner, a couple of politicians, a few generals in uniforms, one former prime minister.

Now there was just Benny, and the wallpaper was peeling and there was dust in the corners. The lone waiter hovered, then vanished back into the kitchen.

'So nu?' Benny said. 'This is bad business.'

'Yeah,' Avi said. He felt reckless. 'You got any coffee?'

'Yossi, bring coffee!' Benny shouted. He said to Avi, 'You want something to eat?' Then shouted, 'Yossi, bring something to eat!' without waiting for a reply.

'Sit, sit,' he said. 'What are you standing up for?'

Benny wasn't a bad guy as far as bad guys went. The waiter showed up with black coffee and a plate of some sort of lamb stew on rice. Avi's stomach knotted and unknotted. He grabbed a fork and dug in without waiting. He tasted lime, parsley, green onions, lamb.

The food went down hot. Benny grinned.

'That's Ghormeh Sabzi just like mother's,' he said.

Avi didn't reply. He chewed on lamb and beans. Benny watched him eat. There was something disconcerting about Benny watching him eat.

'You're too skinny,' Benny said. 'You should eat more. You need a girl to look after you, Avi.'

'I don't need a girl,' Avi mumbled.

'No?' Benny watched him. 'Heard you had one all the same.'

Avi choked on a mouthful and Benny yelled, 'Yossi, water!'

The waiter came over with a jug and glasses and set them down.

'You need to eat slow,' Benny said.

Avi gulped water. Avi said, 'What girl?'

'How do I know? She's your girl.'

Avi shrugged. 'There are just girls, you know?' he said.

'Married almost thirty years,' Benny said. 'What do I know about girls?'

'Cut the shit, Benny,' Avi said. He put down the knife and fork. The plate was empty. 'What do you want?'

'Got a job for you.'

'*Now*?'

'What better time? All the little mice are busy elsewhere.'

'I can't. I'm on this case, Benny.'

'You? Why you?'

Why me, Avi thought. He said, 'Orders.'

'Whose orders?' Benny said.

'Cohen,' Avi said. 'Cohen gives the orders.'

Benny shouted, 'Yossi, pastries!' The waiter was already approaching with a plate and a coffee pot. He refreshed both their drinks. Avi took a pastry.

'It's good,' he said, his mouth full.

'You bet it's good. Best Persian restaurant in the country,' Benny said. 'What does Cohen want?'

'He wants to catch whoever did this. Do you have any idea who did this?'

Benny brooded. 'I told you to stay away from Cohen.'

'I did. He found me.'

'Has he got anything on you?'

Avi didn't answer. Benny said, 'Well, I can think of some

names. Could be the Goldins, could be Aharoni, could be Bogdan and those fucking Russians.'

'Bogdan? I thought you worked with him.'

'Sometimes, sometimes. I like peace, myself. You don't pick a fight you can't win, that's how you stay in business. But there's bad blood between him and Rubenstein. The Russians have no code. Still. I don't know.'

'Come on, Benny, give me something.'

'I still need you to do that job. Same payment as last time. And don't give me that look, Avi. Save those pretty eyes for the girlfriend.'

Avi drank coffee. Avi thought.

'Tell me who you know could pull a job like that,' he said.

'The bomb?' Benny rubbed his face. 'The Abadis, in Jaffa. Their dad, Abu-Ramzi, he had a construction business. The oldest brother, Ramzi, he was playing with nitro-glycerine before he could read. Got a real talent for it, too. The younger brothers, Ahmad and Fuad, they help with the family business.'

'You know them?'

'I don't like bombs,' Benny said. 'Too many things to go wrong. You'll have to ask around.'

'Alright.'

'What do you make of Cohen?' Benny said unexpectedly.

Avi thought. 'When I was a kid,' he said, 'we used to visit my cousins sometimes on their kibbutz. I don't know if my mum liked it much, going there, but me and my dad did. I was only small, and the kibbutz was on a hill, and if you went all the way down to the bottom they had a swimming pool. It was a proper big one, too, Olympic sized, and there was a children's pool with a real water slide. We used to go on Saturday and the grownups would talk and smoke and I played with my cousins. It was nice.'

Benny regarded him with some amusement. 'Is there a point?' he said.

'The pool was at the bottom of a wadi and the wadi still had a brook running through it. When they built the pool they rerouted the water around it but you could still see it where it fell down into a sort of rock pool before vanishing. It went all the way to the sea. It was cooler there, in the shade, away from the pool, so we'd sometimes go over there and just stand and look at the water. And one day when we went, there were all these dark shapes moving in the water. They'd come down the waterfall and into the rock pool and they went round and round and the water churned. They were long and sleek, and if you tried to catch them they slipped right out of your grasp and then they kept going.'

'Eels,' Benny said.

'Eels,' Avi said. 'What I learned about eels is, they start off in saltwater but as they approach the shore they start changing physically, and by the time they get into a river and start swimming upstream they're freshwater eels. And they just keep going upriver. Over dams, weirs, waterfalls. And they hunt all the way. They hide and they ambush their prey. They're killers. And just when you thought you got a handle on them they turn around and go back and you realise, all this time, you only thought you knew what they were about but really you were just staring at your own reflection in the water the whole time.'

'How old were you then, again?' Benny said.

'I don't remember. Six, maybe.'

Benny shook his head. 'So that's Cohen?' he said.

'I guess. I don't really know him.'

'Well, he knows you,' Benny said. 'So you'd better get to work. Word from the top is we're all to lie low and wait.'

The top, Avi thought, being Rubenstein.

'So I don't have anyone I can send for work,' Benny said. 'You know that social club on Allenby?'

'The one near the strip club?'

'That's the one.'

'Right, yes.'

'Make it quick,' Benny said. He took out a thick envelope from his pocket and slid it across the table. 'A taste, Avi. The rest when you finish. You know the drill.'

Avi opened the envelope. Cash, and a photo of a guy. He looked at the photo and slid it back and put the money away.

'Alright. And thanks for the tip.'

'I'm here to help, officer,' Benny said. 'Anything you need.'

Avi stepped out into sunshine past Benny's bodyguards who stood at the entrance to the Shiraz. He nodded, they nodded. Benny had a piece of most everything in South Tel Aviv. Money change, protection, brothels, gambling, drugs. Even black market organ transplants, which was a real growth area. Grey market really, there was no real law against it. Plus he had legitimate businesses like shawarma and juice stands all over the place, the strip club on Allenby, and a lock on greengrocer stalls in the Carmel Market. Anything that dealt in cash and could be used to clean money that was dirty. He didn't touch the bottle recycling business, though. More people died over empty bottles in Tel Aviv than died of fever in the old days. No, that was one war Lior and Yair Goldin won, though it cost them.

He wondered if they were the ones who ordered the hit on Rubenstein. They were the obvious choice.

But he didn't really care.

He had cash in his pocket and an empty film canister that needed filling with something other than film. He was full with whatever that Iranian lamb dish was and hopped up on black coffee. So he stepped out into sunshine and the pedestrian street of Neve Sha'anan, which back in the day was full of good old tradesmen like printers and shoemakers, not to mention ideologues with utopian dreams who left Jaffa to build a new city here, where no city had been.

Now it was full of African refugees and Asian and Eastern European migrant workers and still sold shoes and cheap clothes and cheap vegetables. Laundry hung from the balconies on the second and third floors where people crammed together into apartments too small to contain them. On blankets on the pavements lay pirate DVDs and cassettes. Avi didn't recognise half the titles. He picked up a packet of cigarettes from a stall manned by an old Somali and went in the direction of the old bus platforms. Most of the platforms were gone but a few still hung on unused. He passed the Kingdom of Pork butchers and took a left. He passed the abandoned bus terminals and reached Fein Street.

Avi was aware of eyes on him. The building that sat at No. 1 Fein Street used to hold the Egged Bus Company offices back when the station was in operation. Now the entire complex was taken over by drug dealers, pimps and prostitutes, and if you wanted a heroin fix or a discount blowjob it was the place to go. Avi *was* discerning, and he let his service weapon show as he walked past, and the junkies who congregated outside gave him the finger but that was it.

He knew that inside the building, behind the shuttered windows he was seen and registered. But no one at No. 1 Fein Street really worried about the police. Every time there was a raid people got arrested and then everyone went back to work. The police were like rain, people said, it fell on you every now and then but it didn't damage the crops.

Avi walked past faded peep show halls and apartment blocks where people still lived despite it all when he heard shouting. A guy was running with his trousers down in an alleyway and his dick flapping about and he was screaming murder as he tried to catch up to a woman with long matted hair who was running away from him as fast she could with a man's leather wallet in her hand. She was coming towards Avi so when she was almost on him Avi bunched a fist and hit her quick and hard in the nose.

The woman crumpled to the ground. Avi grabbed the wallet off her. He saw American hundred dollar bills. Who carried that kind of money in this kind of place? The man came up to them, panting.

'Did she blow you first, at least?' Avi said.

The man glared at him. 'No,' he said. 'She wanted cash in hand.'

'That's a lot of money. Pull your pants up.'

'Oh, right.' The man reached for his trousers.

The woman said, 'You broke my fucking nose!'

'I'll break your fucking nose,' the man with the trousers said. He turned to Avi. 'Give me back my wallet.'

Avi flashed him his badge. The man blustered, then said, 'Well, thank you, officer. May I have my wallet back now, please?'

'You're a policeman?' the prostitute said. 'Great. Just great.'

'How much is in here, twelve hundred?' Avi said. 'What are you, some big shot?'

'I do business, what?' the man said.

'And you just fancied a trip to the junkyard to play pin the tail on the donkey?'

'I was just—'

'Forget it,' Avi said. 'Here. This is for you.' He passed the woman on the ground a hundred dollar bill.

'Nice,' the woman said.

'Hey!' the man said.

Avi extracted two more bills from the wallet, thought about it and added a third. He put them in his pocket.

'These are for the tax,' he said.

'What tax!' the man said.

'And this is yours,' Avi said, passing him back the wallet. 'Anyone have a problem with that?'

'Not me,' the woman said. 'Thank you, officer.'

The businessman stared at Avi, then stared at Avi's gun, then nodded reluctantly.

'No problem,' he said.

'That's right,' Avi said. 'Now get the fuck out of here, both of you.'

'I'll blow you for a fifty,' the woman said.

'Another time,' Avi said. He walked on and reached a small shop front with a sign above it that said *Bentovich Books*. There were dusty textbooks in the window, geography books by the long-deceased Y. Paporish with maps that showed countries that no longer existed. Avi pressed the buzzer. An old worn-out face peered at him through the metal bars of the security door.

'Oh, it's you.'

The door unlocked. Avi went in.

The shop was dark and dusty. Books were piled everywhere, paperbacks in English and French vying with forgotten Hebrew novels. Ancient comics dangled from the ceiling on strings. A radio on a shelf played Dudu Zakai singing 'Elad Went Down To The Jordan' and the music, slow and old-fashioned, momentarily transposed Avi into another decade in time.

Hung on the wall was a detailed artist's illustration of the imagined future of Tel Aviv's Central Bus Station. It showed a graceful tower rising into the sky, a sort of fifties futuristic construction decorated with spiral walkways and floating flower gardens, and showed happy, well-fed, well-dressed residents, the men in suits and ties and the women in floral dresses, all smiling and holding hands as they beheld this miracle of engineering.

'Makes you cry, doesn't it?' the proprietor said. He gestured to the street beyond the bars outside. 'You know, only last week someone was murdered just across the road. It's going to the dogs, Avi, and I'm the only one left. And how am I supposed to pay the rent?'

'I'm sure you can figure out a way, Bento,' Avi said.

'It's Mr Bentovich to you,' the man said. He was small and rotund with bright feverish eyes behind thick glasses. 'What can I get you, motek? You want porno? I got some German stuff just come in, real raw, sado. Whips and chains, that sort of thing.'

'What? No.'

'I got some Japanese peeing stuff if you prefer.' Bento regarded him mournfully and without much hope. 'I don't suppose you came in to buy a book.'

'I did not.'

'This used to be a real place,' Bento said. 'All the kids in the neighbourhood used to come in for their textbooks. I used to stock literature. Everyone came here, Hanoch Levin grew up around here, he used to come in here all the time.'

'Really,' Avi said. The music was getting on his nerves and so was Bento. And he didn't give a shit about Hanoch Levin. He took out a hundred shekel bill and waved it at the bookshop proprietor. 'What else you got, Bento?'

'Alright, Avi.'

Bento went round his desk. He pushed a button and a drawer slid out. Bento peered at its contents through his glasses. Avi saw neat little packets of all kinds of things.

'What you after, Avi? I got hash from Egypt, weed from Lebanon, ecstasy from Holland, really top grade, I've got khat, you ever try it? It's what all the old Yemenites who came over in Operation Magic Carpet back in the forties use.'

'The stuff you chew?' Avi said.

'That's it. Gives you a buzz.'

'No. I want the usual.'

'Coke and speed,' Bento said, 'the Policeman's Special. Sure. I got some of that.'

He picked a box of pills from the drawer and a bag of powder.

'Listen, Bento,' Avi said. 'You sell to any Arabs?'

'Arabs? What do I want with Arabs?'

'Jaffa Arabs,' Avi said.

'Listen, bubeleh,' Bento said. 'I don't discriminate. I don't check people in the tsitsiyot, you know what I mean? Jew, not a Jew, what do I care? You look around this neighbourhood recently? I sell meth to Thais and hash to Somalis and weed to rich white kids from Ramat Gan and coke to anyone who's got the money. The only thing I don't touch is the junk. I don't need the balagan. You see what it's like out there? It's like a jungle. I don't touch junk. Here's your order.' He pushed the drugs across the desk.

'Thanks.' Avi laid down cash. He pocketed the product.

'You planning some sort of party?' Bento said. 'This shit will keep you awake for days.'

The music on the radio, mercifully, ended and the news came on. 'Army units are sweeping through the Palestinian Territories today following a car bomb attack in central Tel Aviv,' the newsreader said. 'No organisation has yet claimed responsibility. Police are not ruling out an underworld hit gone wrong, but the Judea and Samaria Division Brigadier General's office has confirmed the army is taking an active role in investigating terrorist links and conducting mass arrests across the Territories. A number of heavily injured victims remain in hospital, one in critical condition. American forces continue to fight in Iraq as the hunt for Saddam Hussein intensifies. The World Health Organisation has issued a worldwide alert on a new deadly virus currently sweeping through Asia. SARS originated in China and currently—'

'It's terrible, is what it is,' Bento said. 'Those poor children on the news.'

Avi laid down a couple more notes. Bento's eyes followed the money. 'Arab customers,' he said quietly. 'Jaffa.'

Bento swallowed. 'You'd have to narrow it down a bit for me,' he said. 'You got a name?'

'Ramzi Abadi,' Avi said.

'Abadi, Abadi,' Bento said. 'No, I don't sell to those, Avi, sorry.'

'Then who does?'

'Listen, what's this about?' Bento said. 'I don't want any trouble, you understand?'

'No trouble,' Avi said.

'There's a guy called Chamudi, he works with the Goldins. Works with all kinds of people. People from Gaza, you know what I mean? You want to move so much as an eighth in Jaffa you have to go through him. Alright? I'm just small time, motek. I don't need *my* shop blowing up.'

'Understood,' Avi said. Bento grabbed the money off the table.

'I hate this place,' he said. 'You know?'

'I know,' Avi said.

'I used to sell books.'

'Whatever you say, Bento. I'll see you.'

'Just take it easy on the stuff, motek.'

4

A TURN FOR THE WORSE

'Not a fucking word' – Avi

All that summer with the piano lessons and that oppressive silence broken by the keys, and the hushed house with the blinds always closed, any chance he got Avi ran out. He ran wild in the neighbourhood that summer because there was no one to tell him not to. He wanted to run. He wanted to break something.

He played with his friends from the neighbourhood, but they had orderly homes to go back to and orderly summer lives in which he could no longer take part. They went swimming in the Kinneret or the Sakhne, or drove down to Eilat with their parents, or to visit the Druze villages in the Carmel, or to the cinema or to the nearby Safari Park.

Avi didn't do any of that.

From time to time they'd play on the road that separated the neighbourhood from nearby Givat Shmuel. There was another group of kids who'd come down most days, from the opposite direction, and when they'd see Avi and his friends they'd raise a battle cry and then storm across the road, waving sticks, and Avi and his friends would run. One day, Avi stood there on the warm asphalt and saw the boys come down with the sticks, and he didn't run. He didn't know why. He was tired of running. He wanted something – anything – to happen. The other boys surrounded him.

'What's this?' one said, poking him with a stick.

'Does it speak?'

They laughed. 'Hey, Goldin! Goldin, come see this!'

They parted way as a boy the same age as Avi ambled over. He was shorter than Avi, and wore glasses, and his hair was dark and cut short in a buzz cut. He looked at Avi curiously.

'Why didn't you run?' he said.

'Why should I?' Avi said.

The boy punched him in the stomach, quick and hard. Avi doubled over. The pain made tears come, but he wouldn't cry, not in front of them. He straightened up slowly.

'That's why,' the boy said.

Avi blinked back tears.

'You hit like a girl,' Avi said.

Someone in the gang laughed and someone else slapped him on the back of the head and told him to shut up, but neither Avi nor the other boy paid it any attention.

'What's your name?' the boy said.

'Avi. What's yours?'

'Lior.'

'Goldin, come on!'

'I'll see you,' Lior Goldin said. Then he and his gang ran off.

Avi lit a cigarette as he walked back to his car. Last night was fun, dancing with Natasha at the Barbie. Last night life was good and he didn't have any worries. Then came the morning and kicked him until it hurt. He needed, he thought, to take stock of the situation. Nothing about it was right but he didn't know what he could do other than follow the road in front of him. He wanted to call Natasha. He wanted to see her.

He leaned against the hood of his car, thinking. He dribbled smoke. A lot of people wanted Rubenstein dead – that was a given. Someone had to give the order and someone had to most likely hire private contractors to carry out the job. He didn't know these Abadis but he figured Benny wouldn't have fed him their name unless it meant something.

Might as well check it out.

He thought of popping another pill but his heart was racing and his vision was getting blurred. Avi blinked until the world came into focus again. No. Better stay clean for a while. Drink some water. It was hot. He blinked back sweat. It was a terrible thing that happened, he thought. He knew that on some intellectual level. The blood on the ground, the collapsed shop, that witness with the look of shock still in his eyes. Just details.

'He's alright,' Lior Goldin declared, the third time the kids came down and Avi didn't run. And that was that. That day he went with them. They walked down to the brook and looked for frogs. One of the kids brought a half-empty packet of cigarettes he'd stolen from his dad and they all took turns smoking. They all coughed and laughed. Then they tossed stones into the brook.

And no one cared that his dad was a police officer, or what happened to him, and no one was going swimming in Eilat. They were just there, the day just was, a perfect summer's day all for them. And Avi forgot about home, for just a little while he could be only himself, just him and his new friends.

It was a good day.

He tossed the cigarette and got behind the wheel and hit the gas. Followed the same route until he was back in the hospital parking lot. His numbness was replaced by a burning rage. It gave him clarity. Clarity was good. He almost ran into the building. Back to the room he passed, where the little girl lay in the bed and the monitor charted the course of her heart as it struggled to beat. He came to the place but it was empty.

'Where is she?' he said. He found a nurse. 'Where is she!'

The nurse shook him off. 'Surgery,' she said. He showed her his badge.

'You can't go in there,' she said.

'What happened to her?'

The nurse looked at him undecided. 'She took a turn for the worse,' she said. 'The doctors are doing all they can.' She touched his shoulder, lightly, and he almost cringed from her touch.

'I hope you catch them,' she said. 'Those animals.'

'Can I see her?'

'I'm sorry. No one can go in.'

She looked at him a moment longer and then turned and walked away. He stared after her. When he stepped back outside he saw Cohen's car sliding into an empty space. Cohen unfolded himself from the driver seat.

'What are you doing here?' he said when he saw Avi.

'She's in surgery.'

Cohen's face softened. 'I know,' he said. 'I came as soon as I heard.'

'I'm going to get them,' Avi told him.

'I know you will. I'm counting on you.'

Avi went back to his car. He stared at the wheel.

He whispered, 'Go get them, then.'

He had no music on the ride across town. He rolled down the window and let the hot air on his face and he thought about that little girl fighting for her life on that hospital bed. He drove through Allenby and when he got to the place he stopped. He checked the glove compartment for the throw gun. Better do it quick. He went down the alleyway to the back. Rubbish bins and a rat the size of a kitten ran away. The door to the place was unmarked. Avi stood flat against the wall. He put on a ski mask and gloves. He waited.

When the door opened it was to let a middle aged man out. The man wore jeans and a chequered shirt and the shirt was tucked tightly into his jeans and his belly spilled out over the belt. The man was in a good mood and sang 'Hava Nagila' softly to himself and did little dance steps. He smelled of booze. Avi slipped in. He hit the bouncer over the head with the butt of the gun and whispered, 'Not a fucking word.'

It was around noon outside but it could have been any hour inside. The bouncer sat down with his back to the wall. He wasn't going to put up a fight. Beyond the antechamber there was a bead curtain and beyond that Avi could hear the clink of chips and men muttering to each other. He could smell cigarettes. He stole across and peered in. There were no windows. There was no bar but a table was set up against the far side of the room with a bottle of whiskey on it and some tea and coffee and plastic cups. There was a samovar next to it. There were several tables in the room but only two were occupied at this hour. Avi saw the man he came for. The man had a stack of chips in front of him on the table. He was frowning at his cards.

Avi went in. He didn't hurry but he didn't go slow. He put the gun to the man's head and pulled the trigger. The blast was loud in the room and the men froze almost comically and the man slumped with his head on the table and his blood on the cards. Avi went out fast. He pulled the mask off in the alleyway and got back into his car and drove away and that was that. His heart beat madly. He screamed and hit the wheel. He hit play on the tape deck and turned the volume up.

He pulled into a junkyard in Florentin where they didn't ask questions. He went to the incinerator and dumped the gun minus the bullets, and then the mask and gloves. You could make just about anything disappear in those junkyards.

Then he went to see a guy he knew.

5

PALESTINE, TEXAS

'The only times around here are old times' – Farooq

Mohammed Farooq was a large and usually jovial man. He lost his smile when he saw Avi come into his kiosk. Avi had parked the car near Bloomfield Stadium. Not far from there was a large construction site where they were building the new police headquarters. He walked past the library and a burned down restaurant. Back in his uniform days he'd worked patrol in Jaffa, which is when he ran into Mohammed Farooq.

Mohammed had a niece he doted on and one day when the niece went to the nearby Alma Beach she was assaulted by a local sex offender well known to the police, who liked going around on the beach looking at little girls. Avi came across both men one night after Farooq had tracked down the offender in question and was in the process of beating the crap out of him. Avi turned on the siren and flashed the lights but that didn't seem to deter Farooq until Avi stepped out and inquired what it was all about. When Farooq explained, and elaborated how the police did nothing despite his filing a complaint, on account that the offender was Jewish and friendly with one of the captains at the station, with whom he regularly played shesh besh, Avi sympathised. In that case, he said, he would be happy to lend a hand. So he and Farooq together made sure the man would never be able to walk again and, having smashed most of his teeth out for good measure besides, Avi carefully explained to him that going to the police wouldn't do any good, and that the next time he saw him he'd kill him outright. Since then he'd used Farooq as a confidential informant from time to time, which was handy in a place like Jaffa, where neither Jewish police nor the various Jewish crime families wanted to go much.

'Mister policeman,' Farooq said when he saw him. 'I was just about to close.'

Avi said, 'You never close.'

The kiosk sat on the corner of Jerusalem Avenue, the main road that ran all through Jaffa to Bat Yam. It sold spirits and sweets and cigarettes and roasted nuts and seed snacks and, if you knew to ask, a range of semi-legal party drugs with labels like 'aromatherapy herbal infusion', 'essential oils' or 'for use as incense only'. The exact chemical makeup of the drugs changed frequently depending on the current legal definitions. Since the kiosk was in Jaffa, it fell under the auspices of the Mualem family, who ran most of Jaffa and Ajami up to the border of Bat Yam, where Moshe 'Big Moysh' Uzan held territory.

'I have a headache,' Farooq said. 'I was just about to close, honestly, Avi. Unless you want a packet of Marlboro, then I can sell you one and let you be on your way.'

'I was hoping to have a chat,' Avi said. 'For old times' sake.'

'The only times around here are old times,' Farooq said.

'How's your niece?'

Farooq softened. 'She's doing well. Just got a medal in junior athletics.'

'Mazal tov.'

'What do you want, Avi? I don't like you showing up here. I thought you left all this behind you now that you're a big shot detective.'

'I'm looking for a guy. Ramzi Abadi.'

'I don't know anything about any Abadi, man! Are you going to buy something or not?'

'Alright,' Avi said. 'Alright. So not an Abadi. So tell me something else, instead. How do I get hold of Chamudi?'

'Who?'

'Chamudi,' Avi said patiently.

'No idea who you mean.'

'I think you do, Farooq. All this shit you sell in here?'

'Hey, man, those are legal highs.'

'Be a shame if I had to call it in,' Avi said.

'Call it in?' Farooq laughed at him. 'Call it in to who? This is Jaffa, Avi, this isn't Ramat Gan.'

'Don't make me ask again,' Avi said. Two young soldiers came in and bought cigarettes. Avi waited as Farooq served them. When they were gone Avi helped himself to a bar of Pesek Zman.

'You going to pay for that?' Farooq said.

'Sure.' Avi took out three hundred shekels and put them on the counter. 'That enough to cover it?'

'Avi… Come on.'

'For old times, Farooq,' Avi said. He said it quietly.

Farooq took the money. He reached for a pen and scribbled a phone number on it. 'You just call it and ask for whatever. It's like ordering a pizza.'

'Thanks.'

'Don't come round here again.'

'I hope I don't have to.'

'And now the news from Jerusalem,' the radio said. 'A manhunt continues across the Occupied Territories for members of the al-Aqsa Martyrs' Brigades, who are suspected of involvement in the bomb attack in Tel Aviv earlier today. The organisation has yet to claim responsibility. Two teenagers were killed in a car crash in the early hours of the morning near Afula. A memorial service will be held tonight in Jerusalem for Israeli astronaut Ilan Ramon, who died in the tragic Columbia explosion above Palestine, Texas—'

'Palestine, Texas,' Farooq said. He switched off the radio. 'You couldn't make this shit up. And this car bomb this morning, why do you have to go blaming us for it? Everyone knows it was meant for Rubenstein.'

'You did all the other car bombs this year,' Avi said.

'Firstly, I didn't do shit,' Farooq said heatedly. 'You blame us and you blame us and you take from us and you take from us until we can't breathe anymore, and then you choke us some more just for the hell of it, until all the air is gone and all we can do is blow up cars because you do not hear our screams.'

'When did you become such a poet?' Avi said.

'Fuck you.'

Avi left him to it. He stepped outside. The smell from a nearby shawarma stall made him nauseated. His heart beat too fast again. He wanted to talk to Natasha. Instead he called Ronen.

'Avi, where are you?' Ronen said. 'It's madness over here. Cohen has us arresting every Goldin accomplice between Bat Yam and Kfar Shmaryahu. Though half of them vanished. And did you hear about the shooting on Allenby? No witnesses, it being a card joint, and the bouncer barely speaks Hebrew and even then only to call us cocksuckers. When are you coming in?'

'I'm not,' Avi said. 'I'm following a lead.'

'A lead? Listen, you didn't get mixed up with Cohen, did you?' Ronen lowered his voice. 'If it's bad—'

'It's kosher,' Avi said. 'I just need a second body for a spot-and-tail.'

'Shit, I don't know—'

'I can clear it with Cohen.'

'No, don't. Where are you?'

'Jaffa, by Bloomfield.'

'Why! Alright. I'll be there in fifteen.'

He hung up.

Avi went back to his car. He waited outside the abandoned Alhambra Theatre and lit a cigarette and thought about that little girl in the hospital bed and then he wondered why Cohen had him chasing a trail while he had the rest of the squad arresting Goldin soldiers.

'I dare you, Avi.'

'What?'

They were outside a kiosk, and Lior Goldin was grinning. 'I dare you to take something.'

'You mean steal?'

'What are you, a chicken?'

Avi went in. The kiosk owner was half asleep behind the counter. Avi's heart beat fast. He kept looking to see if anyone was watching. He reached for the top shelf. Grabbed a nudie magazine.

'Hey, kid—'

Avi burst out of the kiosk running. He ran all the way and Lior ran after him, laughing.

'Oh, man, you should have seen your face!' Lior said. 'What did you get? Whoa, she's hot.' He opened the magazine to the centre spread admiringly.

'When I grow up,' he said, 'I'm going to have all the money and all the pussy in the world.'

'When I grow up,' Avi said, 'I'm going to be a policeman.'

A car honked and made him jump. Avi opened his eyes and saw Ronen leaning out of the window.

'You look like shit,' Ronen said. He parked the car and stepped out with a half-eaten burekas in his hand. He munched contentedly. 'I had to stop for lunch on the way.'

'I can see that.'

'So who are we tailing?' Ronen said.

'Hopefully,' Avi said, 'a drug dealer.'

'A drug dealer in Jaffa?' Ronen said. 'That's like looking for fish in a fish market. And I hate fish. What's he to you?'

'Nothing,' Avi said. 'He's nothing to me.'

6

EVEN COPS LIKE WEED

'You want it you pay it' – the driver

'Hello?'

'Hello. Chamudi?'

'Who's this?'

'My name's Avi. I'm looking for stuff?'

'What sort of stuff?'

'Brown or green.'

'I don't know you. Are you a cop?'

'What? No. Galit gave me your number. She said you're good for it.'

Avi figured there had to be a Galit. There usually was.

'Sorry, I can't help you.'

The phone went dead.

'Is that it?' Ronen said.

Avi stared at the phone. 'You have another idea?'

Ronen looked around him. The burned down restaurant next to the abandoned old theatre. A homeless man was quite unconcernedly taking a shit by the rubbish bins, trousers down and a roll of toilet paper in one hand.

'I know this place,' Ronen said. 'See that courtyard?'

'Yeah?'

'Used to be an old Arab cinema, back in the British Mandate days. You can still see the grand entrance in that social housing block over there.'

'So?'

'So nothing. It's flats now. Hold on, here's one. Hey, you! Over here!'

A gangly teen came out of the gate. He ambled over.

'Yeah?'

'Where can we score some weed around here?'

The teen looked at them in pity. 'What are you, cops?'

'Even cops like weed,' Ronen said.

'Amen to that,' the teen said. 'But I ain't got any.'

'You know Chamudi?'

'Who doesn't? Alright, hold on.'

The teen took out his phone. His fingers danced on the keypad. The phone beeped. The teen put it back in his pocket.

'He'll send someone. Ten minutes.'

'Hey, thanks,' Ronen said. He passed the teen a twenty shekel note.

'Don't mention it. Fuck the police, am I right?'

'Amen,' Ronen said. He turned to Avi, grinning.

'You've got to be fucking kidding me,' Avi said.

'Mr Detective,' Ronen said. 'I told you, it's Jaffa. So what now?'

Avi said, 'We wait.'

'You wait. I've got a Diet Coke in the car.'

Avi waited. Ronen sat low behind the wheel. It wasn't long before a motorbike came along the road and pulled to a stop on the curb. The driver had a black helmet on and he didn't remove it.

'You got the stuff?' Avi said.

'What do you want?' the driver said.

'Just a gram of hash.'

'Hardly worth getting out for. A hundred and fifty.'

'That's a bit pricey,' Avi said.

'You want it you pay it,' the driver said.

'Here.'

Avi passed him the money. The driver opened the bike's saddlebag and extracted a small package.

'There you go.'

'Thanks.'

The driver nodded and rode off on his bike. Ronen started his car and followed.

Avi smelled the hash. It was good hash. He put it in his pocket. Maybe he and Natasha could smoke it together later, when this was over. Just then his phone finally rang.

'Tashi?'

'Motek, I can't talk for long.' He could hear people shouting in the background and Natasha pacing, heels on marble. 'I'm in the house in the moshav the police don't know about. God, I hate it here! There's nothing but chickens and, and, cows outside. They're completely paranoid, Avi. Do you know what's going on?'

'I don't—' Avi started to say. 'I think Cohen—'

'Natasha! Who are you talking to!'

'Get away you fucking psycho!'

'Who is this!' A man's voice down the phone. Avi closed his eyes.

'Avi you fuck, is that you? I told you to stay the fuck away from my sister!'

'You don't get to tell me what to do, Lior, you fucking prick!' He heard Natasha scream. Glass smashed and he heard Natasha laugh.

'Did you say Cohen? Why is that fucker messing us about, Avi? You tell that prick we want a meet, do you hear! And stay away from my sister!'

'Fuck you, Lior!'

'Fuck you, Natasha! Fuck!' Avi heard something else smash and then the phone went dead.

Avi pinched the bridge of his nose. He had a headache.

When he turned eighteen he went into the army. He got a combat unit and served in South Lebanon, before the withdrawal. One day he got back to the base and went to get something from the warehouse when he saw a familiar face behind the desk.

'Lior?'

'Avile!'

They'd not seen much of each other before the army, mostly for reasons Avi preferred not to think about.

'What are you doing here?' Avi said.

'I'm a supply clerk,' Lior said. 'They didn't want me to join but I fought them. My big brother died in the Beaufort. Did you know that?'

Avi remembered the Goldins' home. The photo of a young man in uniform, smiling, that sat on a shelf.

'It's good to see you,' he said, and found that he meant it.

Lior grinned. 'And you, too. Look at you! A proper soldier.'

'It's rough out there,' Avi said, and he meant that, too. Holding the occupied strip of land beyond the border was getting harder every day. There were always incursion attempts and he had to lie in ambush after ambush, holding his gun, ready to shoot. The only shot you took was a shot to kill.

'We're going to do just fine,' Lior said.

After that Avi saw him often.

The car horn woke him. Had he been asleep? He blinked. The pills were fading. He needed something to keep him up.

'Avi, come on!'

'Ronen. What'd you get?'

'He went into a residential block just off Jerusalem Avenue, on Pushkin,' Ronen said. 'Quiet place. Can't tell you more than that. You still need me?'

'I think I'll manage.'

'Good. Because I don't like any of this.' Ronen squinted at Avi. 'It's just one of those days, isn't it?' he said. 'You wonder how many more people will die before it ends.'

'People always die,' Avi said. He thought of something. 'What's the deal with Cohen, anyway?' he said. 'He's taking all this kind of personally.'

'You don't know? He's got a granddaughter same age as those kids. She's sick with something, I don't know what. I guess he's thinking of her.' Ronen shook his head. 'If I were a Goldin right now I'd be getting on a plane to somewhere far away.'

'There's no evidence the Goldins ordered the hit,' Avi said.

'Does it matter, Avi? They're all the fucking same. I'll see you.'

'Thanks, Ronen.'

'Don't mention it. And I mean that. I was never here.'

Avi got back in his car. He drove slowly, cruising.

'All you have to do,' Lior said. 'Is open the gate and let them through. They're good guys, they're SLA. No one's going to ask questions.' They were drinking coffee on the base.

'What are they bringing through?' Avi asked.

Lior shrugged. 'TVs, cigarettes, arak, hash… Does it matter?'

'You trust them?'

'Avile, they're SLA, they need us more than we need them.'

The South Lebanon Army was a Christian militia propped up by the Israeli Defence Forces. Avi knew they were worried about the plans for Israel to withdraw at last from South Lebanon. Twenty years was a long time to be sitting on the border. When Arik sent the troops in back in '82 it was only supposed to be a short-term operation. Three months tops, they said. Now here Avi was, stuck with Lior Goldin.

Goldin had been busy. As a supply clerk he had access to the warehouses, to the drivers, to everyone. It was easy to get things out. And he was friendly with the SLA guys. He had his brother Yair back home to take care of anything they'd brought back.

And what was the harm? Everyone smuggled shit out of Lebanon. They'd been doing it ever since the invasion, and no one wanted to stop a good thing.

'Sure,' Avi said.

A car alarm blared somewhere nearby and Avi jerked. He'd been driving round the old clock tower. The Turks had built it back in the day to celebrate the Ottoman sultan's long reign, and next to it was the dilapidated old prison. Avi pulled into an empty parking space and sat there for a long moment and then he got out and walked to the promenade and stood there staring at the sea.

The air was hot and still. Someone nearby was smoking a joint and the smell lay thick in the air. Laughing girls went past Avi, wearing bikini tops on their way to the beach. An Arab family went past, the woman in a hijab and pushing a stroller, the man talking on the phone and smoking. Two young Orthodox Jews in wide-brimmed fur hats walked past, arguing animatedly. A body builder wearing nothing but shorts strolled by, his chest glistening with oil. Fishermen dangled lines over the wall into the water below. Avi dry-swallowed a pill.

When he got back to the car the radio said the little girl from the hospital had died from her wounds and the body was being transported to the pathology centre in Abu Kabir.

7

NICE AND QUIET

'You must be stupid' – Chamudi

Most crime wasn't difficult and most criminals weren't very smart. It didn't do to overthink things, so Avi just waited. The apartment block was on Pushkin Street, one of a tangle of residential side roads off Jerusalem Avenue all named after dead writers. It was an ordinary housing block with a mix of Jewish and Arab residents, bikes chained outside and no real traffic on the road. It was nice and quiet.

Avi waited, and presently he saw the bike driver again, back from another delivery. He pulled into the street and parked right beside the entrance. Avi walked behind him softly and waited until the guy buzzed the flat and the door clicked open and then he stuck his gun in the driver's back.

'Nice and quiet,' Avi said.

The driver didn't argue. He walked up the stairs. Avi stuck close. There was no point pulling a gun unless you were ready to use it. Avi understood that. The driver understood that. They came to the second floor and to the last door down the corridor. Avi leaned close on the driver's back, his lips almost to the man's ears.

'Do it right,' he whispered.

The driver knocked, three times. The door opened. Avi pushed the driver hard against the door. The door flew back and hit the man who opened it. Avi came in.

'What the fuck?' the man said. His nose bled.

'Police. Against the wall. Both of you. Now.'

'Bullshit, police,' the man said. But he obeyed all the same. Avi was going to cuff the driver, then thought again and hit him over the head a couple of times instead. The driver sprawled on the floor, face down.

'Drag him to the bathroom,' Avi said.

'You do it,' the man said. 'Jew son of a bitch.'

'You must be Chamudi,' Avi said.

'And you must be stupid.'

'That may well be,' Avi said. He kicked the driver a couple of times. There was a small pool of blood around the man's head but he was still breathing. Avi figured he wasn't going to get up for a while. He said, 'I'll make it quick.'

'I'm going to find you again after this,' Chamudi said. He was small and thin. He reminded Avi of the sort of knife you'd take with you into a club, just in case there was trouble.

'Move it,' Avi said.

'Cocksucker.'

Chamudi went through into the living room. Avi followed him. The flat had high ceilings and plenty of floor space. Avi whistled.

'Nice place.'

'Fuck y—'

Avi kicked him in the lower back and sent him flying. Chamudi turned, a knife in his hand from somewhere. He lunged at Avi.

There was no point pulling a gun unless you intended to use it. Avi fired, the shot loud in the room, but he didn't think any of the neighbours would complain. Chamudi crumpled to the floor. Blood spread from his shoulder.

'Don't move again,' Avi said. He kicked the knife out of the way. Chamudi clutched his shoulder.

'You fucking shot me!'

'I just want to ask you some questions.'

'I can't figure out if you're stupid or crazy or both,' Chamudi said.

Avi showed him his badge.

'I'm a cop,' he said.

'We pay the cops!'

'Where can I find the Abadis?'

'Did you try the phone book?'

Chamudi stared at him. 'You didn't even look, did you?'

'Would they be there?' Avi said.

'You are so fucking dumb,' Chamudi said, 'it's a miracle you're still alive.'

'Do you want me to shoot you again?'

Chamudi spat. 'What are you going to do, kill me?'

'What have you got here?' Avi said. He looked around the room. Saw boxes stacked against the wall.

'What this?'

Chamudi said nothing. Avi went to have a look.

Stopped.

'Shit,' he said.

'Yeah,' Chamudi said.

Avi saw assault rifles, grenades, Uzis, sniper scopes, a couple of grenade launchers. They were all army issue.

He said, 'What the fuck?'

Chamudi coughed. 'So we sell some other shit, not just drugs.'

'To terrorists?'

'Whoever has the money.'

Avi thought of Lebanon, how equipment would go missing sometimes. He knew Goldin was stealing arms, explosives. He was getting ready for a war back then, only neither he nor Avi knew it yet.

Avi looked further. Two bricks of heroin. A crate of pills. He opened the fridge and it was full of weed.

He said, 'Shit.'

'So what, you're going to arrest me?' Chamudi said.

'Tell me where the Abadis are and I'll let you walk out of here,' Avi said.

'Where am I going to go?' Chamudi said. But Avi could see the desperate hope in his eyes.

'Tell me,' he said.

'Fuck it,' Chamudi said. 'I don't like those pricks anyway. They have a compound in Ajami, near the cemetery.'

He told Avi the address. 'But it won't do you any good, Mr Policeman. They have the whole compound wired up with booby traps. And they have guns. You send in squad cars you'll have a war on your hands.'

'So how do I get to them?'

Chamudi looked at Avi. He looked at the gun. The hope in his eyes died.

He said, 'You'll make it quick?'

'I promise.'

Chamudi told him. Avi nodded. He put the gun almost gently to Chamudi's forehead and pulled the trigger.

Avi stared at the corpse.

Avi stared at the blood.

Avi said, 'Shit!'

He heard a groan. He turned. The bike driver. The man looked at him.

Avi said, 'Shit!'

Avi shot the driver in the head.

His hands shook. He took out his coke and made lines on Chamudi's coffee table. Bang. Pow. Fireworks like every night on Independence Day.

He knew whose flat this was. The Mualem family held Jaffa. The Arab crime families often worked closely with the Jewish ones. It wasn't like he could take this problem to anyone. You didn't screw with the Mualems or the Rubensteins of this world.

Only, someone did try to take out Rubenstein, and Avi had just royally fucked the Mualems.

There was really only one thing he could do.

He moved fast. The floor was slick with blood and he kept blinking sweat out of his eyes. He took the driver's bag and packed the bricks of heroin inside and weed and pills and he helped himself to the lighter guns and the grenades. He took one of the grenade launchers, too, and slung it over his shoulder in its bag. He stepped over the driver's corpse, carefully. Opened the door, took one last look inside.

What a mess, he thought.

But it was too late to do anything about it.

He took a grenade out of the bag, pulled the pin, tossed it inside the flat and shut the door.

He ran.

The explosion came when he was on the stairs. He stumbled and fell, breaking the fall with his hands. He heard screams. He ran out. He threw the stuff in the back seat of his car and took off. He drove slowly. The skin on his palms felt red and raw. He searched for a radio station. Arik Einstein, singing 'Drive Slowly'. Avi laughed. Acoustic guitar notes filled the car and Avi thought of heavy rain, falling. He didn't even like Arik Einstein.

8

LOVE TO MAYA

'Justice, justice shall you pursue' – Cohen

'I swear,' Avi said. 'I had nothing to do with it.'

Ronen, on the phone, whispering furiously. 'Are you fucking kidding me?'

'Look, man, it's nothing to do with me! Alright? I didn't even go near the place. Whoever did that must be the same people who ordered the hit on Rubenstein. Tying up loose ends.'

'So, what, it's a coincidence?'

'No,' Avi said. 'It's a sign. I'm getting close to the hitters, Ronen.'

'Shit.'

'Yeah.'

Avi almost believed his own story.

'Did you talk to Cohen?' Ronen said.

'Not yet.'

'You should talk to Cohen.'

'He knows where to reach me,' Avi said.

'Where are you, anyway?' Ronen said.

'Um…'

'No, don't tell me. Fucking prick. This mess of a day. I can't wait for my shift to be over. I just want to go home.'

'Love to Maya.'

'Fuck off, Avi.' Ronen hung up.

Avi had driven to Ben Avigdor, a narrow street between Ha'masger Street and the highway. The whole area was a maze of tiny old garages and workshops and industrial warehouses. Avi hired a small garage there paid monthly in cash. On one side of him he could hear a rock band practicing in a loft and across the road a couple of punters were sharing a cigarette outside the Russian brothel. Avi offloaded the stuff he stole from the Arabs and stashed it in his lockup garage. He lit a cigarette. He stared at the bricks of heroin. He stared at the grenade launcher. The burner phone Cohen gave him rang.

'How are you doing, boychik?'

'I've had better days.'

Cohen laughed. '"For what does a man get for all the toil and striving with which he labours under the sun? All his days are filled with grief, and his task is sorrowful."'

Avi said nothing.

'Ecclesiastes, 2:22,' Cohen said.

'Great.'

'It's quite a mess there in Jaffa. I feel like I'm spending all day cleaning up messes.'

'I heard she died,' Avi said. His throat constricted. 'The little girl.'

'Yes. I'm in Abu Kabir right now with the pathologist. Not that he has anything new to say. She died from the bomb. She just took a while. She was a little fighter, Avi. Just like my little girl.'

'Your granddaughter,' Avi said, remembering something Ronen told him.

Cohen sighed. 'That's right. She has a bad heart. It is a terrible thing, when a child sickens. No parent should have to bury their child. It is the curse of our country, I sometimes think. In my more maudlin moments. We are a nation that devours its children.'

'I'm sorry,' Avi said.

'She is a fighter,' Cohen said.

'Listen,' Avi said. 'About Jaffa—'

'Merely another incidence in the brewing gang war,' Cohen said. 'Now the Mualems are going to be dragged in. This can't be helped. "Justice, justice shall you pursue." Deuteronomy. You are on a righteous path, detective, and all shall tremble as you pass. You have my blessing to do what is right. Do we understand each other?'

Avi stared into the distance. 'We do,' he said.

The line went dead.

Avi sat on a crate. Did Cohen *want* a gang war? The rock band next door cranked up the volume, a drummer who couldn't drum and three guitarists and someone wailing into a microphone. In Tel Aviv, *everyone* was in some sort of band.

Avi had a problem. He couldn't go it alone and he couldn't go to the cops.

They were on regila, back home, seven days of freedom, away from the army, away from Lebanon and waiting in ambush and rocket attacks and the constant fear that this time, this time could be it. One night he was sent to a remote observation post on the border where the only two guards on the gate were privates, two recruits fresh from basic training. Avi had got there late and went to sleep and in the night he heard voices and a car starting up. In the morning he went to check on the privates.

'Any problems last night?' he said.

'Nah. A couple of guys in a pickup drove up,' the one soldier said. 'They had guns. I asked them if they were Hezbollah but they said they weren't Hezbollah.'

'You did what?' Avi said.

'It's alright,' the other soldier said. 'We explained this was an Israeli post and they drove off.'

When Avi got to the top of the observation tower and looked out onto the road just beyond the border he saw it was full with pickup trucks and men with guns waving Hezbollah flags. Later, he realised they must have thought the post was deserted. How none of them were killed that day remained a mystery to him. He should have died. Everything after that was a bonus.

He was on regila with Lior, a whole week away from the army, from Lebanon, from rocket attacks and lying in ambush. He was trying to explain all that to Lior over beer. They were in a nightclub and Lior kept looking at the door until Avi finally said, 'What?'

'Nothing, nothing. It's those fuckers from Pardes Katz.'

It was the neighbourhood east of them.

'Yair had a little run in with them. Tensions might be running high.' Lior scratched his nose. He wore round frame glasses. 'We're going to show them what the name of a Goldin means around here.'

It was then that the doors of the club opened to admit a group of four men their age, who swaggered in. Avi didn't know them, but Lior tensed beside him.

'Here,' he said. He passed Avi a knife under the table and Avi took it.

The men looked around until they spotted Lior and then they came over.

'Goldin.'

'Baruch—'

Two of Baruch's men reached over then and grabbed Lior and tried to pull him out of the seat. Lior kicked and bit one of the men on the hand and when the man swore and released him Lior stabbed him in the stomach. The man screamed and Baruch turned with a nasty little flick blade and went to stab Lior when Avi jumped up and stabbed him first, deep in the side. He kicked one of Baruch's soldiers and broke another's nose and then he grabbed Lior and carried him out, quick, his hands slick with blood and his heart beating, his mouth still tasting of alcohol and smoke.

The police came around later. They grabbed Lior but he didn't say a thing, and neither did Baruch and his guys. No one talked to the police. And no one came to ask Avi a damn thing about it. After, Lior handed him a fat envelope filled with hundred shekel bills.

'Not even a scratch on me,' he said with pride.

'What's this for?' Avi said. But he took the money.

Lior said, 'We're going to pay Baruch a visit tonight. You coming?'

'I don't know about this,' Avi said.

'Bullshit, Avi. We're friends.'

So Avi came. They took a boosted car and cruised slowly to a petrol station café which Lior said the Pardes Katz gang used. They came at night and with the lights off and they cruised to a stop. Through the windows Avi could see seated men smoking at tables. Lior reached for a shopping bag on the floor. It had a Super-Pharm logo on it. Lior opened the bag. He brought out grenades.

'Well?' he said.

Also in the car was his brother, Yair, who never said much, and a guy Avi vaguely knew who was called Small Baruch to distinguish him from the Pardes Katz Baruch. Small Baruch drove. Avi joined the Goldins. They got out of the car quietly and kept the doors open. They went to the café and tossed the grenades inside, and then they ran back in the car and took off. The heat and noise of the explosion followed them, illuminating the road ahead in flames.

Avi stared into the distance. His cigarette had burned down to the filter. He wanted to sleep. He wanted to sleep forever. Instead he did another line of coke. Coke was great. It just kept you going. After the Pardes Katz bombing they had a big party at the same nightclub they had the knife fight. By then the place was unofficially owned by the Goldins anyway. They did shots and lines and danced to Dana International. They all got hammered. A day later Avi went back to the army.

Two of the Pardes Katz soldiers died in the explosion that night, and Baruch lost both of his legs under the knees. Two weeks later Small Baruch was killed in a stabbing and someone took shots at Yair Goldin but missed.

Avi picked up his phone and made a call he didn't want to make.

A familiar voice answered.

'Who is this?'

'It's Avi.'

'You have a lot of nerve calling me,' Lior Goldin said.

'I have a business offer.'

'I don't talk on the phone, ya manyak.'

'I'll meet you at the dunes, same place as before. Half an hour.'

Lior hung up. Avi stared at the phone.

Then he started packing up.

9

STILL FRIENDS

'You think presidents can't be rapists?' – Benny

The dunes of Rishon Le'tsion lay just south of Bat Yam, a wilderness of coast that separated Tel Aviv from the ancient coastal towns of Ashkelon and Ashdod. Back when Yossi Banai still sang 'In The Dunes' people went there to hook up; now, if you had a drug shipment to pick or a corpse to get rid of, this was where you came. The only people who lived in the dunes were the homeless who built themselves makeshift huts here and there, and they knew to keep their mouths shut. The police couldn't patrol the area and so it remained much as it was, quiet and wild and the go-to place of choice for traffickers, hitters and the occasional amateur serial killer like Vladimir Pinyov.

During the Goldins' war with the Pardes Katz gang the dunes saw their fair share of bodies. After Pinyov was arrested in 2000 there was some worry that the police would start digging up bodies, and indeed the police did use a bulldozer for a while. But then Pinyov committed suicide behind bars and as the victims were all homeless nobody bothered to look beyond the three corpses they already had.

Avi drove fast to the meeting place. He got off the road into the dunes and thought just how beautiful the place still was. Gulls cried in the distance and once again he could smell the sea. There was no one around for miles or, if they were, they kept themselves to themselves.

He waited. His mouth tasted of ash. It wasn't long before he saw the convoy of cars approaching. Three cars, raising sand. They stopped and men got out.

'Lior,' Avi said.

'You carrying?'

Avi shrugged. One of Lior's guys patted him down, took both his guns. The others stood in a semi-circle, spaced out, guns drawn but not pointing.

'You wired?' Lior said.

'What do you think?'

'I think you're a piece of shit,' Lior Goldin said. 'And I told you to stay the fuck away from Natasha.'

'She's not yours to tell her what to do,' Avi said, and Lior laughed.

'Look at you,' he said. 'You're a mess. Sooner or later you're going to end up dead or in prison. Tashi deserves better than that.'

'I tried to stay away,' Avi said. 'She wouldn't let me.'

'She does have her own ideas about things,' Lior said. 'Avi, why are we here?'

'I need a favour.'

'I don't owe you shit, Avile. In fact, I'm wondering why I should let you walk out of here at all.'

'In the trunk,' Avi said.

Lior nodded. One of his soldiers went to have a look.

'Hey, Lior, check this out,' he said.

Avi waited. Presently Lior came back. He had one of the bricks of heroin in his hand.

'What the fuck did you *do*?' he said.

'If you want it it's yours,' Avi said.

'I know where it's from,' Lior said. 'I know whose it is. I don't need this kind of heat.'

'What's done is done,' Avi said. 'It couldn't be helped.'

Lior stared at him.

'We didn't hit Rubenstein,' he said.

'Someone did.'

'Well, they should have done a better fucking job of it. That bomb went off too late. Almost like they wanted the fucker to get away.'

'So help me end it,' Avi said.

'Who?' Lior said.

'Family called the Abadis, in Jaffa.'

'Ah,' Lior said. 'Yes. We used them a couple of times but I don't like working with Arabs. Why do you think it's them?'

'I don't know it's them,' Avi said. 'But I'm planning to find out.'

'They're certainly who I might have hired,' Goldin said. 'The Arabs are good when you want to keep a certain distance from a job.'

'But it wasn't you,' Avi said.

'No.'

'So?' Avi said.

'I don't know about this,' Lior said.

'Bullshit, Lior. We're still friends.'

Lior stared at Avi.

'Are we?' he said.

He hefted the brick of white powder in his hand.

'I'll take what you've got,' he said.

'I'll call you when I'm ready,' Avi said.

He watched them unpack the drugs and the guns. He drove away, back towards Jaffa. He checked the news. Nothing about the dead girl. President Katsav was meeting with the American Secretary of State, Colin Powell, for a state dinner. Benny once told Avi that he had something on Katsav. Avi said, 'What?'

'Sex stuff. He likes to touch the girls. Sometimes he likes to do more. Whether they want him to or not.'

'Bullshit,' Avi said. 'He's the president!'

'You think presidents can't be rapists?'

Avi just shrugged. He still thought it was bullshit. But you never knew.

It was early afternoon. The flea market in Jaffa was shutting down. In the evening it was transformed into a trendy night spot with bars open and coloured lights strewn above on the rafters, but in the daytime there were still people selling junk on the floor for a handful of shekels in the main square, and more established stalls selling third-hand electronics and kitchen stuff and knickknacks. He parked his car up on the hill. There was an

Orthodox demonstration up there. The Orthodox were always demonstrating up there. There was new construction going up as Jews were increasingly moving from Tel Aviv to Jaffa, and the construction crews kept digging up old graves, and the Orthodox objected to it as a desecration of the dead as those might have been old Jewish cemeteries.

At the top of the hill was Victory Ice Cream and, since it was a hot day, Avi went and sat down and had a cone. At a table next to him a fat kid methodically went through a waffle loaded with ice cream, spray cream, roasted nuts, sprinkles and three types of sauce. The makeup of the clientele was diverse. Ice cream brought everyone, Arabs and Jews, together, if only for as long as it took to eat a banana split.

Avi waited. It was that time of the day when the heat, which had been lying low and oppressive over everything until that moment, finally began to ease. A welcome coolness fell over the flagstones and the protesters' chanting voices took on an ethereal quality, so that Avi felt himself swept away, like Nils Holgersson in that cartoon series they used to show every summer on television, where the tiny Nils rode a white goose across the skies.

Then he saw Fuad Abadi walk into the ice cream shop.

10

A NECESSARY EVIL

'The methods are dirty but the job is clean.' – Avi

What Chamudi told Avi, before his unfortunate and rather abrupt demise, was that the youngest Abadi brother had a sweet tooth; and it didn't matter what day of the week it was, or whether the police were out on the Intifada raging on or if it was the middle of winter or if Maccabi Tel Aviv lost the championship again, he could always be found in the late afternoon at the Victory. Something to do with Umm Ramzi taking him there as a child, perhaps. Chamudi may have wanted to elaborate on that score but he didn't have much time before Avi shot him. He did take the time to describe Fuad Abadi, who was podgy, wore a large gold Rolex on his wrist and was missing his left ear; lost, so Chamudi said, on one of the brothers' jobs up in the Negev. The point was, he was easy enough to spot.

Avi sent a quick message on his phone while he watched Fuad. Fuad, not registering Avi's interest in the slightest, went up to the counter and ordered himself two scoops of ice cream in a cone, one chocolate and one vanilla, with chocolate sauce and sprinkles on. It was when he turned to go that Avi got up behind him. He stuck his gun in Fuad's back, standing close.

'Keep walking,' he said.

Fuad breathed deeply. He looked confused.

'Eat your ice cream,' Avi said.

They walked out of the shop without anyone paying them attention. The fat kid had finished his waffle. A couple argued in a corner in angry whispers. Avi said, 'Cross the road, nice and gentle, Fuad.'

'Who the fuck are you?' Fuad said.

'I just want to talk.'

They were almost by the car. Avi had his finger tight on the trigger. How many more, he thought, before the day was over?

'Get in. It's open.'

'You leave a car open, here?' Fuad laughed. He reached for the handle. Then he swung round and slammed a meaty hand in Avi's face.

The gun went off. The bullet struck the pavement. Avi kicked Fuad between the legs. Fuad fell to his knees. Avi grabbed him by the arm.

'Get in!'

He had to push him. The guy was big. Avi put handcuffs on him. He heard screams. Turned and yelled. 'Police!'

He got in the car and drove.

'You're a cop?' Fuad said. 'Why didn't you say so?'

'What difference does that make?' Avi said.

'Nothing. I just hate cops.'

'Nobody likes cops, Fuad. We're just a necessary evil.'

'Where are we going? The police station?'

'How about your family's place?' Avi said.

'You think they'd let you in, cop?'

'They might if you're with me.'

'I didn't finish my ice cream,' Fuad said.

'You guys do the hit on Rubenstein?' Avi said.

'Who?'

Avi sighed.

'Fine,' he said. 'We'll do this the hard way.'

He didn't have far to drive. He was there earlier in the day. The old Alhambra Theatre, long abandoned. Back in the sixties it was a swinging nightclub. All the greats played the Alhambra: Umm Kulthum, Farid al-Atrash, Leila Mourad. Before that it was a cinema. It was huge, dark, and deserted.

'Come on, man, this isn't the police station!' Fuad said.

'I asked you nicely,' Avi said. He pushed him along. Someone had already broken the lock on the door so they went in.

'Come on, man,' Fuad said.

Lior Goldin and three of his men were already there. Lior had a portable primus stove going. The gas cast a merry glow of light over everything. Lior brewed coffee. He said, 'Sit down.'

There was a single chair. Fuad tried to run. Avi kicked him and Fuad fell, and then Lior's men came and dragged him to the chair.

'Did you do the Rubenstein hit?' Avi said.

'What's it to you?' Fuad said. He started to sweat. 'A job's a job, anyway. If everyone kept taking pops at the independent contractor then who'd be left to do all the dirty jobs?'

'He's got a point,' Lior said.

'Come on, Goldin. You know me,' Fuad said.

'This is out of my hands, Fuad.'

'Then whose? His?'

Lior glanced at Avi. 'He serves a higher power.'

'Come on, man.'

'Listen,' Avi said. 'It's not like that. The methods are dirty but the job is clean. I just want to talk to your brothers.'

'Talk? This is how you talk?'

'I wanted to get your attention.'

'What do we have to talk about?' Fuad said desperately.

'You come in easy. You get time inside. But that's all. You'll be out in no time on good behaviour.'

'There's no fucking way, man.'

Avi put his gun to Fuad's forehead.

'Then this is how it goes,' he said. 'But it doesn't have to go like this.'

It seemed to him he was trying to convince himself as much as Fuad.

'Sure, alright,' Fuad said. 'I'll take you. No problem. You want to talk, we can talk. Shall we go? I left my scooter at the ice cream place.'

'We'll give you a ride,' Lior Goldin said.

11

ABADIS

'Now we wait' – Avi

They went through Ajami, past the Old Man and the Sea, the big restaurant heaving with clients and waiters moving busily between the tables laying down endless plates of dips and salads, reminding Avi he was hungry. The old abandoned beach was on their right as they drove. The city kept planning to put up a park and a promenade there but didn't. They got to the old Muslim cemetery.

Lior sent his guys ahead. He had a sniper, a ginger guy who learned the trade in the army. Lior liked to take army guys. He said they got all that free education, it was a shame to let it all go to waste. So instead of going backpacking in Goa or someplace in South America to trip on acid or mushrooms, they came to work for him. The money was better and so were the drugs.

The Abadi place stood on a plot of land all on its own above the shoreline. It was surrounded by tall plank fences. It was impossible to see what was inside. Avi could hear dogs barking, horses neighing. They could have had a whole urban farm inside there. He took Fuad to the gates.

'Don't do anything stupid,' Avi said.

'My friend,' Fuad said, 'you are the one being stupid.'

Avi couldn't argue with that one. Fuad opened the gate and they went inside.

It was surprisingly nice. Trees grew behind the walls and somewhere to his left Avi could see a stable. Chickens ran through the grass. A house was directly in front of them and he could hear motion inside and then Ramzi Abadi came out onto the porch eating a sandwich. 'Fuad? Fuad, wen kenet?'

Then he saw Avi.

Ramzi clicked his tongue. Two vicious-looking bulldogs came running from behind the trees. Everything happened kind of fast after that. Fuad started to run towards the house. Ramzi pulled out a gun. Avi fired at the dogs. One dropped with a pitiful howl. The other sank his teeth into Avi's leg.

Avi screamed. Ramzi fired at him, the shots hitting the ground and raising dust, making it hard to see. Avi shot the dog and the dog loosened its grip on his leg. The pain sent waves up through Avi's body. He clenched his teeth. More men came out of the trees, carrying weapons.

Ramzi collapsed on the porch, looking confused. Blood spread across his chest. Lior's sniper, finally stepping in.

Then someone must have used the grenade launcher.

Avi screamed again but there was no one to hear it. Explosions rocked the courtyard. Smoke bellowed up and he couldn't see. He ran forward, towards the house. He tripped over Fuad's corpse. Fuad just lay there looking confused. Avi stumbled ahead. He heard screams, curses in Arabic.

He made it to the steps. His leg throbbed. He climbed onto the porch, grabbed Ramzi Abadi's prone body and pulled him inside, using it as a shield.

'Don't shoot!' Avi screamed.

He saw the third Abadi brother, Ahmad, with gun drawn. Avi fired. He hit the television screen. The television exploded. Ahmad fired and Avi felt his arm catch fire. He fired again, blindly, again and again. Furniture exploded, wood chips flying, glass breaking everywhere. Avi didn't stop until he was out of bullets.

He waited for Ahmad to finish the job, but no shot came.

Avi listened. Silence outside now, no barking dogs, no shouting men.

Silence inside. He peered over and saw Ahmad sprawled on the kitchen floor, half his head blown off.

Nothing moved.

Nothing stirred.

Avi fell to the floor next to Ramzi Abadi.

'You…'

Ramzi opened his eyes.

He was somehow still alive.

Avi just wanted to sleep forever.

He pulled out his phone. Called the police and told them where to go. It was only a few seconds.

He let the phone drop. He could barely hold his gun.

'What… now?' Ramzi said.

'Now we wait,' Avi said. He was so tired.

Ramzi moved his head with difficulty, stared at him. 'You tell… Cohen… to go fuck himself,' he said.

Avi went still.

Avi went cold.

Ramzi closed his eyes.

His chest stopped moving.

Avi let the gun drop.

He lay on the floor and waited as the sirens began to sing in the distance.

12

AUTOPSY

'The pain is shared by us all' – Cohen

'What the fuck *happened* there?' Ronen said.

Avi, bandaged, woozy from painkillers. 'It's all in the report,' he said.

'The report is crap.'

The television was on in the station. 'Police have stormed the compound of the Abadi family in Jaffa earlier this evening,' the newsreader said, 'putting an end to the investigation into the criminal terrorist attack that saw a car bomb explode in the centre of Tel Aviv this morning. Six people have now died of the attack and several more are being treated in hospital. Acting on information received from confidential sources, the Serious Crimes Unit in collaboration with the Yamar approached the compound to arrest the suspects for interrogation. In the resulting exchange of fire three members of the Abadi family were killed and one police officer was injured. Chief Inspector Cohen of Serious Crimes spoke to us earlier by phone.'

'Where is Cohen?' Avi said.

'I don't know. Something about his granddaughter.'

Cohen's voice came on the television. 'Officers acted bravely and correctly to resolve the investigation into this heinous crime,' he said. 'We found a significant cache of explosives and bomb-making equipment, with several pipe bombs ready to be deployed. This is a good day for law and order, Margalit. I wish to commend the officers involved in this operation for their dedication and bravery. This will bring scant comfort to the families of the victims, and my heart goes out to each and every one of them. The pain is shared by us all. But as the Torah says, Margalit, "He who sheds another's blood so will his blood be shed."'

'Genesis, 9:6,' Ronen said. 'What?' he said, seeing Avi's look. 'It's one of his favourites.'

'Justice has been done today,' Cohen said. The picture returned to Margalit, looking sombre. 'And now for the weather,' she said.

'I found you half dead, no one else around, dead bodies everywhere, grenades – who the fuck was with you?'

'It's classified,' Avi said. He shrugged, then winced. 'Ask Cohen.'

'That I will not do. What a fucking day. Do you want me to take you home?'

'No,' Avi said. 'I can drive.'

He left Ronen there. It had been hours. He was patched up in hospital, then had to give his statement. But he was treated with kid gloves. He saw the looks they gave him.

He was a hero.

He limped to the car. The painkillers gave him a nice mellow buzz. When he'd come to, Lior Goldin and his soldiers were gone, of course, and with them the weapons Avi stole from Chamudi and all of the drugs.

Lior kept his word. And Avi was a hero.

He drove almost aimlessly. The lights of the passing cars shone softly. The radio played old songs. Chava Alberstein sang to him, telling him how in London despair becomes easier. London isn't waiting for me, she kept saying. I'll be alone there too.

Fuck London, Avi thought. He'd never been to London and he'd never seen New York. Like Chava Alberstein, Avi didn't have any illusions about those places.

He found himself on Ben-Zvi. Jaffa was just up the road. Almost without thinking he pulled into the parking lot and only then realised he'd come to the Abu Kabir Pathology Centre.

It was evening. Avi knocked on the door until someone answered.

'What!'

'Came to see the little girl from the bomb this morning.'

'Why?' the man said. He was small and thin and wore a woven kippa and round glasses. He looked at Avi suspiciously. 'There's no need for that,' he said.

Avi grabbed the little man by the shirt. The man looked at him in pity.

'You look like half a corpse yourself,' he said.

'It's been a long day,' Avi said.

'Look, I don't know anything,' the man said. 'I didn't even bring her in. Dr Ziss did it in person. He's the chief pathologist.'

'And where is Dr Ziss?'

'He went home to his supper, chaveriko. I'm the only one left.'

'Where's the policeman who was here earlier?'

'Cohen?' The man's face brightened. 'He's a good man, a real mensch. Always brings coffee and pastries. Did you know that?'

'He comes here a lot?'

'Job brings him, doesn't it,' the man said. 'But he deals with Ziss. I'm just the guy on the nightshift.'

'Take me to her.'

'I can't. It's not allowed. Go home.'

Avi pushed him. He had almost no power left and they took away his gun. He didn't have much he could use.

He let the man go and looked in his wallet. 'I've got fifty shekels,' he said, desperately. He'd left his money and everything else in his safe house before the raid.

'Sure. What are you, some kind of freak?'

'Just take me to her,' Avi said.

The man led him down empty corridors. Night-time with the dead. Into a cold dark room. The man switched on the light.

'Just a look,' he said.

When he opened the drawer in the morgue there was nobody in it.

'Look, I don't know nothing,' the porter said. 'Maybe they took her for burial already. Like I said, I didn't even see her come in.'

'Maybe she never came in,' Avi said.

He felt sick inside. Something was very wrong. He pushed the porter away. Stumbled outside.

He fished out his phone. He dialled Benny.

'You set me up,' he said.

'I can't talk right now, Avi. Go to bed.'

'You fed me the line on the Abadis.'

'Not on the phone. And I don't know what you mean. Now is not a good time.'

'Where are you?'

Benny sighed. 'Working late,' he said. Avi could hear noise in the background. Men talking in Russian, and a radio playing something, Shlomo Artzi or some shit. Avi concentrated. He heard an engine starting, stopping, something moving – a forklift? Avi did one summer working in a warehouse and he knew the sound.

He tried to think. It was so hard to think.

Benny had a warehouse somewhere, Avi had to meet him there once after a job. Goldin never forgave him for joining the police and then he never forgave him all over again for going with Benny. But that was after the last job he did with Lior, the one that went bad, the one in the dunes where they'd buried that guy only, it turned out, some fucking stupid sixteen-year-old kid was out there just taking a stroll and he saw them, and so Lior did the only thing Lior could do and shot him, right in the back as the kid ran away. Avi tried to stop him but it was too late, and then he hit Lior. They almost killed each other that time. After that they didn't talk again. There was nothing to talk about. Until Avi met Natasha again and she was all grown up.

'Avile? Are you there? Go to sleep,' Benny said. He sounded tired himself, and a little sad. 'Come see me when you're feeling better. Alright?'

He hung up.

Avi staggered to his car. He knew he shouldn't drive. The painkillers and the pain all mixed together. And they took away his cigarettes.

Fuck it. He got behind the wheel and started up again. The warehouse was somewhere near the port.

13

POPPIES

'You did good' – *Cohen*

Maersk containers stacked one on top of the other. A barbed wire fence. Avi didn't have a key or access card so he gunned the engine at the gate. A headlight snapped and the impact jarred him and he cried out in pain. He had lost a lot of blood. He kept his foot on the gas and drove fast, floodlights blinding him, and he could hear men shout. He came to a halt with a screech of the wheels and the smell of burned rubber and just sat there. Breathing came hard.

'Step out of the vehicle, slowly, motherfucker. Keep your hands where I can see them.'

Avi obliged. The warehouse, much as he remembered it. Men with guns, all pointing at him.

Avi said, 'I'm here to see Benny.'

'Who is this clown?' someone said. Avi blinked, trying to see. The lights blinded. A forklift was parked inside.

'Don't shoot him,' someone said. Benny, stepping out of the warehouse. He looked tired. He looked Avi over and shook his head.

'I told you to go home,' he said.

'I can't go home,' Avi said.

'You look like shit, Avi. Why can't you go home, exactly?'

Avi blinked. Tears kept coming. Benny was a vague outline in a halo of light.

Avi said, 'I need to know.'

'You *need* to know?' Benny said. 'No one *needs* to know anything, Avi. What good is knowing? Go home. Get some sleep.'

'No.'

'What do you want me to do, shoot you?' Benny said. 'Come on.'

'I want to know.'

'You're not thinking straight.'

Avi stood his ground. The men seemed to have lost interest and wandered off. Avi could hear the radio inside, Shoshana Damari singing about red poppies. A second figure stepped out of the warehouse and stood beside Benny.

Two silhouettes in a halo of light. Avi blinked.

'Let him through,' Cohen said.

Avi walked like a drunk. Up close he could see Cohen's face, tired, excited. Cohen wrapped his arm around Avi, helped him walk.

'You did well, boychik,' he said. 'You did good.'

Sunsets burned and poppies flowered, as Damari sang. Cohen sang along with Damari. He had a nice voice.

'Did I?' Avi said. 'Did I do good?'

'I already spoke to Commissioner Raphael,' Cohen said. 'You'll be getting a medal of courage. And I think a promotion is in order. How does Inspector sound? There's talk of starting a new, special unit to deal with organised crime. I rather think you'd be good for it.'

'You?' Avi said. There were so many things he wanted to say. He found that none of them would come out.

'The means justify the ends,' Cohen said. 'And poppies always bloom again. Come.'

Avi could see now. The glare of the floodlights abated and the warehouse was quiet and dim. Only the radio played. Cohen led him deeper into the warehouse. Far, far at the back stood a structure made of prefabricated material. It could have been an office. It could have been anything. A man in a white medical coat came out. He nodded to Cohen.

'Don't ask me for this again,' he said.

'I do not *ask*,' Cohen said. The man stalked off.

'Dr Shvartsman is a good man,' Cohen said. 'A little snappy now that it is over, which can be excused. Back in Russia he was a heart surgeon.'

'And here?' Avi said.

'He fell afoul of the law,' Cohen said, 'but don't we all, from time to time? I gave him a second chance. I like to give everyone a chance, Avi. Come. Put these on.'

He gave Avi a medical coat and a mask to wear.

'She's sleeping,' Cohen said.

Avi followed him. What else could he do? He saw the hospital equipment, nurses, a girl in a bed. The girl was hooked up to monitors. She was asleep. Her chest rose and fell. She looked very small and helpless in that room.

'My granddaughter,' Cohen said. 'She has a bad heart. When the heart is sick, the body follows. I could not abide it. She is the light of my life.'

'You?' Avi whispered. He thought of the car bomb. He thought of the children.

'Everything I do, I do for love,' Cohen said. Avi heard the absolute truth in his voice. 'I love this country and its people and the law.'

Avi thought of those children torn to shreds in the explosion.

'The heart,' he said.

'Yes. The children go to her school. I only needed one.'

'How?' Avi said.

Cohen shrugged. 'The girl in the hospital died a brain death but her body kept going. I had her brought here, for the operation.'

'Where is she?'

'Her body will be back in Abu Kabir by now,' Cohen said.

'How?' Avi said.

'Dr Ziss at Abu Kabir has a side line in organs,' Cohen said. 'Kidneys and corneas, mostly. It helps people. We help people. We save lives, Avi.'

'He'll cover for you?'

'All the paperwork is in order,' Cohen said. 'The girl died and was brought to Abu Kabir where an autopsy was carried out. What difference does it make if her body took a slight detour on the way?' He looked at Avi until Avi looked away.

'How can a single life be measured against the lives of many?' Cohen said.

Avi forced himself to go on.

'And the bomb?' he said.

'You solved the case yourself,' Cohen said. 'I had full faith in you. The Abadis were a menace to civilised society. You did well to rid the world of them.'

'You hired them,' Avi said.

Cohen shrugged. 'Rubenstein needed a lesson and I provided one. Now he'll blame the Goldins and the Goldins will retaliate. And thanks to you robbing them, the Mualems will be dragged into it. On which side, I cannot in truth tell you. But it doesn't matter. Both factions have grown too powerful. They will whittle the herd and when the dust settles, someone else will step in to restore rightful order.'

'You?' Avi said.

'Benny,' Cohen said. 'He is a reasonable man for these unreasonable times.'

'You thought of everything,' Avi said. He looked at the little girl on the bed. He looked at her breathing.

He said, 'And me?'

'You?' Cohen slapped him on the back. 'I have high hopes for you, boychik! You keep climbing the ranks and before long you could make Commissioner and I will be calling you Sir. I look forward to that. We need good men, and good men are hard to find.'

'Sir,' Avi said. 'Yes, sir.'

'You look tired,' Cohen said. He walked him away and Avi let him. 'Go home. Get some rest. Make love to that beautiful piece of yours. Natasha. I think she is waiting for you.'

'You think, or you know?' Avi said. The words were bitter in his mouth like Passover maror.

'If you know, you do not need to think,' Cohen said. 'You did me a great service today and I will not forget it.'

'Yes,' Avi said.

He walked out. Benny stood outside. He handed Avi an envelope. It was thick with cash.

'For earlier,' he said.

'Who was that guy?' Avi said. 'At the card game.'

'Rubenstein's accountant,' Benny said. He looked at Avi and shook his head. 'It's just business,' he said.

'Sure,' Avi said. 'Sure.'

He took the money. He walked back to his car.

Somehow he could still drive. He drove through the gate he'd busted earlier. He saw Benny's men were already fixing it. They stared at him as he went past.

He followed the road until he got to the flat. He climbed the stairs and stood at the door. Natasha waited for him inside.

'Oh, Avi,' she said. She came and helped him to the bed. She ran her hands over his side.

'You're hurt,' she said.

'Yes,' Avi said. The flat was dimly lit. Cars passed outside and their lights shone briefly through the blinds.

Natasha kissed him. The light illuminated the heart shape of her face. He thought how lovely she was.

'I'll make us a drink,' she said. She got up and for just a moment Avi was alone. He heard ice clinking in glass. He buried his face in his hands.

'I hate this country,' he said. And then he started to cry.

PART TWO

THE GIRL ON THE BEACH

1974, The North Coastal Road

14

SPRINGTIME

'It's not always safe out there' – Eddie

The radio was turned up high and Shoshana Damari sang about red poppies. She'd been singing that tune since the Nation of Israel was declared and she wasn't going to stop any time soon. Eddie Raphael drove. Cohen rode shotgun beside him. He smoked a cigarette, leaning out of the open window of their Ford Escort cruiser. Springtime, irises and tulips in bloom on the hills. The air just smelled different. Fresher. Good.

The week before while on foot patrol they heard a girl scream on Sirkin, in the entrance to one of the buildings there. Eddie and Cohen ran for it. They were just in time to stop Heavy Ezra from raping the girl. They hauled Heavy off her and they slapped him around some and then Cohen took out his baton.

'Why, Ezra?' he said.

And Heavy just looked at him and shrugged and said, 'It's springtime.'

Eddie watched as Cohen hit. Heavy cowered on the dirty floor. The baton smashed into his face, his mouth. Heavy spat out teeth. Heavy cried. The girl cried too. Eddie walked her down the road, to the next streetlight.

'You want to watch out,' he told her. 'It's not always safe out there.'

'Sure,' she said, 'sure,' and then she walked away, and he didn't think she'd heard a damn foolish word he'd said.

There was a drug station on Sirkin in one of the apartment

blocks. Eddie knew it, and Cohen knew it, and sometimes they'd see buyers coming in or going out, and sometimes they'd see the couriers, but they never did anything about it. Eddie had wanted to arrest the pushers the first time, but Cohen laughed, and explained why it wasn't worth it.

'If you bust them they'll just come back,' he said, 'and if you bust them enough they'll just move down to the next block. You think they're short on empty flats in Hadar, or people who want a fix? Besides, shutting them down or not, that's a tactical decision. It comes down from Area Command or Narcotics. We're just the soldiers, Eddie. We're just the boots on the ground.'

'So what,' Eddie said, 'I just let it go on?'

And Cohen said, 'No, Eddie, you *study* them. You make contacts. A policeman's only ever as good as his informants.' And that evening he organised a sit-down, with Eddie and two of the pushers, Sammy P and Baldy, at the shawarma stand up on Herzl.

Cohen was only a couple of years older than Eddie but it felt like he was born in uniform.

Cohen and Sammy P and Baldy greeted each other with warmth. 'I tell you,' Sammy P said, 'if I had it in me I'd join the force too. Money in the bank each month and no trouble. You can't ask for more.' He wiped tahina off his chin. 'This other business, what is it good for? I tell you, nothing. But we gotta pay the rent.'

In truth Eddie kind of liked him. He knew guys like Sammy P because a lot of them were in the police academy with Eddie and most of them were in uniform now. It was always like that. It wasn't like the police paid well, but at least they paid on time.

Baldy didn't say much. He was quieter. But after they ate and before they left he said something to Cohen and Cohen nodded.

'There's some guys going to rob the jewellery store on Melchett tonight,' Cohen told Eddie.

Eddie didn't ask questions. They waited in the shadows that night and it was just like Cohen said. There were three of them, in dark clothing, bags ready, one of them an older boy who had a toolbox with him and had the door to the store opened in no time. Eddie and Cohen stepped in and caught them right in the act. When they brought them in, even Sergeant Moskovich who had been there since before the war was impressed.

'It was all Eddie,' Cohen said, and he gave Eddie the wink. 'His tip, his arrest.'

Later they had coffee at a place that never closed down by the harbour, and Eddie asked him why.

Cohen shrugged.

'I'm never going to make top rank,' he said. 'It isn't in me. But you, you could be Commissioner one day.'

Eddie laughed, but Cohen wasn't kidding. Eddie didn't understand Cohen. But it didn't really matter if he did or not.

'What are you thinking so much for?' Cohen said now. The car window was down, the warm breeze blew in and Cohen had changed the station on the radio to Reshet Bet, and 'Red Dress' by The Nahal Army Band played. The upbeat music made them both laugh. A little girl in a red dress with two ponytails who stood and asked why, and no one had the answer.

They'd been promoted to a car. The jewellery job didn't hurt. The whole of the North District was theirs, from the Lebanon border to Netanya. Eddie loved it. The north was wide open, the Carmel mountain evergreen, below it in the valleys lay grass-green kibbutzim surrounded by orange trees and avocado plantations and fields of wheat. It was like a pre-war P&O Cruises poster for a holiday in Palestine. They'd just come back from a domestic call in Caesarea and had managed to squeeze in a fish lunch in the harbour before heading back when the Motorola two-way buzzed.

'Calling all units south and coast, we have a report of a female body found in Tantura, repeat, female body found in Tantura, please identify your location, over.'

Cohen picked up the transmitter.

'This is car zero-five, Constable Cohen speaking. We are on the coastal road driving north, we are' – he glanced at Eddie for confirmation – 'ten minutes away from Tantura Beach. Shall we proceed? Over.'

There was a scratching of static before Dispatch came back on the line.

'Proceed to Tantura, secure the scene. The medical examiner is on his way. Over and out.'

Cohen gave a whoop. Eddie pressed down on the gas. He was going to make it in five.

He switched on the siren. The little Ford Escort shot forward, the few small cars on the coast road moving out of its way. They passed Kibbutz Ma'agan Michael with its fish ponds on the sea. On their right rose Zichron on the hill and below it lay the Arab village of Fureidis. He and Cohen had thought of stopping there to buy some olive oil earlier.

Tantura was just ahead and Eddie drove fast. Tantura used to be an Arab village until the War of Independence, and then it just disappeared. Eddie didn't really know how. Some things you just didn't ask. Now it was just a swimming beach where the bodies were buried.

Eddie remembered going there some summers with his parents, eating tomato and cheese sandwiches, begging for ice-cream from the kiosk. They pulled into the small car park at the main entrance, where a nervous attendant was waiting.

'It's not here,' he kept saying, 'it's down by the hirbe. I called the police from here because this is the only phone. Come on already.'

Eddie and Cohen exchanged amused glances. They followed the man. There were a few people on the beach and a family picnicking on the sand, but the man took them left, away from the small bay and its tiny islands that were just as Eddie remembered them, then past tiny guest houses.

There was no more beach now, only coves and rocks and fishes swimming in the shallows, and it was very pretty. The beach attendant was breathing heavily.

'Did she wash up on the shore?' Cohen asked.

The man shook his head and muttered.

'You will see,' he said.

A dirt track ran down from the main road to the sands ahead of them. A broken stone house, the hirbe as the man called it, the ruin, sat on the sand, a small group of hikers beside it. Eddie saw something lying on the beach.

'Why call us if it's just a drowning?' he said to Cohen, keeping his low voice.

Cohen lit a cigarette, passed it to Eddie.

'I think you'll need it,' he said, lighting a second one for himself.

Eddie's sense of foreboding grew and his good cheer dissipated. There was death and he had seen his share of it. Only the month before he and Cohen were called out to Haifa Harbour, where a decomposing body had washed up. And the year before, during the war in the Sinai, he was in the midst of the battle with the Egyptians, until they'd had to run, to give up all the territory they'd won the war before, and he'd seen stuff there.

So he wasn't scared of seeing a dead body. But still. He could tell from the attendant's manner and from the way that group of hikers stood that something was very wrong with this particular corpse.

When they came to the ruin the hikers moved away from them, silently. Avi saw that one of them, a big, tanned guy, had sick in his big black beard, and the two girls with him looked pale and had been crying.

Cohen was very quiet. Eddie looked.

A part of him didn't want to. He saw the long black hair spread across the sand.

The pale, naked skin, the small breasts.

The slim watch on her wrist, the sort of cheap watch you'd get from one of the stalls at the bus station.

He saw the bruise marks and the bra strap wrapped around her neck.

He saw enough.

'You found her?' Cohen said. The hikers nodded.

'When?'

'An hour ago. We came here for a stop, thought we'd make some coffee. Instead we…' The girl fell quiet.

'Did you touch anything?'

'No! I mean…'

'I checked her pulse,' the man said. 'I was a medic in the army. But she was dead. I think I knew, I just didn't want to know, you know?'

Eddie nodded. Cohen said, 'I'm going to have to ask you to step away from her now. All of you. Eddie, can you set up?'

Eddie nodded. He moved mechanically. Marking the crime scene. Making sure no one passed. He stared at the dirt track that led down to the beach. It must be just a turn off from the coast road, he thought. They must have passed it in the car.

'Tyre tracks?' he said. 'Footprints?'

'Yeah,' Cohen said. 'Like in the movies, right?'

He pinched the end of his cigarette between his fingers and pocketed the stub. 'One of us should call Dispatch, let them know to take the turning or the medical examiner's going to be pissed.'

'We're going to have to ask you some questions,' Eddie told the hikers gently. 'Take a statement.'

'Sure,' the girl who spoke earlier said. 'But we don't know anything.'

'Did you see anyone with her?'

'I told you, we found her like this.'

'She was stiff,' the bearded man said. 'I think she died last night. Rigor mortis.'

'Aha,' Eddie said. He couldn't concentrate. He kept stealing glances at the girl on the beach, then felt guilty for some reason, like it was an invasion of privacy. He wanted to cover her with something. It wasn't right that she was left like that, like trash.

'I'll go,' he told Cohen. He jogged down the shore, up and down the rocky terrain, back to the beach, the tiny islands, a fat kid licking an ice-cream cone while his mother dipped her toes in the water and his dad read *Davar* in the shade, the newspaper shading his face from the sun. Eddie found the phone in the office and called in and told them and Dispatch said they'll let the medical examiner know. He was on his way.

Dr Schatz must have been on his way *fast*, because when Eddie got back to the hirbe, Schatz's car was just coming down the track. The first thing he said when he got out was, 'Did you touch anything?'

Eddie shook his head. Schatz patted him on the arm. Schatz spoke with a thick Hungarian accent. They said he'd lived through the Holocaust, surviving on the streets for two years before the war ended. None of his family lived.

They also said he liked to talk to the bodies.

'What do we have here?' Schatz said. 'Give us some room, give us some room!' he said irritably. He knelt by the corpse.

'Who did this to you?' he said. 'You will tell me,' he said, 'you will whisper it to Schatz… Menachem, take pictures.'

The photographer was already out, his Canon snapping photo after photo. Schatz examined the body without touching anything yet.

'Bruising on her arms and chest,' he said, 'A broken nail, bruising on left wrist – you fought him, didn't you?' He hummed as he worked, speaking softly. 'Semen on—' he said, and Eddie turned away. He was sick into the bushes.

Cohen was there when he straightened up. They looked at each other. Cohen nodded.

'It's awful,' Eddie said.

'We'll find him. We'll make him pay.'

'Do you think so?'

They didn't speak again. The rest of the day went by fast. They took witness statements, the photographer came and went, the ME declared the victim dead and ordered her loaded onto the ambulance. By then the place swarmed with activity, officers and detectives had pulled in, and Eddie and Cohen were left forgotten in the hubbub. Cohen lit them two more cigarettes and they leaned against a rock and watched the sun play on the sea, the little fishes leaping in the air from time to time.

'I remember coming here once, years ago,' Eddie said. 'We went in for a swim and only then realised the sea was filled with jellyfish. The small purple ones, you know?'

'The ones that sting.'

'Yeah. They were suddenly all around me. Then I felt the first one, then the next. I started crying, it was deep and I was scared. I was only little. I couldn't touch the bottom and these creatures were everywhere.'

Eddie took a drag on the cigarette and started to cough. He wasn't really much of smoker and he didn't like the smell. It was just that everyone did it and it looked great on the screen, like when Belmondo did it in *The Fingerman*.

Cohen waited him out. Behind them the body was being wheeled away but neither of them mentioned it. They watched the sea.

'So what happened?' Cohen said.

'My father jumped in and pulled me out. I had marks all over later. Like somebody'd been putting cigarettes out on me.'

'That must have been nice,' Cohen said, and Eddie said, 'What?'

'Your father saving you.'

'It was. He's a good guy, my dad. Still is.'

Cohen nodded.

'What about yours?' Eddie said.

'He's dead,' Cohen said. 'Arab sniper took him out during the War of Independence, one shot, straight in the head, right from the top of the Rushamia Bridge.'

Eddie winced. Cohen was so matter of fact about it.

'I was born a month later.' Cohen smiled round his cigarette. 'The day Ben Gurion declared independence.'

'I'm sorry,' Eddie said.

'What for?' Cohen tossed the cigarette into the sea. 'I want to do something, Eddie. I want to catch this bastard. Whatever it takes.'

'We're just uniforms,' Eddie said.

'And then I want to hurt him,' Cohen said.

'I'm not smoking anymore, it's disgusting,' Eddie said.

'Are you listening to me?' Cohen said.

'What do you want me to do?' Eddie said. 'What do you want *us* to do, Cohen?'

'I don't know. Help.'

Eddie said, 'Then let's find someone we can help.'

15

THE MACHINERY OF JUSTICE

'It's all junk. But that's the job' – Cohen

'Yes,' Detective Sagi said. He was only a few years older than them but had climbed through the ranks fast. He had a thick moustache and thick arms and he wore a chequered shirt tucked into his jeans. His notepad and two pens were tucked into his shirt pocket. 'Constable Eddie Raphael, correct? And you're Cohen. Come with me.'

'Yes, sir,' Eddie said.

'The girl was found without clothes or belongings, correct?' Detective Sagi said.

'Yes, sir,' Eddie said. 'Except for her bra. She was, um, strangled with it and it was left on the body.'

'Correct,' Detective Sagi said. 'If not entirely helpful, Constable. I want you to join the others, search the area. See if you can find anything. Her shoes. Her bag. Maybe her ID card will be in it. Maybe you can find a piece of paper on the ground with the name of the killer on it and an address. That would be helpful.' He barked a laugh at his own joke. 'Anything that stands out. Anything suspicious or not. We don't know who she was. We're checking any reports of recently missing persons but in the meantime… Start looking, gentlemen.'

'Yes, sir,' Cohen said.

'Yes, sir,' Eddie said.

Half an hour later Eddie had found three cigarette stubs, two condoms, a man's shoe sized twelve with holes in it, a military water canteen, a broken pen, five bullet casings, a popped balloon in light blue with *Happy Birthday* on it, a tin of sweetcorn, empty, a Coca Cola bottle, also empty, a broken lighter and too many mosquito bites on his arms and face to count anymore and he was fed up.

'This is all just nothing,' he said.

Cohen picked up a bullet off the ground. 'Hey, look, a whole one.'

'You don't want to – oh, come on, Cohen, what are you, a kid?'

Cohen was grinning happily. He pulled the bullet head out carefully and poured the gunpowder from the casing into his palm. 'Did you use to do that too?' he said.

'Sure, who didn't. We'd go looking for bullets on the Carmel where the soldiers did their training. Look for bullets, pick them right off the ground like mushrooms under the pines. Then we'd light up the gunpowder.'

Cohen made a neat tiny pile on the ground and lit it with his lighter. The gunpowder *whooshed*. Cohen laughed.

'I love that,' he said.

'Think any of this is any use?' Eddie said.

'It's all junk,' Cohen said. 'But that's the job.'

'What do you think happened?'

'I think he drove her down to the rocks, and then he raped her, and then he killed her, and then he dumped her body on the sand and got right back in his car and drove away. That's what I think.'

'And her clothes? Her bag?'

'If he was smart he took them with him and burned them.'

'And if he wasn't so smart?' Eddie said.

'Then he tossed them somewhere on the way. Most murderers, they're not so smart, Eddie. They're like policemen. If they were smart they'd be doing something else.'

They kept trudging along but they didn't find anything. Detective Sagi called a halt when it got dark.

'We'll try again tomorrow,' he said. 'You two, you come with me.'

'Sir?'

They followed him in their cruiser. Sagi drove a Fiat. He drove fast.

'You should arrest him, Eddie,' Cohen said. 'He's driving over the speed limit.'

Eddie turned on the siren. He grinned at Cohen.

'How's that?' he said and hit the gas.

Sagi gave them the finger in the mirror. They followed him to Haifa Harbour and parked outside the Beer Fountain right behind him.

'You boys come in,' Sagi said.

'Sir?'

'You can drive me home later.'

Not waiting for them he went inside. Eddie and Cohen followed.

A long counter, polished wood tables, a lot of glass bottles behind the bar. The smell of garlic and smoked pork and cabbage. It smelled good. Eddie realised suddenly that lunch was a long time ago.

At the end of the room sat a group of detectives. Eddie knew who they were. Everybody did. Sagi nodded to the men but stood perched at the bar.

'Three beers,' he said.

'Sir, we—'

'Relax. Shift's over. What a fucking day, huh?'

'Sir, any progress on the case?'

'The case?' Detective Sagi looked amused. 'No, Eddie,' he said. 'Schatz is doing the autopsy. Miller's looking at missing persons. We have a couple of possibles. One girl was hitchhiking from Tel Aviv back to Haifa, only she never made it back that night. Her boyfriend swears blind he dropped her off at the Tel Aviv trempiada, where everyone catches rides from.'

'We're working with Tel Aviv District, sir?'

'We are indeed.' Again Sagi looked amused. 'Teacher soldier, I believe she is. Nothing to be alarmed by. She probably had another boyfriend in Haifa and spent the night with him and she'll turn up. But we'll see. Ah, there you go.'

He pushed the beers at them and took a sip from his own. 'You were quick on the scene today,' he said.

'Just bad luck,' Eddie said.

'This is going to be a long one,' Detective Sagi said. 'Most murders, someone just blows up one day. Just have it all bottled in for too long until they snap. Most murders, they're waiting for you when you come to arrest them.'

'Not this one, sir?'

'Not this one,' Sagi said. 'What do you think, Cohen? I notice you don't talk too much.'

'I think there was another girl that was found two years ago,' Cohen said. 'Jacqueline Smith. English volunteer on Kibbutz Ma'agan Michael. They found her body by the fish ponds. That's what, down the road from where we just were?'

Sagi stilled.

'So?' he said.

'Never found the killer.'

'People die, Cohen.'

'Sixty-eight,' Cohen said. 'Another girl, found in an orange grove near Hadera. On the coast road. Raped and stabbed. Two years before that, another girl, same place.'

'What are you trying to say, Cohen?'

'Who does this?' Cohen said. 'It's like you said. Most people just blow up one day. A murder of passion. A murder of desperation. But this, today? That's something different.'

Sagi turned and looked at him fully.

'You think I don't know about the other girls?' he said. 'You think we were made yesterday? But it's not to say they're all connected. My money's on the boyfriend. It's almost always the boyfriend. A little tip for you there.'

'It won't be the boyfriend,' Cohen said.

Eddie said nothing. He stared between them. Felt the tension, but didn't know what caused it. He tasted his beer.

'We just want to help,' he said. 'We want to do something.'

Sagi and Cohen still stared at each other. Then Sagi laughed.

'You think like a criminal, Cohen,' he said.

'Yes, sir.'

'I'll think about it,' Sagi said to Eddie. 'You two, stick around. I'll let you know when it's time to go.'

'Sir?'

But Sagi went to join the other table, and the detectives

welcomed him with a cheer. They motioned the bartender and a bottle of Jim Beam materialised.

Avi looked at Cohen.

Cohen shrugged.

'Hey,' he said to the bartender, 'you got something to eat?'

The bartender said, 'You going to pay for those beers?'

Eddie said, 'But we didn't order them.'

Cohen laughed. He took a wad of cash out of his pocket. Counted out ten ten-lira notes. 'This cover it?'

The bartender made the money disappear. He said, 'You cops?'

'Hoping to be.'

'Anything else you need?'

'Another beer, please. And a shot of araq for me and my friend here.'

'Sure thing.'

'I don't really drink much—' Eddie started to say.

Cohen said, 'You do tonight.'

The bartender poured them drinks. They touched glasses, l'chaim. Eddie thought about the hundred liras Cohen put down so casually. He didn't want to ask but then it just came out.

Cohen said, 'I work extra jobs.'

'Doing what?'

Cohen shrugged. 'Whatever comes up,' he said.

Eddie didn't pursue it. It was hot inside the Beer Fountain and the alcohol made him warm inside. The detectives at the table were roaring at someone's joke. The bartender went away and came back from the kitchen and put down a big plate of meat in front of Eddie and Cohen and a whole bowl of chopped garlic.

'Costiza,' he said.

'What is that?' Eddie said.

'Smoked white ribs.'

'You mean it's pork? I don't eat pork,' Eddie said. 'I mean, it's not that we're shomrei mitzvot, my parents didn't keep kosher, but pork, I mean.'

The bartender wasn't really listening. He plonked chopped liver on the counter, pickles, white bread.

'Another beer?' he said.

Cohen nodded. Eddie picked at the ribs carefully. The taste was amazing, salty, smoked, fat. The garlic was so raw it stung. It could heal cuts.

He tried not to think about the girl on the beach. He knew right now others were working, Dr Schatz would have finished his autopsy and be typing up his report, other detectives would be talking to the families of missing persons, the reporters would be filing copy for the morning editions, and the whole machinery of justice would be creaking into gear. He knew those detectives at the table, who were laughing and drinking, cared about the girl and her killer. Just as he knew they couldn't make it personal. He picked at the chopped liver. He thought of the cheap watch the girl wore on her wrist, of the bra strap wrapped around her neck, of how her black hair fanned over the sand.

'How do you know about the other girls?' he said to Cohen.

'Everyone knows. They just don't want to know.'

'Why do you care?' Eddie said. He put an accent on the you. Why did Cohen care? Cohen was so cool the rest of the time about stuff.

'Someone has to care,' Cohen said, and Eddie sighed. He wasn't going to get anything more out of Cohen.

It was close to midnight when the detectives were done. Sagi staggered to the bathrooms and came back still zipping his pants.

'Either of you good to drive still?' he said.

'I think I am,' Eddie said, though he was grinning foolishly. Sagi just nodded. He gave him the address, up on the Carmel, a good neighbourhood. Cohen was half-slumped on the bar.

'I'll catch you tomorrow,' he mumbled.

Eddie managed to get in the car and he drove Detective Sagi home. He stopped outside the house. The lights were off and the night was quiet. He shook Sagi's shoulder until the detective woke up.

'Where am I?' he said.

'Home.'

'Alright.'

Sagi stepped out of the car. He stood under the streetlight.

'Come see me tomorrow, both of you,' he said.

He went into his house, and Eddie drove away.

16

RUTENBERG

'She died a soldier' – Mrs Nachmias

'She was supposed to be back the day before yesterday,' the girl said. Her name was Rona, which was short for Sharona. She was perched on a chair at the open reception area of the station. 'We share a room at Rutenberg House, only she never came back.'

'You are a soldier teacher?'

'We both are. We were doing a training course only Esther never came back. We had the graduation ceremony yesterday.'

'Did you report it to the army?'

'I… No, I mean, I figured maybe she was seeing a boyfriend, and we'd already done the course, it wasn't like she'd be missing anything. But it isn't like her.'

'What is her name?'

'Esther Landes.'

They were back at the police station, Eddie with his first real hangover, and it hurt. Cohen seemed unruffled. Detective Sagi was inside with the commanders, so they dumped talking to the girl on Eddie and Cohen. She was only one of several people clamouring to claim the dead girl, and so far all the results were negative.

'What does Esther look like, Rona?' Cohen said.

'Short, skinny, long black hair. Pretty.'

'If we showed you a picture, could you identify her?'

Rona put her hand to her mouth. 'You mean a picture of—'

'Yes.'

She took a breath, nodded. 'You really think it could be her?'

'We don't think anything,' Cohen said. 'We're just trying to figure out who she is. Can I get you a coffee or something?'

'Please, yes. I mean, no. I'm fine. Show me the picture.'

There were teams searching the coast road for the girl's belongings and others going around the bus stops and the gas stations on the way, trying to see if anyone remembered seeing the girl, but neither team so far had any luck.

Cohen nodded to Eddie. Eddie took out the crime scene photograph. He showed it to the girl.

'Oh my God,' Rona said. 'Oh my God, Esther.'

Eddie felt his heart quicken with a rush of adrenalin. Rona started to cry and Cohen comforted. Eddie ran. He burst into the meeting room without knocking, found a room full of officers and detectives staring at him over Turkish coffee and the blue fug of cigarettes.

'We found her,' Eddie said.

Chairs scraped back. Detective Sagi got up first. He motioned the others to settle.

'Show me,' he said.

He followed Eddie outside. The girl was crying. Cohen had his arm around her. Sagi went to her.

'You identify her?' he said.

'That's Esther. What did he do to her?'

'Could you identify her body?'

Rona's crying intensified and Cohen shot Sagi a look of pure hatred.

'Not now, not now,' Sagi said. 'Cohen, get her a coffee. Eddie, take her to Room Two and make sure she's comfortable.'

He marched off.

'Will you come with me, please?' Eddie said. He offered her his hand and she took it. Her hand was wet with tears.

'Come where?' she said.

'We just need to ask you some questions.'

'Poor Esther, I don't... I didn't think it would be her. I was afraid but... I thought she'd turn up, that she's just with some boyfriend.'

'Did she have many boyfriends?' Eddie asked.

'I don't know. She went out with some guys. Dates, you know. I think she was seeing someone back home in Bat Yam. Older guy. She said her parents didn't like him.'

She followed him into the interrogation room and sat down without being asked. Cohen showed up a moment later. He placed a coffee on the table and an ashtray.

'I put sugar in,' he said.

'Thank you.'

Detective Sagi came in and with him Detective Hillel, an older man with a yarmulke and white chest hairs poking out of the unbuttoned top of his chequered shirt.

'We'll take it from here,' Detective Hillel said. He turned to Rona. 'You told Constable Cohen you both stay at the Rutenberg House?'

'Yes, we were there for a training course. Esther got a vacation permit and she went home to Bat Yam but she was going to come back for the graduation ceremony, I told Constable Cohen that.'

Hillel nodded. 'Cohen, go to Rutenberg House. I want a full inventory of the girl's room. Constable Raphael, go with him.'

Rona said, 'You're going to search my room? But why?'

'Your shared room,' Hillel said. He touched her hand in a fatherly gesture that seemed somehow natural, coming from him. 'We need to learn all we can, you understand.'

'Of course, of course—' Rona said.

Detective Sagi inched his head at the door. Eddie got the message and got out, Cohen with him.

'They'll rip her apart,' Cohen said, angry. 'That poor girl.'

'They have to interview her,' Eddie said. 'And they're professionals.'

'We found her,' Cohen said. '*We* found her.'

Eddie said, 'Esther Landes.' His voice was quiet.

Eddie drove fast. Cohen said nothing and they didn't turn on the radio. They came to the Rutenberg House, high on the mountain with the sea in the distance and the Baha'i temple gardens spread out below. It was a colonial-style house, pre-Independence. It had its own grounds, and columns at the entrance. Cohen and Eddie knocked and were let in.

'You can't just go in and search the room, though,' the manager said. She was a tall thin woman with dangling earrings and a teacher's voice.

'It's murder,' Cohen said, and the woman wilted. 'You can call Detective Sagi at Haifa Station, just dial one zero zero. Alright?'

'Well, I suppose...'

'Thank you, giveret. Could you show us to the room...?'

She did. Eddie found that you didn't really argue with a man in uniform. Not if you were a good person, the sort who read the literary supplement in the paper, could quote a line of Alterman, never bought real eggs on the black market during the long austerity years, who still did reserve service in their old unit every year and didn't make excuses about missing work, the sort who raised their children right to love this country. He could tell the giveret was one of those. Most people were, or so Eddie Raphael wanted to believe. Most people were good people, who didn't rape and kill young girls, though he had the feeling Cohen didn't really believe that, and Eddie was beginning to believe it less and less himself.

The room was on the second floor. The window opened onto the courtyard. There were two beds in the room. Eddie and Cohen went through the drawers, the wardrobe, looked under the beds, turned over the mattresses. There wasn't much.

'Grunt work,' Cohen said.

'It might lead to something,' Eddie said.

'It's all junk,' Cohen said and smiled. 'But it's the job.'

Eddie pulled a photo taped to the wall above one of the beds.

'That's her,' he said.

Esther Landes looked happy in the picture. She wore shorts and a white shirt and sandals, and her smile was carefree. Her arm was wrapped around a man who smiled at the camera though there was something hesitant in his smile.

'This must be the boyfriend.'

Eddie turned it over. In pencil, scribbled on the back in a somewhat childish hand it said, 'With Udi before the Red Path meeting.'

'This must be Udi, then,' Cohen said. 'Don't know what she saw in him.'

'What's a Red Path?' Eddie said.

Cohen shrugged. 'Sounds leftist.'

'Anything else?' Eddie said.

'No bag, no ID card, no money,' Cohen said.

'So she had it on her.'

'Yeah.'

'No diary, no little phone book.'

'So she had it on her.'

'Yeah.'

'Anything else?'

'Two school notebooks with more squiggles than class notes, a dress, two pairs of shorts, five pairs of socks, one set of uniforms, bras, underwear, three blouses, five pens, a coffee cup from the kitchen downstairs – Eddie, what are we doing here?'

'Maybe she wrote something in the notebooks,' Eddie said.

'Sure, maybe. The name and address of her killer maybe.'

'What's the matter with you, Cohen?'

Cohen packed everything up to take back with them. 'Not even a letter,' he said.

'Let's just get this back to Sagi.'

'Yeah. Hey, I need you to make a quick stop on the way.'

Eddie stared at Cohen. The man looked angry. He kept staring at the picture Eddie still had in his hand.

'What?' Eddie said.

'It's always the boyfriend,' Cohen said, quoting Sagi.

'You said it wasn't. You said—'

'I wouldn't mind a word with him, that's all. How old was she, Eddie? Eighteen?'

'Nineteen,' the manager said. She appeared in the door, looking shaken. 'She's really dead?'

'I'm sorry,' Eddie said.

'She would have been a good teacher,' the woman said. 'Even if she was a little wild. All the girls go a little crazy when they get here, we're a teacher course, not an army base. They all smell freedom. And the city's just there...'

'You knew her well?' Cohen said.

'As well as any of them. They always sneak out, you know. The cinema or dancing or boys. They're not supposed to but what are you going to do, police them? They're not kids anymore. Have you informed the army?'

Eddie looked at Cohen.

'Our boss will,' he said.

'She died serving her country,' the woman said. 'She died a soldier. I want you to remember that. And the army needs to be informed.'

'I am sure they already are,' Cohen said gently. 'Thank you, giveret...?'

'Nachmias. You'll find whoever did this, won't you, detective?'

'Constable,' Cohen said. 'Constable Cohen. We will do all we can.'

'Good.'

She walked them out. She held herself with a straight back and dry eyes, and she shook both their hands before she let them out.

'She might be worth talking to again,' Cohen said.

'Not our call,' Eddie said. 'Come on, let's get this stuff back.'

'Sure.'

They got back in the car and Eddie drove.

'Only, I still need to make a quick stop,' Cohen said, and he gave him directions.

17

INTO THE TUNNEL

'Tell what?' – Eddie

'You stay in the car,' Cohen said. 'I won't be a minute.'

They were outside a nondescript office block in the lower city. Cohen vanished inside. It was the sort of place that had shipping clerks and money changers and tiny numismatist shops, maybe some import-export offices. Eddie drummed his fingers on the steering wheel. Then he said, 'Fuck it,' to himself and got out of the car. He went inside, to a building that had seen better days, and up scuffed stairs and walls nobody cleaned. He passed doors with no activity and it felt as though the whole building had gone out for their afternoon sleep already, though it was not yet even lunchtime.

Then he heard Cohen's voice coming in through a door on the third-floor landing. When Eddie came close he saw the door was just a little ajar, and he opened it carefully and looked inside.

The office could have been any kind of office, with a desk and a telephone and filing cabinets and an in-and-out tray. The windows were grimy and beyond them lay the lower city and the sea.

A man sat in the chair behind the desk, his arms raised in pleading.

'I told Benzion, I will have the money next week!' he said.

'I know what you told Benzion,' Cohen said. 'But the money's owed now, Mr Bichler.'

'I told Benzion, you can ask him,' the man said. 'He's got cheek, sending you in like this, in uniform.'

'Look, Mr Bichler,' Cohen said. 'I don't know from this or from that. You had an agreement with Benzion. If you make an agreement, you stick by that, that's how my mother raised me.'

'Just tell him that—'

Cohen lifted the phone off the desk. It was a heavy duty, black Bezeq phone, the rotary dial worn with use. Cohen slammed the phone across the other man's face. Mr Bichler fell off his chair and crashed to the floor. Cohen tore the wire from the wall and lifted the phone and hit Bichler with it again and again. Eddie, watching, felt sick inside and yet with a sense of strange excitement he couldn't explain, and it made him ashamed. Cohen sat down over Bichler, straddling him.

'The money, Bichler.'

'There's… In the safe…'

'Well then, open the safe,' Cohen said.

'Let me… go.'

Cohen hit him one more time.

'Get up,' he said.

Cohen waited by the window as Bichler rose slowly to his feet. Bichler shuffled to a Gutman reproduction on the wall and moved it aside to reveal a small safe. Cohen glanced at the door. For a moment, his and Eddie's eyes connected.

'Open it,' Cohen said.

'This is all I have, I can't—'

Cohen strode to the wall and went out of Eddie's view. Eddie heard an intake of breath, a soft whistle.

'I can't, Cohen, this is all I have.'

'How many of these are there?'

'This is it, Cohen. Listen, bubele, you've always been good to me. Why don't you take a couple for yourself? I have a buyer, I just need time, next week, you tell Benzion.' Bichler sounded desperate. Eddie wanted to see. The door creaked and he startled. Bichler said, 'Who's there!'

Eddie went inside. Bichler stood with the safe door open. Cohen stood with an envelope in one hand and a pile of small, perfect diamonds in the palm in the other.

'Officer, help me!' Bichler said.

'Shut up,' Cohen said. He weighed up the tiny diamonds. 'Count yourself lucky, Bichler. It's this or the window, and from the third floor, I don't know, I am not a betting man but you are. You might just make it. What will it be?'

'Take them,' Bichler said, and spat blood. 'I'm ruined,' he said.

'Gambling ruins lives,' Cohen said. He put the diamonds back in the envelope and then he put the envelope away.

'Come on, let's go,' he said to Eddie.

Eddie followed him in a dream. Down the stairs and back into their car. He started the engine.

Cohen said, 'You're going to tell?'

Eddie stared at the road.

He said, 'Tell what?'

They went back to the station in silence. When they got there it was anything but. Senior officers and army officers and plain clothes in the corridors, typists and secretaries and constables and someone from the mayor's office and reporters.

'Quiet!' Detective Sagi roared. He spotted Eddie and Cohen.

'What have you got?'

'Not much.'

'You come with me.' He took them into an interrogation room. 'There's going to be a special investigation team,' he told them. 'I want you attached.'

'Why us?' Eddie said.

'Because you do what I tell you,' Sagi said. 'They're taking this from us and giving it to Tel Aviv on account of that's where she was last seen. They're giving it to some Arab. Chief Inspector Awad. You'll be attached to his team. Do what he tells you, keep your mouth shut, and when that cocksucker fucks up they're going to give it back to me. You got it?'

'Mouth shut, do what we're told,' Cohen said.

'Good,' Sagi said. 'Go home and pack a bag. You're going to Tel Aviv. Do you have a car, either of you? Constable Raphael? Good. Then take it. We'll need the cruiser here. Make sure to keep any gas receipts and you can claim them back from Noga in Accounts.'

'What do you mean, where she was last seen?' Cohen said.

'Tel Aviv spoke to the parents and then they tracked down the boyfriend,' Sagi said. 'He says he dropped her off at the hitchhiking spot the night of the murder and that's the last anyone's seen of her. If I know Awad he's going to lean hard on that boyfriend, what's his name?'

'Udi,' Eddie said, 'we found his picture in her room and—'

'Mazal tov, Constable,' Sagi said. 'But events have moved on. Now fuck off. I have enough of a headache over here.'

'Yes, sir.'

'Yes, sir!'

They left. They looked at each other.

Eddie grinned. Cohen grinned.

'Tel Aviv!' Eddie said.

'Meet you at Central Carmel?' Cohen said. 'At the Carmelit station.'

'I'll pick you up in an hour,' Eddie said.

It occurred to him he didn't even know where Cohen lived. Somewhere in the lower city, if he was taking the Carmelit. It was the pride and joy of Haifa, a pulley car that only had one route, from the harbour up to the mountain top. Eddie caught a bus home, had a quick shower and packed a bag. His own car was a tiny Fiat 500 with a two-cylinder engine. It whirred gently as it tried to climb the mountain.

Cohen was late. Eddie parked and waited. He remembered a job they gave him, his second week as a constable. He was fresh out of the academy. Some Carmelit maintenance workers found a severed human hand in the tunnel. The Carmelit had two tracks and two cars, and when one car went up the other went down. It was a woman's hand, and Eddie and some of the others fresh out of training were sent in there to search for the rest of the body.

They found her in bits, a leg here, a foot there, half a torso, eventually what was left of a head. Eddie remembered the oppressive weight of the tunnel over his head, the strange stops, empty of people, mannequins standing behind glass display windows. Sometimes in the dark someone would shout, 'I found one!'

They were down there for hours.

The next day in *Davar* an inside page notice briefly mentioned the dismembered corpse, but that was it. It seemed a gruesome murder, but Dr Schatz concluded it was probably a suicide. It was amazing what a train full of cars dropping down from a height and not stopping could do to a human body. The detectives worked out who she was eventually, there had been another missing person report though it took a while to come through, and they learned she was some girl from Yoqne'am and they'd been told she'd seemed depressed recently. What secret sorrow she carried within herself she took with her into the tunnel.

Cohen knocked on the window.

'What are you dreaming about, girls?' he said.

'Yeah,' Eddie said. Cohen went around and got in the passenger seat. He wriggled and stretched his legs as far as he could. 'Can this thing even make it to Tel Aviv?' he said.

'Guess we'll find out.'

'I'm going to smoke,' Cohen announced. He rolled down the window.

Eddie said, 'Sure.'

'You want one?' Cohen said.

'I'm good. Thanks.'

Cohen lit up. Eddie rolled down his own window. The little Fiat darted along the avenue and soon they reached the top of the Carmel and the little car sped along the road into the forest. Pine trees grew on both sides of the road and air was fresh and soon the houses vanished and there was only forest. There was something eternal about the old Carmel. So many people have lived and died along its slopes and, to the dead, a few more dead made not a difference. Neanderthals and modern humans lived together in the caves nearby, or so he'd read once, and Phoenicians, Egyptians, crusaders and even Napoleon all came and went – most recently the British. Soon the first of the Druze villages came into view and they passed restaurants and curio shops and were through. At a bend in the road an old Druze in a kefiyah had set up a stall selling coffee and labneh, with a makeshift coal fire for the bread.

'Do you want to stop?'

Cohen nodded. They stepped out and made small talk with the old man and bought two rolled pitas with labneh, za'atar and olive oil, and they ate it next to the fire and had two small, black Arab coffees. In a way, Eddie thought, they were delaying the inevitable moment when they'd have to pass the place Esther Landes died, if that was where she'd died. Eddie hadn't read the autopsy report yet. The file was in the car.

'Can you drive?' he said.

'Sure.'

They swapped places and continued on. Eddie leafed through the file. They were going down the mountain now, past Daliyat al-Karmel and the old Carmelite monastery that everyone called the Mukhraka, the place of burning, because this was where the prophet Elijah slaughtered the priests of Ba'al. There was a statue of Elijah with a bloodied sword raised high stepping on the severed head of one of the foreign priests.

'It says here it's inconclusive where she died,' Eddie said.

'Meaning?'

'Either he took her to Tantura and then killed her or he did it first and then dumped the body. What do you think?'

'I don't think, Eddie. I either know or I don't know.'

'So you don't know.'

'He had to have a car, right?' Cohen said.

'How else would they get there?'

'He could have met her on a bus, or…'

'And talked her into going to the beach at night? Come on.'

'So where is the car?' Cohen said. 'If we found the car we'll find our guy.'

'No witnesses, yet.'

'The boyfriend has a car,' Cohen said. 'Remember? He dropped her off.'

'What kind of a guy drops off his girlfriend to hitchhike at night?' Eddie said.

'Unless he didn't. Unless he did drive her.'

Cohen followed the road, down Bat Shlomo's way, and they saw a group of riders on horses in the distance. Soon they passed Fureidis and Eddie realised that he was wrong, they weren't going to pass Tantura after all, and perhaps that was why they'd both opted to drive through the mountain.

Back on the coast road the little car gathered speed, though there was more traffic. Trucks carrying produce and an old kibbutznik tractor holding up the traffic, moving at its own damn speed, an Egged bus heading the other way, to Haifa, two army jeeps, and plenty of Fiats and Fords heading to Tel Aviv. On a billboard sign a young girl stared out at the sea holding a cigarette between her fingers.

She's young, she's smart! The sign said. *She wants the best and she gets it. She smokes Nelson's.*

'Bialik smoked Dubek,' Eddie said.

Cohen said, 'Yeah?' without much interest.

'"Sing, my bird, of the land, where my living forefathers found death!"' Eddie said dramatically. 'I remember that from school. We did a lot of Bialik.'

'That's nice,' Cohen said. 'Well, not nice, but you know what I mean.'

'Do you think we'll find him, Cohen?'

'I don't know.'

'Who's Benzion?' Eddie said. The words came out before he could stop them. Cohen kept his eyes on the road.

'He's just a guy who helps people out sometimes,' he said. 'Lends them money when they need it, that sort of thing.'

'Right,' Eddie said.

'Is this going to be a problem, Eddie?' Cohen said.

'No.'

'You want to ask me any more questions, Detective Raphael?'

'I'm just a constable,' Eddie said, and he smiled, and Cohen smiled, and then they saw the sign for Tel Aviv ahead and the lights of the big city shone on the darkening horizon.

18

TEL AVIV

'Famous people don't live in Haifa' – *Cohen*

'Why are you still in uniform?' Chief Inspector Awad said. 'You're no use to me in uniform. It's not that you're much use to me out of uniform, either, but I had to take you because everyone plays politics.' He looked at them in what seemed to Eddie suspiciously like amusement.

'What did Sagi tell you? Stay out of trouble and report back to him? Something along those lines?' Awad said. 'Well, you can pass along to that prick that he can kiss my asshole.'

'Yes, sir,' Eddie said, and even Cohen smiled.

'We're going to be based out of the building on Salame in Jaffa,' Awad said. 'It's quiet there since nearly everyone but the Nazi Crimes Division moved to the new headquarters in Jerusalem. The new HQ being where your Detective Sagi no doubt hopes to find himself one of these days. So listen to me, both of you. I don't care about any of this stuff. I'm an Arab, so no one's ever going to make me Commissioner, and that means I can do shit the Jews can't, like focus on actually trying to *solve* the crimes. A woman is dead. I want to put someone in front of a judge for that and I want to see them go to jail and I would certainly *prefer* it if it was the right person who went into the cell. Can you work with that? Yes?'

They both nodded.

'Then be at Salame eighteen, tomorrow morning at eight o'clock sharp. It's the old British police station, you can't miss it. Wear civilian clothes. We're probably not going to need you much, but you never know. I've got to go back to interrogation now. You have a place to stay?'

'I've got an aunt near the Central Bus Station,' Eddie said. He'd called his mum to call his aunt, who agreed both he and his friend could stay since this was for a good cause but they mustn't mind the dog and should each pay ten lira a night to help with her expenses since she wasn't getting any younger. Eddie hoped he could claim it eventually from Noga in Accounts, though he wasn't entirely sure how you got a receipt from an aunt.

'Nice area. Alright. Is there anything else?'

'Is he in?' Cohen said. 'The boyfriend?'

'Udi Raveh, yes,' Chief Inspector Awad said.

'Has he said anything?'

'He has said a great many things, Constable Cohen.'

'Can we sit in on it?'

'You cannot.'

'Can we watch?'

'Keen, are you?' Awad smiled. 'I thought you'd be more eager to hit the town, sample the delights of Tel Aviv in the night-time.'

'On a constable's salary?' Eddie said, and Awad laughed.

'Come on, then,' he said. 'You can tell Sagi I'm looking after you better than my own children.'

He walked them to the observation room. It was dark and cramped and filled with silent men and cigarette smoke. Behind the glass sat Udi Raveh.

Raveh also smoked. He wasn't handcuffed and he looked tired and a little defiant. He was maybe twenty-four, twenty-five. Eddie found that he could barely make out his face. He was what witnesses always called 'non-descript'. He was just some guy.

Awad entered the interrogation room.

'When are you going to let me go?' Raveh said.

'You are in a hurry?' Awad said.

'No, it's just… I'm still trying to come to terms with what happened. I can't believe it's real.'

'Tell me again what happened,' Awad said.

'I told you three times already!'

'Tell me again.'

'Esti came home a few days ago, surprised me. I thought she was still in the army. She got a permit, left early. I was happy to see her, though I wasn't expecting her. She complained my flat was messy. You have to understand, I'm one of those guys, I'm just not good at keeping house. It's just not in me. So Esti cleaned up, then she offered to cook dinner. She's a good cook. Was. Oh, God. She made us something, I forget what. She slept over. Her parents don't like me much. I don't know why. Esti and I met at a demonstration, three years ago I think.'

'Three years ago?' Awad said. 'She was only sixteen.'

'Come on,' Udi Raveh said, 'I'm hardly much older than she is. Was. Oh, God.'

'But you were of legal age,' Awad said. 'She wasn't.'

'You'll forgive me if I don't buy into this bullshit bourgeoisie mentality of yours, Chief Inspector. Esti was an old soul. She understood better than most the injustice that this society inflicts on the people whose land we sit on, and – what, look, she wasn't a kid.'

'What happened after she surprised you?'

'I told you, she made us both dinner. We thought of going to a movie but we were both too tired. We put on some music, I had some cognac, then we went straight to bed.'

Awad waited. His silence enticed words Udi Raveh seemed desperate to provide.

'She stayed with me three more days,' he said. 'Well, she went to her parents, too. And her friend Shosh was going to join us. She's her best friend. Shoshana. They went to school together. Only she didn't come. Then the day Esti was going to go back to Haifa I was going to drive her there, only I had a meeting of the Red Path in the evening and I didn't want to be late, and she insisted she was fine to hitchhike. "What's going to happen!" she said. I wish… I wish I didn't let her persuade me. But it was late and the meeting, it was important, though almost no one came in the end, in fact I'd had to cancel, and by then… I guess she got into someone's car. I left her at the usual spot, at the trempiada, I figured it would be easy for her to get a lift at that hour, someone going back to Haifa from Tel Aviv. I didn't know…'

'What was she wearing?'

'Blue shorts, a white blouse,' Raveh said. 'I told her she should wear something more, travelling like that at that hour, but she just laughed at me. She was wild when the mood took her. You couldn't argue with her.'

'Did you argue?' Awad said.

'Who doesn't argue?' Raveh said.

'What did you argue about?'

'I didn't say we argued! I was just saying—'

'But you did?'

'Fine, we had an argument. But it was nothing. I don't even know how it started. She had moods sometimes. She felt I was distant. I'd been neglecting her on this visit. She wanted to go to the pictures, this new Uri Zohar movie. I didn't want to. I don't care for Uri Zohar and my cat was sick. I wanted to see *Charlie and a Half* but she said she already saw it in Haifa. We had a fight then went to sleep and in the morning I went to check on Epicurus and he wasn't moving. Epicurus, that's my cat, I named him after the Greek philosopher. Epicurus said death should not be feared.'

'Your cat said that?' Awad said.

'What? No. The philosopher.'

'I see.'

'I was very distraught. So was Esther. She loves animals. Loved. Oh, God. We tried to take him to the veterinarian but there was nothing they could do but take him. I didn't have anywhere to bury him so I let them. Poor Epicurus. Poor Esther.'

He buried his head in his hands.

'Let's take a short break,' Awad said gently. He left the room and they watched Udi Raveh sit there alone. Raveh glanced at the window. Then he sat still and stared straight ahead and didn't speak.

'You boys can go,' Awad said. The door to the observation room was open. Eddie and Cohen escaped the dark and the smoke and the smell of sweating men standing too close together.

They got back in the car and Eddie drove through the unfamiliar streets, Cohen holding the map book in his lap, squinting at squares. They got lost a couple of times before finding Har Tzion.

The Central Bus Station was busy with buses pulling in and out, stalls selling watches and cassettes and flowers, people waiting around, soldiers heading back from base and workers late from work. Eddie pulled into Neve Sha'anan but couldn't find parking.

'Park there,' Cohen said, pointing.

'But it's over the lines.'

'If you get a ticket just call Traffic and get it cancelled.'

Eddie parked. The street was busy, greengrocers shouting and hawkers selling the evening edition of the papers and people sitting outside cafes or grabbing a falafel from a stall. Outside a fancy-looking restaurant called the Shiraz he saw parked luxury cars, Volvos of the sort only government ministers used, a rare Mercedes. Eddie spotted a man heading to the restaurant with a girl on his arm. He pointed.

'Is that Haim Topol?' he said.

Cohen started to hum "If I Were A Rich Man" and they both laughed.

'Hey, Topol!' Eddie shouted. 'Topol!'

The actor turned, saw them, waved and ducked into the Shiraz taking the girl with him.

'I think he's the most famous person I ever met,' Eddie said.

'Famous people don't live in Haifa,' Cohen said.

They climbed the stairs to Eddie's aunt's apartment on the third floor. Aunt Sarah pinched Eddie's cheeks and enveloped him in a hug of perfume and menthol cigarettes. Her little dog barked excitedly around them.

'That's Genghis,' she said.

'Like Genghis Khan?' Eddie said, surprised.

Aunt Sarah looked at him blankly. 'Who?' she said. 'No, like Zrubavel Ha'navi, you know, the general? Genghis, Genghis. You know he keeps lions in his headquarters? But I keep a little lion right here, don't I, don't I?' she said. The little dog wriggled in her grasp.

'Thank you for letting us stay,' Cohen said.

'Anything for our boys in uniform,' Aunt Sarah said. 'That poor girl. And you found her? It's in all the newspapers, you know. They're saying this isn't the first girl to die like that. Do you really think it's possible? Someone killing our girls? It's so terrible.' She shuddered dramatically. 'You must tell me all about it, I won't tell a soul.'

'We can't, Aunt Sarah,' Eddie said apologetically, and his aunt laughed.

'Never mind, I was just testing you,' she said. 'I'm late for Mabat on the television and you know you have to keep up with the news. Otherwise how will you know what is happening? Here's a key, mind that you come in quietly if you go out later. Don't use too much hot water in the shower! I made you a couple of beds in the spare room. Come along, Genghis! That nice Chaim Yavin is on.'

She left them there. Cohen and Eddie exchanged amused glances. The room was small but tidy and the two single beds were made like army beds, the thin blankets folded so tightly you could bounce a coin on them.

'What do you want to do?' Eddie said.

'It's not late,' Cohen said.

Eddie buzzed with a nervous energy. There was hunger in his stomach but it wasn't for food. He nodded. They got changed into civilian clothes, the two of them in their white underwear and off-balance trying to put on jeans in that small room until they both had to laugh.

'We're going out, Aunt Sarah!' Eddie shouted on the way out. Genghis barked in reply. Night had settled when they got out on the street. The streetlights burned and the air was warm and perfumed with a smell that was all of it of Tel Aviv and none of it of Haifa. He didn't know what London smelled like, or New York. But Tel Aviv had a smell that said, what's the point of sleep? Come play with us.

'One second,' Cohen said. He went to a phone box, put in tokens, dialled. He spoke briefly.

'Come on,' he said, 'I have to stop somewhere.'

'Are we taking the car?' Eddie said.

'Why take a car when we can walk?'

They went past the buses and the flower shops and an orange juice stand and falafel stalls. Pretty girls in shorts walked up and down the street, an old man leaned against the wall of an alleyway smoking a cigarette, his sunken eyes studying everyone passing by, and on a corner a group of long-haired kids sat with flowers in their hair and played guitars: Rotblit's 'A Song For Peace'.

Girls with long legs and short skirts sat at cafes and the moon shone down on it all like this really was the Tel Aviv of the movies, the Tel Aviv of Uri Zohar and Arik Einstein and *Perverts*, the film they made two years earlier that purported to show this new, carefree, hedonistic city. It was nothing like Haifa, where old Abba Hushi ruled with an iron fist until the very end of the sixties, so much so that his detractors called the city Hushistan. They said that in his time, when a sailor set foot down in Haifa Harbour he had to go to Tel Aviv to find his fun. Hushi stamped down on prostitution, had built the university and the Carmelit, but even he couldn't control the smuggling in and out of the harbour – and some said he didn't want to.

Eddie smelled the city and the city called to him and he thought that Cohen was right. He could rise up the ranks, if he played the game right, if he listened to his superiors and made himself useful and kept his mouth shut when he was told to, and if he did that he could leave Haifa, with its hard-up people and its steep and winding streets and come here, to Tel Aviv, a city where you could be someone other than yourself: a city where you could be free.

They came to the area called the Yemenites' Vineyard near the market, though the market was closed for the night and all the stalls locked. There were more shadows and people in the shadows and a young man, accented in the way of the North African immigrants, approached them and asked if they wanted to buy, and Eddie and Cohen didn't ask what. This was the sort of street they both knew.

Eddie understood, deep inside, though he could not articulate it into words exactly, that he and Cohen were different, that he, Eddie, was privileged somehow. He had never lacked for anything and his Hebrew was more like the ones the newsreaders used on the radio and TV. He was in a combat unit in the army and he'd fought in the last war and early promotion was not a possibility for him but a certainty. And he began to dream of what rank meant, and what it could get you. Somehow, the journey along the coast road from Haifa to Tel Aviv changed his perception, or perhaps it was the dead Esther Landes, reminding him how quickly and violently things could end. She could be wild, the boyfriend said. And Eddie thought perhaps she knew she didn't have long left.

They went deeper into the alleyways and Eddie wished he'd brought his gun but Cohen moved with quiet purpose. Eddie didn't know what Cohen wanted, though he sensed in his partner some longing that could have been ambition. But an ambition for what?

Who are you, Constable Cohen? he wondered. What is it you really want?

They came to a restaurant with young men standing outside who stared at them with sullen expressions.

'Help you?' one said. Eddie looked at them. Looking for weapons.

'They said they'd meet me.'

'Yeah? Who are you?'

'Cohen.'

'You stay here.'

He went inside the restaurant. Eddie and Cohen waited. The young men stared at them and Eddie stared back.

'You stay out here,' Cohen said in a low voice. 'It will only take a minute.'

Eddie said, 'No.' Cohen nodded.

The man came back.

'Alright,' he said.

They went in together.

Two men sat at a table laden with food and drink. They were both smoking. They wore nice suits. One was small and bald and the other thin and with a pencil moustache. Eddie knew who they were. They were often in the papers.

'Come in, come in,' the small man said. He pointed a finger at Cohen. 'I know you,' he said. He moved the finger to Eddie. 'I don't know him.'

'He's with me.'

'Stop giving him a hard time, Midget,' the other man said. His name was Tuvia Oshri. He looked at them both with a sardonic smile. 'What are you, constables?' he said. 'You have to be at least a sub-inspector to sit at this table.'

'Even constables grow up to be inspectors some day,' Cohen said. The man's smile widened.

'Well, let's see it,' he said.

Cohen took out an envelope. Eddie recognised the envelope. Cohen put it on the table and Midget reached across and took it. He opened it and upended the contents on the table. The tiny diamonds Cohen took from Bichler back in Haifa shone.

'Nice,' Midget said.

'Alright?' Cohen said.

Midget played with the small diamonds, moving them like marbles with his finger. He nodded.

Tuvia Oshri took out an envelope and tossed it at Cohen. Cohen caught it.

'Don't insult me by counting it,' Oshri said.

'I wouldn't,' Cohen said.

'He's a smart one,' Oshri said.

'Smart, in Haifa,' Midget said. 'You ever make it to Tel Aviv you give us a call, bachurchik.'

Cohen nodded. He put the envelope away.

He went out and Eddie went with him. It was cooler outside.

'What now?' Eddie said. He was sweating and his heart was pounding and he'd only just realised.

Cohen grinned at him. 'Now we go party,' he said. 'Here.'

He took out a hundred lira note from the envelope.

'I'm not going to take that, Cohen,' Eddie said.

'For your aunt,' Cohen said. 'For the room. That's all.'

Eddie took the money.

'Let's go to Dizengoff,' Cohen said.

'Walk?' Eddie said.

'Fuck walk,' Cohen said. 'Let's take a taxi.'

Back on the main road he flagged one down and they both crammed in. The radio was on, playing 'I'll Pinch You' by the Southern Command Band. The taxi driver sang along with the band, telling the girl in the song that if she smiled at him he'd pinch her, pinch her hard...

'I don't like this song,' Cohen said.

'Where to, boychiks?' the driver said.

'Dizengoff.'

'It's a long street, Dizengoff. Anywhere in particular?'

'Yeah,' Eddie said. 'Anywhere with loud music and girls.'

'You from out of town?' the driver said. He hummed. 'I'll pinch you, girl, I'll pinch you, girl… It's catchy,' he said.

Dizengoff wasn't far. The street was long and the taxi crawled along it. Eddie saw cafes, fashionable clothes stores, bookshops and music stores with guitars in the windows, and everywhere young people walking the pavements. Eddie could smell weed in the air. America had its sixties, he thought: Israel had the seventies.

The taxi came to a place with a sign that said *Tiffany's*. The door was half open. Flashing lights inside and the sounds of Abba. Long-legged girls and pretty boys spilled outside.

'That'll be twenty-one lira,' the driver said.

'Twenty-one!' Eddie said. He couldn't help himself.

'Hey, it's on the meter,' the driver said. 'What are you gonna do, buddy, you didn't want a taxi you got legs, haven't you?'

Cohen paid. They stepped out of the car. The driver said, 'Have fun!' He stuck around, looking hopeful that he'd find another fare. Eddie and Cohen went into the club. The music beat and the disco ball spun, and Eddie felt drunk with the noise and the smell of bodies close together, spilled alcohol, cigarettes, weed. He and Cohen pushed their way to the bar. Cohen shouted and pointed. Two shot glasses of araq and two beers, and the girl next to Eddie turned, laughed, and said, 'What are you, cops!'

'What?'

'I said, what are you, cops!' the girl shouted.

'Off duty!' Eddie shouted.

'Oh!' She looked surprised, then burst out laughing. 'I never kissed a cop before,' she said.

'What!'

She leaned into him and before he could speak again her lips found his and she kissed him, long and slow. When she pulled back they were both a little out of breath and Eddie was smiling.

'I'm Eddie!' he said.

'Eddie the cop,' the girl said. 'I'm Galya. Wanna dance?'

'Sure!'

Eddie downed his araq and felt the warmth light him up. He grinned like an idiot.

Galya took his hand in hers and led him onto the dance floor as Abba were replaced by the Bee Gees. The music pumped and Eddie danced awkwardly, arms flopping and legs hopping, and the girl, Galya, laughed and moved with the music. This was no place for Hebrew songs and Hebrew lyrics: nothing was sombre and nothing was sanctified but the rhythm and beats, the bass and the synth.

He couldn't see Cohen.

He forgot everything, forgot Esther Landes lying dead on the sand. He let the music and the lights take him away.

19

THE GOOD OFFICER AZOULAY

'Are you trying to impress me with your bourgeoisie liberalism?' – *Galya*

When Eddie woke he felt he was still drunk. Dawn light seeped in through the Venetian blinds and he had no idea where he was. It wasn't his bedsit in Haifa and he was pretty sure it wasn't his Aunt Sarah's flat.

Something soft moved against him. He felt hands envelope him, a warm cheek press to his chest.

'It's too early…' she mumbled. Then she started to snore.

Eddie looked at his watch. Six-thirty. He had time. He eased himself out of bed. He had no idea where he was. His head spun. The girl opened her eyes. She smiled when she saw him.

'I'd love to see you again,' Eddie blurted. He tried desperately to remember her name. Galya? Amalya?

The girl said, 'Why?'

Eddie didn't know what to say.

'Can I shower?' he said.

'There's no hot water. Come back to bed.'

'I have to go. It was…' Eddie thought. 'It was lovely,' he said.

'It was nice,' the girl said. 'You look like shit, though.'

'I haven't slept much.'

The girl smirked. 'No, you haven't,' she said. 'Here, take one of these.'

She reached in a drawer, brought out a small bottle of pills.

'What are they?'

'Wake you up stuff. I don't know.'

'Alright.'

Eddie popped two. He went out of the room and found the shower. The water was cold but he didn't mind. When he opened the curtain he saw a man brushing his teeth in the sink. The man took a disinterested glance at Eddie and went back to brushing.

'You're Galya's friend?'

Eddie said, 'Aha.' He grabbed a towel and tried to squeeze past the man until he escaped into the corridor. He went to Galya's room.

'Hero cop returns,' Galya said. 'You look good with nothing but a towel on.'

She threw aside the blanket and lay there on her back looking up at him. Eddie swallowed. Whatever was in those pills had woken him up.

Well, *something* was up.

'How far are we from Jaffa?' Eddie said.

'Don't remember much, do you?' Galya said. Her hair fanned across the pillow and her body was naked against the sheets and God, no, he tried not to think of Esther Landes, not now.

'We're near Town Hall,' Galya said, and into his blank look – 'Kings of Israel Square? The centre.'

'So?' Eddie said.

'You could get a bus, won't take you twenty minutes without traffic.' She ran her hand down her flat stomach, almost shyly.

'So?' she said.

Eddie fell on her and she giggled and bit him on the shoulder. They didn't speak then. She moaned into his neck. The pills must have really been working because he was so hard and he kept going, hard, trying not to think of Esther Landes naked on the beach, his mind lost in the physical act until Galya, without warning, shoved a finger up his ass and Eddie gasped in surprise and came.

'What was that!' he said.

'You were possessed,' she said. She lay beside him panting. 'It was nice though. Now you can go. I still have two hours before I have to get up for my shift.'

'What do you do?' Eddie said.

'I wait tables at a café on Dizengoff,' she said. 'But I'm an actress.'

Eddie lay on his back, looked at the room. A poster for *The Good Officer Azulai*, with Shaike Ofir in uniform saluting. Scented candles scattered around, clothes on the floor, both his and hers. The new Garcia Márquez novel, *One Hundred Years of Solitude* in the softback Am Oved edition, thrown on the bedside table along with a pile of pamphlets for organisations with names like Mazpen and Avant-garde and the Workers Alliance and the Red Path. Eddie reached for the top one, which showed a heroic worker facing the sun with a raised fist salute, in the style beloved by early Soviet artists and kibbutzniks both.

'What's this?' he said.

Galya yawned. 'Literature,' she said.

'What sort?'

'Listen, hero cop, there are people out there, good people, who believe we as a state commit a great injustice,' Galya said. 'That we are sitting on occupied land, that we are heading to a disaster unless workers not just here, but all across the Middle East rise as one, to fight for a fair society where all men and women are equal.'

'You mean, leftist literature,' Eddie said. 'What are you, a kibbutznik?'

'I grew up on a kibbutz, actually,' Galya said. 'But that's not what I mean. The kibbutz movement is as much a part of the problem, sitting on Arab land, on the ruins of villages left abandoned as their residents were forced to flee their homes by the Haganah. What?' she said. 'You know it's true.'

'It's not that simple,' Eddie said.

'It's not that complicated,' Galya said. 'But you have to go work.'

'My boss is an Arab,' Eddie said. He didn't know why he said it, and Galya laughed.

'Are you trying to impress me with your bourgeoisie liberalism, hero cop?'

'My name,' Eddie said, 'is Eddie.'

'I know. And I'm Galya. Nice to meet you.' She extended her hand and he shook it and they both laughed.

'Come over tonight if you like,' Galya said. 'There is a big meeting at eight.'

'Maybe,' Eddie said. 'I don't know…'

'Cops are workers too, Eddie,' Galya said. 'It's at the social club on Pumbedita. You know where that is? It's not far from here, actually.'

'What the hell is a pumbedita?' Eddie said.

'I think it was a city in Babylon, back when there were Jews there,' Galya said. 'Are you going or what? I want to get an hour's sleep.'

He kissed her. It felt nice, kissing her. Then he got dressed and left Galya's apartment.

It was a beautiful day. Not yet hot, but already the sun shone brightly, and the air felt fresh. Eddie asked an old lady how to get to the Kings of Israel Square and once there he caught a bus towards Jaffa.

He just about made it. When he got to the police building he saw his Fiat parked in the empty lot, and Cohen leaning on the car.

'Fucker,' Cohen said without malice.

Eddie grinned sheepishly.

'You made it back to Aunt Sarah's?' he said.

'Genghis tried to hump my leg this morning,' Cohen said.

'I guess he likes you.'

'Come on,' Cohen said. 'Let's go be the dumb fucks from out of town for Chief Inspector Awad.'

'You don't like him?'

'I don't like Arabs much in general,' Cohen said.

'He's a Christian though, isn't he?' Eddie said. 'I'm sure I saw a gold cross round his neck.'

'Still an Arab.'

'You don't think all workers across the Middle East should rise as one, to fight for a fair society where all men and women are equal?' Eddie said.

'What?'

'Nothing,' Eddie said. 'Just something I heard.'

'You look a bit jumpy,' Cohen said.

'Not enough sleep,' Eddie said. It wasn't like he was going to tell

Cohen about the pills Galya gave him, though they made him feel great. He gnashed his teeth.

'Come on,' Cohen said. They went in just as the clock over the reception desk struck eight.

'Can I help you?' a rotund officer said. He munched on a half-eaten cheese burekas.

'We're with Awad.'

'You're cops?' the desk man started to laugh. 'Second floor,' he said.

They went up the stairs, to a room down an empty corridor. When they went inside, Awad and several others were already there.

'You're late,' Awad said.

'We were on the minute!' Eddie said.

'That's late,' Awad said. 'Sit down, stay out of the way.' He went back to the blackboard behind him. There was coffee and pastries on the table and detectives lounging back in their chairs smoking. Eddie and Cohen sat down at the back. Pinned to the blackboards were pictures of Esther Landes, Udi Raveh, and the front page of an amateur magazine Eddie recognised for the worker with the raised fist and the legend, which said *Solidarity, Justice, Resistance: Journal of the Red Path*.

'Let me sum up for the benefit of our colleagues from up north,' Awad said, drawing some laughter. 'One, the autopsy report confirms this is death by strangulation. It was preceded by forced sexual intercourse, and there were traces of semen left on the victim. The victim fought, but was overcome. The time of death was between eleven at night to around three in the morning. According to Udi Raveh's testimony, he dropped off the victim at the trempiada at ten-thirty the night of the murder. We are still trying to find an eyewitness who can remember her being there but, as I think we can all agree, this is likely to prove a futile endeavour. So far, no witness has come forward to conveniently notice a car turning off into Tantura or leaving the scene, no one saw the murder, no one saw the dead girl, and if you believe we'll find a useful witness in this case you may as well play the Lotto. So if you believe the newspapers we *could* have a repeating sex killer on our hands, some ghost who strikes at random every couple of years, and if you believe that you probably also believe Yizhak Rabin really gave up the booze.'

A couple of the detectives laughed dutifully.

'We work within a system of law,' Awad said. 'Not within the realm of speculation. Our job is to identify a suspect and to build a case that is beyond reasonable doubt and could persuade a judge. That is all. The last person to see the girl alive was her boyfriend, Udi Raveh. I think we are all familiar with the statistics of murder in this country and elsewhere. It is always the husband or the boyfriend. So what do we know about Udi Raveh so far? Yes, Shimshoni?'

'Udi Raveh, twenty-five years old, wounded in the Yom Kippur War, where he lost his left foot,' a detective with a butter cookie in his hand said. 'Discharged with distinction and currently a second year history student at Tel Aviv University. Lives on his own, father is in advertising – you know that jingle for milk? "Milk, milk, it makes your skin feel like silk – drink milk!" from the Milk Board? That's his.'

'A true claim to fame,' Awad said. 'Please continue.'

'Right. Raveh is on pension from the army on account of his injury. Besides studying he is a member of a radical group called the Red Path, who split from Matzpen back in seventy-one for not being radical enough, apparently. As we all know, it was only two years ago that members of similar splinter group, the Revolutionary Communist Alliance, were convicted for spying on behalf of Syria, for collaborating with an enemy nation, and for planning terror attacks. They are now serving time in prison.'

'Conclusion?' Awad said.

'There are two possibilities of interest,' the detective said and took a bite from the cookie. He sprayed crumbs as he talked and Eddie looked away. 'One is that Raveh, acting out of jealousy or some other motive, killed the girl. The other, and it is a more far-fetched possibility yet one we cannot entirely discount, is that her murder was planned by the Red Path committee as a terror attack.'

'Correct,' Awad said. 'Personally, I don't love either of these options. One, the man is a cripple, could he really kill the girl and, if so, why? And two, all those Jewish leftist organisations do is publish newsletters no one reads and talk too much. And last I checked it was still free to talk.'

'So what *do* you want, Chief Inspector?' someone else said.

Awad shrugged. 'I want to conduct a proper investigation. Raveh is clearly our prime, and currently only, suspect. So either we clear him, or we find that he could have done it beyond reasonable doubt.'

'A confession, basically,' the detective with the cookie said.

'Unless you find me some evidence,' Awad said. 'Alright. We have already tossed his place and found nothing suggestive beyond communist literature. Sandursky and Elias, you track down everyone he knows. Girlfriends, boyfriends, school friends, army friends. See what comes up.'

'Already on it, boss.'

'Rappaport and Abuksis, you look into the radical groups side of things. Mendel, you look into Esther Landes. Find out who her friends were, who she talked to, who she told her secrets to. She may have had another boyfriend or even boyfriends—'

'You know what those leftists are like, total hippies,' the detective with the cookie said and choked. He coughed, spraying more crumbs. 'I'm fine!' he said.

'The family has asked us to release the body to the army and since the autopsy was concluded we have complied. She will be buried today at the military cemetery on Mount Herzl. May her memory be blessed.'

'May her memory be blessed,' the detectives all mumbled, and Eddie joined them.

'Now get to work.'

The detectives rose. Eddie raised his hand.

'Yes, Constable Raphael?'

'What about us, Chief Inspector?'

'You, yes. I don't fucking know, Constable. Are you good for anything?'

'We're good plenty,' Cohen said.

Awad sighed. 'Did you even get any sleep last night?' he said.

'Sir? I met a girl last night and she's in with this crowd,' Eddie said. 'The leftists, I mean. She invited me to a meeting.'

'The one on Pumbedita Street, at eight tonight?' Awad said. 'What?' he said into Eddie's surprise. 'You think we don't know? They don't make it a secret. I was going to send some men down to sniff about but sure, if you want the job you and Cohen can have it. I hope you're up on your Marx and Engels.'

'The dictatorship of the proletariat,' Cohen said.

'That's the spirit.'

'What do we do now?' Eddie said.

'You can join Mendel. See what friends she had, who she talked to. Maybe she had another boyfriend, maybe Raveh got jealous. If so, at least we have a case. I am going to Jerusalem.'

'Jerusalem, sir?'

'The funeral, Raphael.'

Eddie and Cohen exchanged glances.

'Can we… Can we come with you?' Eddie said.

'With me? What the hell for?'

'We found her,' Eddie said, and saw that Awad softened.

'I know I've given you a hard time, kid,' he said, 'you being that asshole Sagi's eyes and ears on my team here, but let me give you a bit of advice. Don't get attached to the victims. Esther Landes isn't the first girl to die like this and she's not going to be the last. The ones that are coming… They're going to need you, Constable. Both of you. I think you know what I mean, Cohen. I read your file.'

'Yes, sir,' Cohen mumbled, and Eddie shot him a glance – what did it say in Cohen's file?

'Still, sir. She deserves justice.'

'She does. We all do. But justice is in short supply here.' Awad rubbed the bridge of his nose. 'Look,' he said. 'The funeral's at midday. If you two happen to make your way there on your own, no one's going to stop you. Alright? What friends she had will turn up there anyway. Maybe you could do some quiet investigating. With those boyish good looks of yours, Raphael, I'm sure you could make headways. Funerals are a great place to meet girls.'

'Thank you, sir.'

'And I want a report on the Red Path meeting on my desk tomorrow morning. Now go.'

'Yes, sir!'

They left but not before they grabbed two coffees and a handful of cookies for the road, the leftovers from the detectives' breakfast.

'Which one was Mendel, any idea?' Eddie said.

Cohen grinned. 'He was the one eating all the cookies.'

'I don't see him anywhere,' Eddie said.

'Me neither,' Cohen said.

'So what now?' Eddie said.

'Grab some files and let's go to Jerusalem,' Cohen said. 'I'm not sure your car can make it up that mountain road, though.'

'My car can make it just fine,' Eddie said.

20

THE FUNERAL

'The dead don't go away' – Cohen

The car wasn't fine. It struggled valiantly up the steep incline of the Bab el-Wad road while Cohen gritted his teeth and held on to the wheel for dear life.

'We're going to stall,' he said.

'We're not going to stall.'

'We're going to stall.'

An Egged bus crawled past them. Beyond the road lay the burned remains of crudely armoured vehicles from the battle for Jerusalem in '48, now positioned artistically at different points along the way. Yaffa Yarkoni had a famous song about the dead. Everyone had a famous song about the dead. Cohen began to bellow: 'Bab el-Wad... Bab-el-Wad!'

'Stop that!' Eddie said. 'I'm trying to read the report.'

'We're going to stall,' Cohen said.

'We're not going to stall.'

The air grew cooler as they climbed up the mountain. Eddie leafed through the file. He saw Awad had Udi Raveh in interrogation for hours.

Awad: Was Esther a part of your political group?'

Raveh: She was not a member but she had solidarity with the group. We met at a political rally. You are an Arab, Chief Inspector—

Awad: Last I checked.

Raveh: Does it not bother you? That this nation's foundation stone is that it is a Jewish land, for Jewish people? That no matter what you do or how far back your family goes here, you are suddenly and inexplicably recast as both foreigner and minority?

Awad: Does it bother you?

Raveh: You're damn right it bothers me! I want to stress to you that the Red Path is a peaceful protest organisation and we have nothing to hide.

Awad: Your comrades from, what was it, the Revolutionary Communist Alliance? They did not share your peaceful intentions.

Raveh: First of all, these are good people. Secondly, they were framed by the Shin Bet. What, you think Ehud Adiv and that lot are hardened terrorists? What did they really do, Chief Inspector? So they met with Palestinian groups.

Awad: They were members of a spy ring. Adiv personally travelled to Syria using false papers and was trained in sabotage.

Raveh: As interesting as this undoubtedly is, I fail to see the relevance to the fact my girlfriend was murdered.

Awad: Do you?

Raveh: What is that supposed to mean? What goes through your head, Chief Inspector? That I killed her? That this is some sort of elaborate political statement? She was my girlfriend! I loved her!

Awad: You loved her.

Raveh: I loved Esti. She was the sweetest, kindest girl… May I have a glass of water?

Awad: Of course.

Raveh: Thank you. I would not wish death on anyone, only life. Do you understand? The situation in this country is untenable. A land built on injustice is a land doomed to suffer. Surely you of all people must understand!

Awad: Say I do. For the sake of argument, you understand.

Raveh: I understand your position implicitly.

Awad: Very well. Let us say I too agree with what you say. What, then? One could choose to make the argument democratically, run for the Knesset on a political platform, for instance. Influence the system from within. Write newspaper columns. Distribute leaflets.

Raveh: Of course.

Awad: Or one may think this way is naïve. That this is an argument that was settled twenty-five years ago now.

Raveh: Twenty-six.

Awad: Twenty-six years ago. And so the only remaining option is armed resistance. A war to liberate Palestine from its occupiers.

Raveh: Yes, of course.

Awad: To follow Yasser Arafat and the PLO, or to cooperate with the Arab nations such as Egypt and Syria, which have the best chance of freeing Palestine. The Yom Kippur War was a great blow to Israel, for instance. A Jewish spy network assisting Syria would have had a tremendous impact.

Raveh: It is a valid argument.

Awad: Such a hypothetical spy network could also carry out terror attacks. Murder, for instance.

Raveh: The Red Path is a peaceful organisation. You must stop chasing shadows and start looking for the man who killed Esther!

Awad: I am just doing my job, Mr Raveh.

Raveh: You are wasting time.

'Anything interesting?' Cohen said.

'Not really. See, she holds.' Eddie tapped the dash. Then they came to a rise and Jerusalem appeared ahead of them like a crown on top of a mountainous head. Cold white stone and the aura of a locked Torah ark. The little Fiat found the slope and gathered speed. The last approach to Jerusalem always felt to Eddie like the last loop on a ride in the Luna Park. He felt his ears pop.

'Think it's worth fighting over?' he said, pointing.

'Jerusalem is the eternal capital of the Jews,' Cohen said. 'This is not a matter for discussion.'

'Yeah, I mean, sure, just...'

'A lot of good men died here,' Cohen said, and Eddie gave up. But he didn't really like Jerusalem.

'Came here once when I was a kid,' he said, 'and my dad put me on a camel. You ever go on a camel? They spit.'

'I have not been on a camel, no.'

'It's cold,' Eddie said.

'What's in the file, Eddie?'

'Nothing. Raveh says he's innocent, his group just distribute leaflets or whatever, why aren't we trying to catch the real killer?'

'It's always the boyfriend,' Cohen said.

'Until it isn't,' Eddie said.

Cohen glanced sideways. 'You believe him?'

Eddie shrugged. 'I have no opinion. There's only beyond reasonable doubt. And we have no proof.'

'Spoken like a true detective. Anything at all useful in there?'

Eddie looked.

Awad: What about friends?

Raveh: Friends?

Awad: Esther's friends.

Raveh: She had a lot of friends.

Awad: Anyone particularly close?

Raveh: She was close to her sister. But her best friend was Shosh. Shoshana but everyone calls her Shosh. But your guys already spoke to her, didn't they?

Eddie stared at the page. He wished he'd been there during the interrogation. Something sounded off about that line. That last question. The tone seemed to him both too casual and a little desperate. And Awad did not reply, he saw.

'Shosh,' he said.

'A best friend?' Cohen said.

'So he says.'

'How close?'

'It's just weird the way he says it,' Eddie said. 'How he asks if we already spoke to her. We'd only just identified who she was, right? So why would we have talked to this Shoshana yet?'

'I don't know,' Cohen said, 'but it sounds like maybe we should.'

They came to the final rise into the city. The little car crawled along the road. Drivers beeped them as they whooshed past. Cohen gripped the wheel and whistled 'Bab el-Wad'.

When they came into the city the stones began to crowd them in. It was the British who passed the law that the city should continue to be built with local stone. Black-clad Orthodox hurried along the pavements, soldiers patrolled the gates to the Old City, and the little Fiat 500, unencumbered by history or religion, merrily passed them all by until it came to a stop outside a café.

Eddie and Cohen sat down exhausted. The Arab proprietor brought them black coffee, a spread of salads, pitas, humous. Eddie tore a piece of bread. Cohen popped an olive.

'If we do well with this,' Cohen said, 'we could get a promotion.'

'I don't think anyone will do well with this,' Eddie said. He thought of Galya, her taste, her heat, her laughter. He realised he really did want to see her again.

Cohen shook his head. 'Even if they fuck up – when they fuck up – they're still going to have to promote us,' he said.

Eddie stared at the humous.

'I wish she didn't die,' he said.

Cohen said nothing. Eddie said, 'What's in your file?'

'Excuse me?'

'Awad said something about how you'd understand, he read your file.'

'The one in '66,' Cohen said. 'Girl they found dead and naked in an orange grove? She was my cousin.'

'I'm so sorry.'

'Yeah, well.'

'Is that why you joined the force?'

'I don't know. It just seemed like a good job, you know? Stable,' Cohen said, but he looked elsewhere and Eddie could not read what was in his eyes.

'Come on,' Cohen said, 'let's get it over with. I don't like funerals.'

They paid and got back in the car and drove to the military cemetery on Mount Herzl. When they parked they saw the fat detective, Mendel, talking quietly to a man in dark glasses and Cohen said, 'I bet you a twenty he's Shin Bet.'

'You think?'

'I think this is what Awad is so scared of. If this goes political no one's gonna want an Arab on the case. His best bet is to solve it quickly or kick it back to someone else to handle.'

'Like Sagi?'

'Exactly. Unless the Shin Bet take it over.'

They got out and Mendel spotted them and came over. He didn't move fast.

'Awad said you'd be here. I've got proper men keeping an eye, and a photographer. I want to know anyone Raveh talks to, anyone who cries. Anyone who doesn't. You two, stay out of my way. Clear?'

'Sure,' Cohen said.

'We're just paying our respects,' Eddie said.

'Do that on your own time!' Mendel snapped.

They saw the coffin arrive. Soldiers carried the coffin and it was draped in the flag. It was only the army that used coffins, the army and kibbutzniks, anyway. Behind the coffin came the family, other mourners, soldiers. Eddie saw Sharona, the girl who first recognised Esther Landes in the picture. Her roommate at the Rutenberg House. He saw the manager, too, Mrs Nachmias.

Behind them, limping, he saw Udi Raveh. Next to Udi Raveh walked a young, black-haired girl, and Eddie guessed that she must be Shosh. The two of them walked close together, almost intimately.

The coffin was carried in and the mother burst into tears. Eddie saw that Udi Raveh grasped Shosh's hand. They watched Esther Landes being brought to rest. As the coffin was covered the mother gave an anguished cry and fell on the coffin and was pulled back. The grave was covered in earth. An army rabbi read the 'Woman of Valour' section from Proverbs. A woman from the Education Corps gave a eulogy. The father tried to give a eulogy and couldn't speak. He and the mother held each other and cried. The younger daughter stared at the fresh grave. The honour guard provided by the army prepared their arms then stood to attention.

The cantor sang 'God Full of Mercy'. The military rabbi said the 'Plea of Forgiveness'. Flowers were placed on the grave.

The honour guard fired their guns on command, into the air.

All in all it was an efficient and moving operation.

'The ceremony is ended,' someone said. The mother was led away. Udi Raveh and the girl stood over the grave. Eddie looked at Cohen.

'Here,' Cohen said. He gave Eddie a pebble.

Eddie nodded. They went to the grave. They each placed a pebble on the fresh mound of earth. Eddie saw that the girl, Shosh, was looking at him. He nodded.

'You knew her?' Shosh said.

Eddie said, 'I'm sorry.'

He and Cohen retreated and watched the rest of the mourners come to lay flowers or a stone.

'There are journalists outside.'

'And Mendel's detectives inside.'

'Did you see Awad?' Eddie said.

Cohen said, 'I did not.'

Eddie watched the grave and scratched the stubble on his face.

'It doesn't feel any different,' he said.

'What?'

'Now that she's buried. I thought, maybe… I don't know.'

'The dead don't go away, Eddie.'

'Let's just go back to Tel Aviv,' Eddie said. He stared at the white stones. The gravestones and the houses in the distance were the same.

'I hate this fucking city anyway,' he said.

21

THE FIGHT

'You're under arrest' – Eddie

At eight o'clock that night, washed and shaved and with the smell of Aqua Velva out of an ancient bottle his aunt had under her sink about him, Eddie arrived at Pumbedita Street. He was on foot. The social club where in the daytime old men played dominoes and cards still smelled of boiled cabbage and industrial disinfectant, and Eddie saw that despite the promise of what he thought of as a grand meeting of the radical left, not that many people had turned up.

A few people gathered in small groups outside, most of them smoking and most of them holding hand-printed leaflets of some sort or another. A lot of them had moustaches or thick beards and one even wore a Lenin cap, the sort that was popular among academics or the union leaders in the Histadrut. The doors of the club were open and chairs had been arranged in rows inside and a small stage was set up at the back. Eddie saw Galya as she came out and she spotted him. She walked over smiling.

'Eddie,' she said.

'Galya.'

'So you came.'

'I like to learn about the evils of the occupation and the inevitable rise of the felaheen proletariat,' Eddie said.

She punched him in the arm.

'Ow!'

'You're making fun of me,' she said.

'Only a little.'

'The occupation *is* evil,' she said. 'And the felaheen *will* rise.'

'Be careful what you wish for,' Eddie said. A guy came over just then. He was in his late twenties, in jeans and a white shirt, good-looking with an easy smile. 'Shalom, shalom, I'm Shalom,' he said, in what must have been a well-worn introduction for him.

'Shalom, this is Eddie,' Galya said.

'It's very nice to meet you, Eddie,' Shalom said. 'It's always nice to see new people come to our talks.'

'Eddie,' Galya said, 'is a policeman.'

Shalom's easy-going smile didn't go anywhere. 'Everyone is welcome here,' he said. 'After all, what does the police do but keep the shalom? And I'm Shalom!'

'You're so funny,' Galya said.

Eddie hated Shalom instantly.

'We all dream of shalom,' Shalom said.

'Some of the girls certainly do,' Galya said, and Shalom laughed and said, 'Oh, stop it!' He turned back to Eddie.

'Peace, Eddie! True peace, which requires justice! Does it not make you angry, that this is how Zionism ended? Zionism to its founders was a beautiful dream, a heartfelt wish for a permanent home for the Jewish people as a *nation*, a nation like all other nations as Bialik said, with its own policemen, its own prostitutes even. Bialik said that. But how can a nation endure here, when it is built on another nation's misfortune? This is against the universalist-internationalist view of socialism, and—'

He went on like this but Eddie was no longer listening. Sitting inside, in the back of the room, he saw Udi Raveh and the girl, Shosh, speaking in low voices. They sat close together, their heads touching. Eddie strained to look, for they were in shadow and must have thought themselves unobserved, for in a moment he saw Raveh slip Shosh a brown paper envelope and she put it in her bag. Then people started going in, and the two vanished from his sight.

'Will it be long?' he said.

'What?' Shalom said. Eddie must have stopped him in mid-flow. 'Yes, probably. We tend to get quite passionate about justice and peace, small things like that, you know?'

'Hey, I get it,' Eddie said. 'I'm here to listen.'

'Good,' Shalom said. 'There are a few speakers tonight. We have here members of Mazpen, the Red Path, Solidarity, the Communist Party of Palestine, Resist, Avant-Garde and the Communist List here, and more may be coming later.'

'I can't wait,' Eddie said.

'Good. Good!' Shalom said and slapped him on the back. 'Galya, a pleasure as always. I better go start the proceedings now.'

He left them with a wave and entered the social club.

'He's a putz.' Another man came to join them. He was in his fifties, with a full head of hair and a thick beard, and his eyes twinkled like he was always up to mischief and enjoyed it. 'But he's our putz. Galya, it's lovely to see you. Who's your new man?'

Galya smiled. 'Uri, this is Eddie. Eddie, this is Uri Avnery.'

'The journalist?' Eddie said, surprised. Avnery owned and published *This World*, a salacious tabloid almost everyone read, if only for the nudie pictures. The paper was famous for its investigative journalism almost as much as it was for tits, which it featured prominently. Avnery even ran for the Knesset a few years back, if Eddie remembered, though he didn't get elected.

'That's right. What do you do, Eddie?'

'Eddie is a cop,' Galya said. She seemed determined to introduce him that way to everyone.

'A cop? Not the only one here tonight, I imagine,' Avnery said. 'Don't worry, bachurchik, we leftists don't have anything to hide. Are you connected to the Esther Landes murder investigation?'

'What makes you say that?' Eddie said, taken aback.

'It stands to reason. But listen. I'd love to talk to you some more, if and when you can. Someone has to hold the powers that be to account, and in the absence of anyone else that thankless task has fallen onto my shoulders. Me and the team at *This World*. Let me give you my number. You have anything I can use, call me, alright?'

'Sure,' Eddie said. He took the number, scribbled on a piece of torn paper.

'Come on, let's go in,' Avnery said. 'I'm speaking too.'

'Of course you are,' Galya said.

She took Eddie's hand in hers as they went inside. It felt nice, to hold her hand. They found seats at the back. Shalom spoke first. He spoke at length. Eddie lost him at 'Maoist uprising' but picked up again when Shalom began talking about the Landes murder.

'All of you here have heard of this recent tragic event,' Shalom said. 'One of our own, dead. Raped. Murdered. I am talking of Esti Landes.'

Eddie saw people nod, murmur.

'Esti believed in the cause. She was one of the good ones. She was one of us! And today, chaverim? Today they buried her.'

Shalom looked genuinely upset. 'She was our friend and our comrade,' he said. 'You all know Udi, too. Udi, who loved Esther.'

Udi Raveh stood up awkwardly. A murmur of condolences, of 'Stay strong,' and those nearby patted him on the back or shoulders.

'And do you know what they say?' Shalom said on the stage. His voice grew loud, angry. 'Do you know what they say? They say it is us! Us, chaverim! They say that we killed her!'

Shouts. Boos. Fists waving. A photographer snapped a photo and the flash went bright.

'One of our own! And not only that! Not only that, chaverim! They would finger us, and they would frame Udi for it! The state is after us! And all for what? For daring to speak truth to power? For daring to say, the occupation is immoral, it is a cancer in our nation's soul, it is a historic injustice? For that they would incarcerate us? For that they would shackle us? For that they would throw us behind bars? I say no!'

'No!' the audience roared. Galya stood to her feet. They all did. Even Eddie felt himself swept in the rhetoric.

'I say no! No! No!'

They shouted and stomped their feet. Gradually the room quietened. Then the door opened and a man stood framed in shadow in the doorway and the light from the street lamp outside cast him in a glow.

'No?' he said. He spoke quietly, but his voice carried. 'You say no, Shalom? You say *injustice*?' He took a step into the room. He wore black pants and a white shirt opened at the chest and behind him came other young men and they stood there like a guard.

'You shake your fists and you shout and you spit and you caper, Shalom,' the man said. 'And all I hear is me! Me! Me!'

Shalom glared at the man in the doorway. 'Ya'akov,' he said. 'It is always nice to see the Black Panthers join us.'

His tone voiced the opposite. Eddie stared with renewed interest at the new arrivals. The Black Panthers formed three years before out of Jerusalem youth, many of them former petty criminals, all of them Mizrahi Jews. The children of immigrants from the Arab nations, they made headlines in the papers and even ran for the Knesset unsuccessfully, protesting against the systemic discrimination against the Mizrahim. They'd taken their name from the Black Panthers of America. Now they stood in the doorway, in stark contrast to the majority European Jews – the Ashkenazim – who made up most of the radical leftist opposition.

'What matters here is not your little squabbling organisations,' Ya'akov said. 'Who split from who this week, can you tell me? Are the Maoists now separate from the Leninists? Did the Stalinists renounce Stalin yet? You, Avnery, do you get enough Social-Democratic action in between all the tittie shoots in your magazine? You disgust me.'

'Steady on, Ya'akov,' Shalom said. Avnery in the crowd smiled.

'I'm with you guys!' he called, to scattered laughter.

'Me, me, me,' Ya'akov said. 'They're all after you, are they? No thought in your head to the poor girl lying dead in a hole in the ground, to who her killer might be. The police are crooks, but you benefit from the systemic racism of this country just as much if not more. Admit it, Shalom! All you Goldbergs and Isaacsons and Silvermans, you're nothing but piss on my shoes! You're nothing to an Abergil or a Marciano!'

'Hold on, Ya'akov,' one of the Black Panthers said. He reached for Ya'akov's shoulder and Ya'akov shook him off. The mood in the crowd turned ugly. Eddie could feel it. They could all feel it. And he thought, they'd all come here today hoping for a release. All they needed was for someone to kick the valve loose.

'You are all *complicit*,' Ya'akov said.

There was a silence. Shalom looked furious on the stage. Then someone shouted, 'Fuck you!' and cut the lights.

Eddie moved fast, for two reasons. First, he grabbed Galya. He heard the first punch being thrown, a hard *thud*, and then it was on. They didn't even need a reason, not really. It was just something to do on a slow weeknight. Eddie crouched low, dragging Galya with him.

'What happened?' she said. 'What happened!'

'Boys being boys,' Eddie said. 'Come on. I want to get you out of here.'

Someone fell and crashed against the row of chairs in front of them. The man lay on his back and grinned at Eddie woozily with two broken teeth. He spat out blood.

'Fucking Bolsheviks,' he said.

Eddie couldn't stomach it anymore with the jargon. He kept expecting the police officers in the audience – they must have been there, in plain clothes – to intervene. Then he realised no one was going to intervene, least of all the policemen. They'd be right in there punching anyone they could find.

He and Galya crept to the door. The Black Panthers delegation was lost within the social club's hall and the way was clear. Eddie just saw a slim silhouette go past and the door opened and closed softly. He took Galya's hand.

'Come on!'

They dashed out just as a bottle smashed against the wall. Fresh air outside, and he held Galya close.

'Are you hurt?'

She raised her face to him, confused. There were two small cuts on her face from the glass. He kissed her.

'What are you doing!' she said. She pushed him off. He staggered. The shadow he saw earlier was walking away down the street.

'What?' Eddie said.

'These are my friends! My comrades!'

'You can't go back in there,' he said.

'You don't get to tell me what to do!' She tried to walk past him. He grabbed her.

'Go back home,' he said. 'Let them cool off. Please.'

'Why should I listen to you?' she said.

Eddie said, 'Because I care,' and kissed her again, and he felt her warmth in his arms and this time she kissed him back.

'Why?' she said.

'I just do.' He pulled away from her, laughing, saw the shadow almost turning the corner. 'And as I respect you, I will leave you to make your own decision.'

'Hey!'

'I want to see you again!' he shouted. Then he sprinted down the street.

He ran after the girl. She vanished round the corner but he caught up to her in the distance as she walked to Arlozorov. She was small and dark-haired and she walked fast in a pair of flat shoes. She reached Arlozorov before him and hailed down a taxi.

Eddie ran. The girl was just getting into the taxi when he grabbed her arm.

'Hey, let go!'

He pulled her roughly away from the car. The taxi driver began to shout at him when Eddie shouted back, 'Police!'

The taxi driver got out of the car. He was big and fat. He said, 'Get away from the girl, you bastard.'

'Police, damn it!' Eddie said. 'Get back in the fucking car!'

'Let go of me! Pervert!' the girl said.

'No fucking way you're fucking police!' the taxi driver said. 'Get the fuck away from the girl!'

'Fuck this!' Eddie screamed. 'What are you, the one fucking tzaddik in all Tel Aviv?' He pulled out his gun and pointed it at the taxi driver. The girl screamed.

'Get back in the fucking car!'

'I'm calling the police!' the man said.

'I am the police!' Eddie screamed.

The taxi took off. Eddie grabbed the girl's bag. He opened it and rifled through it. Found little bound books, cheap girls' diaries of the sort sold in any kiosk. He opened the first one and looked at the childish handwriting.

Esther Landes, My Diary, it said on the first page.

'These are private!' the girl said.

'Hello, Shosh,' Eddie said. She stared at him and her eyes opened in recognition.

'You were at the funeral,' she said.

'And now I'm here,' Eddie said. 'And you're under arrest.'

22

HOME AGAIN

'Esther Landes is still dead' – Eddie

'It's no use,' Awad said. The light was too harsh in the meeting room. Eddie's eyes hurt and his bones hurt and his teeth kept grinding. His heart beat out of rhythm on all the coffee he'd drunk to stay awake. The room was filled with cigarette smoke.

Esther Landes' private diaries lay open on the desk and they were no longer private. Nothing about her life was private anymore, not since death robbed her of that simple allowance. Now she really was naked. Naked and powerless and pawed over by these detectives, who had spent all night reading her secrets and her innermost thoughts as Udi Raveh and Shoshana Agasi were kept in lockup nearby in separate rooms.

'There's nothing here.'

'What do you mean there's nothing here!' Mendel said. There were cookie crumbs on his moustache. 'This proves it, man!'

'What does it prove, exactly, Mendel?' Awad said. He sat there quietly, his shoulders slumped. And Eddie realised he did not just look tired: he looked defeated.

'That Udi Raveh, that sicko, was fucking Shosh! Look, chief, it's all there! First he tries to get them into a threesome, then Esther comes back early one day, finds her best friend making out with her boyfriend. She's upset, Raveh just starts spouting about not subscribing to bullshit middle class morality, Shosh cries, Esther storms off, he doesn't see her again until she surprises him back from Haifa a few days before her death. They fight, he kills her and dumps the body, then panics and gives his accomplice in crime, namely young Shoshi here, the diaries to hide. Instead, your little spring chicken here catches her.'

Eddie blinked. Mendel winked at him.

'Nice work, kid,' he said.

'Thanks?'

'It was nice work, Raphael,' Awad said. 'Really, it was. But is this it? Just a, what, a sex murder? Not even that.'

'A story as old as time, Chief Inspector,' Mendel said. 'Plus, it takes the political angle off the table. Which means no Shin Bet to stick their ugly faces in. Just us proper policemen.'

Awad nodded. It was clear he did not relish the political side of things.

'Well,' he said. 'It's compelling. Or at least, it goes somewhat beyond reasonable doubt, which is all the judge needs. But it's weak.'

'So we get a confession,' Mendel said. 'That bastard's not even denying it. Sure he fucked her,' he said. 'Just like Esther fucked other guys. He wasn't jealous and neither was she. What's the big deal? he says. Can you fucking believe it?'

'Get a confession,' Awad said.

'You want us to lean on him?'

Awad drummed on the desk with his fingers.

'His friends,' he said. 'They make too much noise.'

'Ashkenazis,' Mendel said like that explained anything; which perhaps it did.

'We'll stick them both in a cell and let them think it over,' Awad decided. 'A few days in a cell, a few weeks… make it uncomfortable. He's a cripple, isn't he? Give him something small, not enough room to move in. Near the sea, hot, humid. Make him sweat and itch until he wants to sing because anything would be better.'

'Do you think he will?'

'I think he will,' Mendel said.

And so they left it.

Later, only Eddie and Awad were left in the corridor outside. It was near morning, dawn was coming up.

'You did good work,' Awad said. 'I will tell your man in Haifa. Maybe you'll get a shove up the ranks.'

'Thank you, sir.'

'You think he did it?' Awad said.

'I don't know, sir.'

'No. Well, it doesn't matter, does it? It's not what you think, kid, it's what you can prove.'

'And Esther Landes is still dead,' Eddie said.

'That she is,' Awad said. 'That she is. Good night.'

And with that he left him.

Eddie was ready to go home. He looked for Cohen but he hadn't seen him since they got back from Jerusalem the day before. He wondered what Cohen was up to, then realised he didn't want to know what Cohen was up to. He saw a door open quietly and two men come out. One man was in uniform and Eddie saw his rank on his shoulder and the man was a superintendent.

The other man was the Black Panthers leader, Ya'akov, from the night before.

They did not see Eddie. The two men were smiling, comfortable with each other. The superintendent took out an envelope and passed it to Ya'akov, and then they shook hands. The superintendent went back in the station and Ya'akov went out, free as a bird. He passed by Eddie and saw him. He smiled and gave him a finger salute and then he left.

And Eddie went home.

He slept and his sleep was dreamless, and when he woke it was daylight again, and somewhere nearby Genghis was barking, and the telephone was ringing, and the telephone kept ringing, and his aunt Sarah was shouting something about why won't anyone pick up the phone, she was watching Chaim Yavin, and the dog kept barking, and Eddie stole awake, still dazed with it all, and he padded out to the landing and picked up the phone, which sat on a table by the door, and he said, 'Yes? What is it?'

'Eddie? It's me.'

It was Cohen and he sounded excited.

Eddie said, 'Cohen? Where the hell are you?'

'In Haifa.'

'What the hell are you doing in Haifa?' Eddie said.

'We got him, Eddie! We got him!' Cohen said.

'Who?' Eddie said.

'The killer,' Cohen said.

'He's in a cell in Tel Aviv,' Eddie said, confused.

'Who is?' Cohen said.

'Raveh! The boyfriend!'

'Oh, him. Forget him. Sagi knew it wouldn't fly. Even before the Commissioner called.'

'The Commissioner called? Who?'

'Sagi. Or rather, he didn't.'

'Who didn't?'

'Exactly. The point is, this Raveh, he's no use without a confession.'

'But I found evidence.'

'A girl's diary, Eddie? Come on.'

'But what if he confesses?'

'He's a fucking war hero, Eddie. He's not going to confess. He's not going to sit in a cell. Not for long. Not with the papers and everyone making a fuss. You know he's been talking to *Yediot* to serialise his story? *That's* why he hid those damn diaries! He's going to put it all out there in the papers. Confessions of a Dirty Socialist. No, Eddie, he's gone, and Awad's gone. I told you an Arab was no good for this.'

Eddie stared at the wall. The dog stopped barking. He could hear Chaim Yavin on the TV and smell his aunt's menthol cigarette. He said, 'Cohen, what the fuck are you talking about?'

'I'm saying come home. I'm saying we got him.'

'Got *who*!'

He heard Cohen on the line. He heard phones in the background, people talking, the sounds of a police station.

Cohen said, 'His name is Elisha Barnea.'

PART THREE

'MY NAME IS ELISHA BARNEA'

1974, Police HQ, Haifa District

23

THE SUSPECT

'All he has to do is confess' – Cohen

He sat in the interrogation room and his lips moved without sound. He was tall, stooped, with a thick mane of hair. He was handsome. Eddie thought he was handsome.

'What is he doing?' he said.

'He talks to himself,' Cohen said. 'I think.'

'Why him?'

Eddie had driven back to Haifa. He stopped at a petrol station outside Zichron Ya'akov on the way and drank black coffee from a paper cup and stared at the lights on the hill. Beyond the coast road the sea lapped against the shore, and Eddie remembered the one time he saw a whale. Whales didn't usually come this way but one summer, in Tantura, he saw one rise out of the sea and he never forgot it. He didn't smoke but he did pop another of Galya's pills. They were some sort of diet pills.

He was washed and he was shaved. The air was warm and a warm breeze blew in from the sea. He finished the coffee and drove with the window open, one arm trailing over the doorframe. He drove straight to the police station. Sagi patted him on the shoulder when he saw him.

'Welcome home,' he said.

Eddie wasn't sure what had happened. A subtle coup had taken place, the balance of power shifting from Tel Aviv back to Haifa along with the investigation. He stared at the man in the interrogation room.

'Who is he? What is he?'

'He's a driver for the council. He was seeing Esther Landes, casually. They went on a handful of dates. Her roommate, what was her name—'

'Rona,' Eddie said.

'Rona, right. She said she lent Esther her high heels a couple of times, this fellow's tall and Esther didn't want to feel short next to him so she borrowed the high heel shoes.'

'How did you find him?'

'He found us. Came into the station and said he knew Esther, he wanted to help catch her killer. He said they were friends. No one thought much of it. The officer on duty made a note of the visit and told him thank you. It was Sagi who found him again. He was going through everything, going back, trying to find a witness who saw her, anyone she knew in Haifa.'

'He didn't like the boyfriend angle?'

Cohen smiled. 'He didn't like the Tel Aviv angle,' he said.

'Right.'

'He did his job, Eddie,' Cohen said. 'That's all. And he did it right. He saw something that didn't add up. Why this guy. Where did he come from? So he went looking. Barnea has a history. Sagi got his military record. He had problems in the service. He was in the Paratroopers Brigade but he didn't fit in, he got into fights. The psychologist there said he had borderline personality disorder with psychopathic traits. He was moved elsewhere. He fought in the Six Day War and then in the Golan Heights during the War of Attrition. Now he drives for the council and still lives with his parents, they made aliyah from Libya.'

'So what?'

'So Sagi thinks he met up again with Esther after she came back from Tel Aviv. Took her in the car, drove to the beach. Now this is where it gets interesting. Sagi's been talking to everyone who knows this guy. A few girls he's been out with. They say he has problems. Can't get it up, you know? Got angry and defensive a couple of times. He's a big guy, too. Not someone you want angry at you. So what Sagi reckons is, he takes her to the beach, they start to make out, he wants to go in, she says no, he gets angry. Or maybe *she* wants him to go in, he can't do it, he gets angry.'

'There was semen on the corpse,' Eddie said. He felt sick.

'Maybe that's the only way he could get it done,' Cohen said.

'This is bullshit,' Eddie said. 'You know it's bullshit, Cohen.'

'It's not bullshit.'

'It's weak as shit. It's circumstantial.'

'Sure. It's circumstantial. Unless he owns up to it.'

Cohen looked at Eddie and there was nothing friendly in his eyes at all then, there was nothing at all in them in fact. It made Eddie scared.

'All he has to do,' Cohen said, 'is confess.'

Eddie looked away from him. He looked at the man in the interrogation room. Elisha. He had long fingers. He drummed on the desk and looked from side to side like he was searching for an exit but was just now beginning to realise there wasn't one.

'You think he will?' Eddie said.

'He has to.'

Eddie waited while Cohen lit a cigarette. It was quiet in the police station. Why did they just leave the suspect there like that? Somewhere a telephone rang. Cohen's match whispered against the strip of the matchbox, then fizzed into life. Eddie heard the drag of smoke, the rattle of matches, the suspect's tapping on the desk.

He said, 'Why, Cohen?'

'Why what?' Cohen said.

Eddie said, 'Why are you doing this?'

Cohen looked angry. He blew out smoke. He said, 'Because he fits.'

'Fits what!'

'He could have killed the others.'

'You still think there is a, what, someone out there raping and killing a girl every couple of years? That's insane.'

'It's not insane, it's the seventies.' Cohen stared at the suspect. Elisha. Eddie felt the need to keep saying his name to himself. 'He fits. He could have done the others. It would take a loner. Someone a little off. Someone with a car. He would seem normal.

He would *be* normal. Until he can't hold it in again. He could have done it.'

'You said this to Sagi?'

'Sagi doesn't want to know. He doesn't want me to mention the others. We have to get him for Esther Landes, he said. Listen, Eddie. There's a lot riding on this guy. Awad was never going to carry it and that Udi Raveh doesn't fit. Not for the others, and not for Sagi's ambitions. And with the newspapers all over this everyone wants a quick end. So he has to confess. Do you understand?'

Eddie stared at Cohen.

'I understand,' he said.

'Sagi's just sweating him right now,' Cohen said. He was smiling again. 'Then we take turns. Ask him questions, doesn't matter what. Just make sure he doesn't leave that room, and he doesn't sleep. No one but us goes near him. No family, no friends. No one. There's only one way that guy goes out of that room.'

'I said I get it,' Eddie said.

'Yeah, well,' Cohen said. 'It's nice to have you back.'

24

THE DATE

'We're just trying to understand what happened.' – Eddie

The clock ticked twelve. The seconds hand crawled along the face. It reminded Eddie of an insect.

'The clock isn't right,' the man across the table said. He was agitated. 'It's showing the wrong time, Elisha knows it is.'

'You're Elisha,' Eddie said.

'Yes?' the man said. 'Elisha doesn't know why he's here. Why do you keep Elisha in prison?'

He had bags under his eyes now and his hands shook. He was right about the clock, of course. They kept changing it to keep him disoriented. How many hours has he been awake now? Earlier Sagi had a go at him, then one of the other detectives. Now it was Eddie and Cohen's turn.

'We're just trying to understand what happened,' Eddie said. 'When you took her out.'

'Elisha told you,' Elisha said. 'Elisha didn't see her.'

'When did you last see Esther Landes?' Eddie said.

'Esther was nice,' Elisha said. 'She smiled at me. She liked to smile. We went to a movie, I think. *Charlie and a Half*, with Yehuda Barkan. Very funny. Did you see it?'

'Yeah,' Cohen said. 'It was funny. The girl in it, she's pretty.'

'Pretty, yeah,' Elisha said. 'Elisha liked her.'

'Does Elisha talk like this all the time?' Cohen said.

'Like what?' Elisha said. He looked genuinely confused.

'You like pretty girls?' Cohen said.

'Who doesn't?' Elisha said. He tried to smile but it sat awkwardly on his face.

'You liked Esther?'

'Elisha liked her. She was nice.'

'You fuck her?' Eddie said.

'What?'

'Did you fuck her? It's a simple question.'

'Please, I just want to go to sleep,' Elisha said.

'So you didn't fuck her?'

'We didn't make love,' Elisha said. 'But love is love.'

'What does that mean? You hold hands? You kiss? You feel her up under the shirt?'

'Did she have nice tits?' Cohen said.

'How far did you go, Elisha?' Eddie said. 'Did you go all the way?'

'*All* the way,' Cohen said. 'Did you like it, when she screamed? Did you get hard, finally, when you wrapped her bra around her neck? When you twisted? You had your dick out, didn't you. You got so excited you came on her. Didn't you? I said, didn't you!'

Cohen slapped him. The slap came fast and unexpected and Eddie flinched. Elisha Barnea looked at them with helpless, dog-like eyes.

'Please,' he said. 'Why are you doing this?'

Eddie sat back in the chair. Cohen relaxed, reached for a cigarette. The silence lengthened and the clock ticked and ticked.

'You were in the Six Days War?' Cohen said.

'I was in the army, same as everyone,' Elisha said.

'I was there too,' Cohen said. 'Where did you serve?'

'The Golan Heights, mostly,' Elisha said.

'Yeah, I was there,' Cohen said.

'I was a reservist,' Elisha said.

'I was, too,' Cohen said.

Elisha blinked. 'I try not to think about it much,' he said. He had a soft voice, Eddie noticed.

'What did you do before that?' Cohen said. 'When you joined up you were in the Paratroopers Brigade. Combat unit, elite. Then you got transferred to artillery. Not very glamorous, artillery. So what happened?'

'I don't know,' Elisha said. 'It was a long time ago. Please, can I sleep now? I just need a little rest.'

'Soon,' Cohen promised. 'Tell me what happened. You got in a fight or two?'

'I served my time,' Elisha said. 'I just saw too many friends die. I guess it does something to you.'

'Does it make you angry?' Cohen said.

'Angry how?'

'Like you want to do something bad. Like you want to hit out.'

Elisha Barnea shook his head. 'No,' he said. 'Elisha doesn't like war. Bad things happened but that's just that, they happened. My friends died but Elisha lived. So I have to live.'

'Have a job, meet girls…'

Elisha smiled. 'Everyone will tell you,' he said. 'I'm a gentleman. I have no problems with the girls. The girls like Elisha.'

It was weird how he slipped into talking about himself in third person. Eddie wondered what really happened in the war. He was battle touched, they called it. Guys who came back different. He wondered what Elisha was like before the war.

'Your parents,' he said. 'They came from Libya?'

'Tripoli,' Elisha said. 'They love this country. I love this country. I fought for this country.'

'You live in Acre?'

'Sure.'

'How did you meet Esther Landes?'

'At the Rutenberg House. In the library there. I like to read.'

'What do you read?' Eddie said.

'I took out Moshe Shamir's *He Went In The Fields*,' Elisha said. 'You know it?'

Eddie nodded. 'Everyone knows it,' he said.

Cohen stirred. 'This how you see yourself?' he said. 'The sabra, like Uri in the book? What do they call it, "handsome of locks and of countenance"?'

'This is my country too,' Elisha said.

'Uri was a kibbutznik,' Cohen said. 'In the story. Salt of the earth. A new Jew. And you're, what? A half-Arab from Africa.'

'Elisha is as good as anyone!' Elisha said. He was agitated. He banged on the table. 'As good as anyone!'

'Do you like Ashkenazi girls, is that it?' Cohen said. 'Or do you hate them, Barnea?'

'Elisha doesn't hate.'

'Hate enough to kill one?'

'I did nothing!'

Eddie put a hand on Cohen's arm. He leaned forward.

'You met Esther in the library?' he said.

'In the library, yes. We got to talking.'

'You really do have the locks,' Eddie said. Elisha ran a hand through his mane of hair.

'And the countenance?' he said, smiling.

Eddie smiled back.

'Did Esther like it?'

'Sure,' Elisha said. 'What's not to like.'

'What did you talk about, the book?'

'A little. She didn't like it. She said it represented the twisted death-idolisation of the founding generation, how Uri is destined to die. She talked with big words sometimes. I hadn't read the novel yet so I didn't know he dies. And his girlfriend's from the Holocaust. It's very sad. Elisha offered to buy her a coffee. She said yes.'

'What were you doing in the Rutenberg House?' Eddie said.

'I was doing a training course. I'm going to be a youth councillor.'

'A youth councillor,' Eddie said.

'Yes. I want to give back to society.'

He sounded so earnest. Suddenly Eddie didn't want to do this anymore, he couldn't. This babyish man who still looked at him, across the table, with eyes full of trust, as though despite everything Elisha Barnea still believed it would be alright in the end, as soon as Eddie and Cohen realised it was all just a big misunderstanding. Then he could go back to Acre, and be a youth councillor, and chat up the girls with his easy smile and big puppy eyes and his mane of lustrous hair. He really was a handsome man, Eddie thought.

'So you were there for a course, Esther was there for a course, you hit it off... Then what?'

A shy grin came on Elisha's face. 'Then what?' he said.

'She was quite spirited,' Cohen put in. 'Adventurous. You knew she had a boyfriend?'

'What's a boyfriend?' Elisha said. 'I didn't see a boyfriend.'

'We know she had sex with all kinds of men.'

'That isn't true! She was not like that. I think she was lonely, she was struggling to fit in the army.'

'You knew how she felt.'

'Elisha knew how she felt, yes. Elisha felt bad for her. Such a pretty girl, and so nice. We went out a couple of times. The last time she came with me to Acre. I have a car, on account of the council job. We went out to a café, with my brother and his wife. They have a new baby.'

'And after?' Cohen said.

'After, what?'

'Did you fuck her?'

Elisha stared at Eddie, as though hoping he'd help.

'He didn't fuck her,' Eddie said.

'No,' Cohen said.

'Maybe felt her up a little?' Eddie said. 'Did you, Elisha? You're driving back to Haifa, the beach is right there, somewhere quiet to stop, something romantic on the radio... What's that Dan Almagor song, "When You Say No"? You know that one? What does "no" even mean, right? You like that song, Cohen?'

'I don't like that song,' Cohen said. 'I think when she says no she means it.'

'But does she?' Eddie said. 'Did Esther really mean *no*, do you think, Elisha? She didn't, did she? She *meant* yes. She *meant* it like an invitation.'

He sat back, said, 'What do you listen to, Elisha?'

'Just the radio, I guess.'

'You had the radio on?'

'You stopped the car?' Cohen said.

'You leaned over, maybe kissed her?' Eddie said.

'A quick squeeze?' Cohen said. 'Nice tits, were they?'

Elisha didn't say anything. Cohen sat back with a big grin on his face.

'You *wanted* to fuck her,' he said.

'Please,' Elisha said. 'Let me sleep. I am so tired.'

'But he didn't fuck her,' Eddie said. 'Right, Elisha? You drove her back. You dropped her off. You're a gentleman, you said so.'

'Elisha is a gentleman, ask all the girls,' Elisha said.

'You wanted to fuck her,' Cohen said, remorselessly. 'But you couldn't, could you? You can't get it up.'

'Did she want you to?' Eddie said. 'She did, didn't she? She came on to you. She knew what she was doing. Out on a date with this older guy. She wanted to see it. Did she open your belt? Slide her hand in? She knew what a cock was for.'

He hated himself, and at the same time he never felt better, more righteous. It was like they were getting to him now. Eddie couldn't stop.

'But you couldn't do it, could you?' Cohen said. 'It's not how you're wired. So you did what, said sorry? Drove her back and dropped her off, polite as you please? And she was understanding, wasn't she? Maybe she blamed herself. Yeah. She must have. Was she not attractive enough for you? You made plans to see each other again.'

'Elisha didn't see her again,' Elisha said. 'Maybe if…' But he fell to brooding.

'If she hadn't died,' Eddie said.

'You were going to hook up again,' Cohen said. 'You *did* hook up again. Her boyfriend dropped her off at the trempiada in Tel Aviv. She got a ride. A girl like that, she'd get a ride. And you *were* in Haifa that night. You were in the Rutenberg House. You had an exam.'

'Yes.'

'On, what was it? Civic knowledge, was it?'

'Yes.'

'You finish your exam, you see her. Surprise! She has nothing to do. Her roommate's not there, none of the girls are. They got a day off from the army. So what's a young girl going to do? She's not going to go to *sleep*.'

'You take her out?' Cohen said.

'A fourth date,' Eddie said.

'*The* date,' Cohen said.

'This time you both know what's going to happen. You drive slowly. The music's playing. The window's rolled down, the air is warm. The coast road, with the moon in the sky and the sea in the distance.'

'Neither of you say much,' Cohen said. 'It's the anticipation, isn't it? Knowing what's coming. Makes me hard just thinking about it.'

'Makes *her* wet,' Eddie said.

'Stop it!' Elisha said. 'Stop it!'

'You took her to Tantura, and she didn't say no, did she?' Cohen said.

'Did she?' Eddie said.

'She couldn't wait to have your cock inside her,' Cohen said.

'Your big fat cock,' Eddie said. 'But you couldn't get it up, could you? And you got angry.'

'You scared her,' Cohen said.

'She tried to fight you off then,' Eddie said.

'It wasn't like that!' Elisha said.

'Then how was it!' Cohen said.

'It wasn't nothing! I wasn't there!'

'You took her bra off and you strangled her with it!' Cohen screamed. 'You choked her and you choked her and you felt her, under you, thrusting, shuddering, she *wanted* it, didn't she, Barnea, and *you* wanted it, you wanted to show that fucking bitch! You shot up all over her, didn't you! Came on that bitch as she died.'

'No! Stop it!'

'And then, when you came, you realised what you'd done,' Eddie said. Compassionately.

'Did anyone see you? Would anyone *know*?' Cohen said.

'Maybe you didn't mean to kill her,' Eddie said. 'You just wanted to make her stop. Maybe she laughed at you. At your… disability.'

'Stop it…' Elisha said. He grabbed his head in both hands and moaned.

'So you stripped her. What wasn't off already,' Eddie said.

'Dumped everything back in the car. What did you do with? Drop it somewhere? Burn it? Well, it doesn't matter. It doesn't matter to Esther Landes, she's dead.'

'Dead,' Eddie said.

'And you just left her there,' Cohen said. 'And drove off home like nothing happened.'

Elisha Barnea buried his face in his hands. Eddie tensed, waiting, hoping.

'I didn't do it,' Elisha said. 'It didn't go like that. I never saw her that night. I never...'

Eddie let out a breath he didn't realise he was holding. Cohen stood up. He loomed over Barnea. He slapped him again, hard and without warning. Barnea rocked in the chair.

'Five minutes,' Cohen said. 'Don't you dare go to sleep.'

He left the room.

Eddie, gently, said, 'Is there anything at all you can tell me?'

Elisha looked at him with dull, wounded eyes.

'My name is Elisha Barnea,' he said. 'And I am an innocent man.'

25

DAY TWO

'Everyone jerks off' – *Cohen*

'He almost broke,' Sagi said. 'Nice work, both of you.'

'You really think he did it?' Eddie said.

'Oh, he did it,' Sagi said. 'And he's going to confess. He *wants* to confess.'

Eddie looked at the prisoner in the interrogation room. He didn't think Elisha Barnea looked like he wanted to confess.

'I'll have a word with him,' Detective Hillel said. He pulled up his sleeves.

'Not in the face,' Sagi said.

Hillel said, 'Do you think I was born yesterday?'

Eddie watched. Cohen smoked. Hillel went in the room. He grabbed Barnea by the hair. He pulled. Barnea toppled backwards, fell to the floor. Hillel squatted on his chest. He slapped him. He had hands like a harbour porter. He slapped Barnea again.

'I told him not the face!' Sagi said.

Hillel picked Barnea up by the hair. He dragged him up. He pushed him against the wall. His fist sank into Barnea's stomach. Barnea dropped to the floor again. He gasped for breath.

'That's better…' Sagi muttered.

Hillel didn't say a word. His woven yarmulke sat crooked on his head. He worked Barnea over quietly, methodically. The only sound was of Hillel's breathing and Barnea's crying, but there was no one to heed his cries. There was no one to comfort him and tuck him back into bed. No one to tell him this was just a bad dream he was having.

Eddie felt sick. Eddie watched. Cohen smoked. The smoke ebbed in the room. Sagi scratched his arm. The clock on the well ticked and ticked and then stopped.

Hillel straightened. He left the interrogation room. Eddie heard the bathroom door in the corridor open and close. Barnea stayed on the floor. He gasped for air. His jeans turned dark as he started to piss himself.

'Oh, for God's sake—' Sagi said.

Barnea cried.

'Sir?' Eddie said. 'Do we get him cleaned up? He needs food, sleep.'

'I want him like this,' Sagi said. He clapped Eddie's shoulder. 'Go, get some rest, both of you. Come back in eight hours. If he's still here you can have another go.'

Cohen nodded. Eddie nodded reluctantly. They left just as Hillel was coming back in.

Outside the night turned cold. A couple of uniformed cops rolled in with a man in handcuffs.

'Hey, Cohen!' the man said.

Cohen smiled. 'What they get you for this time, Meshulam?'

'They say I stole some panties! I didn't steal those panties, Cohen! I was just smelling them!' He laughed.

'We found him in one of the house gardens up in Denya,' one of the uniformed cops said. 'He was peeping in the teenaged daughter's bedroom and jerking off.'

'He was wearing these on his head,' the other cop said, brandishing a pair of pink girls' underwear. 'Can you believe this shit?'

'They don't like this sort of thing up in Denya,' Cohen said.

'I was going to put them back on the line, Cohen! Honest!'

'I believe you, Meshulam,' Cohen said.

'Come along, pervert,' the first cop said. Meshulam laughed again and the two uniforms walked him into the station.

'You want to get a drink?' Cohen said.

'I haven't even gone home yet,' Eddie said. 'Who does that?'

'What?'

'Peep on women, jerk off. Wear their panties on his head.'

'Everyone jerks off, Eddie.'

Eddie said, 'I'm going to bed.'

He went home. The room felt strange to him, even smaller than he remembered. He tried to sleep but a dog was barking outside, he heard a bottle rattle along the pavement, someone's radio on upstairs, playing Schubert. Somewhere, Syrian artillery was firing. There were shouts, people running. A mortar hit close, threw dirt in the air, he heard screams, ran, saw Elisha Barnea with blood on his face trying to drag half a corpse out of a hole.

Is this what it was like? Would it make you murder? No one talked about how you were all trained to kill people and sent out to kill people but that was just war, that wasn't… Then Esther Landes was leaning over him, with seaweed in her hair, and she was smiling. She leaned in to kiss him and he held her and saw her face change, become fearful as he wrapped her bra round her neck, as he squeezed and squeezed…

He woke up sweating. The sheet was wet. He smelled that shame smell, like when he was a teenager and had wet dreams. Keri laila, they called it, the 'thing that happens at night'. The Orthodox said you had to wash it off for it was an impurity, a corruption. Eddie just left it.

Outside it was daylight. It started to rain when he got to the station. Cohen was outside, smoking a cigarette.

'Well?' Eddie demanded.

'"I do not speak because I have the power to speak",' Cohen said. '"I speak for I have no power to keep silent." Rabbi Kook.'

'Is this a new thing you're doing?' Eddie said.

'I found this book of quotations in the Rutenberg House library,' Cohen said. 'I'm trying it out.'

'What were you doing in the Rutenberg House?'

'I went to the library,' Cohen said, as though it were obvious.

'And what did you find, besides the good Rabbi Kook?' Eddie said.

'I found nothing,' Cohen said.

'He was there?'

'He was there. But no one saw Esther. And he has no alibi for what he did after the exam.'

'This is bullshit, Cohen.' Something occurred to him. 'Did Sagi send you there?'

'No.'

'You went in your own time? Why? What did you hope to find, Cohen?'

For the first time he saw something slip in that careful mask Cohen always wore. Eddie saw something desperate.

'*Something*,' Cohen said. 'Something to say…' He brooded.

'Yeah,' Eddie said.

They went in. Sagi stood with his back to the wall, holding a paper cup. He shook his head when he saw them. He pointed them silently at the interrogation room door.

'I'm going to get some sleep,' he said. 'Keep him awake, keep talking. You can do that?'

They went in. Cohen closed the door softly behind them. They took their seats. Elisha Barnea sat in the chair. He blinked at them.

'One minute,' Cohen said. The clock wasn't ticking. He went and tinkered with it. It started ticking again. It was set to some random time, Eddie saw. He looked at Elisha.

'Can I get you anything?' he said. 'Coffee?'

'No more coffee,' Elisha said. 'Elisha just wants to sleep.'

'Soon,' Eddie said. 'Just tell us what you know. That's all we ask.'

'Cigarette?' Cohen said.

'Sure,' Elisha said. He took the offered cigarette and dropped it. His hands shook. Cohen helped him, put it to his lips, lit it for him. He sat back and watched Elisha smoke. They let the silence permeate the room.

'I didn't do anything,' Elisha said. He was desperate to fill the silence. 'I didn't hurt her.'

'Maybe she liked it,' Cohen said. 'We read her diaries, you know. You weren't her first. Maybe she liked it rough.'

'Do you like it rough?' Eddie said.

'Maybe it just went too far, that's all,' Cohen said. 'An accident. Maybe she wanted you to choke her. Is that what happened? She wanted you to choke her?'

'I didn't... no!' Elisha said.

'You kill people? In the war?' Eddie said.

'Elisha doesn't talk about the war,' Elisha said.

'You threatened a guy with your service weapon?' Eddie said. He'd read it in the army file and he was curious. 'Why?'

'I didn't want to be there anymore.'

'You kicked a door in.'

'I was provoked.'

'Provoked how?'

Elisha shook his head. 'I don't like to think about it,' he said. 'Elisha just wanted out of the service, after the war. But they wouldn't let me.'

'You saw psychiatrists?'

'Psychiatrists!' Elisha said. 'They don't know.' He looked to Cohen. '*You* were there,' he said. 'You know.'

'It's war,' Cohen said. He shrugged. 'It's finished and you're alive and... and that's it, that's all there is to it. Then you go back to normal life.'

'I did,' Elisha said. 'I went back to normal life.' He tried to smile. He could barely move his lips. His cigarette turned to ash, untouched in the ashtray. 'I have a job, a car. Friends.'

'No serious girlfriend, though,' Eddie said. 'No wife. No kids.'

'You have a wife? You have kids?'

'No,' Eddie said. Cohen shook his head.

'I'm too young to settle down,' Elisha said. 'Maybe when I find the right girl...'

'Maybe you did,' Eddie said.

'Maybe you left her on the beach in Tantura,' Cohen said.

'What did you do with her clothes? Her bag? Where are her shoes?' Eddie said.

'I want my brother,' Elisha said. His eyes threatened to close. 'Please...'

'Stay with us,' Cohen said. 'Hey, Barnea! Wake up!' He slapped him, hard.

'Why are you doing this?' Elisha said. 'Please, just make it stop.'

'Then tell us,' Cohen said.

'I told you,' Elisha said.

'Then tell us again.'

Eddie sat back. Round and round they went. Elisha's training course. Meeting Esther. Going on the dates. Driving to Haifa that night for his exam.

'Did you hope to see her?' Cohen said.

'Did you make plans to see her?' Eddie said.

'I thought she might be there,' Elisha said. 'I don't know. I didn't know they finished early and she went home. There was no one there. I didn't know they had their graduation ceremony the next night. I didn't know anything. She wasn't there. I drove home.'

'What would you have done if she was there?' Eddie said.

'If she was there? I'd say hello. Maybe ask her out for coffee. That's all.'

'You liked her.'

Elisha mulled it over. 'Sure,' he said. 'She was nice. But I have lots of girlfriends.'

'We spoke to some of them,' Cohen said.

'So you know.'

'Why did you come to the cops?' Eddie said. 'Why did you offer to help?'

'Why wouldn't I?' Elisha said.

'You barely knew her,' Eddie said. 'By your own account.'

'I thought maybe there was something I could do.'

'You could tell us what really happened.'

'I don't know what happened.'

Cohen brought out photos. Elisha flinched. So did Eddie. Where had he gotten these?

'Crime scene photos,' Cohen said. 'Menachem took them.'

'Who's Menachem?' Elisha said.

'He's the photographer,' Cohen said.

Eddie just stared at the pictures. He could hear the sea in the distance, the waves lapping at the shore. The hikers standing around, out of shot. How still it was. Esther Landes stared up at them and her hair was spread against the wet sand in a fan. Eddie said, 'Excuse me.' He got up and left the room. He went into the men's room just in time. He threw up in the sink.

He couldn't do this anymore, he thought. He wiped his mouth, rinsed it with soap. He went into the observation room. Hillel was there. He looked at him without an obvious expression.

'Needed a piss?' he said.

'Something like that. Sir, what about the boyfriend?'

'What about him?' Hillel said.

'Is he still a suspect?'

'You can't try him,' Hillel said. 'So that's that.'

'And this guy?'

'This guy you can try,' Hillel said.

'But did he do it?' Eddie said.

'You did it,' Cohen said, on the other side of the glass.

Elisha shook his head. 'No,' he said. 'No.'

'Look at her,' Cohen said. 'Look at her!'

Elisha started to cry. Cohen lost control. He got up and lashed at Elisha. He hit him, quietly, expertly. Hillel nodded.

'There's a promotion in this for both of you, you know,' he said.

Cohen stood over Elisha.

'Let me help you up,' he said. He helped Elisha sit in the chair again.

'Can I get you a coffee? Another cigarette?'

'Why are you doing this?' Elisha said.

'You drove her to Tantura. You went down a dirt track to the beach. You made out. You fought. You dragged her out of the car. You wrapped her bra around her neck and twisted. You came on her. Before, or after?'

'I don't know...'

'You stripped her naked. You left her there. You drove home. Tell me. I said, tell me!'

'I don't know! I don't know!'

'You know!' Cohen screamed.

Eddie rubbed his face.

'Keep at it,' Hillel said. 'That's all you can do. He'll crack. Sooner or later he'll crack.'

'Is no one asking to see him? How are we keeping him here?'

'We wrote it down under suspected sexual harassment. Some girls complained.'

'About him?'

'Some other guy, but it doesn't matter. He's ours to keep.'

'And the family?'

'His brother's been trying to reach him,' Hillel said. 'We arrested him too.'

'Arrested him? For what?'

'Maybe he knows something. Maybe he's an accomplice. But he's not going to help our friend in there. Not until he tells us the truth.'

'The truth,' Eddie said.

'Be'ezrat Ha'Shem,' Hillel said. 'Right, get back in there.'

Eddie went back in there.

'Sorry for that,' he said. 'Elisha, I really want to help you.'

'I know you do,' Elisha said. 'I can see you're a good person, deep inside. Not like him.' He nodded at Cohen.

'Just tell us what happened,' Eddie said. Almost begging. 'Tell us the truth.'

'The truth?' Elisha said. 'I don't know what truth it is you want.'

'You know,' Eddie said; and that admission sat between them.

'Just write it down,' Cohen said. He had a pen and paper. He had a lot of things. He put them on the table. 'Tell us what you know.'

Elisha picked up the pen. He began to write. His letters were rounded and a little childish. Large. Eddie read upside-down.

I met Esther Landes in Haifa during my youth councillor training. I thought she was pretty. I met her at the library. We had coffee together. I—

'Go on,' Cohen said.

'You're doing well,' Eddie said.

I liked her. I thought she liked me. We arranged to meet again the next evening. We went to see a movie. After, we went for ice cream.

'What cinema did you go to?' Eddie said.

'The Palace,' Elisha said.

'Lots of room at the Palace,' Eddie said. 'It's a big old place.'

'Lots of room for privacy,' Cohen said.

'If you want to be alone with someone,' Eddie said. 'In the dark.'

'Who hasn't made out at the Palace,' Cohen said. 'Am I right?'

'Elisha is a gentleman,' Elisha said.

'So you keep saying,' Eddie said.

'Gentlemen don't strangle pretty young women and leave them like garbage on the beach,' Cohen said.

'Keep writing,' Eddie said. 'This is good.'

We watched a movie like I said. Then after the ice cream we said good night. The third time we went to Acre. I drove her there and back.

'Go on,' Cohen said.

'I don't know,' Elisha said.

'What's to know?' Eddie said.

'Just write what happened,' Cohen said.

'After you saw her again,' Eddie said.

'That last time,' Cohen said.

'That night she came back from Tel Aviv,' Eddie said.

And that was another thing that bothered him, Eddie realised. If Esther Landes got a ride from Tel Aviv then why hadn't the driver come forward? Her picture was in all the newspapers. If you'd given Esther Landes a ride from Tel Aviv to Haifa you'd remember it. You'd remember *her.*

So why had no one come forward? Why did no one *see* her again after Udi Raveh dropped her off?

'I don't know,' Elisha said. 'I don't know. I am sorry she is dead. I am so sorry…'

A tear fell on the page and smudged the ink.

'Write that,' Eddie said.

I am so sorry…

'Why are you sorry?' Cohen said.

'What's to be sorry for?' Eddie said.

'If you didn't do anything,' Cohen said.

'What did you do?' Eddie said.

'We *know* you made out with her,' Cohen said.

'We know what happens when you try to make love,' Eddie said.

'Can't get it up,' Cohen said.

'How far did you go?' Eddie said.

'Did you feel her up? Did she suck your dick?'

'Did she jerk you off?'

'Did you stick your fingers up her cu—'

'Stop it! Stop it!' Elisha said. He started to bang his fists against the sides of his head.

The door opened. Hillel stood in the door.

'Get out, both of you,' he said.

'No, no, please, no,' Elisha said.

Eddie and Cohen got up. They went out. The door shut.

They heard the first punch being thrown.

26

THE SHOES

'He who knocks on the door shall receive an answer'
– An Arabic proverb

Eddie thought he'd barely slept but when he woke the sunlight draped across the dusty carpet and the clock by his bedside said eleven o'clock. The telephone outside rang. It had woken him up from a deep sleep and no dreams he could remember. The phone kept ringing. Eddie padded to the landing.

'What!' he said.

'They found her things,' Cohen said.

Eddie dressed hurriedly. Cohen was outside in their police car by the time he got down the stairs.

'Where?' Eddie said.

'Not far from Tantura.'

'Son of a bitch,' Eddie said.

Cohen lit a cigarette one-handed. He drove fast, turning on the siren so people would get out of the way. They passed the Baha'i gardens, which were constantly under construction. The terraces ran up to the temple with the famous golden dome. Eddie didn't know much about the Baha'i. They were just another part of Haifa, like the Templers who built the German Colony directly to the north of the gardens had been. Some of the Templers sided with Nazi Germany during the war and they all eventually vanished, Eddie didn't know where. Their former town was now a near-abandoned industrial zone.

Cohen turned on the radio. Abba came on with 'Waterloo'.

The song made Eddie think about Galya back in Tel Aviv. He had tried to reach her on the phone but she wasn't in, her flatmate said she was 'in a lecture or something'. Eddie realised he'd wanted to talk to her, wanted to hear her voice again. Cohen was humming alongside Abba to the song. His fingers tapped on the steering wheel.

'You're in a good mood,' Eddie said.

'We're going to get that bastard,' Cohen said. 'I can feel it in my bones. Oh yeah! Waterloo!'

He laughed. Eddie stared out of the window. They drove through the evergreen forest, past Kibbutz Beit Oren, and Cohen said, 'You know, the Palmach used to train here during the British Mandate, Yitzhak Rabin and those guys. They were going to take on the British, the Nazis, the Arabs, anyone. With nothing much more than wooden sticks and some guns that were old when the Turks still ran things around here.'

Eddie nodded, but he wasn't really listening.

'Now they run things, the old Palmachniks,' Cohen said. 'Rabin's prime minister, Peres is Security Minister, all the generals from the old order. You know what generals like, Eddie? They like to eat, they like to fight, and they like to fuck.'

'Aha,' Eddie said.

'Are you even listening to me?'

'Aha.'

'Fuck you,' Cohen said. 'I'm just saying, they've run this country for nearly thirty years. It won't last.'

Eddie stirred. 'Then who? Menachem Begin and that lot? Or the Black Panthers?' He laughed.

'Yes,' Cohen said.

'Bullshit,' Eddie said.

'You'll see.'

They passed caves in the mountain. An archaeological dig was set up and Eddie saw bones in a pile of dirt. They'd been digging skeletons out of the ground of that land for a long time, he thought. And they were still doing it now. He felt broody. When Cohen wasn't looking Eddie palmed a pill and dry swallowed. He missed Galya, he realised. He wondered if she even thought of him.

He felt better when they finally got to the place. Under an interchange near Hadera. Two uniformed cops in a cruiser like theirs were already on site, along with Dr Schatz and the photographer, Menachem.

Dr Schatz nodded when he saw them.

'You're Sagi's boys, aren't you,' he said.

'Sir?'

'It's alright. I don't mind. It's his case and he's got the Commissioner breathing down his neck. Not that I think he dislikes it. Did you see his photo in the paper yesterday? He can't wait to go up a rank. They're talking about divvying up North District, at which point he could end up heading all of Haifa. If he can make the case.'

'And?' Cohen said. 'Can he make the case?'

'Let's see now,' Dr Schatz said. 'Come. Menachem, photos!'

Eddie and Cohen followed him. On the ground Eddie saw a black army kitbag. Next to the two policemen was a third man, looking nervous, sporting a thin moustache and a farmer's tan in a short-sleeved chequered shirt.

'You found it?' Cohen said.

'Yeah, I mean… Yeah.'

'Who are you?'

'His name is Oren Karmi,' one of the policemen volunteered. 'Said he came down here last night, found the bag, didn't think much of it until this morning when he heard on the news about the ongoing investigation. He thought he'd phone it in, and got us. We've been looking at every piece of junk between Hadera and Haifa for days.'

'What were you doing here last night?' Eddie asked, curious. The man mumbled something.

'What's that?'

'I went for a hike.'

'A *hike*?' Eddie said.

The policeman smiled. 'It's a quiet stretch,' he said. 'Sometimes people come here to do things they don't want other people to see.'

'I don't—' Eddie said. Then, 'Oh.'

'Hey, I wasn't… I'm not!' Oren Karmi said.

'A homosexual? Do we look like we care?' Cohen said. 'You know anyone who went to prison for fucking a guy?'

'Not prison, maybe, but—' Karmi said, then stopped himself.

'We just want her stuff,' Cohen said. '*Is* this her stuff?'

Schatz looked through the bag with gloved hands. He pulled out a diary. It looked familiar. He opened the page carefully. Eddie recognised the same handwriting he'd seen before.

Esther Landes, My Diary, it said.

'Shit,' Eddie said.

'We found her clothes, too,' the policeman said. He brought out four sealed evidence bags. 'White shorts, a shirt, underwear, a pair of high-heeled sandals.'

'The contents of the bag include a diary, earrings, a change of clothing, a purse with an ID card and an army card both issued to Esther Landes, one book, *He Went In The Fields*, several personal photographs—' Dr Schatz looked up. 'Do you need any more?'

'No,' Cohen said.

'May her memory be blessed,' Karmi said, and his eyes teared up.

Dr Schatz frowned as he dusted for fingerprints. 'You need any of this now?' he said.

'The diary,' Cohen said.

'The shoes,' Eddie said.

'The *shoes*?' Dr Schatz said.

'The shoes,' Eddie said.

'The book is a library book?' Cohen said.

Schatz opened it. The stamp card was affixed to the front endpaper.

'Rutenberg House,' he said.

'Thanks, Doc.'

Cohen took the diary.

'Don't lose it,' Dr Schatz warned.

Eddie took the bag with the shoes.

'Thank you,' he said to Karmi.

'Me? Why?' Karmi said.

'For not just leaving her there,' Eddie said.

'I couldn't, you know?' Karmi said.

'I know.'

They got back in their car. Cohen burned rubber. They made the journey back to Haifa in half the time. Into the police station, where Sagi was waiting.

'I spoke to Schatz already,' he said.

'There is nothing in the diary,' Eddie said. He read it all through the drive back. 'It stops in Tel Aviv, before she goes back to Haifa.'

'But he doesn't know that,' Sagi said. 'So use it.'

'Us, sir?'

'It's your turn. I want to see you work.'

'But sir, it's not—'

Cohen saluted smartly.

'Yes, sir,' he said.

'See?' Sagi said. 'He gets it. And there I was thinking you were the smart one.'

'Sir,' Eddie said. 'I have a question.'

'He who knocks on the door shall receive an answer, as the Arabs say,' Sagi said.

Cohen nodded and it looked to Eddie like he was going to write it down.

'What is it, Raphael?' Sagi said.

'It's just… If she came back from Tel Aviv, like we say. And if she got to the Rutenberg House, and she met Barnea there…'

'Yes, Raphael?'

'Then why did we find her travel bag under an underpass in Hadera?' Eddie said.

'What?'

'If she got back, she would have left the bag in her room before going on a date,' Eddie said.

'Ifs and buts!' Sagi said. 'What about the shoes, Raphael? The shoes are the nail in his coffin! *Why* would she be hitchhiking with high-heeled sandals that we know she borrowed from her roommate especially to go on a date with Barnea? These shoes are going to send that son of a bitch to prison for a very long time!'

Eddie didn't know what to think. He nodded.

'Yes, sir,' he said.

'Good. Now go in there. He seems to like you, Raphael. So make him fall in love with you. Let him tell you his life secrets. Let him confess. He *wants* to confess.'

'Yes, sir,' Eddie said.

27

HE WENT IN THE FIELDS

'And that was when what happened happened.' – *Elisha Barnea*

'Please,' Elisha Barnea said. 'I can't take it anymore.'

'Then tell us what happened.'

'Tell us and you can rest.'

'Tell us and you can sleep.'

'Tell us, Barnea.'

'You hit me,' Elisha said.

'No one hit you,' Cohen said. 'We're the police, we don't do this sort of thing.'

'I'm going to tell,' Elisha said.

'Tell the wind,' Cohen said. 'Tell the trees. Tell Yasser fucking Arafat for all I care, Barnea. But there's only one way out of that door and it's by telling us what really happened that night between you and Esther Landes.'

'Nothing happened.'

'You were there?'

'I was… I was at the Rutenberg House like I told you. I thought maybe she was there. I asked someone for directions to her room. But she wasn't there, so I left. I swear. I didn't see her.'

'You're a tall guy,' Cohen said.

'I guess?'

Elisha blinked sleep-starved eyes at them. He had the deep stare of an orphan.

'Esther was small. Short, I mean.'

'I guess?'

'She wanted to look good next to you,' Cohen said. 'She wanted to stand tall.'

'So what?'

'Let's leave that for the moment,' Eddie said. 'Can I get you anything, Elisha? A coffee? A sandwich?'

'I just want to sleep.'

'I know you do. I want to help you. I really do want to help you.'

'Thank you,' Elisha said.

'You grew up here? Your parents came from Libya.'

'I grew up here, I am from here.'

'What do you think of the government?' Eddie said. 'Of Rabin?'

Elisha stared at him, confused. 'Of Rabin? He was Commander in Chief during the war. I never met him. I was just a simple soldier.'

'But he's a sabra, a real one. A Palmachnik. If anyone is handsome of locks and countenance it's Yitzhak Rabin.'

'I don't follow,' Elisha said.

'Not like you,' Eddie said, mercilessly. 'Not some Mizrahi Redskin like you and your parents, brought over from Africa, crammed into tenements in Acre. He's someone who speaks proper Hebrew and yes, I hear how you speak it, how hard you try to speak like them. And your hair, how hard you try. You do, don't you? But you're not a Moshe Shamir character, those fields are not there for *you* to walk in.'

'Why are you saying these things?' Elisha said. 'This is Elisha's country as much as anyone's. Elisha fought for it. My friends died for it. Their blood watered the earth.'

'You're just an Arab,' Cohen said. 'An Arab who thinks he's a Jew. They don't have people like *you* in power, do they, Barnea?'

'Makes you angry,' Eddie said.

'Makes you mad,' Cohen said.

'And you see one of theirs, and you think, why don't I pluck that fruit from the tree? Why don't I get a bite?'

'Did you bite her?' Cohen said.

'I don't even know what you are talking about!' Elisha screamed. 'All you do is talk and talk and talk! I'm just like you, I'm a citizen, I have rights!'

'Do murderers have rights, Eddie?' Cohen said.

'The right to life in jail,' Eddie said.

Cohen brought out the evidence bag. He slammed a high-heeled sandal on the table. Elisha startled.

'She wore these for you!' Cohen said.

'It's true,' Eddie said quietly. 'She borrowed them to wear when she was with you, so you wouldn't be so much taller than her.'

'You,' Cohen said. 'No one else.'

'You,' Eddie said. 'Just you.'

Elisha Barnea began to cry.

'She had them on that night, when she died. Because she did meet you that night, Elisha. She came back to the Rutenberg House and there you were. And she went and put on her high-heeled shoes. And then she went out with you. Out for a drive. A drive she never came back from.'

'Where did you drop her stuff off?' Eddie said.

'I don't know! I don't know!'

'You drove to Hadera,' Cohen said remorselessly. 'It was a nice night. You had the window down. The wind in your hair. Blood under your nails. You found a quiet underpass and dropped her bag and shoes and panties and all, over the side. But you didn't look in her bag, did you? You didn't know she had her diary there. She wrote about you. Did you know that? Do you know what she said about you, Elisha? Do you know?'

'I don't know!'

'I'm scared of him, she wrote,' Cohen said. 'He scares me but he also excites me. I feel like he could hurt me if he wanted to, and sometimes I think he wants to, but then I want him more.'

'She was having problems with her boyfriend,' Eddie said sadly.

'He was fucking her best friend,' Cohen said.

'What an asshole, right?' Eddie said. 'But still. Why would she be scared of you?' He looked across the table at Elisha and felt nothing. 'Unless she had a reason to. She had a reason to, didn't she, Elisha? She had a reason to be scared?'

'Not scared enough,' Cohen said.

'Only at the end,' Eddie said. 'But then it was too late, wasn't it.'

They let the silence sit. They watched the prisoner. He cried without sound.

Cohen put pen and paper on the table.

'Maybe write her a letter,' he said. 'Tell her how you feel.'

Elisha cried.

'Give him a moment,' Eddie said.

Cohen stood, stretched. 'Sure,' he said. 'You want anything from the kiosk?'

'I'm good,' Eddie said.

Cohen left. Now it was just the two of them in the room. Just Eddie and Elisha.

'Why are you doing this?' Elisha said. 'Why?'

'It's our job.'

'But you don't have to do it,' Elisha said.

'I do,' Eddie said.

'Then what's the point?' Elisha said.

'I don't know,' Eddie said. 'I don't know that there is a point.'

Elisha nodded. He took a deep breath. He wiped his nose on his sleeve.

'OK,' he said.

'OK?'

'Sure. I went to the Rutenberg House for my exam like I said. I went looking for Esther after, like I said. I ran into her. She'd just got back from Tel Aviv.'

'What time was it?'

'I don't know. Late?'

'OK.'

'She was happy to see me. She got changed. I don't know what she wore. She came down and we went for a drive. We both knew what we wanted to do. Make out. Maybe more. I drove along the coast road. I found that turning into Tantura. I came there before, a couple of times. Is this good?' He looked shy. 'So far?'

'It's good,' Eddie said. 'It's good.'

'We made out. I wanted to… you know.'

'Fuck.'

'Make love,' Elisha said. 'She didn't want to. She hit me and I… I don't know. We fought. I pushed her out of the car. Her bra was already off.'

'Yes?'

'She struggled. I was angry.'

'Yes?'

Elisha nodded. 'And that was when what happened happened,' he said.

'What happened?'

'You know.'

'Can you say it?'

'Do I have to? I am so tired,' Elisha said.

'Write it down,' Eddie said. 'That's all you have to do.'

'Write it?'

'Tell it like you told me.'

'If you think so,' Elisha said. He picked up the pen. He began to write.

My name is Elisha Barnea—

'Good,' Eddie said. 'Good.'

Elisha nodded. He wrote and he wrote. There was no coercion.

'And sign,' Eddie said. 'At the bottom there.'

'OK.'

Elisha signed. He looked at Eddie with those big, bruised, hopeless eyes.

'I did good?' he said.

'You did good,' Eddie said.

'I am so tired,' Elisha said. 'So very tired, you know.'

'I know,' Eddie said. He could feel them behind the glass – Sagi, Hillel, Cohen. He took the signed confession from Elisha Barnea's hands.

'Now you can sleep,' Eddie said.

PART FOUR

SMALL TIME CROOKS

1976, Wadi Nisnas to the Grove of the Forty

28

WATERLOO

'Justice prevailed' – Cohen

'You did alright, then,' Rubenstein said. He folded the newspaper neatly across his knees.

The headline screamed, 'Barnea Found Guilty of Murder.'

'I suppose so, yes,' Cohen said. 'Justice prevailed and all that.'

Kaveret's 'I Gave Her My Life' played on the radio and Benny lit a cigarette and watched the pretty girls go past on the pavement outside. He didn't give a shit about Elisha Barnea.

Haifa, he thought. What the fuck was he doing in Haifa.

This Cohen was a strange one, Benny thought. For one thing he was a policeman. He'd arrested Rubenstein once, a year or so back. That's how they met.

Benny grew up with Rubenstein in Jaffa, just across from the police station near Bloomfield Stadium. They weren't going to end up in prison like some of those old fuckers who ran things, leftover black marketeers from the fresh egg-running years of austerity. Rubenstein had ambitions, and Benny appreciated ambition, and where Rubenstein went Benny wanted to follow.

But he didn't know about this Cohen.

'It's a shame they didn't win the Eurovision,' Benny said.

Rubenstein looked up, irritated. 'What?' he said.

'Kaveret. They came seventh place. It's not bad.'

'Who won, then?' Rubenstein said. Rubenstein's family was Romanian. Benny didn't know, maybe they rooted for the Romanians in the contest, only Romania was behind the Iron

Curtain and nobody *there* was going to be singing on a stage in Brighton or anywhere else in the West, for that matter, not anytime soon.

'Abba,' Benny said. 'With "Waterloo".'

'Who?' Rubenstein said. But even he had to know Abba.

'I'm just saying,' Benny said. 'It's a good song.'

'"Waterloo"?' Cohen said.

'"I Gave Her My Life",' Benny said. 'You know it's really a political song? It's against Golda and how there's enough room for two countries, for us and the Palestinians.'

'What *are* you talking about?' Rubenstein said.

Benny knew Rubenstein didn't like being in Haifa any more than Benny did. Their patch was Tel Aviv, where they crept around the old boys like Midget and Oshry, those two fuckers who ran the market stalls and the diamond trade and any grab-and-run and burglary and who knew what else.

Yet here they were in Haifa, sitting with a cop.

Officially, Benny supposed Rubenstein was what the cops called an intelligence source. Only Benny was pretty sure Cohen wasn't filing any reports on this meeting.

Which was what this was, a business meeting.

They sat in the café and watched the diamond shop across the road.

'That's him,' Cohen said.

Benny watched the old guy come out of the shop. He was a little fat man and he was wrapped in a thick fur coat and he smiled and waved to someone in the shop before he got into his car and drove off. His name was Herring.

'So, what?' Benny said.

'He lives up in Denya,' Cohen said.

Rubenstein stood up. 'Alright,' he said.

'Alright, what?' Benny said.

'We'll do it.'

'Alright,' Cohen said.

So that was that.

'Come on, Benny, let's go,' Rubenstein said. He left cash on the table. Benny followed him to the car.

'What are we doing here?' he said.

'Let's go see some cousins of ours,' Rubenstein said.

Their next stop was in Wadi Nisnas in the lower city, though they got lost twice trying to find it and Benny had to hold the map book in his lap. It was an Arab neighbourhood, the 'cousins' Rubenstein talked about. They parked and found the falafel stand. Pierre Malik was already sitting there.

He waved a hand at the selection of salads on the counter. 'You want anything?' he said. He was a small intense man with thick black hair. He bit into his pita. Tahina sauce turned his lips white.

'I'm good,' Rubenstein said. He sat down and Benny followed. Benny noticed Malik's men sitting around the place. In fact no one else was sitting at this particular falafel shop but for Malik's men.

'You won't eat with me, Rubenstein?' Malik laughed. He patted his lips delicately with a paper napkin and tossed the rest of the pita on the plate. 'Alright, then. What *do* you want, if it isn't falafel?'

'I want brown,' Rubenstein said.

'Yes, well,' Malik said. 'Do you have the money, is the question.'

'You can get it from Lebanon?'

'I can get it.'

'What about the war?' Benny said. The war in Lebanon had just broken out but it looked set to be an ugly one.

'I'm doing this for the war effort,' Malik said. 'I'm not some criminal. No offence.'

'You're selling hash for the *war effort*?' Benny said.

'Sure. The Phalangists are my family. Those fucking Arabs are going to get what's coming to them.'

'But you're an Arab,' Benny said.

'Fucking never!' Malik said. 'I'm a Maronite.'

Benny didn't get it. The Lebanese were worse than Jews, he thought. They had so many factions and minorities and they all seemed to hate each other. The Phalangists were Christian and they were a powerful minority, but more importantly they had access to the vast fields of marijuana in the east of Lebanon and that was what Rubenstein wanted. Which was all that mattered, when it came down to it.

'Do you have the money?' Malik said.

'How much can you get?'

'How much do you want?' Malik said.

'How do you bring it over?' Benny said.

'What are you, a cop?' Malik said. 'I have people to get it across the border.'

They discussed quantities and haggled over the price. Malik ordered coffee and baklava. Benny nibbled on a pastry. Malik and Rubenstein shook hands.

'That's a big move for you, Rubenstein,' Malik said. 'You get into the drugs you're going to be stepping on some big boys' toes in Tel Aviv.'

'Let me worry about that,' Rubenstein said.

'Trust me, I won't lose sleep over it,' Malik said.

They left him there and got back in their car. Benny was uneasy. They *didn't* have the money for a move like this. Not unless tonight went well.

He guessed this was why they were in Haifa. It was a bit of a no man's land, and it was the gateway to the north and to that lucrative Lebanon border. But if they got into the drug business like this then Pierre Malik was right, they weren't going to go unnoticed for much longer.

Right now they were just small time crooks. But Rubenstein wasn't planning on staying that way forever.

29

THE RAID ON ENTEBBE

'Be like Shaike' – *Cohen*

Things started to go wrong as soon as they set out on the job. The car wouldn't start. Rubenstein popped the hood and Cohen messed about in there and on the third try it started. The plan was simple. They drove up to Denia, under a starry sky. It was a wealthy neighbourhood up on the Carmel. The house itself was a two-storey building with a front garden. There was a light on in the upstairs bedroom. They parked the car and waited and watched the house.

Benny fidgeted.

Benny had a bad feeling about the robbery plan.

Later, the lights went out. Still they waited. The radio was on. There was the usual news report. A memorial for Yoni Netanyahu, the commander who died in the Entebbe raid, was to be held in Jerusalem. His brother Benyamin, a young economist living in America, spoke movingly of his brother. The girl from the Baader-Meinhof gang was found hanged in prison in Germany. Prime Minister Yitzhak Rabin was accused of holding a dollar account in the United States, against Israeli law. Tensions remained high after the general strike by Israeli Arabs in March and the subsequent armed response by police and military forces.

The usual.

Arik Einstein came on singing 'Maybe It's Over' from the *Good Old Land of Israel* album, and Benny hummed along with the song.

Something about how the country used to be just mosquitoes and swamps back in the day.

'Yeah?' Rubenstein said. 'Tell that to the Arabs.'

'Fuck the Arabs,' Cohen said.

Rubenstein nodded.

'Let's go,' he said.

They stepped quietly out of the car. They wore blue workmen's overalls. Benny's heart beat faster. He didn't like this plan. He didn't like Haifa. He didn't like – well, it didn't matter what he liked or didn't like. They went to the house. They put on ski masks that covered their faces. The mask itched. What was he, a Baader-Meinhof?

Rubenstein opened the kitchen window and they climbed in.

The house was quiet. It was dark. No dog, Cohen said. There was no one downstairs. Rubenstein went up first. Cohen and Benny followed.

The floor creaked. The door to the first bedroom on the landing was open and a night light glowed, illuminated three children asleep. Rubenstein trod softly past the children's room and into the second bedroom.

Mr and Mrs Herring were also asleep. Benny gripped the Uzi. Rubenstein and Cohen went to the bed.

Rubenstein nodded. Cohen held a sock in his hand. The plan was to gag and tie up the couple. It was a simple plan.

Just then Mrs Herring opened her eyes.

She stared at the masked men.

She screamed.

Mr Herring woke up. Rubenstein hit him over the head with his pistol as Cohen tried to gag Mrs Herring. Mrs Herring bit his hand and Cohen swore and slapped her. Benny held the Uzi but what was he going to shoot? He heard footsteps behind him and turned.

Two small girls and a boy stared up at him and started to scream.

'What the fuck do I do!' Benny yelled.

'Calm them down!'

Cohen was wrestling Mrs Herring. Mr Herring was lying back with his forehead cut open and blood dripping on the bedsheets.

'Hey, kids,' Benny said desperately. 'Don't cry. Mummy and Daddy are just playing.'

The kids screamed louder. Cohen slapped Mrs Herring again. He tried to pull something off one of her fingers.

'Goddamn it!' Rubenstein said. He prodded Mr Herring with his pistol. 'Where is the safe!'

Mr Herring's head lolled on the pillow.

Cohen said, 'You hit him too hard.'

'Where is the safe!' Rubenstein yelled at Mrs Herring. She started to jabber at him in Yiddish. Benny couldn't understand a word she was saying.

'Hey, kids,' Benny said brightly, 'let's play a game! Do you know where Daddy keeps his diamonds?'

The boy pointed to the wall, crying. The painting on the wall was by Anna Ticho. Benny lifted it carefully. Behind it was the safe.

'How do you open it?' he said.

Rubenstein prodded Herring.

'He's out,' he said.

The kids cried. Mrs Herring let out another torrent of Yiddish. Who the hell still spoke Yiddish? Cohen balled up the sock he was going to use as a gag. It was too late to do any good.

'I got her ring,' he said.

'Let's go,' Rubenstein said. 'Sorry, kids.'

Benny grabbed the painting.

'What are you doing?' Cohen said.

'What?' Benny said. 'It's an Anna Ticho.'

They ran downstairs and out of the house. All the lights were on in the neighbouring houses. Benny could hear police sirens in the distance.

They jumped into the car and drove away at speed.

'Fuck you, Cohen,' Benny said. 'We didn't even get into the safe.'

He'd hated dealing with the children. Benny liked children. He and Ofra were planning on starting a family soon.

Cohen opened his palm. Showed them a diamond ring, with a fat cut diamond that shone even in the light of the street lamps.

'This isn't going to buy shit,' Rubenstein said, disgusted.

'I'm sorry, Aryeh,' Cohen said.

'You should be sorry.'

'I'll make it up to you,' Cohen said.

'I need a deal with the Lebanese,' Rubenstein said.

'Fuck it,' Cohen said. 'Go back.'

'You what?'

'Turn back! Right now!'

The car swerved. Rubenstein grabbed the wheel until his fingers were white. He didn't say a fucking word. Benny knew and Cohen knew. This wasn't the sort of thing you walked away from. Not if you were stupid enough to go back.

They drove back to the house. They left the car running. Cohen kicked the door open and they ran upstairs. This was no time for finessing a window.

Mrs Herring screamed when she saw them all over again. Mr Herring was still out cold.

Benny sweated. Benny heard the sirens coming close.

The kids screamed.

'Shut them up!' Rubenstein said. He stuck the Uzi in Mrs Herring's ribs.

'Get up,' he said, and his voice was low and Mrs Herring stopped screaming. You kept your mouth shut when Rubenstein looked at you that way.

He wasn't crazy, he was just cold.

'Kids, kids,' Benny said. They screamed like they'd seen a monster. He tried to think what to do as Rubenstein pushed their mother out of the room.

Benny cleared his throat.

He started to sing.

The only song that popped into his mind was 'Hatikvah'. He tried desperately to think of the words some drunk Russian poet came up with, which somehow became the national anthem.

'As long as the tears fall from our *eeyyees*,' he sang, the music slow, heavy, the music of army bands and official ceremonies, with more than a tinge of a Slavic tune, 'like a rain of *aaalms*, how does it go, wait, I know the line, right – as long as scores of our *peeeooople*, still end up in the *groouund*!'

The children stared at him.

They *had* gone silent.

Rubenstein pushed Mrs Herring at Cohen. Cohen took her downstairs. Rubenstein slapped Mr Herring until the man blinked awake in confusion.

'You'll hear from us,' Rubenstein said. 'No police or she's dead!'

Benny went past the kids. Rubenstein followed him. They ran down the stairs and into the car. Cohen was trying to shove Mrs Herring into the back seat.

Rubenstein said, 'Just knock her out,' and Cohen nodded. He hit her with his gun. She dropped and was still on the seat.

'The painting!' Benny said.

Mrs Herring had fallen over it.

'It's an original,' Benny said.

'Forget the fucking painting,' Rubenstein said.

The sirens wailed close. Cohen said, 'Aryeh, you go. Find somewhere quiet and call the house. Benny, you come with me.'

'This is fucked up,' Benny said. But he followed Cohen.

Rubenstein burned rubber getting out of there. How did everything go so wrong? Benny ran after Cohen. He had the urge to shoot the man in the back.

But they were stuck with him and whatever this was.

Cohen stopped between two buildings. He tore off the ski mask and quickly removed his overalls, and Benny did the same.

'Good, good,' Cohen said. 'Toss them in the bin over there.'

Cohen started to whistle. He rooted in his pockets. He tossed something to Benny and Benny caught it.

It was a badge.

'Listen,' Cohen said. 'You don't speak, and if you have to speak you mumble. You watched *The Good Officer Azulay*? So be like Shaike. Got it? Just shut up and follow me and we could end up with the money so Rubenstein doesn't kill me.'

He marched out of the little alley just as two police cars pulled to a stop with their lights flashing.

30

THE GOOD OFFICER AZULAY

'Oui' – Benny

'I came as soon as I heard the call,' Cohen said. 'Do you want to tell me what is going on here, Mr Herring?'

They were in the living room. The children were crying and Mr Herring had a bandage round his head and he sat heavily in an armchair. The room was filled with old wooden furniture, more European than Israeli in style, and the blinds were drawn. Two police officers stood by the broken door.

'Come, come, Mr Herring,' Cohen said. 'There is no use prevaricating. Tell me what happened?'

'I can't,' Mr Herring said. 'They said…' He fell quiet.

'Where is your wife?' Cohen said.

'They took her!' One of the two little girls blurted out. 'The men, they took her!'

'Took her where, sweetheart?' Cohen said.

'I don't know,' the little girl said, and she started to cry again. Benny stood there very awkwardly. This really wasn't anything like *The Good Officer Azulay*, which he'd seen at the Alhambra Cinema in Jaffa when it came out.

In the movie Azulay was a kind-hearted but hapless policeman who never made rank. He was so useless that the top criminals of Jaffa got together to try and help him keep his job, but even they couldn't do it. There was no place for a policeman like Azulay in the Israeli Police Force, the film seemed to say.

Benny clutched the badge Cohen gave him and he kept his mouth very firmly shut.

'Your wife was kidnapped?' Cohen said gently to Mr Herring.

Herring nodded at last. 'Yes… yes!' He started to spill it out then. He seemed confused. Men broke into the house. Did he see their faces? No, they wore masks. They wore blue overalls he thought. They were armed for sure. They wanted diamonds but one of them hit him too hard and he passed out. As he was coming to, the men were gone, and he thought they'd been saved by God. Then they came back. He heard them break down the door. Yes, that door, right there. The front door. They came up the stairs and took his wife. His poor wife.

Mr Herring started to cry. What did he ever do? What did she? He paid his taxes, he was an honest man, he looked after his children and prayed to God every day. He gave to charity. He was blameless and upright, a man who feared God and turned away from evil. Just like Job. And like Job, he was visited by misfortune.

'They said not to talk to the police,' he said. 'Oh, Batya, Batya!'

'We'll get your Batya back,' Cohen said. 'Don't you worry. This one, here?' He indicated Benny. 'He's a special negotiator, from France.'

Benny spluttered.

'A special negotiator?' Mr Herring said, confused.

Cohen sighed. 'He is on a formal visit from the Police Nationale as an observer. I've been tasked with showing him around. We just happened to be passing through when I heard the call and we came immediately. He is an expert on negotiating with kidnappers and terrorists.'

Mr Herring looked at Benny with wonder.

'Oui,' Benny said. He nodded vigorously. 'Oui.'

'The French have great experience in dealing with this kind of situation,' Cohen said. 'We will handle it discreetly. Ofer?'

'Sir?' one of the policemen said.

'We need to keep this quiet,' Cohen said. 'You understand?'

'Yes, sir,' Ofer said.

'Good,' Cohen said. 'No reporting to anyone. Let's make this seem like a routine visit. You guys leave the house and get back in the car. Drive away, but loop back and park nearby. I will handle communication. With luck, we'll catch these bastards in the act. But the main thing is to get Mrs Herring back safe.'

'You know best, Cohen,' Offer said. He nodded to the other policeman and they both left.

'What do I do?' Mr Herring said. He looked at Cohen helplessly. 'What do I do now?'

'Now we wait,' Cohen said.

The children were still crying. Cohen motioned them to come to him. He sat down on the sofa. The children sat around him. Cohen reached for a book. He opened it and turned the page and smiled, and the children snuggled close to him as if already spellbound by his presence. There was a little red mark on his hand from where Mrs Herring bit him, but no one but Benny seemed to notice it.

The book was a worn-out copy of *Chipopo in Egypt* by Tamar Bornstein-Lazar. Cohen began to read, and his voice was melodic and kind, and Benny watched in wonder as soon the children forgot the violent events that had only just transpired, and the loss of their mother, and were carried in their imaginations by the whacky exploits of the talking monkey, Chipopo, and his little friends. Benny went to the kitchen and made coffee and carried a cup back for Mr Herring.

'Thank you,' Mr Herring said.

Benny said, 'Oui.'

He hoped bloody Rubenstein would bloody call. It was the middle of the night. The children fell asleep where they were, one by one. Cohen sat back with the book face down on his chest. He looked wistfully at the children.

'You have a beautiful family, Mr Herring,' he said.

'Thank you,' Mr Herring said helplessly.

The telephone rang. Cohen snatched the receiver.

'I don't want to wake up the children,' he said. He passed the phone to Mr Herring.

'Hello?' Mr Herring said.

A voice on the other end.

'Where is my wife?' Mr Herring said. 'What did you do to her!'

The voice again. Mr Herring grasped the receiver.

'I don't have that kind of money,' he said.

The voice again. Threatening. Cohen took the receiver out of Mr Herring's hands.

'Listen to me,' Cohen said into the phone. 'You will not harm a hair on Mrs Herring's head, are we clear? This is what will happen. We will meet you with the money. You will bring Mrs Herring. There will be no cops. Who am I? That is not your concern. We will make the exchange. Where? There's a picnic area not far from here, at the Grove of the Forty, do you know it? Then find it on a bloody map. It's quiet, there will be no one there this late at night. We will meet there in one hour. Are we clear? Good. Goodbye.'

Cohen hung up.

'Do you have the money?' he said to Mr Herring.

Mr Herring paled. 'I have some in the safe upstairs, but it's... But I...'

'This is your wife's life here,' Cohen said.

'But it's...' Herring sagged in defeat. He led them upstairs. Unlocked the safe. Benny stared as Mr Herring removed stashes of dollars, francs and Israeli lira and put them dejectedly into a plastic shopping bag.

'And the rest?' Cohen said.

'The *rest*?' Herring said. 'You don't understand, this isn't mine, it's sold on consignment, these stones came from South Africa for polishing and they're going to Antwerp on the next ship—'

He stared at Cohen helplessly.

'The *stones*,' Cohen said.

And that was that.

They left the kids to sleep. Cohen went outside and spoke to the policemen waiting in the car that was parked across the road. Benny watched him, but Cohen spoke quietly. The two policemen left their vehicle and Benny saw Cohen slip something into their hands when they left. They walked away on foot. Cohen got in the car and started it.

'No police,' he told Herring. 'Just us. We will get her back. This I promise you.'

'You are an angel,' Mr Cohen said.

Benny pinched the bridge of his nose very hard and said nothing.

They drove. It was not a long drive through the mountain. The Grove of the Forties was quiet and secluded just like Cohen said. Ancient oaks whispered in the breeze. Benny saw Rubenstein's car already parked. Mr Herring started to blubber.

'Strength, Mr Herring,' Cohen said. 'Strength, now.'

He stopped the car and they got out.

It was dark on the mountain. Rubenstein stood in silhouette, a gun in his hand. He turned the headlights on and the light caught them in its glare.

'You came alone?' Rubenstein said.

'We came alone,' Cohen said.

'You have my money?' Rubenstein said.

'You have Mrs Herring?' Cohen said.

Rubenstein grunted. He switched off the headlights and opened the back door of his car and pulled out Mrs Herring. Her wrists were tied in rope and her mouth was gagged.

'Batya!' Mr Herring cried.

'Don't move!' Rubenstein said. 'My money?'

Cohen lifted the shopping bag.

'I have it right here!' he shouted.

'Come forward slowly. No weapons.'

Cohen advanced, holding the bag up. And Benny stood there, not saying a fucking word, and he watched this play performed under the dark night of the Carmel, with the ancient trees of that grove, sacred to the Druze, the only other witnesses.

Cohen came, with diamonds and cash. Rubenstein took a step, holding on to Mrs Herring.

They stopped. No words were exchanged. Mr Herring stood mutely next to Benny, and he too didn't say a fucking word.

Then it was done.

Cohen handed over the bag and at the same time Rubenstein pushed Mrs Herring. She fell and rolled down as Rubenstein got back in his car and gunned the engine.

By the time Mr Herring got to Mrs Herring, the kidnapper, the money and the diamonds were all gone.

There was one further thing after they drove Mr and Mrs Herring back to their house. Mr Herring wanted to make an immediate complaint to the police.

Cohen nodded seriously all the while the man spoke. Then he put his arm around him.

'They know where you live,' he said.

And that was that.

Benny never fucking opened his mouth the whole time until they left the Herrings' house and got back in the car. Then he let out a huge breath of air.

'I don't *ever* want to be a policeman again,' he said, and he tossed the badge back to Cohen.

'It isn't even real,' Cohen said, and then he burst out laughing. He drove like a wild man out of the sleeping neighbourhood. By then the sun was beginning to rise, and Benny saw the sea spread out below them, and the ships dotting the harbour, and he thought even Haifa could be beautiful sometimes.

They met with Rubenstein in the flat. He sat at the kitchen table with his shoes off and counted cash. Benny stared at the diamonds on the table. They weren't the biggest stones, and they weren't the most beautiful, but fuck if right then they didn't look good: they looked real good.

'I spoke to Malik,' Rubenstein said, not even looking up. 'The deal is on for tonight.'

Benny lit a cigarette and opened the window. He felt the wind on his face. Cohen stood in the doorway.

'Where did you keep her?' he said.

'In the car. Drove up to the forest and parked. She pissed herself a couple of times. Ruined the seat. That was a stupid thing to do, Cohen, what you did tonight.'

'But I came through, didn't I?'

Rubenstein looked up then. 'I can't make you out,' he said. 'What are you, a policeman or a crook?'

You can be both, Benny thought but didn't say.

'I'm not a crook,' Cohen said.

'Then what?'

'I keep order,' Cohen said. 'What I did for you today, you will remember it, Rubenstein?'

'I will remember it.'

Cohen nodded, and then he left. Benny heard the door close softly.

'Do you trust him?' he said.

'No,' Rubenstein said, 'but then, he is a cop.'

PART FIVE

'THE WATCHER IS PURE IN THOUGHT AND DEED'

1976, Haifa

31

A GOOD DAY

'What about Esther Landes?' – Ruth

Einav paced the small living room of the urban commune. She drove Ruth mad. Ruth had put on Dudu Zakai's *In A Clover Field* album on the record player earlier and was trying to just listen to the music, but Einav was making it impossible with her pacing.

Ruth just wanted to be lost in the music. Their small flat was filled with that honeyed kibbutznik voice singing. He was a shmutznik just like them, a blue-shirted, white shoelace knotted through the shirt kibbutznik from Hashomer Ha'tzair, the Young Watchers movement. Zakai was singing about how as soon as he'd climb down from the tank and dust the dirt from his uniform he'd whisk his love away to a clover field, and Einav squirmed a little against the thin mattress. She thought of the tenth commandment of the Watchers: 'The watcher is pure in thought and speech and deed (does not smoke, does not drink, observes sexual probity)'.

She thought she wouldn't pay too much mind to the last part if Dudu Zakai came and knocked on their door. She stared at his album cover, at his dreamy eyes and his mane of ginger hair. She'd show him her clover field, she thought.

Einav kept pacing.

Ruth said, 'What!'

'What?' Einav said irritably.

'Can't you sit still?'

'I need the toilet,' Einav said.

'So ask the neighbour,' Ruth said. Their own toilets were blocked, had been for a week.

'I can't go in a stranger's toilet,' Einav said. She hopped in place. 'I really need to go, Ruthie.'

'Pee in the sink,' Ruth said.

'I don't need a pee! I need a Number Two.'

'Why didn't you go in the leadership's office earlier?'

'I didn't need to earlier, did I!' Einav snapped. 'That's it,' she said. 'I'm going home.'

'What do you mean you're going home?' Ruth said.

'I'm going back to the kibbutz. I'll be back tomorrow.'

'It's the middle of the night!'

'It's not that late, Ruthie. You're always so dramatic. And I really need to go.'

'Let me ask the neighbour. He'll let you use it, I'm sure.'

'He's a creep. He'll listen behind the door.'

'And what, on the kibbutz in the children house you had your own toilets? What are you, the Queen of England?' Ruth laughed. Einav was just being silly. It was after eight. The others were out on an activity with their youth groups. Ruth would have quite liked to have the commune to herself for once. It was her first time away from the kibbutz, doing a year's service for the movement before joining the army. There were so many firsts: opening a shared bank account, using money at all, doing the shopping, cooking and cleaning and working with the kids in the youth group... Grown up stuff.

Sharing the small flat wasn't bad, either. She was used to sleeping four in a room and showering together when they were kids and sharing everything, it was just the way you grew up on a kibbutz. But if Einav went then Ruth would have the whole flat to herself for just an hour or two, just her and no one else around, a rare moment of privacy.

Still, she couldn't let her just go off like this because she needed the *toilets*.

'You're being silly,' she said.

'I'm going,' Einav said. She slipped on her sandals and grabbed a bag she'd put on her bed.

'What are you going to do, hitchhike?' Ruth said.

'Yeah.'

'What about Esther Landes? Remember her?'

'They caught the guy who did it, didn't they?' Einav said. 'Some loser. Nothing's going to happen to me. Anyone tries anything I'll kick them where it hurts.' She made a ferocious face at Ruth and Ruth laughed.

'You worry too much,' Einav said. 'I'll see you in the morning or something. Ciao!' And she walked out and slammed the door behind her.

Ruth shrugged. There wasn't anything you could do when Einav got an idea in her head. And Ruth *did* have the whole place to herself now.

She covered herself in the thin blanket and closed her eyes and thought about Dudu Zakai.

She was asleep when the others got back. Evyatar made coffee on the stove and Liora lit a cigarette, she was a bit of a rebel, and she smoked it inexpertly out of the window. Ruth put the pillow over her head and tried to go back to sleep.

Evyatar and Liora talked, because they always liked to talk and they were still buzzing from their activity, both of their youth groups were up late that night doing a fire ceremony, and they'd been busy for weeks twisting cloth in wire and setting up pulleys and so on, so when Evie lit the flame it shot out across to the fire display and lit it up. They sounded happy and smelled of campfire smoke and it took them hours to go to sleep.

Ruth was the first to wake up. The sun shone outside and when she looked out of the window she saw the shops opening and people going to work.

It felt so strange to her, to be in a city. Back home on the kibbutz there was nothing but the grass and the trees and the flowers and the ringing of bicycle bells on the narrow roads. A little slice of heaven that she wasn't ready to give up.

Next year she'd join the army, but for now she felt driven to share the values she had grown up on, of communalism and love of nature, of justice and fellowship, with her young charges, who were from the poorer neighbourhoods of Haifa, mostly, and had lives very different to her own. She really felt she was starting to connect with them, and making progress.

She yawned and started cooking coffee and saw that again Evie and Liora had left their mugs in the sink unwashed and so she washed them, tidying up a little. They had a group meeting about doing the chores only last week, and even made a rota, but she guessed they forgot: they often did.

'Hey,' Evyatar said. He shuffled to the kitchen. 'You missed a great fire ceremony last night.'

'Was it good?'

'It was great! The kids really worked hard and it paid off. Hey, where's Einav?'

'She went back to her kibbutz last night. She said she needed to use the toilet.'

'She did what? Why didn't she use the neighbour's?'

'She said she didn't like him.'

'She doesn't even know him. Well, when is she back?'

'I don't know,' Ruth said. 'You know what she's like.'

'Yeah, well.' Evie scratched his curly locks and stretched. 'Can I have some of that coffee?'

'Sure.'

A few minutes later Liora joined them and they all had breakfast together. None of them really knew how to cook but Ruth could make eggs and Evyatar could cut a salad like one of the kibbutz elders, every tomato and cucumber cut into tiny pieces. They got some cheese from the fridge and Liora volunteered to go down to the bakery so they had fresh bread.

It wasn't like being on the kibbutz, where everyone ate together in the giant dining room, where hardboiled eggs and fresh bread and vegetables for salad were available every day of the week, but it was nice.

After breakfast they all left the flat together to go to the leadership office, they had a meeting to attend about the end of year activities for their youth groups. They took the bus. And the sun shone down and the sky was blue and Ruth gave up her seat for an old lady who had all her shopping with her, and she felt good. It was going to be a good day, she thought.

32

THE WAIT

'I thought she must be home' – Ruth

Einav still hadn't come back in the evening.

It was a night off for all of them so they relaxed in the commune.

Liora leafed through a magazine while Evie sketched. He was pretty good, and said maybe he could go to school to learn art, though it depended on what the kibbutz would need him for. If the kibbutz needed a teacher then Evie would study to become a teacher, and if they needed a mechanic he'd be a mechanic. But he was free to sketch in his spare time, and there were many artists on the kibbutz Ruth grew up on, there was a guy who did sculptures in concrete and the pathways of the kibbutz were littered with his work, and someone else was a poet who had two books published.

Ruth was restless. 'Does anyone have Einav's number on the kibbutz?' she said.

'Doesn't she have a boyfriend?' Liora said. 'Check the notebook.'

Ruth checked the notebook, which had all their numbers and things scribbled in. Einav had written down two telephone numbers – she wrote in a rounded, curly script that was easy to spot – so Ruth tried the first one.

'Hello?'

'Shalom, I'm looking for Einav,' Ruth said.

'Einavy's not here, she's in Haifa,' the woman on the other side of the phone said. 'Hey, Enrique! Einavy's still in Haifa, right?'

'She said she'd come down for Friday dinner!' a man's voice said in the background.

'It's not Friday yet, Enrique!' the woman on the other side of the phone said.

'Then she's in Haifa!'

'Yes,' the woman said, going back to the phone. 'She's in Haifa on the commune. She's doing a voluntary year for the movement, we're very proud of her. Aren't we proud of her, Enrique!'

'Very proud!' the man bellowed in the background.

'Who is this?' the woman said. 'I don't recognise your voice. Is this Miri?'

'No,' Ruth said. 'I'm Ruth.'

'Ruth, Ruth. Fanya's daughter?'

'No,' Ruth said. 'I'm Einav's friend from the commune. That's where I'm calling from.'

'Oh,' the woman said. 'But isn't Einav with you?'

'No,' Ruth said. 'She went back to the kibbutz yesterday.'

'Back here? But I haven't seen her. Enrique, did you see Einavy?'

'No, she's in Haifa!' Enrique bellowed in the background.

'She's not,' Ruth said. 'I thought she must be home.'

'I haven't seen her,' the woman said. Ruth figured she was Einav's mother. 'Maybe she went to stay with Ilan? Ilan's her boyfriend. Hey, Enrique, did you see Ilan today?'

'Ilan? Why would I see Ilan!' Enrique said. 'He works in the orchards!'

'It's a friend of Einavy from the commune! She says Einavy isn't there, she went back to the kibbutz yesterday!'

'Maybe she's staying with Ilan!' Enrique shouted.

'That's what I said!' the woman said. She came back to the phone. 'You know what she's like,' she said. 'She'll turn up. I'll check with Ilan. How are you up there in Haifa? Are you managing alright? I know it's sometimes difficult, going to a new place, the city in particular, but you're doing such important work.'

'It's fine,' Ruth said. 'I'm enjoying it.'

'We really must come up and visit,' the woman said. 'Ruth, Ruth, of course, Einavy mentioned you.'

'Ruth?' Enrique shouted. 'Fanya's daughter?'

'No! From the commune!' the woman said.

'Alright, thank you,' Ruth said. 'I just wanted to check.'

She said goodbye and hung up. But she felt apprehensive.

Half an hour later she tried the second number from the notebook but it just rang. She called Einav's mother back, who confirmed that was Ilan's number.

'They must be out, the two of them,' she said.

That made sense so Ruth let it drop. The next day she met with her youth group and the day was busy, two of the kids had a fight and when she tried to separate them she fell and hurt her elbow. The kids felt bad for it but Ruth was shook up, and the rest of the day went in a blur, like she was just going through the motions.

She was relieved to get back to the commune. It was a hot, muggy day, too, and she just wanted to have a shower and forget about it.

When she got in, the telephone rang. It might have been ringing for a while. Ruth picked it up and an angry man's voice said, 'Who is this?'

'Who is *this*?' Ruth said.

'It's Eitan,' the man said. 'I'm looking for Einav, she didn't come to her youth group activity today.'

Eitan was the leadership coordinator. So Ruth explained what happened.

'This isn't the first time she's done this,' Eitan said. 'They're going to get a piece of my mind on that kibbutz of hers.' And he slammed the phone down.

Ruth went and had her shower and then she lay on the bed. It had been a strange sort of day. She supposed Eitan would call Einav's kibbutz and this time she'd have to show up, because a call from the coordinator was a big thing.

Liora and Evie showed up a little later, they had dinner together and then went to sleep.

The knocks on the door woke them up the next morning.

33

POLICE

'Their love, their hatred and their jealousy too are lost' – Ecclesiastes

They came without warning. One moment Ruth was fast asleep. The next she was bolt upright in the bed, the knocks violent and hard, like they were going to break the door down to get in.

'Open up! Open up! Police!'

'Police! Open up! Open now!'

Ruth ran to the door. Her fingers shook on the lock and the door shook with the impact of the blows outside. When she finally managed to unlock it they barged right in. They didn't wear uniforms.

One of the men pushed her against the wall. Ruth's palms slammed against the concrete wall. Liora and Evyatar were treated the same way. The policemen searched them.

Ruth felt their fingers on her naked skin. She tamped down horrible revulsion.

'What is this!' Evyatar said.

'Shut up!' a policeman said. They let Ruth go then and started ripping the commune apart, pulling out drawers in the kitchen, turning over the mattresses, looking everywhere, touching everything.

'What's... What's going on?' Ruth said. She didn't know if she could sit. She was still in just her underwear and a T-shirt. The policemen looked right through her. Two of them held Evie against the wall but they let Liora go.

'Is it about Einav?' Ruth said.

Liora said, 'Einav? Why would it be about Einav?'

She still didn't get it, Ruth thought. Ruth saw a policeman with sad eyes by the kitchen window. He lifted the ashtray Liora sometimes used. It had a half-smoked cigarette in it. He picked it up and smelled it.

'Hashish?' he said. 'Is that what you do here, in this *commune*? Sex and drugs?'

'What?' Liora said, outraged. 'We're in the movement, we're Young Watchers! My father is the secretary of our kibbutz! You can't treat us like this!'

'We can do what we want,' the man with the sad eyes said. He looked at Ruth and she thought he looked almost apologetic.

'Where is your roommate?' he said.

'She's not here!' Liora said.

'I can see that,' the man said. 'Yes, I can see that clearly.'

'Cohen, what do you want done with them?' one of the other policemen said.

'Take them to the station. Not her.' Her pointed to Ruth and she shuddered.

'Search the flat and bag what you find,' Cohen said.

The policemen marched Evie out first, in handcuffs. He looked like he was going to cry.

Liora went next, kicking and cursing at them the whole time until one of the policemen slapped her, and then she really lost it and they had to pin her by the arms and lift her up, and Ruth could hear her screaming all the way down the stairs.

Then it was just Ruth and the policeman with the sad eyes whose name was Cohen. She didn't like the way he looked at her.

'Maybe you and I could talk,' he said.

'It's about Einav, isn't it?' Ruth said. 'She's dead.'

The certainty washed over her then.

She said, 'I warned her, I warned her not to go!'

She felt the tears come but she didn't want to cry, not in front of him.

'Let's talk somewhere else,' the policeman said. 'Ruth. Can I call you Ruth? We got your names from your leadership coordinator. Can I get you a coffee, maybe?'

'Why aren't you arresting me?' Ruth said. 'Why did you arrest the others? Why?'

'Arrest them? We're only taking them in for questioning. No one's been arrested.'

'Where is Einav?' Ruth said. 'What happened to her?'

'Let's go get a coffee,' Cohen said gently. His men were busy tearing up what was left of the apartment. Cohen picked up the Dudu Zakai album and looked at it without much interest. He slid the record out of the sleeve, checked there was nothing else inside, shrugged and put it down again.

'"For the living know that they shall die and the dead know nothing",' he said, '"and they shall have no more reward for they are forgotten". Ecclesiastes.'

'She's dead?' Ruth said. Not wanting to believe it. 'But how? What happened?'

'Come,' he said, not unkindly, and she didn't think to question it. She pulled on shorts and followed him out of the flat and down to the street where the sun still shone and people were still out and the bakery smelled of fresh Jerusalem bagels and coffee, as though nothing had happened, as though the world had not stopped at all, not even once, to think and wonder at the death of her friend.

'"Their love, their hatred and their jealousy too are lost",' Ruth whispered, '"and they have no part left in the world and in all that is done under the sun". I did Bible Studies too.'

'You do that, on the kibbutzim?' he said.

'It's in the national curriculum,' Ruth said stiffly. 'Everyone does it.'

He took her to a quiet café where he seemed to know the owner. They took a table in the back. He ordered for them both. She wondered why his eyes looked sad, what he had seen or done to get that look. She waited for him, waited to learn the fate of her friend, not willing to push, perhaps. She didn't know if she wanted to know.

For as long as she didn't ask and he didn't say then Einav would still be counted, still love and hate and envy, though she had never envied anyone, not for as long as Ruth knew her, Einav always followed her own path.

But as long as Ruth didn't ask, Einav would not be forgotten by the living, and she would still have a voice under the sun.

She drank the coffee when it came and it burned her lips. Why was she not in the station with the others? Cohen, too, took a sip. He looked at her and said, 'Tell me what happened.'

So she told him what happened. She told him about that evening Einav left, and then she told him about calling the kibbutz and trying to find her, but she wasn't there. But no one seemed worried, and she had her activities with the movement, and so she didn't ask again.

'Like in the midrash of the four sons,' she told him then, surprised. 'The wise, the fool, the evil one, and the one who didn't know to ask. I didn't know.'

'Then ask,' he said.

'What happened to her?' Ruth whispered.

But Cohen seemed unwilling or unable to tell her. He stirred sugar into his coffee and looked at her with those big sad eyes of his.

'What was she like?' he said, and Ruth could not help but notice the past tense in his question, and she couldn't hold it back anymore and she cried. She felt the tears come silently, and Cohen said nothing, and he let her cry.

'She was smart,' Ruth said. 'She was funny. She made me laugh. She was stubborn. She always knew best. She went her own way. I don't know that she would have stayed on her kibbutz. It's not so good to be a kibbutznik and always go your own way, you need to place your interests secondary to the will of the membership, and we had fights about this, on the commune, sometimes she found it hard to share, and do things like her share of the housework and...'

She blinked back tears, said, 'But it's nothing, it was nothing! She was kind, and generous, and she...'

'I understand,' Cohen said. 'But what about the others?'

'We're like a family,' Ruth whispered.

'What about the boy? Evyatar? Did he sleep with her?'

'What? No! She had a boyfriend and, it's not like that, none of us—'

'A commune, though,' Cohen mused. 'All living together in that small place. Everyone knows the stories about the kibbutzim, all of you growing up together, boys and girls in the same dormitories, showering together… Did she ever do drugs?'

'Drugs? No! The Young Watcher doesn't…' And suddenly she laughed. 'You know what they say, about the tenth commandment? The Young Watcher drinks, but doesn't get drunk. He smokes, but not drugs. He gets off, but he doesn't get her pregnant.'

The laugh felt bitter. She was all over the place. She stared at the coffee.

'What happened to her?' she said again. And this time she thought she was ready.

'She was found this morning,' Cohen said. 'In an avocado grove just outside Kibbutz Ma'agan Michael, on the coastal road. She was raped and murdered. I'm sorry.'

Ruth closed her eyes and the world spun. And Einav no longer had a part left in the world and anywhere under the sun. Someone took that from her.

'Who did this?' Ruth said.

'I don't know.'

'Isn't it… Where did they find that other girl? Esther Landes?'

'Not far from there,' Cohen said; reluctantly, Ruth thought.

'How was she killed?' Ruth said.

'Esther Landes?'

'Einav.'

'He hit her over the head. Broke her skull. Esther was strangled.' He looked at her with eyes that reflected her own strange helplessness back at her. 'Before that, Jacqueline Smith, a volunteer on the Ma'agan Michael. Raped and murdered, found by the fish ponds there. Before that… Anyway. Who can prove anything?'

'You knew Esther Landes?' Ruth said.

'I was involved in the case.'

'But you arrested someone for it. He's in prison.'

'Yes.'

'Who did this to my friend?' Ruth said.

'I don't know,' Cohen told her.

'And you think it's, what, me? Evie? Liora?' She laughed in his face. 'You're crazy.'

'I didn't say that.'

'So why did you put handcuffs on him!'

'Because he's a suspect, Ruth. And we're trying to find the truth.'

'The truth,' Ruth said, disgusted. She got up and put some money on the table. 'For the coffee,' she said.

'I will get it,' Cohen said.

'No,' Ruth said. 'You won't.'

She walked out. She could feel him at her back, watching her. She kept waiting for him to follow, to stop her. She was a suspect, wasn't she? She stepped out into sunshine.

Her friend was dead.

And no one was going to ever do a goddamned thing about it.

PART SIX

'YOU WON'T BREATHE IN THIS COUNTRY'

1977, The West Bank

34

THE PARTY

'All the faces are different and all the shit is the same' – Cohen

'Ladies and gentlemen, nothing less than a coup!' Haim Yavin said.

It was the first time the television used an election poll. They got the idea from ITV in England. Sylvie lit a fresh cigarette and stared at the black-and-white screen sitting on the bar. The bar was crammed with newsmen and full of smoke, and she felt a headache coming on.

'That can't be right,' Gabi said beside her. He squinted at the TV. 'He didn't just say that.'

Sylvie tried to feel some of the excitement in the room but it wasn't in her. Israel had been ruled for nearly fifty years by the labour movement, its unions and political arm. No one thought their bitter rivals from the days before independence would ever take power.

But if the television was right then Menachem Begin, fresh from another heart attack that left him thin and weak, was to be the new prime minister. Begin, who ran the Irgun back in the days when they fought the British. The Irgun carried out revenge killings; its men threw bombs at buses carrying Arabs; carried out lynches and put bombs in busy markets, train stations and cinemas; kidnapped and killed British soldiers and policemen.

That Begin.

Since Independence he'd become a politician, running for PM and failing each time. His Likud party followed old Revisionist dogma: they were free market capitalists, both-sides-of-the-Jordan nationalists, the eternal underdog of the one-ruling-party nation that had thought itself secure.

'Now the vilde chayes are in charge of the zoo,' someone said, but quietly.

The wild animals. And maybe, Sylvie thought, that attitude, more than anything, explained this sudden, unexpected win.

Israel had changed. The new immigrants from the Arab and African countries who had been crammed into camps and hopeless towns on the edges of nowhere had found an unlikely champion in the Polish-born Begin. He understood their helplessness and their rage, their faith and their hope. When Golda Meir said of the Black Panthers that they were 'not nice' it was Begin who spoke with and for them. He understood that niceness was not a privilege they could afford.

And now he was going to be prime minister.

It was a story. It was a huge story. But it wasn't a story for Sylvie Gold.

There'd be a hundred takes in all the papers tomorrow. Right now the Wolf Fort, as the Likud headquarters building was known, would be packed full of hundreds of sweating, smoking, cheering supporters unable to believe they had finally made it into power. And over in the Labour offices Rabin would be hitting the bottle and Peres would be chain smoking sadness, and didn't they both hate each other anyway?

Now they'll just have another reason for hatred.

'Sylvie, are you coming?'

'What?'

'To the party,' Gabi said.

Sylvie looked at him blankly. 'What party?' she said.

'*The* party,' Gabi said. 'Come on!' He took her arm and she let him drag her to the door.

They had a problem hailing down a taxi. People were congregating on street corners, some in shock, others celebrating like it was Independence Day or Purim all over again. Whistles and foam spray and flags, all it was missing were the plastic hammers people hit each other over the head with. Gabi finally hailed down a taxi. Forget getting one when you were a woman, Sylvie thought.

The taxi driver had the radio on and it was tuned into the news because all the stations just carried the news. They got in at the back.

'Can you believe it?' the taxi driver said. 'We finally have a voice.'

'Where are you from?' Gabi said.

'Me?' the driver said. 'From Hatikvah.'

'I mean originally.'

'Iraq,' the driver said. 'Mum and Dad came over after the war.'

'Why do you like Begin? He's a Pole.'

'Pole shmole,' the driver said. 'He's a good Jew. He understands the plight of the man on the street. Not like those parasites from the Histadrut. It's a new era for us. It's going to be great. Where can I take you?'

'The Salome Hotel,' Gabi said.

'Ah…' Sylvie said. '*He's* holding a party?'

'*The* party,' Gabi said.

'But how did he know they would win? No one knew they would win.'

Gabi shrugged. 'You don't need to win to have a party,' he said.

He was Baruch Mizrahi. He was a poor kid from a poor family who'd made good in this new Land of Israel. After the army he started in construction, and now he had a chain of hotels and office blocks and he was often in the papers. He was often in *their* paper, because Sylvie had just got the job writing for *This World* after she wrote to Uri Avnery looking for work, and Avnery hired her.

This World loved stories about glitzy parties, shady characters, politics and tits, not necessarily in that order. Sylvie would have been happier writing for somewhere more respectable like *Ma'ariv* but you took the job you were offered. She was twenty-two, the guy she was going to marry had died in the Yom Kippur War, and the rent on her flat wasn't going down any time soon.

So now she wrote the 'Dear Ruthie' column of readers' letters, and a gossip column, 'A Little Bird Told Me'. It was shit work for shit pay, and she thought Avnery was a pig, but he mostly paid on time. What Sylvie needed was a real story, something with meat and bones on it, not some old shit no one cared about like how Moshe Dayan, when he was the Defence Minister, was blackmailed by a mother whose daughter Dayan fucked a few times when she'd asked him for a favour. Dayan was always fucking someone or other behind his wife's back when he wasn't robbing archaeological sites to sell relics on the black market.

That one-eyed prick, she thought. The one-eyed prick with the one-eyed prick, Avnery called him. Avnery didn't like Dayan. *This World* published the story in three instalments, while all the respectable newspapers ignored it. No one cared where Dayan stuck his junk.

The taxi crawled along the road thronged with Begin and Likud supporters. At last it edged into the Salome's parking lot and they got out, and Gabi paid, because at least Gabi could claim expenses. The parking lot was heaving with taxis and official cars and it was clear what sort of person came to this party just by the number of official drivers standing around with a smoke in their hands.

Sylvie and Gabi went inside and followed the foot traffic to the party. Two goons in suits stood politely at the entrance and they stopped them from coming in.

'Do you have an invitation?'

'We're from *This World*,' Gabi said.

The goon on the right stared at him like he was a piece of gum he'd found under his shoe. The goon on the left ran his eyes up and down Sylvie's body and then smiled.

'You can go in, doll,' he said.

'Hey, what about me!' Gabi said.

'Get lost before I break your arm,' the goon said. 'This way, miss.'

'Thank you,' Sylvie said. She mouthed an 'I'm sorry…' to Gabi, waved and went in. A disco ball broke light into pretty dots overhead and, on the stage, a young girl was singing something beautiful. Her voice haunted the events hall. She was nineteen, maybe twenty, with black hair and huge dark eyes, with a voice that was bigger than her, bigger than anyone. She had the sort of talent a small country like Israel could never contain, a smile that when it came felt like the sun, and something sad around the eyes, like she already knew she was always going to make the wrong choices in men.

'He got Ofra Haza?' someone said. 'Who else did he hire, the Trackers?'

'Actually,' his companion said, 'they're performing next.'

The man who spoke shook his head and Sylvie, glancing at them, recognised him vaguely: a minor politician with a much younger woman on his arm. A waitress went past with a tray of drinks. Sylvie grabbed a glass and sipped. She listened to Ofra Haza sing and wondered if she could fit this into her gossip column somehow. Not Haza, she was just a kid fresh from the army. But the Trackers, who were a nationally celebrated trio of comedians. Performing at *party*? Just how much did Mizrahi pay them?

Haza finished her song and Sylvie clapped. Everyone else was too busy schmoozing. There was an air of wild abandon, of anything goes in the room. This was a new era, a new dawn. And these people were going to be in charge now.

The Trackers came on stage. They started one of their skits but Sylvie had never found them very funny so she stopped listening. She perched herself at an empty table and tried to put names to faces and a story to the names.

'Hello there,' a smooth voice said. A smooth man in a smooth business suit came and perched himself beside her and gave her a beaming smile. 'Why are you sitting alone?'

He had a thick French accent on his Hebrew and the charm of a snake-oil salesman. Sylvie said, 'Congratulations, Mr Knesset Member.'

His smile widened. 'You heard?'

'*Oui*.'

'You speak French!' he said, delighted. 'What is your name, please?'

'Sylvie.'

'C'est magnifique! I am Shmuel, but I am sure you know. Shmuel Flatto-Sharon. But call me Sammy.'

'Alright, Sammy. How does it feel, to win the elections?'

He laughed. 'I only won one seat,' he said. 'I'm my own one-man party. I guess I'll have to cosy up to that old bird Begin and hope he gives me a portfolio for my services. It is an honour to represent the country in these unparalleled times as we look to the future for progressive and business reform—'

'Was it expensive?' Sylvie said, cutting him off. He looked hurt.

'What was expensive?' Flatto-Sharon said.

'Buying your seat in the Knesset.'

He smirked. 'You think I bought it?'

'Everyone knows you bought it.'

'Who is everyone, pretty lady? There's only you and me here, and why waste the night talking politics? Everyone pays everyone, that's how deals get made and an economy works. Waitress!' He snapped his fingers. 'Two glasses, please.'

Sylvie was surprised to find that she liked him. It was rare to find an honest crook. She knew he didn't so much make aliyah from France as flee his home country for embezzlement. He stole millions and now he was a politician, and he only ran for office so he could try and pass a law prohibiting extradition. There was no way the French could touch him now. She raised her glass to him.

'When you play the game, at least play it well, right?' she said.

'Exactly! Oh, Sylvie, if only there was somewhere private we could go and talk…' he said.

'You're not my type,' she said regretfully.

He looked wounded. 'Too old?' he said.

'Too honest.'

He laughed. 'Then *au revoir*, Sylvie. Until next time.'

And just like that he was gone. Soon he was hot on the heels of a blonde in a red dress, so that was that.

'Alright, Eddie,' someone said. She turned and saw two men with the unmistakable look of cops at a party, which is to say, they looked like suspicious waiters. One went one way and joined a group of older men standing together smoking cigars. The other came and stood by her table.

'It's weird,' the man said. 'All the faces are different and all the shit is the same. You're Sylvie Gold, aren't you. I like your "Dear

Ruthie" column. Would you mind if I sat down? It's been a long day.'

She looked at him curiously. 'Sure,' she said, 'sit down. You are...?'

'Cohen,' he said.

'Cohen?' she said.

He nodded.

'Alright, Cohen. So how do you know who I am?'

'I asked.'

'You asked.'

He smiled. 'I ran into your colleague outside. He's getting all the drivers drunk and pumping them for the dirty on their bosses. Smart guy, that Gabi. Smart enough to carry a big flask, too. He said you were in here and asked me to keep an eye on you. So here I am.'

'A regular knight in shining armour,' Sylvie said.

'Just a tired policeman,' Cohen said.

She looked at him and took a sip of wine as she thought.

'You want something,' she said. She stared at him.

'Most guys want something,' she said. 'Usually, the same thing. But you I can't figure out.'

He shrugged it off. He lit a cigarette and offered it to her and she took it from him and he lit another for himself. They sat in companionable silence, and she thought he was a man easy to sit in silence with.

'See those men over there?' Cohen said after a while. He pointed, the cigarette burning between his fingers. Sylvie followed to where a gaggle of men stood close together with glasses of whiskey and lit cigars in their hands.

'Yes?' she said.

'That one there, that's my partner, Eddie. We worked that murder that was in all the papers a while back, the Esther Landes case.'

'You did?' She looked at him in a new light. 'That was a big case. Didn't they put someone away for it? What was his name?'

'Barnea,' Cohen said. 'Yes. His name was Elisha Barnea.'

'That's right. Didn't he say it was beaten out of him? The confession? He still says he didn't do it.'

'The prisons are full of people who say they didn't do it.'

'True.'

'I got a promotion out of uniform. I work intelligence in Tel Aviv now. And Eddie, he got put on a fast track to officer. See that man he's talking to?'

'In the bad suit?'

'That's our first commissioner of police, Izzy Moon. He's in business now. That guy standing next to him, that's his partner, Shamir.'

'The guy who looks like he would sell you home insurance and then set your house on fire if you asked?' Sylvie said, and Cohen laughed.

'That's the one,' he said. 'He's a convicted forger. Sixteen times. What you would call "a person known to the police", I think.'

'Interesting,' Sylvie said, and she leaned forward a little, because Cohen clearly had something in mind, and Sylvie could smell a story when someone served it to her on a plate and put it right in front of her nose. 'So what is the former police commissioner doing in business with a convicted forger, Cohen?'

'Now there's a question,' Cohen said.

Sylvie stared. There was a fourth man standing with the others and him she knew.

'That's Genghis,' she said.

'That's right,' Cohen said, and he looked like he wanted to spit.

'Wasn't he Rabin's security adviser until a few months ago?' Sylvie said.

'I believe so.'

'And what does he do now?' Sylvie said.

'I am sure I can't tell you,' Cohen said.

There were all kinds of stories about Genghis. Disturbing ones. He kept lion cubs. He once murdered two Bedouins in cold blood. He was friends with Oshri and Midget from the Yemenite Orchard mob. She shuddered. Cohen was leading her somewhere and wherever it was it was bound to be dangerous. She looked at him again.

'You won't tell me?' she said.

'You could start at the Tabu,' Cohen said.

Sylvie was going to press him for more but just then Ofra Haza went past them, holding a gym bag and looking tired, and Cohen's attention shifted, and a desperate, longing look came into his eyes.

'Ofra!' he said. 'Ofra!' He got up and followed her at a trot and Sylvie saw Ofra Haza give Cohen the look women always gave men who followed them, appraising for danger, but she put on her smile and it was then that Sylvie knew the girl was going to be a star. She watched Ofra Haza and Cohen walk out of the hall.

The party was only getting started but Sylvie had had enough. She watched the men Cohen had pointed out to her, Moon, Shamir, Genghis. They had no business being in business together. Then she saw the host of the party come and join them. Mizrahi, the construction magnate. He was Genghis' subaltern in the army, if she remembered right. She watched the men backslap and conspire. She stubbed out her cigarette. She left.

35

THE TABU

'Now the floodgates will open' – The woman at the typewriter

Sylvie was up early with a cup of coffee and a cigarette, then she went out. The morning rose over a transformed Tel Aviv that still looked very much the same. The old power may have fallen but the street cleaners still had to clean, regardless of political orientation, and people still had to go to work on a Wednesday. Sylvie hopped a bus and got off just the other side of the Kiryah, the closed military base that housed the army's High Command. Across from army HQ was the Tel Aviv Museum of Art, and attached to it was brand-new Brutalist building that housed the Ariela Library, and that was Sylvie's first destination.

She found the archives and got herself settled at a microfiche reader and she loaded up old newspapers, going through them methodically. The first person she looked up was Commissioner Moon. She made notes as she worked.

Yizhak 'Izzy' Moon was third generation native to the land, having been born during Ottoman rule in Palestine. His father was a timber trader, his grandfather a rabbi. He studied in London, served in the British Army during the Second World War, fought in North Africa in the second battle of El Alamein, and was honourably discharged with the rank of major.

In '47 he was tasked by Ben Gurion to plan the future police force of the new Israeli state, and the following year he was appointed to lead it. He served for a decade, following which he became an ambassador to Austria. On his return to Israel from diplomatic service he became embroiled in a libel case between Ben Gurion's son and a civilian group that alleged widespread police corruption.

Moon testified in the trial, only to then go on trial himself, for offering false testimony. He was convicted and sentenced to a suspended prison term and a fine, but was shortly after pardoned by the president at the time, Shazar.

Since then he was in private business.

Alright, Sylvie thought. So that was one down.

She tried to look up Giyora Shamir, the guy Cohen said was Moon's partner. There was less on him. *He* was never the ambassador to Austria, and his only role in the newfound Israeli Police Force was to be periodically arrested by them.

Strictly white collar, though. Forgeries, mostly, cheques and suchlike, with occasional old-fashioned fraud.

How he and Moon first met, or how they came to be business partners, she had no idea. She checked the company register and found that they owned a limited partnership called Keep, which told her nothing very much. She went outside for another coffee and another cigarette and hopped another bus to the Tabu.

The Land Registry Office was in a gaggle of other government offices. Everyone just called it the Tabu, a corruption into Arabic of the Turkish word Tapu, or land deed. Sylvie just knew this sort of thing, if not much else about land ownership, though she was hoping to buy the flat she lived in one day. She went to a busy room with telephones ringing where a woman with blue-rinsed hair punched a typewriter like she was Muhammad Ali.

'Help you?' the woman said, not looking up.

'I'm Sylvie Gold, from *This World*,' Sylvie said. 'I'm a journalist.'

'Yeah? So?'

'I'm trying to find some information.'

'Yeah? So?'

'So can you help me? Find it? The information?'

'I don't read that trash,' the woman said. 'Nothing but gossip, and all that bare flesh. It's not decent.'

'I don't like it much either,' Sylvie said, 'but it's a job.'

'This is a job,' the woman said. 'What you call that trash I don't know.'

A man in glasses came wafting past. He was thinning on top and he smiled good-naturedly at Sylvie.

'Don't pay any attention to *her*,' he said, nodding at the woman on the typewriter. 'She was just up too late last night watching the elections.'

'Thirty years I've voted for Mapai,' the woman said. 'I voted for Ben Gurion, then Ben Gurion again, then Ben Gurion again, then—'

'Ben Gurion again?' Sylvie said.

The woman looked up sharply. 'That's right,' she said. 'Then Levy Eshkol, then Golda, then Golda again. And now this. Those hooligans in charge.'

'She worries it will give us too much work,' the man explained, though Sylvie didn't understand what he meant. He put out his hand. 'Eliezer Menachemi, and how may I be of assistance, Miss Gold?'

Sylvie explained, and Menachemi nodded. 'Let me see if I can pull it up for you,' he said. 'Take a seat. It may take a while. Coffee? Tea?'

'No, thank you.'

He nodded and vanished into the stacks of filing. The woman kept punching the keys. Sylvie sat down. A radio was on somewhere down the corridor, and Yehudit Ravitz was singing 'Forgiveness'.

'She has quite a voice, hasn't she?' Menachemi said, reappearing. The woman at the typewriter muttered under her breath and didn't look up.

'It's the racy lyrics, you see,' Menachemi said, nodding at the woman at the typewriter. 'She doesn't approve.'

'It's disgusting. And on the radio too! It's pornography is what it is.'

'I like it,' Menachemi said. 'She has a nice voice. Regarding your query, Miss Gold, I'm afraid there isn't anything I can help you with after all.'

'I'm sorry?' Sylvie said.

'There is nothing in the files. No title deeds, no land registration, no transaction.' He shrugged. 'I'm sorry, but it doesn't look like any kind of story worth printing, does it?'

'The Mystery of the Missing Transactions,' the woman at the typewriter said and laughed to herself. 'Put that in your rag of a paper, why don't you.'

'I don't understand,' Sylvie said. 'But he told me to—'

'Who told you what?' Menachemi said. Sylvie just shook her head.

'There's nothing?' Sylvie said.

'I'm afraid so,' Menachemi said. 'Now, if there wasn't anything else, I was about to go to lunch.'

'He must have known I wouldn't find anything here,' Sylvie said. She was half-talking to herself. Since Ori died in the war she had got used to talking aloud when she was alone, not to pretend that he could hear her, because Ori was dead and that was the end of that; but somehow the sound of her voice in the empty flat kept her company and didn't make her feel so lonely, and the habit stuck. 'So why would he send me here?'

'This is where all the land ownership and transactions are registered and recorded for the State of Israel,' Menachemi said, a little pompously Sylvie thought. 'So if this Keep Ltd. of yours are not trading land here, then they won't… Unless, of course… It's possible, I suppose. Yes. Yes.'

He nodded quite seriously.

'What!' Sylvie said.

'He means the West Bank of the Jordan,' the woman at the typewriter said in disgust. 'But is it quite impossible, it really is. We won't register it, it is occupied land, not territorial land, and really I have too much work to do, far too much work to do. Only now the floodgates will open.'

'The West Bank?' Sylvie said. 'Why would they be buying land in the West Bank?'

'It's ours now, you see,' Menachemi said, with an apologetic air.

'But the government wouldn't allow any settlement there!' Sylvie said, and the woman at the typewriter looked up at her and adjusted her glasses and said, 'But which government, dearie?'

'I really must be off to lunch now,' Menachemi said. 'I am sorry I couldn't be more help.'

He nodded to her and left.

Sylvie was left alone with the woman in the room.

'But I don't *know* anything about land in the West Bank,' Sylvie said.

'You are not going to leave me in peace, are you?' the woman at the typewriter said. 'Here.' She pulled a piece of paper and scribbled a name and number on it and snapped her fingers for Sylvie to take it.

'He might talk to you,' she said. 'He's a talker, that one, but he's not stupid, so maybe he won't. Try fanning those eyelashes of yours at him. He likes that.'

'What am I, a peacock?' Sylvie said and the woman unexpectedly laughed.

'Good luck with whatever this is,' she said. 'Don't get lost on the way to Hebron.'

'Hebron?' Sylvie said. 'Who the *fuck* goes to Hebron?'

36

THE LAND

'It's easier when it's occupied land and you have the men with the guns on your side' – *Sami*

'Is this Sami van Aarden?' Sylvie said.

'Depends who's asking,' the voice on the other end of the line said.

'My name's Sylvie Gold. The woman at the Tabu gave me your number.'

'Is that Chava?' the man said, sounding delighted. 'She's always trying to fix me up. She has the soul of a saint. Sure, this is Sami. What can I do you for?'

'Can we meet? I have some questions.'

'Meet? Sure. You sound pretty. But questions, those I'm not so sure about.'

'I'm a journalist.'

'Now I'm even less sure.'

'For *This World*.'

'Oh, why didn't you say so!' He laughed. 'That's not really a proper newspaper. Listen, sweetheart, I have a few things to take care of first. Why don't you meet me at Café Tamar in a couple of hours? We could get a coffee, get to know each other better... How does that sound?'

'That sounds wonderful, Mr van Aarden.'

'Please, call me Sami.'

He hung up and Sylvie went and got a cheap falafel at a nearby stall. She wasn't quite sure just what she had. A company belonging to the former No. One Policeman and his crook partner, who Cohen seemed to suggest dealt in land, only they had no land registered.

It was a mystery, and Sylvie realised she didn't much care for mysteries.

And just *why* did Cohen put her on this trail? What did he get out of it?

She made her way on foot to Sheinkin Street, found the café and waited over a coffee and cigarette. The coffee wasn't very good but Sylvie wasn't going to complain. The landlady, Sarah Stern, was known to have a temper.

The place was quiet at this time of day. Sylvie spotted a couple of journalists from *Davar*, whose offices were nearby, and a minor poet. But then who wasn't a minor poet in this land that was so very full of poets, all writing in a language brought back to life with sheer pig-headedness, that no one else spoke or understood? She watched the poet drink his cognac and was startled when she felt a tap on her shoulder and turned to see a smiling man hovering over her.

'Miss Gold, I presume.'

'Mr van Aarden.'

'I told you, call me Sami.' He sat down across from her. 'Hey, Sarah, can I get a coffee when you have a moment?'

'Aha.'

Sylvie looked at him in surprise. 'She likes you,' she said. 'She doesn't like anyone.'

'What's not to like?' Sami van Aarden said. In person he was not as she'd expected. Middle-aged, with thinning blond hair and a little bit of a potbelly. His face and arms were tanned. He wore a small gold crucifix on his chest.

'So you're a land dealer?' Sylvie said.

'Not exactly.' He looked her over. 'Why should I talk to you?' he said.

'What kind of a name is Sami van Aarden?' Sylvie said.

'Samuel van Aarden,' he said. 'It's Dutch. But in Israel you can call me Sami.'

'You're Dutch?'

'Do I sound Dutch?' he said. 'My parents were from Utrecht. My father was Jewish, and after the war ended he and my mother decided to come here. It didn't work out for them but then what does ever work out in life? She was a painter. What about you, Sylvie? That's an unusual name. Are you French?'

'I was born there,' Sylvie said. 'In France. My older sister was born in Germany. My parents are from Poland. They came to Israel after the war, only it took them a long time to get here. Long enough to have a couple of kids on the way. So that's my name. And that's your name. Samuel in Holland, Sami in Israel. And in the West Bank? What do I call you there?'

Sami smiled, and she got the sense he smiled easily, but there was a hardness behind his eyes and for a moment she felt afraid.

'You been yet?' he said.

'No.'

'It's quite a land we got there. Enough room for a man to breathe. Fertile, empty. Empty but for the Arabs.'

'I thought the purchase of land there is forbidden for us.'

'You're not entirely wrong,' Sami said. Then he said, 'It's complicated.'

'Complicated how?'

'I can talk to you off the record,' Sami said. 'My name doesn't appear in this.'

'I can do that,' Sylvie said.

Sarah Stern came over with his coffee. Sami beamed at her and waited until she left. He took a sip and made a face. Sylvie laughed.

'The Six Day War,' Sami said, 'was essentially a land grab operation. From a pure military standpoint the occupied lands are buffer zones against the enemy states. But land's land, Sylvie Gold. You can buy it, you can sell it, and you can damn well build on it.'

He ticked items on his fingers one by one.

'We got the Golan Heights from Syria. The whole Sinai Peninsula from Egypt. And the West Bank from Jordan. That's a lot of land. A land of opportunity.'

'Opportunity?'

'The opportunity to make a lot of fast money,' Sami said, and he was no longer smiling.

'I like that you met me here on Sheinkin,' he said. 'He was a land dealer too, Sheinkin. You see, buying land for us isn't just a business. It's a *duty*, a calling. To redeem the land of Israel for the Jews. What do you think we're going to do with the West Bank, now that we finally have it? We're going to settle it. We're going to *build*. So that's where it starts. Where it ends I don't know.'

Sylvie thought of all that land. They were already building in Sinai – Ophira, Yamit, new towns coming into being on the shores of the Red Sea by 'soldiers without uniforms' as the army, early on, referred to their new occupants. Facts on the ground, a statement to the world that they were there to stay, for all that the Sinai was a land under military occupation. In the Golan, too, they were building new kibbutzim behind the new demilitarised zone that the UN patrolled. But nothing in the West Bank, not yet.

She realised Sami was right. It was inevitable that settlement would happen there, it was inevitable all along. And the Jewish method from before independence was always two-fold: buy land when you could, occupy it when you couldn't. The kibbutzim used the notorious 'fence-and-tower' system under the British: they would come to a plot land in the night and build a watchtower and a fence around it and, under the law of the time, they could not be evicted then.

'We make our borders by agricultural occupation,' Sami said. 'The Romans did much the same thing in their time. And I'd rather be on the side of the Romans.'

'What you're saying,' Sylvie said, 'is that some people are already speculating in land in the West Bank.'

'For sure, yes.'

'Betting that when the government *does* approve it – as the new people in power surely will – they can sell the lands back to the government and make a killing?

'A *killing*,' Sami said.

'Even if buying land there right now isn't legal?'

'It's not not legal,' Sami said. 'The West Bank has the same legal framework as we do, more or less, based on the old Ottoman law. There are ways to make it work. You just have to convince the landholders to sell.'

'And how do you do that?' Sylvie said.

'There are all kinds of ways,' Sami said. 'All kinds of ways. It's easier when it's occupied land and you have the men with the guns on your side.'

She looked at him in a new light then.

'And you're one of those men?' she said.

He shrugged. 'I'm just a middleman,' he said. 'I get paid for my services. There are all kinds of buyers. But I can't give you names.'

'Moon,' Sylvie said. 'Shamir. Genghis.'

Sami took that in. He showed no expression but he blinked.

'I don't get involved with Genghis,' he said. 'And you shouldn't, either. Not if you don't want a bomb on your doorstep or a gun to your head.'

'He's really that bad?' Sylvie said.

'He's worse,' Sami said. 'And he's friends with people you don't want to meet, believe me.'

He got up, went to the counter, exchanged a few words with the owner and paid. When he went back to Sylvie she could see he had already dismissed her.

'Go back to your gossip column,' he said. 'Forget we had this talk, Sylvie Gold. You have a pretty face and it would be a shame if something happened to it.'

He patted her on the shoulder and left.

Sylvie looked to the counter, where the owner was polishing the counter with a dirty rag. She looked at Sylvie with contempt.

'Well?' she said. 'Fuck off out of here already.'

So Sylvie left.

37

THE BELL

'Just don't fall down the hole' – *Avnery*

The phone woke her up in the night. The clock on the bed stand said midnight. Sylvie picked up the phone.

'Hello?' she said.

'Sylvie Gold?' The voice was male, breathy. 'I'm going to fuck you up, Sylvie. Do you like living, Sylvie? Because I'm going to fuck you up until you scream and beg for mercy. I'm going cut you up and when you're lying on the floor begging me not to kill you I'm going to stick my big fat d—'

Sylvie slammed the phone down. Her heart raced. Everything was quiet. She got up and tiptoed to the window. Nothing outside. A car went past. She saw a dark car parked on the other side of the street but there was nothing unusual about t—

The phone rang and she jumped. She ran to it, listened.

Silence on the line, scaring her, somehow, even more.

'Hello?' Sylvie said.

'...kill you, you dumb bitch.'

The line went dead. It was a different speaker, this time.

Sylvie looked out again. Nothing. She listened for footsteps on the landing. Was that someone quietly climbing the stairs, or was it just the wind?

The phone rang.

'Listen you dumb cunt, you're messing with the wrong people,' the voice said. It was a different voice again. 'You think we don't know where you live? Are you looking out of the window right now, Sylvie Gold? We can see you. You fucking cunt whore bitch fuck—'

Sylvie hung up the phone and then she left it off the hook. She sat on the edge of the bed and shivered. She reached under the bed.

There was a small shoebox under there that she hadn't opened in three years. The lid was covered in dust. She lifted it carefully and looked inside.

Photos, her and Ori when they were together. Ori in uniform, smiling at the camera, his arm around her. Ori and his dog. After he died she couldn't bear to look after the dog and it went to a farm in the Galilee. Ori died in Yom Kippur, became just another name to add to the roll call every Memorial Day. She hated the pomp and ceremony, one day of manufactured sadness followed like clockwork the next day by the celebrations for Independence Day.

Hebrew had a special word for it. *Scholl*, which was something like bereavement, but in Israel bereavement took on a national aspect, accompanied by the sound of military trumpets, echoes on the mic, quotations by Bialik or Shlonsky, the cry of peacocks and the howl of jackals in the distance.

She felt under the photos and found the gun. She didn't have a license for it. It had belonged to Ori, and she found it one day, shortly after he died.

She pulled it out, felt in the box, found some bullets.

She put the box back under the bed.

She sat at the kitchen table, watching the door, and cleaned the gun and then she loaded it with bullets.

She sat there for a long time but the building was quiet and no one came up the steps to her door, and eventually she got back into bed. She slept for a few fitful hours, the gun by her side.

In the morning she felt groggy. She put the phone back on the hook without thinking and it immediately rang. She picked up.

'Cunt bitch whore!'

She hung up and pulled the wire from the wall.

She made coffee.

When she left the flat she had the gun with her, just in case.

She went to the office. There was hardly anyone in. She went to see Avnery. He sat behind his desk.

'Nu?' he said when he saw her. 'What's the news?'

She told him about the case, and how she started to dig, and about the phone calls.

'So what do you want to do?' he asked her when she'd finished.

Sylvie said, 'I want to keep digging.'

Avnery sat back.

Avnery smiled.

Avnery said, 'Then keep digging. Just don't fall down the hole.'

Sylvie went to her desk. She picked up the phone. She called Sami van Aarden.

He picked up after a few rings.

'You son of a bitch!' Sylvie screamed into the phone.

'What? Who is this?'

'It's Sylvie Gold, you bastard. You set them on me? You fucking ratted me out!'

'Hold on, hold on,' Sami said. 'Slow down. What are you talking about? I didn't give your name to anyone.'

'Yeah? Then why am I getting threatening calls in the middle of the night!' Sylvie screamed. It made her feel so much better, letting the bastard have it.

'I didn't tell anyone I met with you,' Sami van Aarden said. 'Why the hell would I? I don't want my name in any of this.'

'Then how, motherfucker! How!' Sylvie said. 'I'm going to fucking bury you.'

'No one's burying anyone,' Sami said. 'Let me think. Wait. You said you went to the Tabu, right?'

'Yeah, so?'

'Was there anyone there beside Chava? Anyone else you talk to?'

Sylvie tried to think. 'There was this guy, Menachemi,' she said. 'But he was sweet, and very helpful.'

'Him?' Sami said. 'I'm sorry, Sylvie, but he was probably on the phone as soon as he left you. Did you mention any names?'

'I asked him to look up Keep Ltd.,' Sylvie said. 'That's all.'

'You rang a bell, Sylvie Gold. You rang a bell, and the thing about that is, it makes a fucking noise. I had nothing to do with it. Don't call me again.'

He hung up.

Sylvie replaced the receiver. She lit up a smoke.

Cohen got her into this, she thought.

He's gonna have to do some explaining.

She called a policewoman she knew. Constable Keren Carmeli answered the phone.

'Sylvie!' she said, sounding delighted. 'I haven't heard from you in a while. You want to go out tonight? There's a new place opened in Dizengoff.'

'There's always a new place opened in Dizengoff,' Sylvie said. 'But maybe. I owe you a drink. Listen, Keren, you know a guy called Cohen?'

Keren laughed. 'Sylvie, there are like a million guys called Cohen.'

'A policeman. Said he worked Intelligence in the district.'

A short silence on the line. 'Yeah, I know him,' Keren said. She sounded cautious.

'What's he like?'

'He's not so bad,' Keren said. 'Not like a lot of the others. You know, the commanders, they like to pinch your ass and stuff like that. Corner you in a room when no one's looking. He doesn't do *that*.'

'So what *does* he do?'

'Nothing, Sylvie. Nothing I know of. It's just that, well, you know what it's like in a small force. There are always stories.'

'Stories?'

'I really shouldn't be talking out of turn.'

'What kind of stories, Keren?'

'Look, he's an intelligence officer, right? I mean, that's all it is. It's not a nine-to-five, morning briefing, paperwork kinda job. I mean, is it? So he's got to be out there, mixing it up with all kinds of people. That's all I'm saying.'

'He's dirty?'

'I didn't say that.'

'You implied it, Keren.'

'Who isn't dirty, Sylvie? Come on. All I'm saying is, be careful.'

'Where can I find him? If I went looking?'

'Did you not just hear me when I said, be careful?'

'I just want to talk to him,' Sylvie said.

'You owe me a drink tonight,' Keren said.

'I'll buy you three,' Sylvie said. 'With little umbrellas and canned pineapple slices and *everything*. Promise.'

'Alright, but you didn't hear it from me. He's got a pad on Ibn Gabirol near the Bar Yehuda bridge. You know the bridge?'

'I know it,' Sylvie said.

Keren gave her the rest of the address and Sylvie wrote it down.

'Thanks, Keren,' she said.

'You owe me.'

Sylvie left the office. She waited at the bus stop. She kept looking around her but she didn't see anyone.

A part of her just wanted to let it be. What did it matter about the West Bank? Why should she stick her neck out?

But she could smell a story and once she did there was no turning back. She wanted to know what Keep Ltd. were doing in Judea and Samaria, as the government had started to call the occupied territories on the west of the Jordan. Were they backed by the government? The army? Who did they buy from? Who did they sell to? With the names she had – Moon, Genghis – there had to be some sort of official sanction.

So what was the catch?

The bus came. She sat at the back and watched the doors. She got off a few stations down and walked the rest of the way. Traffic zipped along the road to the bridge. It went over the Yarkon river but she didn't get that far. She found the apartment block, found the number and pressed the buzzer. There was no answer. Sylvie kept her finger on the buzzer.

'What! Goddamn it, who is this!'

It was a woman's voice. Sylvie released the buzzer.

'It's Sylvie Gold,' she said. 'I'm looking for Cohen.'

'Cohen isn't here.'

'Do you know where I can find him?'

'No.'

'Could I come up?'

'Why the hell would I let you come up!'

'Because I'm not going to leave until I find Cohen?'

'Are you sleeping with him?' the woman said. 'I don't give a fuck if you do.'

'I'm not sleeping with him,' Sylvie said. 'I don't even know him.'

'So what the fuck do you want?'

'I want to talk to Cohen.'

'Well, he's not here. So fuck off.'

Sylvie sighed. She was about to turn back when the intercom crackled into life.

'Who did you say you were, again?'

'Sylvie Gold. I'm a journalist.'

'You write "Letters to Ruthie"!'

Sylvie sighed.

'Yes,' she said.

The door buzzed.

Sylvie stared at the door.

'Well, come on up, then,' the woman said.

38

THE STORY

'No one saw' – Na'ama

Sylvie trudged up three flights of stairs. The left door on the top floor was open and a young woman stood in the doorway. She was a few years older than Sylvie, maybe late twenties.

'Can I see your ID?' she said.

'My I… sure,' Sylvie said. She showed the woman her ID card and the woman let out a breath of air.

'You really write "Letters to Ruthie"?' she said.

'I really, really do,' Sylvie said.

'Well, come on in. Cohen isn't here. I'm Na'ama. Do you want a coffee?'

'Sure, thanks,' Sylvie said.

'I might have some biscuits in the cupboard,' Na'ama said. She vanished towards the kitchen.

Sylvie took a look around the flat. The shutters were closed over all the windows and the flat was dimly lit, with only a stray ray of light breaking through to illuminate the motes of dust standing still in the air. There was an ashtray on the coffee table and a vase with incense sticks. There was a sofa and an armchair, both looking like they came from the flea market in Jaffa, brown with spots, and a mint pot on the windowsill with a few wilting leaves.

'Is this Cohen's place?' Sylvie said. For some reason she hadn't pictured it like that.

'He comes and goes.'

'He around much?'

'Not much. He's kind of letting me crash here for a while.'

'I like what you've done with the place.'

Na'ama came over with two mugs. 'It's instant,' she said.

'I don't mind. Thanks.'

'Let me see about the biscuits.'

She went back into the small kitchen, came back with a few chocolate digestives heaped on a plate. Sylvie took a sip from the coffee. She looked at Na'ama. Her nails were made up but her hair was unwashed. Sylvie looked at the eyes. Something bruised and vulnerable there. Sylvie knew the look.

Women often stopped her if they recognised her. And they always had a sad story to tell.

'So how do you know Cohen?' Na'ama said.

'I don't, really,' Sylvie said. 'He kind of dumped me in some shit and I'm trying to figure out what he's got coming out of it.'

'He does do that, sometimes,' Na'ama said. 'He is not a good man, you know. But he's been good to me.'

Sylvie waited. No one buzzed up a person they didn't know in the middle of the day just to offer them bad coffee and stale cookies. She figured Na'ama will get around to it on her own.

'So you do, what?' she said.

'Not much,' Na'ama said, and she gave Sylvie a tired smile. 'I'm enrolling at the university next semester. History. I'm just… killing time until then, I guess.'

'You and Cohen an item?' Sylvie said.

'No, it's not like that. Well, sometimes it is. But he's not around here much. He has his work, you know.'

'So I heard,' Sylvie said. 'It's nice of him to let you stay here.'

'It is.' Then Na'ama started to cry.

Sylvie waited it out. Na'ama cried quietly and then she wiped her eyes and tried on a smile that didn't take.

'I'm so silly,' she said.

'You're not,' Sylvie said.

'I thought of writing to you so many times,' Na'ama said. 'But who would believe me? And who would care?'

'Believe what?' Sylvie said gently.

Who did that to you, she thought but didn't say.

'I was in the army,' Na'ama said. 'I was working for Central Command. Just a typist, but it was fun, there was always something to do and I got to stay in Tel Aviv. Then one day I get a call. The commander had asked for me personally. I didn't even know he knew who I was. He was always so busy, he was a hero in the war, he was in the papers, he knew Chaim Topol personally. It was after the Six Day War but before Yom Kippur, so there was that real euphoria still. We had all of the West Bank and Central Command was in charge of all that. I was flattered, you know? I was just a typist and there was this war hero, asking for me by name.'

Sylvie just nodded.

'So I went over to HQ. It was the end of the day. All the desks were empty. The general met me. He was so nice. Full of compliments. Kept telling me how pretty I was. We went into his office and he shut the door and then he locked it.

'"Come on, Na'ama," he said. "Let's stop playing games."

'"Games, sir?" I said. I didn't know what he meant. He went and sat behind his desk. I stood at attention. He stood up. Then he just sort of leaned over and made a grab for me.

'"What are you doing?" I said. "Stop that, sir."

'"We're just having a bit of fun, aren't we?" he said. He came round the desk. He grabbed me and started unbuttoning my shirt. I pushed him away. "Stop it, please," I said. "Stop it."

'He laughed. "You're such a tease," he said. I tried the door but it was locked and he just laughed again, like I was being funny. He reached for something on the wall and pulled down a folding bed. "Just lie down," he said.

'"Go away," I said. "Please, stop this." I tried to fight him but it wasn't in me and he was so strong. He pulled me on the bed and took my clothes off and then he lay on top of me. I just froze. I remember the bedsprings creaking and thinking won't anyone come to check on us? But no one came to check. No one saw. Then he was finished and he got up and he looked at me like I was in the way. "Well, get dressed," he said. He lit a cigarette and unlocked the door and then he just left me there.'

Sylvie touched Na'ama's hand gently; that was all.

'I got dressed,' Na'ama said. 'I left. I went home. I didn't know what to do. My brother and his girlfriend saw me when I came in. They kept asking what was wrong. I said nothing was wrong, nothing. Then I started to cry and they got it out of me. They were furious. I told them I'll go to the police and report it. My brother and his girlfriend just looked at me like I was mad. "Him?" they said. "Who will believe you over him?" But I did it. I went to the police. That's when I met Cohen. He listened to my story. He didn't say much, but I could see he was angry. He believed me. He left me there and he went away, for an hour, two hours, I don't know. I don't know where he went. When he got back he just told me I couldn't do it. They would destroy me in court, in the papers. My rapist was too powerful. For my own sake, I had to let it go. But Cohen promised me he'll get him one day. He promised me that, and I believed him. I think he almost lost his job. I don't know what he did that night but I heard that after that they demoted him back to constable and exiled him to Haifa. So that was that. When I got back to the army the next day they told me I was reassigned to a camp in the Negev. About a month later I got a cheque in the post. It was from the general. Payment for services received. I never saw him again after that night.'

'What was his name? Who was it?' Sylvie said.

'General Zrubavel Ha'navi,' Na'ama said. 'Genghis.'

'Genghis…' Sylvie said.

She hugged Na'ama. The woman felt strong in her arms.

When they let go Na'ama smiled and it lit up her face.

'Thank you,' she said. 'I never told this story to anyone after that night. I guess I needed to. But I bet you hear stories like this all the time.'

'I do,' Sylvie said. 'But it doesn't make them any less awful.'

'I went through a rough patch,' Na'ama said. 'But I'm starting at Tel Aviv University soon and I'm really looking forward to it. And I've been saving up when I could. Maybe I'll move out of here.'

'What you said,' Sylvie said. Something bothered her at the back of her brain. 'Central Command was in charge of the West Bank?'

'Still is,' Na'ama said. 'Nothing happens there without Central Command's say so.'

'What did you do there, exactly?' Sylvie said.

'I was just a typist,' Na'ama said.

'Yes, but where?' Sylvie said.

'Oh, the Administrator for Abandoned and Government Land office in the Civilian Administration Department,' Na'ama said.

'The what?' Sylvie said.

'It was just a lot of paperwork,' Na'ama said. 'You know, all the land in Judea and Samaria. It's the office that deals with land registration and permissions, and all that stuff. It was pretty boring. Why?'

'And Genghis was in charge of all of that?' Sylvie said.

'Sure. Why, is it important?'

'Maybe,' Sylvie said. Then she said, 'Thank you.'

She left Na'ama the way she'd found her, standing in the doorway.

Cohen had been right, of course. There was no way the police would have done anything. Na'ama was right to let it go.

Sylvie wished it wasn't like that, but it was. And she was angry now. How many other girls had there been? How many more young women did Genghis summon into his office just before he locked the door and pulled down the camp bed? And no one did anything.

39

THE BAR

'They find you' – Shmuel Flatto-Sharon

Night had fallen. Sylvie looked over her shoulder as she walked. She checked reflections in the shop glass windows. That man moving behind her, was he following her? Someone bumped into her then hurried on. Sylvie's heart beat faster as she approached her building. Was there anyone waiting in the shadows? She made it through the front door and up the stairs.

She locked the door behind her with a sense of relief. She mixed arak and grapefruit juice in a glass and drank it too quickly. Her head hurt with images of the flat she'd just left, the smell of cheap incense, the taste of bad coffee and old nightmares.

She wasn't going to get answers in Tel Aviv. She thought of the Green Line that ran all across modern Israel like a Caesarean scar. She tended to think of the West Bank as somewhere far away, but it wasn't. The line ran all the way from near Afula in the north to Be'er Sheva in the desert. The line passed not too far from Tel Aviv, it ran the same longitude as the coast road to Haifa. The West Bank was just there, so close you could throw a stone and hit it. How many people lived there now? Two, three million? She knew what happened during the War of Independence, everyone knew. How did her father put it once? She was only small, and she'd asked him, this German immigrant survivor, in his heavy, still-accented Hebrew, as their bus slowly went past a ruined abandoned village – what happened to these people? Where did they go? And her father looked serious and adjusted his glasses and he said, 'They were escaped.'

The Arab villagers were encouraged to flee by the newly formed forces of the Israeli state. Then the bulldozers came in and levelled their houses to ensure they would have nothing to come back to. Then the land was settled. Some of the kibbutzim that came in their place used the rubble from the villages to build their new homes. Now the refugees sat in camps in Syria and Lebanon and the West Bank and Gaza. Their numbers swelled. They pressed against the borders, demanding to be let back in. But that wasn't going to happen. And that wasn't going to answer her questions, which were of a simpler and more sordid sort.

What kind of scam were Genghis and his partners pulling?

It was a story that could make her. And then she wouldn't have to work for shitty *This World* anymore. She could write for a real newspaper like *Yediot*.

She plugged in her phone without thinking, intending to call Keren and cancel tonight. But as soon as she plugged it in the phone rang, and Sylvie froze.

The phone rang and rang. Sylvie didn't have the courage to answer it.

The phone stopped ringing.

The silence was jarring. Sylvie went to the window. Was the car parked out there the same as the other night? Were those shadows in the seats, watching her window?

The phone rang.

'Hello!' She snapped it up this time.

Heavy breathing on the line.

'You fucking bitch, you're dead,' the voice said.

'Eat shit, asshole!' Sylvie screamed. She slammed the phone down and yanked the wire from the wall. She sat on the edge of the bed.

She wasn't going to get the answers she needed in Tel Aviv, she thought.

To find out the truth she had to go over the line.

***

She walked head down through the dark streets, the gun in her purse, moving quickly, not stopping. Past a flower seller with the smell of roses, past a shawarma stand with the smell of lamb fat. Past men smoking cigarettes on a corner, past the fumes of buses. She bought a ticket and got on the bus to Jerusalem. She sat at the back and watched anyone coming on board and anyone standing outside. There, was that the same man she saw earlier? He was smoking on the concrete. Then he tossed his cigarette and walked away.

An old Arab man sat beside her holding grocery bags. Two Orthodox women in the seat in front of them exchanged recipes. A group of teenage soldiers got on the bus with their guns on their backs, chatting excitedly. The bus made its slow way out of the city. Sylvie watched the bus stops go past, one by one. The city receded from sight. Instead there were fields, then low-lying hills, then the mountains. The red Egged bus huffed and puffed its way up the mountain road. Sylvie stared at the skeletons of the armoured cars, so carefully placed. The radio played throughout the bus.

'Your forehead rhymes with eyes and light,' Arik Einstein sang in words that made even less sense than usual. It was the lovelorn song of a man in love with another's wife, like King David pining for Bathsheba. Arik probably fucked just as many married women as not, though he didn't write the song, it was more prosaically written by a Tel Aviv poet for his friend's wife, or so the gossip went. Arik couldn't find an original word in him anyway, and Sylvie was sick of all his songs where women were always little girls and were always captive by the man, but fuck if she wouldn't fuck him anyway, he was like a long tall dick in hippie clothes.

The West Bank ran all across the country like a mirrored half; but Sylvie knew her destination lay south. Jericho, Hebron, Bethlehem, Jerusalem: that stretch of land cried out from the pages of the Bible with a messianic fervour, demanding to be filled and made Jewish once more. If any land deal went down it would be somewhere there, in the Judean Mountains. She just knew it.

She disembarked into the night in cold, white-stone Jerusalem.

The bustle of people calmed her. Orthodox in suits and coats, patrolling soldiers. She made her way to Fink downtown.

Going inside didn't help Sylvie's anxiety. The place was small, warm. It smelled of goulash soup and cigarettes. She saw three journalists from the *Jerusalem Post* at one table, Golda Meir perched on the bar.

Sylvie took a stool and sat down. Her hands shook. Golda looked her way, blew out smoke. The ashtray before her was full of stubs.

'What can I get you, giveret?' the bartender asked.

'A dry martini,' Sylvie said. It was the first item listed on the small menu. The bartender nodded approvingly. Sylvie stole another glance at Golda.

'What?' Golda said. 'I'm not the prime minister anymore.'

'I like your nails,' Sylvie said, then blushed at her own idiocy. But Golda smiled.

'You're not from around here, are you?' she said.

'Tel Aviv,' Sylvie said.

'Come on, kid. No one's from Tel Aviv, not really.'

'Haifa,' Sylvie admitted. She had so many questions to ask Golda. Did she authorise a land deal for Keep Ltd. back when she was in charge in '74? Genghis would have been *her* chief of Central Command. What was it like to be the first woman prime minister, maybe the last? Sylvie had so many questions.

'Golda, your table's ready,' the bartender said. He shot Sylvie a disapproving glance.

Golda coughed. It was a bad cough, the sort that age and smoking use as marker for bad things to come. From the look in Golda's eyes she knew it. She patted Sylvie on the shoulder as she left the bar.

'Good luck, kid,' she said.

The bartender served her dry martini. Sylvie sipped. She hadn't eaten and she felt light-headed. Her hands shook in her lap. The bartender placed a coffee mug of goulash soup and a side of bread on the counter without being asked. Sylvie nodded thanks. She didn't trust herself to speak.

She ate quickly though the soup was hot. It burned her tongue.

Fink's was there since the first British administrator of Jerusalem went out looking for a drink and realised there weren't any to be had. Sylvie smelled expensive aftershave and felt a presence by her side. A man glided onto a barstool smoothly and smiled at her with what he obviously thought was charm. He had the twinkling eyes of a cheerful conman and a fantastic head of hair.

'*Bonsoir*, Sylvie,' the man said.

It was Shmuel Flatto-Sharon, the newly-minted Knesset member she met at the election victory party. It felt like a lifetime ago.

'*Monsieur*,' Sylvie said. There was a bit of beef stuck in her teeth. She tried to dislodge it with her tongue. Flatto signalled to the bartender. A dry martini appeared as if by magic. He raised the glass to her.

'L'chaim,' he said.

Sylvie realised she'd eaten all the food. The bartender took it away. Sylvie raised her glass and clinked it against Flatto's.

'What are we drinking for?' Sylvie said.

'Chance encounters and the promise of the night,' Flatto said. Sylvie couldn't take him seriously. She laughed, and he seemed delighted.

'It is not so unusual for a journalist and a politician to meet at a bar frequented by journalists and politicians,' Sylvie said.

'You are a journalist?' His smile didn't waver but there was a new hardness to his gaze. 'You did not mention.'

'You did not ask.'

'You are… chasing a story?'

'Perhaps.'

His smile widened. 'Is it about me?'

'No, Sammy! Why would it be about you?'

'Because,' he said, and he leaned in theatrically, 'I am *fascinating*.'

Sylvie laughed again. She couldn't help it. And the dry martini didn't help either. She noticed it had been replaced with a fresh one. She felt a little flushed already.

'Can I ask you something?' she said.

'You can ask me anything,' Flatto said.

'What do you know about land deals in the West Bank?'

He sat and regarded her with amusement and took a sip from his drink before answering.

'Do you always start conversations like this?' he said.

'I didn't start the conversation.'

'*Touché*, Sylvie.'

'You don't have to tell me.'

'On the record? I know nothing and care even less. Off the record? It's nothing but bad business.'

'How so?' Sylvie said. She bit into an olive.

'Eh, this land, it is too... disputed. You've got to buy fast and sell fast, but the sellers are slow and the only buyer's the government. And you don't know if you'll get to keep it. What if I wanted to build a casino in Jericho, for example? I like to build big buildings, you know. Big projects! I built the Dizengoff Centre, you know.'

'I know.'

'You've been to the grand opening?'

'It is the talk of Tel Aviv,' Sylvie said. She wasn't lying, either. The modern shopping mall was really the first of its kind in the city. It was advertised as a place that you'd never have to leave because everything you needed was inside. But the building still stood empty apart from the Mashbir department store.

'So you understand! I bought the land, the land is mine, there is no dispute. But say I build that casino – and I like casinos, Sylvie, they are good business, and I can't open one here because of the law. Say I open it over the Green Line, though. It is a different law. Good business, right? I will need land. Say land near Jericho. Who owns this land? Who, Sylvie?'

'I don't know.'

Flatto clapped. 'I don't know! Exactly! So many owners, who knows who they are? Would they sell me? And if they do, are they really the owners? And if they sell, what if there is another war or, even worse, peace? Do I give my land back? No, you see? It is no good. It is a business only for, how do you say?'

'Crooks?'

He shook his head at her. 'No, no,' he said. 'Much worse. Idealists. Though you could be forgiven for confusing them.'

Sylvie's drink was dangerously low. She lit a cigarette. She felt light-headed.

'What idealists?' she said.

His eyes twinkled. 'You don't know?' he said. 'Yes, well. They like to keep a low profile, as you say. They do not *advertise*. It is a bad business when you must be like a spy, eh? Like the Mossad!' Flatto laughed, but there wasn't much humour in it. He signalled the bartender for another round.

'Two drinks limit,' the man said.

'Another round, Rothschild!' Flatto said. The man considered, then shrugged and made them drinks.

'What spies?' Sylvie said.

'Not spies,' Flatto said. 'But the work's dirty all the same. Himanuta.'

'What?'

'Himanuta,' he said again, patiently. 'It's Aramaic for loyalty. It is the name of a company registered in London, which makes the sort of land deals the Jewish National Fund can't or won't do openly. They're not crooks, Sylvie. They just have to act like they are. Or so they tell themselves, I guess.'

'I never heard of them.'

'Like I said, they don't advertise.'

'So how do they buy the land?' Sylvie said. If they were a branch of the Fund they'd have money. It would be both government money and private donor money.

'There are ways. They do it quietly. And they like to use intermediaries. Less paperwork. Less of a trail.'

'Like Keep Ltd.?'

Flatto smiled. 'I hope you are paying for the drinks at least, with all that I'm laying out. Of course, we could reach some other enjoyable arrangement…'

A part of Sylvie was tempted. She felt warm, giddy. Flatto had his charm. He was what he was and he didn't try to hide it.

'I'll think about it,' she said.

'Don't think too much, Sylvie. It will make your head hurt.'

'Keep Ltd.,' Sylvie said.

Flatto shook his head. 'There are all sorts. They can put

pressure on the sellers to sell and get the land cheap. Then they turn it around to the government for a healthy profit.'

'I thought the government made buying land in the West Bank forbidden.'

'Nonsense, Sylvie. The plan was always to settle. Create a buffer, if nothing else. Not just around Jerusalem. In the soft belly of the country, too, where all that good land is. And of course in the holy sites. Hebron in particular. There are already a handful of settlements. How many more do you think there'll be now that Begin is in power?'

'How do I find these Himanuta people?' Sylvie said.

Flatto leaned close. She could feel his lips on her ear and she shivered.

'You don't,' he said. 'They find you.'

40

THE MONEY

'It's a death sentence, selling land to Jews' – Youssef

Sylvie made her escape when Flatto went to the bathroom. Cold air blew as Sylvie stepped outside. Golda coughed cancer in the corner. The streetlights burned and every passing figure was a shadow. She hurried on unsteady legs to her hostel in the Old Town. The city was a labyrinth, the ancient alleyways twisting and turning. Washing hanging on a line. Old men playing backgammon in a courtyard. The sound of dice against the wood. Graffiti on one wall, *Free Palestine*. Giant rats ignored her as she passed the rubbish bins. Footsteps behind her and she turned but saw no one and she walked on faster, until she came at last to a white stone building amidst all the white stone buildings that said *Hostel* on the gate and she went in.

Coloured lights strewn overhead. A bored receptionist gave her a key. Sylvie went upstairs and lay on the bed in her clothes.

She woke up to sunlight and a pounding headache. Something rustled at the door. Sylvie reached in her purse and found her gun.

'Who's there!' she shouted.

There was no answer. She got up and found an envelope had been slipped under her door. She picked it up and turned it over in her hand.

'Son of a bitch,' she said.

She sat on the side of the bed and opened it. Inside she found a surveyor map of some two hundred dunams, a mimeographed, hand-written list of apparent stakeholders in a venture and amounts given by each, and finally an address in East Jerusalem.

She stared at the papers for a long time.

'Alright, then,' Sylvie said.

She washed her face in cold water in the sink and downed a couple of headache pills.

Out on the main road she found parked taxis and settled on one with a young Arab driver who was leaning nonchalantly against the hood, smoking. Sylvie lit a cigarette of her own and approached him. She gave him the address.

'Sure,' he said. 'I can take you there.'

'I'll pay for the whole day,' Sylvie said. She had a feeling there was more to come.

They haggled over the price until it was agreed.

'I'm Sylvie,' Sylvie said.

'I'm Mohammed. Well, get in.'

He drove fast, beeping when people didn't get out of his way fast enough. They went through Jewish neighbourhoods and Arab neighbourhoods. They came to a poor part of town where garbage collected in corners and the roads were broken and there they stopped beside a solitary two-storey building made of weathered stone.

'Here?' Sylvie said.

'That's what it says,' Mohammed said.

Sylvie stepped out of the car. The light was bright. Dusty grass grew out of the cracks between the stones. The house had a small garden and a tethered goat that chewed the grass behind the broken fence. The goat glared at Sylvie. Sylvie closed her fingers on the gun in her purse.

She went to the door and knocked. Nobody answered and she tried again, louder. She saw a curtain twitch in the upstairs window. She looked up.

'I'm a journalist with *This World*,' she said. 'I just want to talk.'

The curtain twitched, then closed. Sylvie waited. She heard feet coming down the stairs. The door opened.

'How did you find me?' the man said. He was unshaved, his

hair ruffled. He looked to both sides of the street. 'Who is that in the car?'

'A taxi driver. Someone gave me this address.'

'Who!' he said. 'Come in, quick. Let me see some ID.'

She showed him her press pass. The inside of the house felt airless and oppressive. All the windows were closed. The rooms were empty. She followed him into a kitchen that had a plate of half-eaten foul and pita on a low table, but no chairs. The man shook a pack of Noblesse out with shaking fingers and put one in his mouth. He said, 'They're trying to kill me.'

'Who's trying to kill you?' Sylvie said.

'Fatah, the PLO,' the man said. 'Sons of bitches. I'm trying to get out of the country, go to America or Germany. Somewhere I won't have to put up with all this bullshit.'

'What's your name?' Sylvie said.

'Youssef. You?'

'Sylvie.'

'That's a nice name,' he said distractedly. 'How did you find me?'

'I don't know how,' Sylvie said. 'Someone must know you're here.'

'Those bastards,' Youssef said. 'They're watching. And I'm low on cash. They never paid me what they owed.'

'Who didn't?'

'Moon and that piss face he works with. Shamir. They still owe me half.'

'You sold them your land?'

'Sure. I mean, what was I going to do, you know? I'm sick of this fucking place. I want to see Disneyland.'

'Disneyland?'

'With the rides and everything?' Youssef said. 'Fuck this place and everyone in it. No offence.'

'None taken,' Sylvie said. She took out her pen and notebook. 'Do you mind if I make notes?'

'What's to make notes of?' Youssef said.

'Just tell me your story.'

'What's to tell? They came round, they wanted the land in

my village. This was a few years back now. Some deal they had with the administration that they wanted to build villas for their generals. They offered shit money, but what was I going to do, tell them no? Who else was going to buy it? So I agreed. Others in the village didn't agree but that wasn't my problem. Moon gave me some cash and a cheque only the cheque bounced. Meanwhile the fucking Fatah heard about it and they've been trying to kill me. They shot at my house, killed my sister's dog by accident. Second time I was driving, someone took pot shots at me. So I figured it's best if I vanished. It's a death sentence, selling land to Jews. So I'm hiding here for now, but I can't get the rest of my money, and Moon's no longer taking my calls. Fucking Jews. Shouldn't have trusted them.' He looked at Sylvie with wide eyes.

'I don't know what to do,' he said.

Sylvie got what she could out of him and then she left him. When she stepped outside a lone dog barked. The curtain upstairs in the house twitched. Mohammed waited by the car.

'Where to now, boss?' he said.

Sylvie looked at her papers. She looked at the scribbled stakeholders list.

'Fucking Cohen,' she said with feeling. She knew she was being set up. But the cheese at the end of the maze was a newspaper story, and she couldn't turn down a story any more than a mouse could turn down the cheese.

'What?' Mohammed said.

'Let's go,' Sylvie said.

They left that lone house and its occupant behind them. Still in hiding, still waiting for a cheque that will likely never come. Youssef in hiding, dreaming of Disneyland. They drove east, away from Jerusalem, following the old Jericho Road that led down, down to the Dead Sea. It was startling how quickly the hills could turn to desert, how quickly one began to spot Bedouin encampments on the side of the road, camels dozing in the sun, but it wasn't long before they reached the turn and followed it, still high on the hills, to a small industrial estate and a sign that said, *Ma'ale Adumim*.

'I don't like coming up here,' Mohammed said. 'It's Bedouin country.'

But it wasn't any longer, Sylvie saw. The industrial area lay almost fallow. Concrete foundations stood without factories on them, and prefab workers' huts were distributed haphazardly around. A fence was already falling apart. Signs in Hebrew promised apartment blocks coming any day, creating jobs and housing. There was a lone guard by the open gates. He ambled over, bearded, armed, wearing a parka.

'Help you?'

'I'm looking for Motti,' Sylvie said.

'Motti who?' the guard said.

She looked at the list. 'Motti Mordechai. It lists this as his address.'

'Motti Motti!' the guard said, delighted. 'Go straight, then left. You can't miss it.'

'Thanks,' Sylvie said. Mohammed gunned the engine and they cruised into the industrial estate, the wheels raising dust. She saw a kiosk, apparently open, and was reminded she'd had no food yet but she didn't want to stop. Here and there people milled about, and one small factory was open and belching steam. They went straight and then left and found a construction crew and a man directing them.

Mohammed stopped the car again. Sylvie climbed out.

'Are you Motti?' she said.

'Depends who's asking, meidele,' he said, then he burst out laughing. He had a big laugh and a big gut and an honest, open face.

'Wait,' Sylvie said. 'You're really called Mordechai Mordechai?'

'A name so good they used it twice,' the man said. 'My dad had a weird sense of humour. But everybody calls me Motti. Can I help you with anything?'

'My name's Sylvie Gold. I'm from *This World*.'

'Oho!' Motti said. 'A journalist! I've been trying to drum up attention but no one's bothered to come until now. Come! I'll give you the tour. You want some coffee?'

'I'd love some coffee,' Sylvie said.

She looked at him in bemusement. 'Attention to what?' she said.

'The factory!' Motti said. 'Arik, bring coffee!' He clapped his hands. One of the men hurried to oblige.

'What are you making here?' Sylvie said.

'*Will* be making,' Motti said. 'Cars.'

'*Cars*?'

'Homemade Israeli cars,' Motti said. 'Just like we used to. This nation has a proud tradition of car manufacturing! Susita, Carmel, Sabra! Do you remember the Sabra Sport? It was a beautiful car. Beautiful!'

'Susita?' Sylvie said. 'Didn't they say camels would chew up the fibreglass?'

'Come on,' Motti said. 'That was just a story.'

'Why here?' Sylvie said.

'It's cheap,' Motti said. He spread his arms. 'And there's space to breathe. Plus, we're reclaiming our land, you know? Sure, I could open a factory in Naharia or somewhere, but this is settlement, this is a mizvah. Don't look at it like it is now. One day a city will rise here. There will be schools and hospitals and tree-lined neighbourhoods where kids can play. One day it will be beautiful here.'

Sylvie looked around her at the dusty industrial park and the workers milling by the unfinished foundations.

'Sure,' she said.

She accepted the coffee gratefully. 'Motti,' she said, 'did you put money down on a company called Keep Ltd.?'

He looked at her closely but said nothing for a moment.

'Do you mind me asking?' she said.

He shook his head. 'No, of course not. Is this why you're here?'

'It is, but I do like your car factory.'

He smiled. 'No one believes, but I tell you the Susita will ride again. I should have known no one will come. But it's still a good story. Maybe you will write it?'

'Maybe,' Sylvie said. 'But about this company?'

'Sure, yes,' Motti said. 'Well, there's not much to tell about that.

I know Izzy Moon socially. You know how it is. A good man. He got into land in Samaria and Judea early and they had rare permission to build a neighbourhood for some of the army generals. They wanted to build it in Herodion. You've been?'

'Not yet.'

'You should. It is beautiful there. Anyway, they needed investors for the scheme and I was more than happy to put some money down for it. I think reclaiming the land of Judea is a moral obligation.'

'So you were one of the original investors?'

'Sure. Me and a bunch of other guys. Settlement is inevitable and getting in early on the land was a smart move.'

'So it paid off for you?' Sylvie said.

'Well, no,' Motti said. 'Not yet, anyway. The deal never really worked out for one reason or another. But it's difficult, you know. A lot of the private land's disputed and if you find the owners, can you convince them to sell? And so on. The important thing is to keep trying.'

'Thank you,' Sylvie said.

'Not a problem.' He smiled at her. He seemed the sort of guy who smiled easily. 'Hey, you don't think there was something not kosher about it, do you? I mean, these guys, they have impeccable credentials.'

'I don't know,' Sylvie said. 'It's what I'm trying to find out.'

'There was a big construction guy involved, too,' Motti said. 'Mizrahi. He built all those hotels.'

'Right,' Sylvie said.

'It will work out,' Motti said. He reached out his hand and Sylvie shook it. Motti's hand was rough and warm.

'Thanks,' Sylvie said again. Then she took off.

A lone telephone box stood by the side of the road. Mohammed stopped the car and Sylvie went in. It was boiling hot. She rooted around for phone tokens, put them in.

'Mizrahi? Sure,' Gabi said when she called. 'But you didn't hear it from me.'

'Hear what, Gabi?'

She could hear the office in the background behind him, typewriter keys running, animated conversation, spoons clinking against the side of mugs. The office, in full swing.

'It's going to be in all the papers soon enough,' he said. 'Someone in the police leaked it to Avi Valentin at *Ma'ariv*. Son of a bitch got the scoop on us.'

'What scoop, Gabi?'

'They call it the List of Eleven. The police have been sitting on it for a while now. Eleven figures the police link to organised crime. Mizrahi's on that list.'

'Alright.'

She hung up and collected a spare phone token. It was hot now, and they drove with the windows open, the dry hot wind of the desert blowing through the car.

A small car dawdled behind them. It didn't go fast enough to overtake and it didn't turn at any of the exits. It was just there.

'Do you think it's following us?' she asked Mohammed.

He shrugged.

'There is only one road,' he said.

The road was narrow and ill-maintained. They were going west now, small Arab villages on either side. They passed a monastery to St Theodosius. A sign pointed up: *To The Cave Of The Magi*.

Ancient land. The road to Bethlehem. But she wasn't going that far. They came to a village called Za'tara. Sylvie looked at the surveyor map.

'There,' she said, pointing. Mohammed nodded. He drove through the small village until they came to a house on the edge and there he stopped the car. Curious kids came out to watch them. Sylvie stepped out, feeling very visible and very out of place.

A man came out of the house and stood there watching them.

Sylvie said, 'Abu Ali?' – going by the name someone had scribbled on the map.

The man came forward. He shooed away the kids.

'Yes?'

He looked at her with distrust.

'My name is Sylvie Gold, I'm a journalist.'

Abu Ali seemed to relax, only a little. Sylvie looked back at the road but the car behind them had vanished.

So maybe it was just nerves, she thought. That's all.

'What do you want?' Abu Ali said.

'I want to ask you some questions. About this.' She showed him the surveyor map.

'I am not selling!' Abu Ali said. Almost shouting. Sylvie sweated. She saw people come out to watch.

'I just want to know what happened,' she said. 'Can we go inside?'

He stared at her. Mohammed started speaking rapidly in Arabic. Abu Ali nodded. Then he smiled. Then he motioned them in.

'What did you tell him?' Sylvie said.

'That you were a crazy Jewish lady from Tel Aviv who has a bug up her ass about land deals,' Mohammed said. 'And you write for a big newspaper.'

'I only write for *This World*,' Sylvie said.

'"Letters to Ruthie",' Mohammed said. 'I know.'

'You *read* it?'

'I buy it for the pictures.'

He looked at her innocently until she laughed.

'What do you do when you don't drive a taxi?' she said.

'Studying pharmacy at the Hebrew University, and organising for the Communist Party,' he said.

'I didn't know that,' Sylvie said.

'You didn't ask.'

They went inside. Abu Ali brought coffee. Out of the window Sylvie could see the land, and boundary markers of the sort used by surveyors. She pointed them out.

'He put them there,' Abu Ali said.

'Who?'

'Sami the Dutchman.'

'I know him!' Sylvie said. She shouldn't have been surprised at the name and yet she was.

'Day after the elections he drove up to see me. I found him out there, planting markers in my land. He looked at me and he said,

"You know who's in power now? Now me and Begin are in charge. You'll do what I tell you to do." This is what he said to me.'

'He came here before?'

'He came here before,' Abu Ali said.

'He wants the land?'

'He doesn't give a shit either way. His bosses do. They sent him. They want me to sell out. But this isn't my land. This is my village land. Our land. We've sat here for generations. And they want me to sell it to them for nothing. I won't sell. They will have to kick me out by force.' He looked defiant but scared.

'They threaten you before?'

He shrugged. 'They had soldiers come around once, twice a week for a while. Then it went quiet for a long time. They want me to sign but I won't sign. What do they need this land for? Don't they already have all the land?'

'They offer you money?'

'A pittance.'

'You saw it?'

Abu Ali looked confused.

'Saw what?' he said.

'The money they offered.'

'No,' Abu Ali said. 'Why would I see money?'

Sylvie thought of the cancelled cheque Youssef, now hiding in Jerusalem, couldn't cash. She thought of the money Motti, now in his unbuilt car factory, put down and never got back.

What if there *was* no land deal? Sylvie thought.

What if there had never been a land deal?

She thanked Abu Ali for the coffee and his time. He saw her out of his house. She sat in the car next to Mohammed and thought.

Was that really all it was?

41

THE AGENT

'Land is a tricky business' – The property agent

She sat with Mohammed in the shade of the Herodion. The ancient citadel had stood there, more or less, since it was built by Herod two thousand years earlier. Now it was evidently an archaeological dig, only no one seemed to be around. They sat with pitas and olives they'd sourced in the village on their way and ate their late lunch and looked over the desert. 'You figure it out yet?' Mohammed said.

'Figured what out?' Sylvie said.

'Your story. What you were chasing.'

'I'm not sure. I think so.'

She watched the road. A plume of dust in the distance.

'Is that a car?' she said.

'I think so.'

'It's coming here.'

'There's only one road,' Mohammed said.

'You're really a communist?' Sylvie said.

'I am.'

'You're connected to the PLO?' Sylvie said.

He looked at her sideways. 'I might be.'

'You won't tell, will you? About that house we saw in Jerusalem?'

He laughed, but there wasn't any humour in it.

'That guy in there needs to get out fast, if he's going to get out at all,' Mohammed said. 'But one way or the other it won't be my doing.'

'Good.' She felt a weird sense of relief and didn't quite know why. The plume of dust grew larger and she could hear the motor now. Faint, but getting louder.

'They'll come, you know,' Sylvie said. 'They'll build more towns, pave new roads, make it just another part of Israel.'

'You say they when you mean you,' Mohammed said. 'This isn't my land. I grew up near Haifa. The people in the refugee camps, in Gaza, in Jordan, here – they ran here. Their kids are born here. But their land, their heart? It's your land now. Who will give them *that* land back? Who will give us our heart? Now you try to take away even their refuge.'

'I suppose,' Sylvie said. She felt listless. No doubt Mohammed was right, she thought. But you couldn't think that way. This was her country. She had nowhere else to go.

She said, 'I grew up in Haifa.'

She could see the car now. It crawled up the side of the mountain. Sylvie reached in her purse, found the gun.

They watched the car come their way. When it reached the spot it stopped. The engine hissed in the sun. When the door opened a young man came out. He wore a cheap suit despite the heat, and a trilby hat that looked out of place for both the country and era, as though the man were an encyclopaedia salesman from the time of the British Mandate.

Sylvie held her finger on the trigger of the gun.

The man came over. He stopped a short way from them and stood with his back to the view.

'You've been following me,' Sylvie said.

The man wiped sweat from his forehead.

'You're a hard woman to track down,' he said.

'State your business.'

The man looked at her and he said, 'I've had gun pointed at me before.'

'Then you'll know to keep it brief.'

'I don't mean you harm,' the man said. 'I'm from Himanuta.'

You don't find them, Flatto said. *They find you*.

Sylvie tensed. She cocked the gun.

'Whoa, whoa,' Mohammed said.

The man from Himanuta just stood there, like he had all the time in the world.

'I don't know what you think I am,' he said. 'I'm just a property agent.'

'I know all about you,' Sylvie said.

'Do you?' He extracted a pack of Marlboros from his breast pocket. 'Do you mind if I smoke?'

She noticed the gold wedding band on his finger. He didn't wait for an answer but lit up and regarded her.

'You're looking into Izzy Moon and Keep Ltd.,' he said.

'What if I am?'

The man shrugged. 'What I have to say is off the record. Do you want to hear it?'

'Say your piece.'

The man laughed. 'Very well,' he said. The smoke ebbed lazily from the cigarette and rose above into the ancient citadel. 'They've been in this business since a while back.'

'So I understand.'

'How much did you figure out?' the man said.

'Enough.'

'Yes,' the man said. 'You see, my job is to acquire land that is not so easy to acquire, and to do it quietly. Intermediaries are best. Keep had connections, sanction. They had the military leadership at the time on their side.'

'Genghis,' Sylvie said.

'Yes. They were ideal. For that purpose, we advanced them a considerable amount of money to acquire land: in Nebi Samuel, in Latrun, and here. For each deal the paperwork was signed and money deposited. We were quite hopeful. But land is a tricky business.'

'I see,' Sylvie said. She was indeed beginning to see now. She put the gun back in her purse and lit a cigarette of her own. She squinted in the sunlight, saw the man from Himanuta in silhouette against the desert.

'Did you acquire the land?' she said.

'We did not.'

'The deals fell through?'

'For one reason or another, yes,' the man said. 'Every time.'

'And the money advanced?' Sylvie said.

The man shrugged. 'It was written off,' he said.

Sylvie exhaled.

'Moon's partner, Shamir,' she said.

'Yes.'

'He's a convicted forger.'

'Yes. In hindsight that should have been a concern.'

'They showed you documents? Memorandums of understanding and so on?'

'They did.'

'But you suspect they might have been faked.'

The man smiled tightly round his cigarette.

'I am sure I couldn't say.'

'So why are you telling me this?' Sylvie said.

The man tossed his cigarette on the ground and crushed it with his foot. He looked up one last time, briefly.

'You've got a guardian angel watching you,' he said. 'That's all. If you write the story, just leave us out of it.'

He reached in his pocket and drew out an envelope and tossed it her way, already turning to go. Sylvie caught in in mid-air. The man was nearly by his car when she called after him.

'What's your name?'

He turned.

'It doesn't really matter, does it?' he said. Then he got in his car and was gone.

She watched him make his slow way down the mountain and soon he was gone from sight. Back to Jerusalem and to an office where names meant nothing.

She opened the envelope.

Copies of understandings and agreements, mentions of large sums of money. Nowhere did the name Himanuta appear.

'Alright, then,' Sylvie said.

She got back in the hot taxi with Mohammed.

'Where to?' Mohammed said.

Sylvie sat back and closed her eyes.

She thought, It's over.

'Let's go back,' she said.

42

THE HUNT

'I'm one of the good guys' – Genghis

The sun set quickly over the desert. The citadel was far behind them now. They drove across the desert to Jerusalem. The sands vanished by degrees, replaced with shrubbery, then trees. The air grew cooler as the sun set. Streaks of blood criss-crossed the horizon.

They came to an army checkpoint ahead. The road closed and soldiers stood armed on both sides. They signalled them to stop.

Mohammed stalled the car. Rolled down the window.

'Your papers, please.'

They handed over their IDs. The soldier went and spoke to an officer. They both looked at the documents. The officer went to a command car, used a radio, spoke. Sylvie couldn't make out what he said.

The officer came back to the car.

'Could you step out of the vehicle, please, giveret?'

'What's this about?' Sylvie said.

'Please step out of the vehicle.'

'I'm an Israeli citizen,' Sylvie said. 'You have no reason to pull me over.'

'Step out, please.'

She glanced at Mohammed. Glanced at the glove compartment, where the envelope was. He gave her the briefest nod.

Sylvie got out.

The officer leaned in through the open window.

'You can go,' he told Mohammed.

'Hey!' Sylvie said.

Mohammed didn't need to be told twice. He gunned the engine. The soldiers opened the barrier and the taxi vanished up the road to Jerusalem.

'What is this about?' Sylvie said.

'Come with me, please.'

She followed him. She didn't feel afraid, but she was curious. The officer got in a jeep and she got in next to him.

'I'm a journalist,' she told him.

He nodded but said nothing back. They drove off-road, up the mountains into the woods. Night slowly settled. A sense of inevitability took over Sylvie. That this was how it was always going to end.

They came to a group of logwood cabins in a clearing. She heard a dog barking, smelled campfires, heard the chattering voices of men. There was a guard on the gate and he let them in. The officer stopped the jeep and waited for her to climb out. Then he drove back out and was gone.

'Sylvie Gold,' a voice said. A thin, hatchet-faced man in civilian clothing came out of the shadows. 'You're a hard person to track down.'

'Mr Ha'navi,' Sylvie said.

'Call me Genghis,' he said. 'That's what everyone calls me.'

Sylvie tried to tamp down a shudder of revulsion.

'What do you want?' she said.

'Want? Nothing,' he said. 'I think you have the wrong impression of me. I'm one of the good guys.'

She was a journalist, Sylvie reminded herself. She was a journalist and this was a story. She took out her notebook and pen.

'Is this an interview?' Genghis said. He looked amused.

'It can be. Isn't this why you brought me here?'

'Invited,' he said. 'Invited here.'

'If you want to call it that. What is this place, anyway?'

'An old hunting lodge,' Genghis said. 'I think some British officer built it back in the day. Do you know what is a tragedy, Sylvie?'

'What is?' Sylvie said.

'The state of wildlife in this country,' Genghis said. 'Back in '64 – you were only a kid then, you wouldn't be expected to know this – the government was concerned about the spread of rabies. To try and stop it we engaged in a programme of mass poisoning of the common jackal. A wonderful animal, the jackal. I love to hear them sing at sunset, when their calls rise into the darkening skies.'

'You are quite the poet, Mr Ha'navi.'

'I told you, call me Genghis. I am not a poet, Sylvie. Merely a man who loves his country. In '64, the Ministry of Agriculture scattered tens of thousands of poisoned chicks throughout the country. They decimated the jackal population, and along with them destroyed the habitats of wolves, mongoose, wildcats and leopards. Did you know we have all these animals in this land? Majestic creatures, that should have been allowed to roam, free like Jews. Did you know jackals are monogamous? They live in pairs, make families, and each family controls a territory. They are much like us.'

'Are you monogamous, Genghis?'

He smiled at her. 'I love my wife,' he said, 'I love women.'

He moved before she could stop him. His hands were all over her, patting, searching. He ran his hand on her groin and she tried not to scream. He took her purse and looked inside it carefully, found the gun.

He raised it up. 'You know how to use it?'

Sylvie said nothing. She felt sick inside. He'd touched her like it meant nothing to him. He did not even think it, to him it was his right.

'Where is it?' Genghis said.

'Where's what?'

Sylvie forced out the words.

'The papers,' Genghis said.

'I have no idea what you're talking about.'

'I know what you're doing,' he said.

'What am I doing?'

'You're trying to besmirch the name of good men. I can't let that happen.'

'What are you going to do to me?' she whispered.

'Do?' he looked surprised. 'Nothing.'

He handed her back the purse but kept the gun.

'You don't understand,' he said earnestly; as though nothing had happened. 'It is irresponsible to spoil a man's good name. And for what? Mistakes were made. That is all. But the thrust of the project is good and worthy. We must settle this land. We must reclaim it!'

There was sweat on his brow. He wiped it with his sleeve.

'Come,' he said. 'We are going hunting.'

'I would rather go back,' Sylvie said.

'Come, come,' he said, laughing, as though she were a little girl who had said something amusing. 'There are wolves still in these hills! I would like to bag a wolf.'

He went and picked a hunting rifle that was leaning against the wall.

'Come,' he said again.

The edge of the wood pressed against the campsite. Cedar and pine and cypress. It was dark in the woods. She stepped hesitantly. She turned and saw him in silhouette, the gun held at an angle.

Sylvie ran.

Pine needles caressed her skin. Branches broke underfoot. She stumbled over a root, regained her balance.

A shot rang in the dark forest.

A cloud of swifts, startled by the shot, rose into the air. Something moved in the trees behind Sylvie.

She ran.

She heard nothing and nobody, only the pounding of blood in her ears, her own heartbeat too loud. Her lungs burned. She had to quit smoking. It was all so quiet and—

A shot. She fell, lay on the ground, inhaled pine and earth.

He would say it was just an accident.

He would say she got lost in the woods.

She heard movement behind her, a rustling of pines. Someone stepped on a branch and it snapped. Sylvie crawled, quietly, quietly. She blinked sweat out of her eyes.

A hare stood on a rock and regarded her with a quizzical

expression. How silly it all was, it seemed to say, how funny that this was how she died. And all for what? A good old-fashioned scam? You had to laugh, it seemed to say.

Fuck you, Sylvie silently said to the hare. She got to her knees. She made as small a target as possible. Movement somewhere behind her, but it was farther away. She looked and in that split second the hare was gone.

Sylvie ran.

She sprinted from starting position, just as she had done at school. She ran, through the brambles and branches and trees in the dark, and she wasn't going to stop, she was never going to stop, she staggered over a rock and just kept going and the ground began to slope and she let it carry her onwards, and for a moment she was like a free bird, flying.

She burst out of the trees and onto an asphalt road. A car screeched to a halt, its headlights shining, illuminating a rest area a moment before it came to an abrupt halt.

'Oh, thank God, thank God,' Sylvie said.

'What the fuck do you think you're doing!' an angry voice said from inside the vehicle. The driver leaned out of the window. 'Are you fucking crazy!'

Sylvie ran to the car. She pulled the door handle until she nearly jerked the door open. She got inside.

'Drive!' she said. 'Just drive!'

'Hey, are you alright?' the man said.

'Go!'

'Shit,' the man said, but he mercifully put the car back into gear and it creaked into life, and he pressed on the gas. Sylvie watched the empty road move ahead, illuminated by the headlights, and for a moment she thought she saw a hare on a rock, standing there on its hind legs and watching her quizzically. Then it was gone.

'Are you alright? What happened to you?' the driver said. 'Was it Arabs?'

Sylvie sank back in her seat. She closed her eyes.

She shivered.

She said, 'Just drive.'

43

THE MEETING

'Can it run?' – Sylvie

She crawled into her bed in Tel Aviv as the birds began to chirp outside her window and the first rays of light tapped on the glass. She plugged in her phone. It was mercifully silent. The driver who picked her up wanted to take her straight to the police station. Sylvie nixed it. She called Gabi from a payphone and woke him up. He drove from Tel Aviv and picked her up from the first bar she'd found, near a youth hostel where no one spoke Hebrew and no one paid her any attention.

Gabi didn't ask any questions. He dropped her off at her building, insisted on going up with her, left her at the door.

She fell into bed and slept for what felt like hours.

When she got up her whole body ached and she kept having flashbacks to Genghis' hands on her, to the dark of the forest, to the smell of pine resin. She threw up in the sink. She washed and scrubbed herself until the water ran cold. She brushed her teeth but she couldn't get the bad taste out of her mouth.

She went into the kitchen, made instant coffee, and smoked two cigarettes.

'Fuck this,' she said out loud.

She was alive. And she had the story.

She went down the stairs. Nobody stopped her. She went to the office. Inside it was busy as always. She ignored everyone. She sat at her typewriter. She started to write.

As she was typing the mail came in and someone placed an

envelope on her desk. She tore it open. All the evidence was there. Mohammed, she thought with relief. He got it back to her.

She kept typing. An hour and a half later she was done.

She went into Avnery's office.

She put the pages on his desk.

She lit a cigarette and waited.

Avnery read. He turned the pages slowly. From time to time he marked a line with his pen, circled a word, made small corrections. At last he finished.

He looked up and smiled.

'It's good,' he said.

'Can it run?' Sylvie said.

'It can run.'

Three hours later they had the front page laid out and her byline was on it.

Sylvie held the proof in her hand.

Fraud, extortion, corruption. It was all in there.

'It's beautiful work,' Avnery said.

The phone in his office rang.

'Just a moment,' Avnery said. He went to his office and listened on the phone for a while.

When he came back he'd lost the smile.

'They want to meet tonight, at my house,' he said.

'Who does?'

'Ha'navi and the rest. They know about the story.'

Sylvie felt sick.

'They can't,' she said.

Avnery sighed. 'I will hear them out,' he said. 'These are not men you can ignore.'

'I'm coming too.'

He didn't argue. They left the office soon after. Avnery drove. His home was nice, Sylvie thought, if a little untidy.

The knock on the door came soon after. Avnery answered it. In came Genghis, Mizrahi, and a third man Sylvie vaguely recognised, then it hit her: the policeman who was Cohen's friend, the one she saw at Mizrahi's party.

'You must put a stop to this, Uri,' Genghis said.

Mizrahi glared at them both. 'My name is being dragged through the mud by *Ma'ariv* and that Avi Valentin cunt,' he said. 'I'm going to sue them. You publish, I am going to sue you, too.'

Sylvie stared at Genghis. He seemed barely aware of her presence.

'Eddie?' he said.

The third man coughed. He was younger than the others, but he had authority.

'You know me?' he asked Avnery.

'You're Inspector Eddie Raphael.'

'Chief Inspector,' Eddie Raphael said. 'It's soon to be announced.'

'Congratulations,' Avnery said.

'You can't publish, Mr Avnery. These men are right.'

'Why can't I?' Avnery said.

'Come on,' Eddie Raphael said.

'It is for the good of the country,' Genghis said.

'I will sue you, you fucking cunt,' Mizrahi said.

'Mr Mizrahi, please,' Avnery said.

Sylvie realised she may as well not have been there. No one paid her the slightest attention. The three men remained standing. Avnery was sat on his sofa. The three men were arranged spaces apart, all facing him. Sylvie was physically on the sidelines.

'I want my gun back,' she said.

'What?'

For the first time they seemed to notice her.

'I want my gun back, you son of a bitch.'

Genghis stared at her. The cold in his eyes made her shiver but she held his gaze.

He suddenly laughed.

'This?' he said. He took out a gun. It was her gun. He held it loosely, but the barrel pointed at Avnery.

Genghis looked back at Avnery.

'You won't breathe in this country,' he said.

Avnery slowly nodded.

Genghis laughed. He tossed the gun to Sylvie. She caught it awkwardly.

'You go near me again,' he said. 'I'll have my friends take care of you.'

The men left.

Avnery sat on the sofa. Sylvie leaned against the wall. Her hands shook. She put the gun away.

'Well?' she said.

Avnery looked at her. Then he looked away.

'I'm killing the story,' he said.

PART SEVEN

LEBANON

1982, Ramat Gan to Beirut

44

HOLD BACK THE RAIN

'This isn't Switzerland' – Cohen

Chocolate Mint Bubblegum sang 'Easy, Easy Dancin'' on the radio.

Rubenstein said, 'Turn that disco shit off.' He rotated the dial on the radio and Benzine came on with drums and guitars on 'Friday Night'. Rubenstein drummed his fingers on the passenger window to the tune, singing along about partying all night.

Benny, driving, didn't say anything. Rain fell on the windshield and he squinted to see the road. The streetlights cast orange pools in the gloom. Summer rain, unexpected and hot. He rolled the window down, let his arm dangle out, into the rain.

The music ended and the news came on. 'Israeli forces shell Beirut for the second week as Operation Peace for Galilee continues under heavy fighting—'

There was no point finding another station. They listened to the news, reports of the war across the border. Arik promised it would be over in weeks.

Benny wasn't so sure. And Rubenstein smelled opportunity.

Ramat Gan. Quiet leafy streets, suburban homes, a woman walking her dog outside, kids waiting under a bus stop. Nice place, so close to the city and yet a world away. Benny would have moved here if only there weren't so many crooked cops already there.

He found the house. It was a nice house.

Cohen stood in the front garden, smoking a cigarette. He shook

Rubenstein's hand, shook Benny's. Benny looked up – a kid in the upstairs window looked down on them.

Benny said, 'Who's that?'

'Sagi's kid. Avi.'

Benny waved. The boy withdrew. Rubenstein said, 'So?'

'In the garage,' Cohen said.

They went in. Chief Inspector Sagi wiped his car with a hand cloth. It was a red Lotus convertible. He was listening to the small radio, plugged on top of the fridge in the corner. Yehoram Gaon, singing 'The Last War', promising the little girl in the song that this war would be the last.

Cheerful, Benny thought.

Sagi straightened when he saw them.

'You want a beer?' he said.

'Sure,' Benny said.

'Help yourself.' Sagi gestured to the fridge. Benny helped himself. No one else did. Benny withdrew to the wall. He was just the driver.

'So you're Rubenstein?' Sagi said.

Rubenstein nodded. Sagi looked him over.

'You don't look like shit.'

Rubenstein nodded. Words never bothered him, Benny knew. When the police had him in for interrogation no one was cooler than Rubenstein. He just didn't give a fuck.

'I read your file,' Sagi said. 'You're just a small time crook. Robberies, market stall extortion. Why should I give a shit?'

'He's Ashkenazi,' Cohen said.

'Romania, isn't it?' Sagi said. He had cold eyes, Benny thought. Cold eyes and a nice suburban home.

'On my father's side,' Rubenstein said. 'Mother's from the Caucasus.'

'Makes a change from all the schwartzes,' Sagi said. 'Still.' He looked Rubenstein over, dubious.

'I think he's the guy,' Cohen said.

'You think,' Sagi said.

'Oshri and Midget are in prison,' Cohen said. 'There's a vacuum

Yehezkel Aslan's trying to fill. Do you really want another one of those running Tel Aviv?'

Rubenstein said, 'I will kill Aslan and his wife and his brother and his partners if they get in my way.'

Yehezkel Aslan ran south Tel Aviv after the Yemenite Orchard gang got done for murder, finally.

'Oh, they *will* get in your way,' Sagi said. 'And no one is talking about killing anyone. What we need is *stability*. And you're still just a small fish in a pond.'

'"God ordains strength out of the mouths of babes",' Cohen said. 'Psalms.'

'I said fish, and you're mixing up my metaphors,' Sagi said irritably. 'We'll cover you, but you have three months to show me you're not just dressing up for Purim. Goddamn it,' he said, 'I volunteered to go back to reserves but the army told me I was too old. I should be shooting fucking PLO right now in Lebanon.'

Rubenstein nodded.

'Nice car,' he said. Then he pulled up the garage door and went outside.

Benny put the half-drank beer down and went to join him. Rubenstein lit a cigarette. It stopped raining. It was still hot.

'Rain in the middle of summer, can you fucking believe it,' Rubenstein said.

'Three months,' Benny said.

'It's doable,' Rubenstein said. Cohen came out then. He bummed a cigarette off Rubenstein.

'He likes you,' he said.

'He's a cunt,' Rubenstein said.

'But he's a boss,' Cohen said.

'What's your angle, Cohen?'

'Keeping the peace,' Cohen said. He blew smoke. 'Fucking Lebanon,' he said.

'Fucking Lebanon,' Benny said, with feeling.

Rubenstein clapped Benny's shoulder. He had a grip on him.

'What?' Benny said.

Cohen smiled, tight-lipped.

'*What*?' Benny said.

'You're going,' Rubenstein said.

'Like fuck I am,' Benny said. 'They shoot people there.'

'This isn't Switzerland,' Cohen said. 'But what can you do?'

They were on either side of him, shoulder to shoulder. Benny realised he'd been had. Rubenstein said, 'Come back with what we need, or don't come back at all.'

Cohen said, 'This is how fortunes are made, bubele.'

Benny said, 'How do I get there?'

'Cohen will take you to the border,' Rubenstein said. He tossed the cigarette on the manicured grass.

'I'll see you on the other side,' he said.

Shoshana Damari sang 'Poppies'. Benny said, 'I am sick of this old shit. Put something foreign on.'

'Do it yourself,' Cohen said. They were in Cohen's car.

Benny twiddled the knob on the radio. They were past Haifa now, heading north. A scratchy signal, at last: Radio Monte Carlo out of Lebanon playing Duran Duran's 'Waiting For The Night Boat'. Benny thought of too many nights spent in the dark doing the same thing. The Christians shipped hash in fishing boats to Israel. The arrangement has been good for everyone. The war threatened to disrupt the trade – unless they could use it to their advantage.

Benny said, 'They met on a kibbutz, you know.'

'What?' Cohen said.

'Duran Duran. They were volunteers on a kibbutz.'

'Why do you know all this shit?' Cohen said.

'I read it in *Monitin*. I like music.'

Cohen muttered something Benny preferred not to hear. They rode in silence the rest of the way. The sky in the distance became busy with lights. Convoys passed them on the road, soldiers heading to battle. Benny said, 'Pull up, I need a piss.'

He stood behind a bush, thinking. He had a gun. He could just shoot Cohen and run. But that wouldn't solve anything. The last communication he had from Pierre Malik was that he was heading into Lebanon to join the fighting. His uncle ran one of the biggest

Christian militias. Ever since Operation Freedom For Galilee started the shipments stopped, and this was very bad for business. Rubenstein had to use the reserves and those were going fast.

Someone had to establish the situation in the middle of the war. Someone had to bring back a shipment. Benny supposed Rubenstein trusted him, as much as Rubenstein ever trusted anyone. And he further supposed that he was dispensable, which was no doubt why they chose him.

'Fuck it,' he said, and zipped up his pants. He got back in the car.

'Chose not to run?' Cohen said. 'Can't say I would have blamed you.'

Benny kept his thoughts to himself. They drove on, north, to the Galilee, until they reached a military base and were flagged down by the guards.

Cohen flashed them a badge and a name, a second-rank general. They were waved through. Benny could see explosions far in the distance, hear choppers overhead. Soldiers and trucks, tents, guns. Everyone looked tense. When they got out of the car he felt conspicuous in his civilian clothes and the civilian car.

'Cheer up,' Cohen said. 'What's the worst that could happen?'

A military aide came to meet them. He led them to a command tent where men stood talking intently around a map spread on a table. The general turned, saw them. Shook Cohen's hand.

'I will be with you in a moment,' he said. 'Grab a coffee.'

They went to the side of the tent. The general spoke for a while longer, then dismissed the others. He gestured for Cohen and Benny to come over.

'I'm pissing black coffee at this point,' he said.

Benny sipped his. His asshole was clenched so hard he didn't think it would ever unclench. He lit a cigarette with hands that shook only a little. Three other men came into the tent.

He recognised the first one before Cohen called him by name.

'Eddie,' Cohen said. They shook hands. 'It's good to see you.'

Eddie was in uniform.

'Superintendent Raphael,' Benny said. He knew Cohen's former partner was the newly appointed deputy police commander of the entire Galilee region.

Eddie nodded. Benny realised he had miscalculated the situation. A general and two senior police officers in the mix was above his pay grade. Whatever Rubenstein had cooked it was bigger than Benny.

He looked at the other two arrivals. One was young and in army uniform. The other was middle aged, pot-bellied, and in civilian clothes. He had Security Services written all over him.

'This is Nir,' Eddie said, introducing the young soldier. 'He'll be your escort into Lebanon.'

'Sir,' Nir said, saluting. Benny felt very tired then.

'Call me Benny,' he said.

'Yes, sir.'

Benny nodded at the other civilian. 'Who's he?'

'That doesn't matter,' the man said. 'Not to you.'

'What's this really about?' Benny said.

'You do business with Pierre Malik?' the man said.

'Who?'

'Come, come. His uncle is Tony Malik. He's the leader of the second biggest Maronite militia in Lebanon and we need his help in order to take Beirut.'

'So?' Benny said.

'We can't invade Beirut on foot,' the general – Leider, his name was Leider – said. 'We need local forces or it looks bad for us, politically. And they're not cooperating so far. Fucking Phalangists. You'd think they'd be grateful. So all we can do so far is shell the shit out of Beirut and wait.'

'So?'

'So when God drops dogshit on your doorstep you do what you can with it,' the man from the Security Services said. It was clear to Benny who the dogshit was in that analogy. 'You're going to go to Lebanon and meet with Commander Malik and convince him to help us with the invasion.'

Benny started to laugh. They waited him out.

'What are you, high?' Benny said.

'You will be doing your country a great service,' the general, Leider, said. Benny stared at the lot of them.

'I don't even know where Pierre is,' he said.

'We got word to the militia,' the man from the Security Services said. 'Nir here will take you to the meet. Pierre trusts you?'

'We're on good terms,' Benny said weakly.

'We turned a blind eye to your activities,' the man said. 'Since the political impetus has been to support the Phalangists, and they require funding, ammunition, weapons. Now the situation's changed. It is… fluid. Arik promised this will be over quickly. If it's not, and we get bogged down in Lebanon… Well, one can't read the future but one can try to prepare for it. You understand?'

Benny understood implicitly. He revised the costs of any future deals upwards. How much were they all going to bleed him and Rubenstein for the drugs?

Then he thought, what if the IDF did get bogged down in Lebanon and there was a *direct fucking route* from the source of production straight to Tel Aviv?

He nodded.

'I will do what I can,' he said.

'For your country,' Leider said. He saluted him. Benny saluted back.

Benny said, 'What if I get caught? Or if I'm killed?'

'Either way, we don't know anything about you,' the man from the Security Services said. 'Clear?'

'Clear…' Benny said.

Then somehow Benny was outside. There was another, beat-up car, with no license plates. Eddie Raphael and General Leider were gone and so was the man from the Security Services. There was only Cohen.

Benny said, 'This is bullshit.'

'Listen,' Cohen said, 'there is no more of this kilo here, kilo there business, no more using Arabs. When the shipments start coming next they'll be in tonnes. So sure, you'll have to grease a few more palms. But you'll have the army bringing it right in, and the police giving you an escort all the way to the warehouse. So what, you're going to argue *percentages*?'

'And that guy? What is he, Mossad or something?'

'Or something,' Cohen said. 'They don't care. There's a separation of interests here. They need sources in Lebanon. If you can get them intelligence, you can do what you want. Can you do it?'

'Talk to Malik? I don't know, Cohen. I was happy dealing with a middleman.'

'There are no more middlemen,' Cohen said. He reached for Benny's shirt, grabbed it by the lapel and turned it over.

'What the fuck are you doing!'

'Checking the labels.' There was a knife in Cohen's hand. He sliced the label off. Benny flinched.

'Give me your ID card, everything,' Cohen said.

'This is insane.'

Benny complied in a daze. The soldier, Nir, gave him a bullet-proof vest to put on.

'What is that?' Benny said.

'Soviet or something,' Nir said. 'Got it off some PLO guy. At least, I think he was PLO. It's hard to tell who anyone is over there. Here, put a helmet on, too.'

Benny put on the helmet. Cohen saluted him.

'Good luck,' Cohen said.

'Fuck you,' Benny said. He climbed into the car next to Nir.

'Let's just get this over with,' he said.

Nir started the car. They rode down the hill, along the road and took a turn past a rusted sign leaning on its side. A broken fence marked the border.

'Welcome to Lebanon,' Nir said.

45

ANYONE OUT THERE

'Heroin. That's where the real money is' – Pierre

They drove north-easterly. It was surprisingly quiet. Nir said, 'This part's more or less secured, it's just us and the Maronites in charge now, but you have to watch out for ambush or IEDs still.'

'How did you end up doing this?' Benny said.

'I just do what they tell me,' Nir said.

'You're active service?'

'Yes, sir. I was in the advance on Beirut until Leider ordered me back.'

'You're good at this, then.'

'As good as anyone. When we got here, I had twenty-four men in my platoon. Five minutes later I hear a sound, I look up, something blows up. When I got up again half my platoon was lying on the ground and we were down to twelve. Five dead, the rest air-lifted to hospital. It's hairy out here. But we're only in South Lebanon here, sir. It's the Free Lebanon State. We shouldn't have any major problems.'

'You smoke?' Benny said.

'No, sir.'

Benny lit up. He saw a doll on the back seat.

'Where did you get this car?' he said.

'I don't know, sir. One of the villages, I would say.'

They drove past cherry groves and sleeping villages. A dog barked in the distance. Twice they came to a roadblock. Soldiers, too young, fingers jumpy on the trigger. Both times they got waved through.

'Just so long as we don't go to Beirut,' Benny said, tried to make a joke of it.

'No, sir, we do not want to go there,' Nir said.

Benny's guts hurt. There was something awful about being over the border like this. He didn't know this place, what to do, how to be. But he noted how open the border was, noted the drivers on the road, the army trucks going back and forth, and he began to see what Cohen and Rubenstein had already seen, and it was that South Lebanon was an open funnel into Israel now. Whatever happened next, however the invasion ended, it wouldn't be business as usual anymore.

Cohen was right.

They needed to go right to the source.

It wasn't that much farther before Nir slowed down. The road ended here and a dirt track began. They passed a ruined building and a shelled field still guarded with a wire fence. A dead goat lay rotting by the fence. Nir drove without lights. It was very quiet.

They came to the edge of an apple orchard. Nir flashed the lights, twice, and waited.

A convoy of cars came slowly along the dirt track. A black Mercedes with armoured cars on either side and men holding weapons. They came to a stop. The men fanned out. Benny took a breath.

'Fuck it,' he said. He stepped out of the car and waited.

The door of the Mercedes opened. Two men came out, one older than the other, and Benny recognised Pierre with relief. Pierre was smiling. He hugged Benny, slapped him on the back.

'Look at the balls on this one!' he said. 'I told those fuckers I will only deal with you. Hey, Benny, let me introduce you to my uncle. Uncle Tony, this is Benny.'

'Benny,' Uncle Tony said. He shook Benny's hands. He had rough hands and thick gold rings. He said something in French to Pierre.

'You speak French, right?' Pierre said.

'Comsi comsa,' Benny said.

Pierre said something to his uncle in French, then Arabic. Benny picked up a word here and there. Tony Malik nodded.

'I'll speak,' Pierre said.

'Suits me,' Benny said. 'So what's happening, Pierre?'

'It's good news, Benny,' Pierre said. 'You know where our drugs come from?'

'Sure,' Benny said. 'The Bekaa. But it's FatahLand.'

The Valley of the Lebanon, they called it in Hebrew. The Romans, when they were still around, called it the bread basket of the empire. It was said that if you spat a pomegranate seed there it would grow into a tree. But it was on the Syrian border and controlled by Palestinian factions displaced from Jordan back in Black September. From what Benny read in the newspapers they had training camps there for half the hippy terrorists in the world, from Baader-Meinhof to the Japanese Red Army to the Nicaraguan Sandinistas. Smoking hash, shooting guns, plotting revolution. The Israeli newspapers called it FatahLand.

'That's the good news,' Pierre said. 'The PLO's been kicked out to Beirut and, soon enough, they'll be kicked out of the country altogether. We can take the whole valley.' He said something to his uncle, who shook his head.

'If not all of it, then enough,' Pierre said, as though mollifying him. 'Those PLO cunts have been running half the drugs out of the Bekaa to Europe and trading hash for guns from the IRA, and the Syrians have been using the army to ship the other half, but everyone's got a piece of the Bekaa. We had a share, and now we're going to have a much bigger share, because we have you guys behind us. We have the IDF. You understand?'

'Yeah, I get it,' Benny said.

Uncle Tony said something. Pierre nodded.

'Tell those Mossad guys we'll give them all the information they need,' he said. 'We have the same goals. Liberate Lebanon from the Palestinians and restore Christian rule. My uncle's party could take power with Israeli backing. He could be the next prime minister. Hell, Benny, maybe I could be a minister myself, in the new government.'

'How much are we talking about here?' Benny said.

'Tonnes,' Pierre said.

'What am I going to do with tonnes of hash?' Benny said.

'Sell them,' Pierre said, and looked at Benny a little funny.

'We'd have to ship them overseas to make a real profit,' Benny said.

'You have your guys in Los Angeles, don't you?' Pierre said.

Benny stopped.

'You know about Los Angeles?' he said.

Pierre grinned. 'Plus,' he said, 'we don't just have hash. The Syrians really invested in the valley. They brought in experts from Turkey to teach the farmers how to properly grow poppies. I'm talking opium, Benny. Heroin. That's where the real money is.'

'That's real money,' Benny said. So this is how it was, he thought.

'It's all set up already, isn't it,' he said. 'You and Cohen and Rubenstein. It's already agreed.'

'Of course,' Pierre said. 'But you still have to shake on it.'

'Oh, I'll shake on it,' Benny said. 'Listen, they told me to tell your uncle, they need you guys to go into Beirut, take over the city. We can't do it. It has to be a Lebanese force.'

Pierre said something to his uncle. His uncle shook his head.

Pierre said, 'You can tell them you asked.'

'Alright,' Benny said. He couldn't wait to get the fuck out of there. He stuck out his hand.

'We have a deal?' Pierre said.

'We have a deal.'

Uncle Tony reached out to shake Benny's hand. Then there was a hole in the middle of his forehead. Uncle Tony looked surprised. He fell to his knees and pitched over.

'What the fuck!' Pierre screamed. He pulled out his gun and began to fire. Benny dropped to the ground. The Phalangists began shooting in all direction, but suddenly bright lights blinded them and then a hail of bullets mowed them down. Benny felt bullets ping around him, hit the earth on all sides of him. He crawled desperately towards the car, which was already moving.

'Nir!' Benny screamed. A foot pressed him into the hard ground. He saw Pierre run to the car, grab the door and get in. He had a gun in his hand. Benny couldn't make out what he said but it was enough to convince Nir, apparently. The car shot out of there, followed by bullets. It was hit several times and the back window was smashed but Nir kept hold of the wheel and the car raced out of there and vanished into the dark.

Benny stopped crawling.

There were no more gunshots, and the silence was eerie. He very carefully reached for his gun.

Someone kicked him hard in the ribs and then kicked the gun away. Benny groaned, turned over. He saw indistinct shapes, men wearing ski masks, holding guns. He waited for a bullet. But the gunshot didn't come.

They pulled him up. He was still alive. They tied his hands behind his back roughly. He watched as the men went through the Phalangist corpses, one by one, and shot them once in the head each time. Confirm kills. Benny felt sick. Then the men put a sack over his head and he couldn't see anything. They dragged him to a car. He heard doors open and close. They shoved him into a small space and shut the boot on him. He heard the engine start, the car thrumming, then the bumps in the road as they sped away, taking him elsewhere.

46

HUNGRY LIKE THE WOLF

'Everything is political' – Alexei

From time to time Benny heard gunshots in the distance and the sound of mortar. The ground was uneven for a long time and then it was straight for a while and then it was bumpy again. Twice the car slowed down and he heard muffled voices, but both times they went through and continued on their way. He couldn't hear inside the car other than the faint notes of a radio playing Arabic music.

The fact that he was alive was not good news. It meant they wanted him for something. Torture? Interrogation? And he didn't know who they were. A rival Christian faction? PLO? PFLP? Druze? Amal? Armenians? The Red Knights? Syrian intelligence? Iranians? Communists? KWP? Japanese Red Army? Those last were behind that mass shooting in Lod Airport a few years back. Or Marxists? Benny hoped it wasn't Marxists. His cousin Ezra was a Marxist and he was a right pain in the ass. Well, he was still alive, so that was something, anyway. He needed a piss. The car didn't stop. After a while Benny pissed himself. He didn't feel bad about it. He was fucked if he was going to hold it in.

The sound of distant fighting intensified and he heard explosions, too close for comfort, more gunshots, people shouting. Then then car slowed down and finally came to a stop. The engine idled.

When they opened the boot Benny got a glimpse of unvarnished brick walls, men with their faces wrapped in keffiyehs, a few clouds in the sky and stars. But the stars were whited out by the light of explosions. The sky above Beirut was like a fireworks display on Independence Day celebrations. But Benny didn't think anyone was celebrating.

They pulled him out, and one of them said, 'Ya kalb!' when he smelled Benny's piss. The pushed him roughly on the ground, dusty, some empty buckets lying around, empty sacks, a leaking tap in the corner of the yard. Armed men everywhere. They dragged him in, to what was once a villa, past a living room still stuffed with sofas and cushions. A radio set sat in the middle of the room manned by a team of two, sending out signals. A man who must have been the commander stood waiting. He gestured at Benny.

'Shu?' he said.

Benny's captor said, 'Israil.'

A wide smile spread across the commander's face, then he spat on the carpet. He nodded to a set of stairs.

Benny knew he was fucked then. They knew who he was, what he was. And they let him see their faces. He wasn't getting out of there unless it was in a coffin.

They dragged him down to the basement. There was a door and more guards. A guard unlocked the door. They pushed him in, cut the ropes and shut the door on him.

The lock turned, and that was that.

'Kus em em emak,' Benny said, with feeling.

'That's no way to talk about our hosts' mothers,' a voice said in the dark. At least that's what Benny thought it said. His Arabic wasn't up to much, though he'd picked up bits from the people he worked with.

People like Pierre, who fucking *stepped* on him, running to save his own life.

'Falastin?' the voice said. It sounded curious more than alarmed by Benny's appearance. 'Masihiun? Iran? Red Army?'

It said the last one in English.

'La, la,' Benny said. No, no. 'No Arabic,' he said at last, in English.

'Parlez vous Francais?'

'Comsi comsa,' Benny said, then thought better of it. 'Non,' he said.

'English?'

'A little English,' Benny said in English.

'Me, too,' the voice said. 'A little English.'

A match flared in the dark. The speaker lit a candle. There were no windows in the basement. There was a bucket of dirty water to one side. The speaker was an older man, his hair silver at the sides. He sat on a chair and wasn't bound.

'You?' Benny said. 'Lebanon?'

'No, no,' the man said, laughing at though the idea was absurd. 'Alexei Ivanovich, Consular Attaché, Soviet embassy. Call me Alexei, please.

'This doesn't look like the Soviet embassy,' Benny said.

'That it is not, sadly,' Alexei Ivanovich said.

'You're a prisoner?' Benny said.

'You are very observant, Mr...'

'Benny,' Benny said.

'Mr Benny. I find you quite intriguing. You are not French, not an American, and not Lebanese. I would say Israeli, but you are not in uniform, and they are hard to kidnap. One of the foreign mercenaries working for the Phalangists? Italian?'

'Israel,' Benny said bitterly, and heard Alexei's sudden draw of breath.

'Ah... They know?'

'They know,' Benny said.

'Then you are out of luck, my friend,' Alexei said.

'What are they going to do with us?' Benny said.

'Do?' Alexei said. 'Nothing. We are only useful as hostages against our respective governments. They will keep you alive if they can, but if not, a corpse still has a value of exchange.'

Benny thought of Sigali, who was three. She'd be asking where Daddy was. His wife knew better than to ask questions. But she'd know something was wrong when he failed to come back. At that moment he felt scared deep inside. Not for himself but for Sigali, for his family. Everything he did was for them, or so he told himself. Benny was honest enough not to have too many illusions.

What he did he did for the money, but money was only good when you could spend it. He'd promised Sigali a Barbie doll, just like in America, one where you could brush her hair and had all the accessories, even though his wife said she was too small and what if she tried to swallow the tiny handbag or something?

'I have a wife, a little girl at home,' he said miserably.

'Then they will miss you,' Alexei said. 'Do you play cards?'

'Cards?' Benny said.

'I have a pack of cards. Do you know Rummy?'

'Sure,' Benny said, 'I know Rummy. But I'm going to sleep. I had a very long day.'

'It is good to sleep when you can,' Alexei said.

'Where are we?' Benny said.

'Somewhere outside Beirut, I think,' Alexei said. 'They moved me a couple of times already. I never see where.'

'Where did they kidnap you?'

'Beirut. I stopped at a kiosk to buy cigarettes. Do you have any cigarettes?'

Benny took out the flat-pack, crumpled in his pocket. He shook two out. Alexei lit them from the candle and passed one back to Benny. The smoke filled the windowless basement but Benny didn't mind.

Alexei took a long, grateful drag.

'What will happen to you?' Benny said.

Alexei shrugged. 'The Soviet Union does not negotiate with kidnappers,' he said.

'So, then what?'

'So I wait. Maybe I live. Maybe I die.'

'That seems very Russian,' Benny said, and Alexei laughed. 'And you, Israeli? What will happen to you?'

Benny said, 'We're too stubborn to die.'

'Everyone dies,' Alexei said. 'In Lebanon, everyone dies. I wish they'd sent me to Cuba instead. This country was fun once. Nightclubs, good beaches. Now, all this shit.'

They smoked the rest of their cigarettes in silence.

***

Benny slept fitfully. His head hurt and his trousers dried unpleasantly on him. There were constant booms in the night, the sound of sporadic gunfire in the distance, times where the ground shook and he wondered if he'd be buried down here alive, in this basement, in this prison. When he woke it was as dark as before. He groped around for the bucket and pissed. He could hear the guards on the other side of the door. Alexei snored. Benny felt the walls but they were solid. He tried to sleep again but couldn't.

After a while the door opened and a guard shoved food at them and shut the door again. An electric light came on overhead. A bare light bulb, dangling from a wire.

'They must have turned the generator on,' Alexei said. 'Good morning.' He nodded affably to Benny.

They ate with their hands. A pita each, and something out of a can, unheated, that Benny didn't even recognise. He just shovelled it in and swallowed. He figured he needed his strength. He drank the dirty water they'd provided them. After the meal he and Alexei shared Benny's last cigarette. It had only been a day, less than a day since he'd left home and gone to that meeting with Cohen. But it felt like a lifetime.

'What does a consular attaché do, anyway?' Benny said. 'Are you a spy?'

'Sure,' Alexei said. 'We're all spies, don't you know?' He looked at Benny closely. 'What do you do?'

'Import-export,' Benny said.

'Aha.'

They played Rummy. Benny lost twice.

'If I were a spy,' Alexei said, 'I might make a pitch to recruit you.'

'Recruit me? For what?' Benny said.

Alexei shrugged. 'If we get out again, who knows? The Soviet Union likes to keep a close eye on the Middle East.'

'You don't let the Jews out,' Benny said. 'Like that guy Sharansky, the refusenik.'

'Should he not be happy in Russia?' Alexei said.

'And you support Syria,' Benny said.

'Syria is a socialist nation,' Alexei said. 'We support socialism, wherever it may be. You would blame us for that? Doesn't America do the same for their interests?'

'I don't know,' Benny said. 'I'm not very political.'

'Everything is political,' Alexei said.

They played another round of Rummy. Benny won. Alexei said, 'We could pay you, of course.'

'Pay me for what?'

'For information.'

Benny laughed.

'I like you, Alexei,' he said. 'But I don't think either of us is getting out of here alive.'

Alexei shrugged. 'We do, or we don't,' he said.

'Are you really a spy?' Benny said.

Alexei shook his head. 'Like James Bond,' he said. 'No. I handled visas, cultural events, that kind of stuff.'

The door opened without warning. The guards came and got Benny. They hit him a couple of times, just because, then dragged him up the stairs. Benny didn't complain.

He saw their commander in the living room of the villa. The guards pushed Benny onto the sofa. It was still covered in linoleum.

'Shalom,' the commander said.

'Excuse me?' Benny said.

The commander laughed. When he spoke it was in perfect Hebrew.

'I'm from Haifa,' he said. 'I studied in the Hebrew University in Jerusalem. I had a lot of Jewish friends.'

'So what happened?' Benny said.

'The Six Day War happened,' the commander said. 'And suddenly I didn't have too many friends. One night I crossed the border into Jordan, and the next day I was in a training camp.'

'So you're a Palestinian,' Benny said.

'Yeah.'

'PLO?' Benny said.

'No,' the man said. 'We're a new group. But it doesn't matter to you.'

'No,' Benny said. 'I suppose it doesn't. What are you going to do with me?'

'Nothing,' the man said. 'Keep you as insurance. Be good and you won't be hurt. Try anything and we'll keep you as a corpse.'

'Seems fair,' Benny said.

The commander looked at him closely.

'You're pretty calm,' he said.

'No, no,' Benny said. 'I'm shitting myself.'

'Try not to do that,' the man said. 'There's a bucket for that.' He lit a cigarette. 'Want one?'

'Sure.'

The commander passed him the lit cigarette and lit another.

'Why were you meeting with Tony Malik?' he said.

'Does it matter?' Benny said. 'Tony Malik's dead.'

The man considered the question.

'Does it matter?' he said. He blew smoke in the still room. The windows were boarded over and it was dark. 'It does,' the man decided. 'It matters. He was the second most powerful Christian commander, an ally of Israel. You work for Mossad?'

'Fuck, no,' Benny said.

'But they let you in.'

'Maybe. I don't know.'

Benny didn't know what to tell him, what not to tell him. He figured he was dead either way. But the man didn't seem bothered.

'You don't know,' he said, 'because you are just a drug dealer. Because the Zionist Entity is a parasitic state that feeds on the suffering that drugs brings. They profit from it. And Tony Malik, Allah rest his soul, was one of the biggest drug lords in Lebanon until my men took him out.'

Benny smoked. Benny nodded.

'You profit from it too,' he said softly.

'We profit from the trade only to fund our war!' the man said.

'That's what the Christians told me, too,' Benny said.

'Maybe they meant it too,' the man said.

'Maybe we can make a deal,' Benny said. 'I came here for a seller, I don't care who it is. You control the flow of drugs out of the Bekaa? Great, I'll buy from you. If you will let me go I will—'

'Arrange the money?' the man smiled. 'Everyone has a hand in the rice bowl of the Bekaa,' he said. 'Christians, PLO, Druze...

With the Syrians taking the biggest portions for themselves. You think we can't find buyers? We have men everywhere. In Europe, in South America. This war has sent our people across the world like dandelion seeds. But they do not forget where they come from, and what they owe. No,' he said. 'You're not going free.'

'You didn't ask me my name,' Benny said desperately. It bothered him, that the man didn't even ask him that. He felt despair, for a moment he thought he could talk his way out of this.

'We know your name,' the man said. 'Mr Rubenstein.'

Benny didn't react. They had good information, he realised. Someone who knew about the meet, about the arrangements. Probably someone inside the Phalangist militia. The only thing they missed was that Rubenstein would send him in his place.

Fucking Rubenstein, Benny thought. And he swore that if he ever got out of there, one day he'd let Rubenstein have it, even if he had to wait years.

'You will send word?' Benny said.

'About you? Why?' the man said. 'The people who sent you already know. As this unholy invasion continues we will have more hostages, and more power over the Zionist Entity. If you are lucky, we might swap you for our own imprisoned men in a year or two.'

Benny just nodded dumbly. He had no more spirit left to fight. He felt hollow inside, useless. He wasn't even a person. Just an uncashed cheque kept in a safe.

'Good,' the man said, seeing that. 'You'll do fine.'

He nodded to the guards. They came and hit Benny a couple more times and then dragged him down the stairs again and tossed him back in the cellar.

The door locked.

'Well?' Alexei said.

Benny just shook his head. 'He was almost *nice* about it,' he said. 'That's the worst part.'

'Daoud? He's not a bad guy, for a kidnapper,' Alexei said.

'And he knew everything.'

'That you're a drug dealer, you mean?' Alexei said. Benny looked up sharply. Alexei's eyes twinkled in the candlelight.

'What else would you be?' Alexei said. 'This is what Lebanon *is*, Benny. The market to which all come. I've seen people like you every day during my posting here. Arabs, Jews, Corsicans, South Americans, Galicians, Irish, Turks… The more this country makes the more the buyers want, and the more the buyers buy the more everyone buys guns. Guns before food, Benny. That is the rule in Lebanon. And the drugs buy the guns, they buy the big houses, the nice cars, the government posts, the police and the army, what is left of them. When you see a Mercedes drive down the street, it was paid for with hashish. It is in the very air you breathe. You can smell it, can't you? It draws you like nectar draws a bee, and you are seduced and helpless before it.'

'It's just *hash*, Alexei,' Benny said. And, 'Do you know where I could buy some?'

Alexei laughed.

'Just walk out that door,' he said, pointing, 'and ask the first person you see.'

'I'll be sure to do that,' Benny said.

47

RIO

'Even a long day ends' – Alexei

They were not given food again that day. Benny tried to sleep but sleep came hard and the night was filled with bombings in the distance. He could hear more now. He heard dogs barking, he heard car engines when they came and went. He thought he heard a woman shouting, the bleating of a goat, gunshots, a radio playing Duran Duran's 'Save A Prayer'. In the night he heard Alexei get up and stumble in the dark. He hit the bucket and cursed, then squatted over it and defecated.

'I don't feel well,' Alexei said.

Benny got up. He lit the candle, which was burning low. In its light Alexei's face looked wan and old. Benny went to help him. He pulled him off and Alexei hung on to him. Benny led him back to his place on the floor and helped him down and sat down with him.

'Please, I do not want the light,' Alexei said. His forehead shone with sweat. 'I do not like to be seen like this.'

This personal vanity in the midst of their situation touched Benny. He got up and got a dirty cloth and carefully poured just a little of their water on it and went back. He mopped Alexei's face, the back of his neck.

'You're hot,' he said.

'I will be alright… in the morning,' Alexei said. 'The nights, they can be hard here.'

Benny heard the whistle of mortar in the sky outside. He said, 'They're hard out there, too.'

'That they are,' Alexei said. 'I wish I was back with my Olga in Moscow. We have a little apartment not far from Dzerzhinsky Square. It is many stairs to reach it but it is ours, and Olga…' He fell quiet.

'She is very pretty?' Benny said.

'Ugly as sin,' Alexei said, and tried to laugh. 'But she loves me.'

'It is good to have someone who loves you,' Benny said.

'This is the problem with you Jews,' Alexei said. 'With everyone in this place. You love too much. You love the land, and hate each other.'

'That we do,' Benny said. He kept applying the damp cloth to Alexei's skin, and was relieved when he soon felt Alexei's temperature ease.

'If they come, you should stay… behind me,' Alexei said. 'I will… look after you.'

His eyes closed.

'Sure,' Benny said. 'I'll do that.'

'I'll… tell them.'

Alexei fell asleep. He started to snore. Benny sat with his back to the wall. He stared at the door to the cellar.

He wished he had a gun, so he could shoot them all.

In the morning they got another tray of food and some water. After they ate, Alexei seemed better. He said, 'I am sorry for the night. Sometimes they are hard.'

'They've kept you here long?'

Alexei shrugged. 'A month, I think. Maybe more. But it is all one long day. From when it starts, to when it ends.'

'How will it end?' Benny said.

Alexei shrugged.

'Even a long day ends,' he said philosophically.

They played more Rummy. Alexei told Benny of Moscow, how the buildings rose above you, how no one had more than another, and no one starved, and you were never far from a book of poetry or a hot samovar. He made it sound pretty. When Benny mentioned Stalin, Alexei just said, 'Stalin is dead,' and that was that. Benny told him of Tel Aviv, the sun, the girls. A city of beaches and white walled homes. Of freshly squeezed orange juice and lamb fat on the grill. Of the movie theatres that were just like in Europe, of the coffee houses and discotheques.

'It sounds bourgeois,' Alexei said, but he smiled as he said it.

And Benny said, 'But it is bourgeois,' and they both laughed.

Outside the invasion continued, but Benny had no idea how it was going. Maybe Israel will save him, he thought. They'd crossed the border to bring order and stability to Lebanon, to end the reign of the PLO, to establish the Christian leader, Bachir Gemayel, as president, to have, as Begin promised them, 'forty years of peace'. They'd crossed the border for all those reasons or none of the above. Benny wasn't sure exactly why. The official reason was the assassination attempt on the Israeli ambassador in London. But everyone knew it was just an excuse.

Maybe, sometimes, wars just built up until they had to happen. And maybe he'll be rescued, Benny thought. Maybe he'll be some kind of hero when they find him, when Israeli tanks roll over that neighbourhood and liberate it from the… whoever it needed liberating from. Maybe he'll be in the papers. Just like Oshri and Midget were always in the paper with famous people, generals and singers, before they went to prison. Just like Yehezkel Aslan was now, Aslan with his restaurant where all the famous people came, Aslan with his hold on the drugs and gambling in Tel Aviv. That fucking guy.

Benny didn't want to be in any papers. Benny just wanted to do business. Why was it so hard to just do business in this world? You bought stuff, you sold stuff. No one had to die. And if they had to die they had to die, so you made it simple. Not like this shit. Maybe Lebanon was just a turf war that got out of control. What did he know. He had no idea who these people were. He just wanted to buy a tonne or two of decent hashish.

There was no more food and no one came. He heard the guards outside the door. They were always there. The bucket was filling up. Did they ever empty it? They had to. He pissed in it. The smell was awful. Alexei was sitting in the chair. Benny paced. He stank. His clothes were dirty. He realised he had blood on them, maybe Tony Malik's. He paced.

'Stop pacing,' Alexei said. He sat in the chair staring at the door.

But Benny couldn't stop pacing. His skin itched. His muscles ached from the hard floor. There wasn't enough air. He was hungry. Alexei stiffened in the chair.

'What is it?' Benny said.

'Hush.'

Benny stilled. He didn't hear anything. Then he heard shouts, cut short by gunfire. He heard running overhead. It was all muted. He heard the guards behind the door. Then he heard two bursts of machine gun fire and two bodies fall to the floor. That thud of impact.

He heard someone move behind the door, quietly. The key moved in the lock. Benny looked desperately for a place to hide but there was nowhere to hide. He looked for a weapon. He would fight them. They won't take him just like that, he thought. He would try and kill them, maybe he could kick one before they shot him in the head.

The door opened. Benny did nothing. A man in grey fatigues stood in the doorway with a submachine gun. Benny raised his hands. Alexei stayed sitting in the chair.

The man looked at Alexei.

'Comrade Ivanovich?'

'Da,' Alexei said.

The man nodded. He pointed the submachine gun casually at Benny.

'Nyet, ne strelyai,' Alexei said. He got up. Looked at Benny almost apologetically. He patted him on the shoulder.

'Ostavte ego,' he said to the man with the gun. The man shrugged and turned to leave. Alexei followed him.

Benny stared after them. He heard muted voices, a vehicle starting up in the distance, then nothing but silence.

After a while he took a step, and then another. He had to climb over the corpses of the guards and up the stairs.

In the living room the radio set was still running. Benny heard echoey voices on the line, repeating code words he didn't know, asking for a reply that wasn't going to come. Several men lay on the floor in pools of blood. They had been shot quickly and expertly in the chest and head and dropped where they were.

The commander lay on the sofa. There was a neat hole in his forehead. It might have been the sole neat thing in the entire country, Benny thought. The commander lay on the sofa and the sofa was still covered in the linoleum sheet and so, if the family who owned the house ever came back, they could use their sofa just as good as new. But Benny didn't think the people who owned the house were ever coming back.

He saw no one alive.

He didn't know what to do.

He was free.

He stepped outside.

The yard, a car still in it. The wheels were shot out. It was day. The sun hurt his eyes after the gloom of his prison. A chicken darted into a break in the grey brick wall.

Who the fuck *were* those guys? he thought.

Everything felt so quiet.

He went back inside. He took a pistol off the dead commander, a second one from one of the fallen men. He searched for ammo. Looking for a bag, he found the kitchen. He fell on the bread and cheese, stuffing his face. Then his guts gave out and he half-ran half-hopped but it couldn't be helped, and he dropped his trousers and shat out his guts on the kitchen floor.

When it was done he washed his hands in the tap. The water still ran. There was no soap.

It was still so quiet. He found a backpack, stuffed it with the remaining food, magazines for the guns. He went to the radio set. Turned the dial, searching for Israeli signals, anything in Hebrew. He thought of trying to call out, but what would he tell them?

It was so quiet. Why was it so quiet?

He stepped outside. Blinked against the light. Then he saw shadows fleet against the sun, like birds but faster.

They flew over in silence. The sound followed too late.

Things fell from the air, from the planes.

An explosion threw up a house. The ground shook. Benny fell. Bricks and frames flew in the air. He curled into a ball, covered his head with his hands.

He heard the planes come back a second time.

Benny screamed.

Another house exploded. The planes strafed bullets. They whistled past like awful mechanical bees. Benny screamed but no one could hear him. The roof of the house behind him caved in. The planes came back a third time. Benny hid behind the car. The planes dropped bombs. Clouds of ash and flames rose high, blooming like flowers all around him.

Benny screamed. The planes climbed high and sped away.

In moments they were gone.

48

CARELESS MEMORIES

'You are a long way from home' – *Uncle Ali*

When Benny stepped out into the streets his ears rang and it was no longer quiet. A man wiped the frame of a collapsed car with a dirty cloth, over and over. The car had no windows, no doors, no wheels anymore, but he kept cleaning it. A cat, skinny and starved, ran under Benny's foot. He saw a little hand stick out of the rubble of a collapsed building, saw a woman trying to reach her only to be pulled away, to be pushed down the road, as more and more people emerged, some carrying bags, some carrying nothing, many carrying children in their arms, others pulling them behind them. Women in high heels and expensive dresses, men in rags, men in suits, men in fatigues, some carrying guns, most unarmed. Those who could find a car found one and drove away, packing as many as they could inside, but there were not many cars.

The rest walked. Their faces were stained with dust. Many were wounded. Men, women, children, they followed the road, between the ruined houses, past toppled apartment blocks, shops where the shutters had been pressed down like paper. Benny stood there, unmoving, unsteady, until someone pushed him, shouted, 'Imshi! Imshi!' and went past him, startling him out of his stupor.

Benny walked like the others. He took one step and then another, one foot on the ground and then the next. It was all he could do. He realised he was invisible among this diaspora, not knowing who or what they were: Shi'ite or Sunni, Christian or Druze, or a mix, in this town whose name he didn't know. In the distance smoke bellowed, a bombardment that now didn't seem to cease at all, that might have been there all along in his captivity. But it was far, and he thought maybe it was Beirut.

If so he was a little outside of town. Just enough to get away, perhaps. He followed the road. They reached the outskirts of town when there were shots fired. He couldn't see where they came from. A woman went down and didn't get up, and the little girl with her knelt by the body, crying, 'Mama! Mama!' but someone, another woman, came up to her and grabbed her arm, pulling her along. They left the dead woman behind and walked on, dust rising before them from the feet of the others ahead, and all the time the fire burned and the smoke rose on the horizon. More fighter jets went past. Once Benny saw, in the distance, a column of tanks drive against the fading sun, and he broke free and started to run towards it, and a man grabbed him, shouting and pointing, and the tanks went on and Benny kept marching, on and on, the most alone he'd ever been, until there were no thoughts left in him, and even the music that he loved was wiped clean from his mind.

The sun set but the night was lit by fires, and on they marched. They came to a place in the road where corpses hung from ropes over the trees and they kept on marching. A kilometre farther and there were shots fired again and two people died and one was hit in the chest and fell, and they left them there and kept going, and Benny, in a moment of lucidity, wondered who they were: were they lawyers, were they plumbers, were they cooks or cleaners, shopkeepers, teachers, poets, painters? That he couldn't know. He didn't know these people, their language, their loves and hates, but he knew their fear. He felt it. And he walked on, and on, not knowing where, not daring to stop, not daring to even think there was a destination in mind.

They came to a village that was bombed and saw bodies in the rubble and walked on, saw more tanks in the distance, somewhere, the night lit up, and mountains far ahead, and on they went, and Benny saw a road sign, pointing west and east, with inscriptions in Arabic and English. One direction said *Beirut* and the other *Damascus*.

On and on they went. He wanted to stop. He could not go on,

not any farther. At one point he collapsed and lay in the dirt and a woman came and pulled him up and told him something. Benny just nodded, mute, and kept on walking. The woman had a little girl with her and when the girl could not walk Benny carried her a while, and then the woman took her, and when hidden snipers shot at them again they ran and hid, leaving the dead behind, pressing on, away, away.

They came to a temperate valley and Benny saw fields, and the air smelled clean and he could not see the fires. There were few people left now, they had split north and south through this valley, and Benny couldn't see the woman or her child anymore, and he wondered if he had dreamed them. He came to a stone villa standing in a field and there stood men with guns and looked at him. They raised their guns to shoot.

'Israel,' Benny said desperately, 'Israel.'

The men looked at each other and didn't lower the guns. But they didn't fire.

One of them came closer, prodded him.

'Ata medaber ivrit?' he said.

Benny stared at him, not believing he was hearing Hebrew. Not knowing if this was friend or foe, and they could shoot him, or sell him for a hostage, or let him free. He didn't care, not anymore.

'I want to buy some hash,' he said.

Then he collapsed, and the world became a pit and he tumbled inside it.

'No, don't get up,' a voice said in English. It was the rough voice of a heavy smoker. Benny could tell even without the smell of smoke in the room. He sat up and opened his eyes, then winced at the pain in his feet and thighs.

'You walked from Beirut?' the man said. He scratched his beard with the barrel of his pistol.

'Not Beirut,' Benny said. His throat hurt. 'But not far, I think.'

'You are a long way from home, my friend,' the man said. 'I am Ali Khalil, but you can call me Uncle Ali.' He waved the gun. 'Or, you know, just Uncle, if you prefer. That's what everyone calls me.'

'Why is that?' Benny said.

'I'm like an uncle to everyone,' Khalil said, as though it were obvious.

'You know who I am?' Benny said.

'You know who *I* am?' Khalil said.

Benny shook his head, which was a mistake. His head hurt. He said, 'No idea, but since I'm still alive, and not in a cell, I'd say you have some sympathy to my side. I'd also guess you're wealthy, because I'm betting the men I met were working for you. So they found me and they brought me here. And now you're trying to decide what to do with me. As for what you do, I don't know. You grow pot?'

Uncle Ali laughed. 'This is the Bekaa Valley,' he said, 'everyone grows pot.'

'So, what, you're a Christian?' Benny said.

'La,' Uncle Ali said. 'Shi'ite.' He regarded Benny, put the gun in his lap and lit a cigarette.

'You want one?'

'Sure,' Benny said.

He took a drag. It hurt on his lungs and he coughed.

'I have no sympathy to Israel,' Uncle Ali said. 'My people have always been the most oppressed in Lebanon, and we will suffer more with this invasion, unless we fight. By rights I should sell you to the Syrians. They pay a good price.'

'So what's stopping you?' Benny said. Figuring this might be his last cigarette. Figuring he should enjoy it.

'I'm not in the business of being a Shi'ite,' Uncle Ali said. 'You're on my land now, and it is no one else's land. Not the government in Beirut, not the Party of God's, not the Syrians', either, much as accommodations had to be made with them. Anyone come to my land, they must come in peace or they will be met with bullets.'

'You sell drugs,' Benny said.

Uncle Ali drew on the cigarette. His fingers were stained with nicotine. 'Isn't this why you came, Benny Pardes?' he said.

Benny sat still.

'So you do know who I am,' he said.

'I make sure to know things,' Uncle Ali said. 'I heard of what happened with Tony Malik. Word was the Gemayels had him taken out, the Christians have been fighting each other for years.'

'It was some other squad,' Benny said. 'They wanted me for a hostage. There was a Russian guy, too.'

'I heard the Russian prisoners were all let go suddenly,' Uncle Ali said, and smiled again. 'You know anything about that?'

Benny shrugged. He looked for an ashtray and Uncle Ali passed him one. Benny said, 'Russians do as Russians are.'

'True,' Uncle Ali said.

'So?' Benny said. 'What happens now?'

'Can you walk?' Uncle Ali said.

'I can try.'

Benny swung himself out of bed. He stood up, held on to the bed for support, then straightened. His mouth tasted of ash and everything hurt, but he was alive, and what else mattered?

'Where are we going?' he said.

'Come, come. Let me show you around.'

Benny hobbled after Uncle Ali. Out of the room into a cool corridor, past doors and down stairs. The house solid, made of stone, weathered with age. On the ground floor a group of children sat in the large living room, assembling and disassembling M-16s. They didn't look up. Benny could smell cooking coming out of the kitchen. His stomach growled and Uncle Ali laughed.

'We will eat soon,' he promised. 'It is almost lunch time.'

Outside, Benny smelled lavender and roses. Several vehicles were parked in front of the villa, which sat alone in the midst of extensive fields. He saw the mountains rise on both sides, hemming the valley in between them. Chickens ran underfoot. He saw tractors and trailers, a couple of jeeps and an untethered plough. He saw barbed wire coils, bags of fertiliser and a forklift.

He took a deep breath. The air was clear. It was so quiet. For a moment he felt as though the past few days had been nothing but a dream. It felt so peaceful; it felt like paradise.

'Come,' Uncle Ali said, and he went to the doors of a large barn and threw them open. Benny went in with him.

It was dark inside and the walls were bare, but Benny didn't pay any attention to that. The only thing he saw were the piles of pure, fine, black hashish. They were everywhere, on the floor, against the walls, piles as high as Benny's waist; and along long wooden tables, young women with their heads and faces covered in tight scarves were sifting more powder, running their hands patiently over and over the giant sieves. Sacks of finished product piled up, one on top of the other, tied with string. The girls barely glanced Benny's way. The warehouse stretched, on and on.

'You said you wanted to buy some hash,' Uncle Ali said.

'I... yes.'

'This is hash.'

Benny swallowed. 'I can see that,' he said.

He could more than see it. He could breathe it. The dust was so fine it was in the air. It settled on his face, his clothes. He felt light-headed.

'It doesn't matter who you are in Lebanon,' Uncle Ali said. 'It doesn't matter if you're a Christian or a Muslim or a Druze. It doesn't even matter which ports you control, Beirut or Sidon or Tripoli, or what land routes you hold from here to those ports. You still have to come to the Bekaa. You still have to come *here*. You understand me, Benny?'

'I came,' Benny said.

Uncle Ali clapped him on the back. 'Then let's go to lunch,' he said. 'I don't like to keep my wife waiting. She gets angry if I'm late.'

Benny followed him out. He tried to brush the hashish dust off himself but it had stuck. They went back in the house, into the kitchen and to a long table laden with food. Children and their mothers and Ali's nephews and sons were all there. Benny sat down.

'Let's eat,' Uncle Ali said.

After lunch they discussed details.

'I need to get hold of my boss,' Benny said. 'Do you have a radio?'

'Why don't you use the phone?' Uncle Ali said.

'The phones work?' Benny said.

Uncle Ali shrugged. 'They work,' he said.

Benny tried the phone. The phone worked. He tried to place a call. How did you place an international call to an enemy country? Uncle Ali got on the phone to the operator. He said a few words. Benny tried to think. He gave them Rubenstein's phone number.

The phone rang. Uncle Ali passed the receiver to Benny. Benny waited. A familiar, cold voice came on the line.

'Yes?'

'It's me,' Benny said.

'Where the fuck have you been?' Rubenstein said.

'I'm coming home,' Benny said. 'Tell them I need a clear run. Blue pickup truck, no plates.'

'I'll send Cohen.'

Rubenstein hung up. Benny stared at the phone.

'Asshole,' he said.

He went outside with Uncle Ali.

'You understand what will happen to you if you don't come back?' Uncle Ali said.

'Oh, I understand,' Benny said.

They stood and watched Uncle Ali's men load the bags onto the truck.

'Here,' Uncle Ali said. He tossed Benny the keys.

'You're just giving me a tonne and a half of hashish,' Benny said, the idea still nebulous in his mind. It seemed fantastical, but then what didn't, in Lebanon?

'And lending you my truck,' Uncle Ali said. 'I like this truck.'

'I will get it back to you,' Benny said, 'and enough money to buy whatever new car you want.'

'Just get me my money,' Uncle Ali said.

They shook hands.

'That border will be open for a long while yet, I think,' Benny said. 'Open border, easy minds.'

They shook hands.

The men finished loading. They covered the back of the pickup truck with tarp and secured it with ropes. Benny climbed into the driver seat. He put in the key. The thrum of the engine starting was like a cry of freedom. Benny put the truck in gear. He waved to Uncle Ali. Uncle Ali's men stood there with their guns and watched him drive off. Benny hit the accelerator and sped down the dirt track, throwing up a cloud of dust. He hit the road south.

Tanks and armoured cars passed him on the road, all going the other way. Benny honked and waved. The soldiers stared at him in bemusement. He flashed them a V.

As he drove he saw marks of the battles that took place here. Ruined houses, a burned tank lying on its side, fields bombed into desolation. At another site he saw a small TV crew, and a woman taking pictures. Benny slowed down to watch and the woman aimed her camera at him.

'Sylvie Gold, *This World*,' she said.

The shutter clicked, clicked again. Benny turned his face. He hit the gas again.

Farther along the road a jeep came driving towards him, and it slowed when the driver spotted him. The driver signalled. It was Nir, his escort to the meet with the Maliks.

Benny gave him the finger. Nir did a U-turn and followed Benny and the truck. When they came to an army roadblock Nir drove ahead and cleared the way. The soldiers let them through. There was one other roadblock and then a clear road and a clear sky, and when he came at last to the border post Cohen stood there, waiting.

Cohen opened the gate and Benny drove through.

'Welcome to Israel,' Cohen said.

PART EIGHT

HAVA

1985, Tel Aviv

49

MELA

'All this fuss' – Hava

Hava washed the dishes. The water was hot, scolding the way a mother scolded. She scrubbed and scrubbed the plate, the tips of her fingers white where they pressed against the china, the palm flesh red.

Her wedding ring was in the soap dish on the counter. She'd picked the kids up from school earlier. Now the boy was outside and the girl was watching television, *Krovim Krovim* maybe, judging by the laughter track. It was hot outside but the apartment felt cool.

Hava scrubbed, rinsed, put the plate onto the drying board and picked a coffee cup. Nobody called on the phone. The birds whistled outside the window. Cars went past on the road below. She could hear the boys kicking the football outside, *whack, whack* against the wall. She wondered if there was anything in the newspapers.

Ehud was away again. He was always away. The kids saw him more on the television than at home. He was always interviewing someone important. He was always on the television. Well, he did what he had to. He worked. She remembered how handsome he was when they met. He had seemed so sophisticated. And he was besotted with her. She looked good, too. She always wore sunglasses. And she'd smiled a lot. Her mother always told her to smile.

She scrubbed the coffee cup. When did she get up that

morning? Six-thirty, maybe? Made breakfast for the kids, took them to school, then drove to work. It felt good to be at work. She liked working. She liked the hush of the bank, the air conditioning, the crisp suit she wore. She liked to dress nice. Money had a whisper to it, an air that was like, she tried to think of what she meant. Like when you were a kid in the library, maybe, that hush of books, the soft tread of the librarian, that book smell. Money wasn't like that, it smelled different and the hush of it was of a different pitch. Maybe like when you put a seashell to your ear, like the boy liked to do, and then hear the faint cry of the ocean far away. Like waves trapped in a seashell. That's what it was like.

She liked it. She liked the tread of her heels on the hard floor of the bank. The spray of perfume she always put on before leaving the apartment. The perfume lingered, followed her. It made an impression. You had to look and smell right. To give the right impression. She loved crossing the lobby and going behind the glass window, the safety of it, her and the world separated by glass. She liked counting out the money and filling the forms, the filing too. She liked the whisper of the pen across the paper. When she was at the bank she wasn't anyone's mother, she wasn't anyone's wife. She was in a world apart, a world that was made for her, where she mattered in a different way.

She even liked the customers. Every customer had a story and a face to go with that story. You could tell so much about a person by the numbers in a column, their incomings and outgoings, their profits and loss.

Take Mela Malevsky, for instance. When she first saw Mela across her desk, when the older woman sat down and folded her hands over her handbag in her lap and looked at Hava and smiled, you could see in her eyes and in every line etched in her face that she'd lived.

Mela spoke English with an accent. She didn't speak much Hebrew but that was fine with Hava. Mela was visiting from New York and she wanted to put money into her new account. She was thinking of investing, she told Hava. She wasn't shy with it but she still seemed a little unsure. She wanted to put back into the country. Into Israel. She was planning to visit often. Her husband was a dealer in pearls. She had three children, three grandchildren too, she showed Hava their pictures, smiling proudly but a little self-consciously. She was such a nice woman, they had really connected that first time, and Hava helped her with the transaction and then, with a little regret, said goodbye to the client as she left.

She washed the coffee cup and put it on the drying board. The *whack! Whack!* of the football outside. Kids shouting. A car honked in the distance. The girl laughed in front of the television. Hava picked up another plate to clean.

She'd got used to seeing Mela when she came to visit. She always stopped at the bank. She kept quite a lot of money there really. They always talked, learned more about each other. Mela was very impressed that Hava's husband was so famous, a journalist, on the television. And Hava just felt a connection with the older woman. Something she couldn't quite articulate. She didn't have many friends. Family friends, yes, couples friends or her husband's friends. But not so much just for her. Eventually she suggested going for a coffee and, why not? Her life didn't revolve around the bank. She sat with Mela at a café, she was still working for the bank in Jerusalem then, and they had talked for hours, and laughed a lot. Mela never talked about the Holocaust, about what happened to her there.

She came to Israel two or three times a year, usually. Sometimes she brought little presents from New York. Small, but tasteful. A new perfume for Hava, one that smelled of America, not Israel. A scarf. Ehud was always taking off somewhere like New York or Paris, there was some talk of sending him to America but he said it was punishment for being so opposed, publicly, to the idea of a peace accord with the Arabs. He just didn't believe in it. He was a good husband. A good father. A good man. She told herself that. He was a public man.

She told Aviva that. Aviva laughed. Aviva always laughed. Aviva laughed a lot.

Aviva said, 'All men are bastards, even my one, and he's a poodle.'

Aviva was her best friend. Why was she thinking about Aviva now? She scrubbed the plate but it still wasn't clean. She put more soap on. Her hands were so raw but she didn't even feel it. She kept scrubbing.

Aviva said, 'This friend of yours, she sounds nice.'

For a long time Hava felt as though she and Aviva were like two children born together and separated by some malevolent force since childhood, yet somehow they found each other again. They had lived together in the same block of flats in Jerusalem. Hava worked in the bank and Ehud for the television and the kids were small and Aviva lived in the block with her own daughter and her own husband and they started talking and then spending more time together.

Aviva wasn't pretty, not like people said Hava was pretty, or at least glamorous, but there was something about her. Aviva was like a woman people don't notice but then can't not notice, once they'd realised. Once she'd let them. She could move so quietly through the world and yet upset it when she wanted to. She worked in a pharmacy she owned with her husband, but the business wasn't doing so well. She didn't like to talk about it, she said.

'Let's not talk about money,' she's said.

But Hava loved money, it was her job, the moving it and changing it and putting it here and putting it there. And Aviva always did talk about money, even as she protested, how the pharmacy wasn't doing well, how it was hard to pay the suppliers, how she would need to make a plan. They talked about investments, which was something Hava was really into now. The Tel Aviv Stock Exchange was really exciting just then. People were talking about new technologies, telephones you could put in your car, computers you could have in your home.

She started putting some money into stocks. Only a little at first, then a little bit more. Taking a chance. Risking her money. It was so thrilling. In the mornings she'd make the kids breakfast and take her Valium and take them to school and then go to work and then come home and pick them up from school and make dinner and help with their homework and clean and wash and give them their bath and make sure they brushed their teeth and say good night and kiss them to sleep and watch television with a glass of wine, sometimes even with Ehud, who liked to watch himself on TV.

Hava said, 'Maybe one day I'll be on TV.'

Ehud said, 'What do you need that rubbish for? You're perfect just as you are.'

But in between she'd play the stock exchange. She went up, she went down. She put a little bit more in. Then a little bit more again. There was no harm.

Aviva and her husband had to sell the pharmacy. They weren't paying the suppliers. The suppliers all threatened to sue. Aviva did something, she was hazy on the details, but it made them stop. Some sort of arrangement. Hava didn't really press her. Aviva had a way of getting out of things. She got by. She was scrappy. She was stealing money from the suppliers, maybe. Borrowing, she said. When they found out, they wanted to call the police.

'So why didn't they?' Hava said.

Aviva said the suppliers were stealing money from the government. Everyone was taking so she was taking too, that was all. She said she told them it's better not to involve the police. They agreed. So it went away quietly, but Aviva and her husband still had to sell the pharmacy to pay back some of the money.

Well, it was a minor thing. So you borrowed some money. So what? She paid it back. Hava admired Aviva. She didn't let the world push her around. She played it at its own game. Hava wished she could be like that. They couldn't be more different, really. It was nice to meet up with Mela the next time she came to visit. She was thinking of investing quite a lot of money. Did Hava have any ideas? Hava admitted she'd been playing the stock exchange. Her own money, she said. She'd been doing very well. Very well. But she didn't push it. She watched Mela's bank balance grow with each visit.

She needed more soap. Which plate was she holding? The girl was watching television. The boy outside, the football going *whack! Whack!* against the wall. She'd lost her train of thought. Would Ehud call? Will he be home tonight? She rinsed the plate and put it away. Aviva hadn't called.

She thought – which of them had brought along the rolling pin?

She wished the radio was on. She should turn on the radio, listen to something nice. Arik Einstein, maybe. She used to like Arik Einstein. Well, everyone did. But she didn't anymore, not since the thing. But maybe there'd be something else on.

She should turn on the radio and find out. But her hands were wet. She was always worried about touching anything electric with wet hands. She could turn off the tap and dry her hands but there were still dishes in the sink, there were always dishes.

She didn't have big dreams. She scrubbed up well, like they said. She kept Ehud company when he went to functions. She knew people. For a moment she thought of the man she was seeing every now and then. He was a member of the Knesset, a politician. He had a family too. What they had worked for both of them. She was sure Ehud had women on the side too. Why couldn't she have someone on the side? It wasn't complicated, she and the man. Just bodies, and a little affection. She saw him in Jerusalem when she could. Sometimes he saw her when he came to Tel Aviv. Hotel rooms, always. In between the kids and the job. When they could.

She scrubbed the cutlery. A fork. A knife. It had been Ehud's car. Their car. She liked to drive. She told Mela not to play the stock exchange.

'Keep your money in the bank, where it's safe,' she said.

It was good advice. Mela listened to her.

Why was she thinking about Mela? She wished the kids would stop it with the ball already. Sometimes she wanted to scream. It was so hard being perfect. A perfect wife, a perfect mother. Always with the sunglasses on and the nice clothes and the trail of perfume. Someone who is seen. Aviva was the opposite of her. With that big hair and those big glasses with the thick lenses and a husband who wasn't on TV. Hava hadn't liked living in Jerusalem. She was from Tel Aviv, from the sun and the sea. Jerusalem was cold and so were the people. She was so glad to have met Aviva.

The teaspoon was smudged. Why wouldn't it come off? She rubbed and rubbed. She needed the Brillo pad. She reached under the sink. She was going to scrub it until it was clean. She couldn't stand mess. The tyres, they couldn't have kept the tyres. They were in the car. Hava was driving. She enjoyed driving. The sun had set and it was dark. Aviva and Mela were in the back seat together. Which one of them brought the rolling pin? She couldn't remember. It was a nice drive. Three friends together. Just to talk things over.

She should check her horoscope, Hava thought. Aviva got her into astrology. She was very interested in it, how the movement of the stars could influence your health, your wealth. At some point they both left the apartment block in Jerusalem. Aviva got a job at a warehouse, she was a manager, she was well liked there she said. Aviva was back in Tel Aviv. Mela came to visit twice a year, maybe three times.

She said, 'Hava, I think some of my money is missing.'

Ehud's car. Why was it Ehud's car and not her car or the family car? Ehud's car. Just like she was Ehud's wife. Did she even love him? He thought she and Aviva were lesbians for a while, that she was cheating on him with Aviva. Like women couldn't just be friends! He didn't like Aviva. He tried to forbid Hava from seeing her. Aviva, who was her best friend!

Aviva said, 'Mela, we need to resolve this situation.'

The windows were open in the car. A warm breeze. Few lights. Hava had driven without purpose. She found herself going towards the sea. Tel Baruch, which was not a good area, it was a place for prostitutes, at night the sands were haunted with lonely women and desperate men, anyone from army generals to yeshiva boys went to them, it was the quiet of the place, the isolation and privacy. Why did she choose Tel Baruch? It was a terrible place.

That's not true. She'd told Mela they'd go to the Mandarin. It was a nice hotel. They'd have a drink, all together. Work things out. So why did she go past it? Why did she turn down the dirt road to the sea?

'My money,' Mela said, 'what happened to my money?'

Hava wanted to explain to her friend. It was just a mistake in the accounts. Was it worth making such a fuss about everything? It would cause everyone problems. Surely Mela could be made to understand? Hava tried to be reasonable. The radio was on. Arik Einstein singing 'How Good You Came Home'. She loved his voice.

'Come on, Mela,' she said, 'we're all friends here.'

'My money is missing,' Mela said, 'it is a lot of money.'

It was what, fifty thousand dollars maybe? It was hardly a lot. Barely enough, even, Hava thought. She kept investing in the stocks but the money just kept vanishing into that hole, and eventually she had to tell Ehud, and they had to sell the flat. But it was still not enough. She tried to explain to Mela.

'Mela, listen, everything can be resolved, the important thing is to calm down—'

'Calm down?' Mela said. She was breathing hard. 'Hava, how can I calm down? I don't understand what happened, I trusted you—'

'Calm down!' Aviva said. Was it Aviva in the back seat that night? Was it Hava who drove? Who brought the rolling pin?

'Mela, it's not stealing, it's borrowing, we can work it out—'

Arik Einstein on the radio and the dark sea nearby where furtive men had hurried sex with women who took it for just a transaction, didn't Mela understand? It was just ins and outs, just profits and loss, numbers in a column that didn't mean anything.

'Mela, calm down—'

'Thieves, thieves!' Mela shouted.

Why did she have to shout? Hava hated shouting, everything in life had to be done quietly, you didn't want the neighbours talking, you always—

The rolling pin smashed into Mela's head.

It was just to calm her down. It wasn't… It was just a tap. Mela? Why did you have to check? Mela, why did you go behind my back? We don't want to worry the bank, Mela. It was just a bit of money. You gave me power of account, didn't you? And if you didn't, and Aviva wrote it instead, the signature still looked like yours. Enough to borrow. That is all.

'Such a bitch!' Aviva said.

She was breathing heavily. It was dark and quiet outside. Tel Baruch, with not even a prostitute in sight. Hava stopped the car. You had to do everything with purpose, this was always a rule with her. To be methodical, neat. Her father was a trader, it was such an embarrassment growing up. To be in trade. But she got out. She was a respectable woman, a society woman. So what if she and Ehud had problems? Everyone had problems. They had beautiful children. A lovely kitchen, with all the latest accessories. She scrubbed and scrubbed, her hands raw in the water.

'Quick,' she said, 'let's take her out.'

They pulled Mela out of the car. Was she still breathing? There was blood on the back seat. There was blood on the sand. Mela looked ridiculous sprawled across the sand. The waves lapping gently against the shore in the distance. That smell of the sea. The city seemed so far away. This was how it had always been, will always be. Three humans alone against a vast darkness. The stars were so cold in the skies overhead. She got into the car and started the engine again. This is how it had to be. Who was driving? Was it her or was it Aviva? Who brought the rolling pin? She reversed.

Whack! Whack! went the football outside.

She stopped, shifted gear. Ehud's car. Drove it forward.

Whack! went the ball outside.

And again. And again.

The girl was watching TV. She could watch it for hours. And the boy, she worried about the boy, he wasn't always… He wasn't always present, she thought. Such a loving family. When her father died, how did she feel? She barely spoke to her mother. She stopped the car and stepped out.

'What now?' Aviva said.

'She had an accident,' Hava said, 'she was run over, maybe a truck hit her. What was she doing wandering out here on her own?'

She felt sad. She liked Mela. Mela never talked about the Holocaust, about what happened over there. That silence of a generation. It was only fifty thousand dollars, she wanted to tell her. What difference did it make? Mela's husband was rich. Not like Hava's, all Ehud wanted to do was talk about Arabs on TV. He loved the cameras. He loved the sound of his own voice. How much she hated him sometimes.

'There's blood on the tyres,' Aviva said. 'I know a place.'

Hava hugged Aviva.

'All this fuss,' she said.

They got back in the car. Mela didn't look like nothing, lying there on the sand. Hava could see the lights from the nearby airfield in the distance. Only a short drive and they were back on the road. This never happened. This never happened. I know a place, Aviva said. Hava drove until they got there. They changed the tyres.

There were no more dishes in the sink. She stared at the suds of soap in the water. She shut the tap.

'Mummy?' The girl said. 'I'm bored.'

'Go play with your brother outside.'

Hava made herself a drink and took a Valium. She wondered if Ehud would be home. He did love her. Didn't he? Some prostitute found the body. At first she thought it was another prostitute who was killed by her pimp. Then the police identified the body. They informed Mela's family. Her husband in New York, the kids. Hava felt sorry for them. It was in the papers, but it wasn't big news. A dead tourist. It looked like an accident. It was sad, but such things happened. It didn't even stay in the papers a week.

The kids weren't kicking the ball outside anymore. Hava waited for the phone to ring, for anyone to call, but no one did. She looked at the family photos on the stand. They were so happy together, smiling for the camera.

50

THE QUESTION

'Let's not talk about it' – Aviva

'Listen, Aviva,' she said. 'Somebody called me.'

'Who?' Aviva said.

'I don't know. Some woman. She said she knew me from Mela Malevsky.'

'What did you say to her?'

'Nothing. I hung up. I got scared.'

'You don't have anything to be scared about, buba. Don't open your mouth. Don't say anything. It will go away. It's been months already. It was just a hit and run. The papers said so. Let's not talk about it. I read in the horoscope that today is a good day to make new plans. Who knows, you will meet a new man, you will fall madly in love, Hava.'

Hava laughed.

'I love you,' she said.

'How are the kids?'

'Good, good. You know. The same.'

'I know,' Aviva said. 'You know, I studied engineering. I could have been an engineer, Hava. Then Avi came along and I thought I should get married and start a family, so there was no point studying anymore, was there. I thought, Avi and Aviva, it was a good match.'

Aviva often talked about her aborted degree. How many languages she spoke. How she could have been someone of consequence. They both could. In another life, maybe. Not in Israel.

Not where men were men. But they had both made independent lives for themselves. Aviva with the pharmacy, Hava with the bank. They had dreams. They had things they both wanted. Hava said, 'Aviva, I'm scared.'

'Don't be scared, buba. Don't be anything. Let's go see a movie tomorrow. I miss you.'

'What's showing?' Hava said.

'We could go see *Out of Africa* with Meryl Streep. It's so romantic. We could talk then.'

'I need to ask Ehud.'

'You do *not* need to ask Ehud.'

'I mean, with the kids and all.'

'The kids can look after themselves.'

'Is there anything else on? I don't have the paper.'

She heard a rustle on the other end of the line. Was that Aviva looking in the newspaper? Was it something else, a scratch on the line? She was being paranoid. Aviva said, 'There's *Irit Irit*.'

'What's that?' Hava said.

'It's a new comedy. With that what's his name. Hanan Goldblatt from the children's shows. My daughter loves him.'

'Oh, him,' Hava said. 'I don't know. I heard stories.'

'What sort of stories?'

'Just stories.' The gossip from her husband's friends. 'He likes young women,' Hava said, 'and doesn't much care how he gets them, if you know what I mean.' She heard he invited young hopefuls to train with him then did things to them, the things he liked to do.

'Men are pigs,' Aviva said, but for once wasn't interested in gossip. 'The movie looks funny,' she said.

So they left it undecided. Hava didn't much like Israeli films. What was the point of watching Goldblatt when you had Meryl Streep and Robert Redford for the same price?

For a moment she indulged in a fantasy where it was her in Africa that Robert Redford was kissing. They'd look good together, she thought. But Aviva was still talking, and Hava had to go get the kids.

Nobody called. Nobody followed her. Nobody cared about

what happened, and sometimes she even convinced herself it never did. Which of them brought the rolling pin? Which of them drove? She took a Valium and downed it with a glass of Goldstar. She made dinner, put the kids to bed, watched Ehud on TV.

After the news she felt restless. She decided to go for a drive. The kids were asleep. Ehud would be back any minute. She went downstairs. He asked about the new tyres. What did she tell him? She couldn't remember. He wasn't that interested. She drove into the night. The streetlights shone bright. She saw young people going out. A young couple hand in hand. A group of teenagers going into the cinema. People sitting behind restaurant windows eating candlelit dinners. Why couldn't she have some of that? A semblance of freedom. When she was young, what did she dream of? Who did she want to be? She no longer knew, she was a prisoner, held hostage by Ehud and the kids. She put the radio on, looking for something good, something foreign. 'Money For Nothing', the Dire Straits. Where would she go? She didn't usually like to drive alone at night. She always worried something would happen. But she needed to get out. She needed to be free.

Maybe she could talk Ehud into going on holiday. A family getaway. Greece, maybe. The kids could have too much ice cream, she'd sunbathe on a lounger in a bikini with her sunglasses on, watch people and be seen. Have a cocktail to go with her Valium. It just gave her a nice buzz in the morning, what else was she supposed to do? She was so lucky to have Aviva in her life.

A red light ahead and she stopped and waited. Only a few cars on the road and the lights shone on humid air and the trees cast down pools of congealing shadows, why was she thinking like this, the light changed to green and she pressed on the accelerator and the car shot forward, over the lights with a—

Bump—

No, no—

Onto a smooth road, she could go anywhere, to Jerusalem, to Haifa, just pick a direction and—

Bright sudden lights behind and in front of her. The wail of a siren made her stomach clench with sudden fear. A voice on a megaphone: 'Stop the car, Mrs Nahari, stop the car!'

Flashing lights, that awful siren, she wanted to run but they were blocking the road. She slowed down, stopped by the side of the road. She sat and waited. The radio was still on, too loud now with the engine stopped, some foreign band wailing. She stabbed the button, shut it off.

Steps outside. A figure leaning. A fist knocking on the window. She rolled it down.

'Mrs Nahari? Hava Nahari? Step out of the vehicle please.'

Torch light in her face. She blinked.

'Do I know you?' she said.

'Step out of the vehicle please.'

'Why? I wasn't speeding.'

He yanked the door open.

'Please,' he said.

She stepped out. She felt calm now, strangely. She said, 'Do you mind if I light up a cigarette?'

'Mrs Nahari, you are under arrest for the murder of Mela Malevsky.'

Hava burst out laughing. 'But this is ridiculous,' she said.

How was she so calm? It didn't feel real. 'Do you know who my husband is?' she said.

'We know,' the man said. She could see his face now, in the headlights.

'We met,' she said, wonderingly. 'At some function or other. At Soldiers' House, I think. It was in benefit of lone soldiers. You're…' She clicked her fingers. 'Cohen something,' she said.

'Come with me, please.'

'I can't,' she told him. 'I have things to do. The children are at home. Ehud is waiting for me.'

'Then he will wait,' the policeman – Cohen – said.

He took her arm. He held her gently, but she felt she couldn't tear her arm away or he would do something. Maybe something bad. She let him walk her to a police car. She let him lower her into the back seat and shut the door on her. But she couldn't go to the police now, she thought, it was absurd, she had work in the morning.

She sat back. She felt so relaxed all of a sudden. Better than beer with a Valium chaser. They had nothing on her, she could feel it. A policewoman drove her. No one put handcuffs on Hava. They wouldn't dare, she thought. She'd call Ehud when she got to the station. She'll be home by morning. They'll laugh about it.

'Coffee?'

'Please. Do you mind if I smoke?'

'Not at all.' He pushed the ashtray across.

'Do you have cigarettes?' he said.

'Yes, I…' She looked for her handbag but it wasn't there, of course. They took it off her.

'Here,' Cohen said. He pushed a pack of Noblesse cigarettes across and a box of matches on top.

Hava said, 'Noblesse?'

'I'm on a policeman's salary, Mrs Nahari.'

She shook a cigarette out of the pack and struck a match to light it.

'Call me Hava,' she said through smoke. 'No one calls me Mrs Nahari.'

'You don't like it?' he said.

'What?'

'Being called Mrs Nahari?'

'I don't mind.'

What was he getting at? She looked at his eyes. He didn't have kind eyes. She didn't like him all of a sudden.

'Your husband is well known, of course,' Cohen said.

She stared at him. He didn't say anything more.

'Yes?' Hava said.

'What?' Cohen said.

'You were going to say something?'

'No,' Cohen said.

'I am not my husband,' Hava said. When would people ever realise this? She was her own woman, she was a person by herself! She said, 'You must let me go. My children will be worried. I don't understand what you are charging me with.'

'The murder of Mela Malevsky,' Cohen said.

'That is ridiculous! She was hit by a truck!'

'That's what we thought at first, sure.'

He sat back in the chair. Stretched out his legs. Waited. The silence lengthened, thickened with the smoke.

'Your people already interviewed me,' Hava said. 'I knew her from the bank.'

'You did,' Cohen said.

'So what's changed?'

He shrugged. 'Why don't you tell me?' he said.

'I have nothing to tell you, don't you understand!'

'That's alright,' Cohen said. 'I have nowhere else to be.'

Hava said, 'You're a lousy cop.' She laughed in his face.

Cohen said nothing.

'This will be all over the news tomorrow,' she told him. 'My husband *is* the news. And you'll be lucky if they let you direct traffic after this is over.'

'You know,' Cohen said, 'she was a guest here.'

'What?'

'Mrs Malevsky. She was a guest in our country.'

'She was a sweet woman and I was sorry she died,' Hava said. She watched him closely. What was he getting at?

'We have a duty of care to our guests,' Cohen said. 'I couldn't keep her alive. But I can put the person who did it behind bars.'

'What is wrong with you?' Hava said.

'Did she ever tell you what happened to her during the Holocaust?' Cohen said.

'No. She never talked about it.'

It was hot in the interrogation room. When will they let her out? Where was Ehud? Why was she being kept there?

'I sometimes think, what would I have done if I were there?' Cohen said. 'Would I have fought? Would I have tried to run? Would I have gone quietly on the trains to the ovens? What would you have done, Hava?'

'I would fight,' Hava said.

'Yes,' Cohen said. 'But then, that's what we all want to think, don't we.'

Silence again. She couldn't bear it. She couldn't understand him. What did he want? Did he want her to confess? It was so silly. What would she confess to? She had done nothing wrong.

'We know about the money,' Cohen said.

'What money?'

'The money you stole from Mrs Malevsky's account.'

'I didn't steal any money.'

'What would you need money for?' Cohen said. 'A woman like yourself. A nice house. A nice family. A good job. You had everything, Hava.'

She didn't like how he used the past tense.

'I work hard. I look after my family. What I have I made for myself,' Hava said.

'Like the pioneers who built our nation,' Cohen said. 'With their own two hands. Who collected rocks and dug ditches and planted trees. Who lived in tents until they could build houses. Like that?'

'Are you making fun of me?'

She lit another cigarette. Her hands shook.

'You smoke a lot?' Cohen said.

'Sometimes.'

He nodded.

'She had three grandchildren, you know,' he said.

'I know. It's awful, what happened.'

'What happened, Hava? Do you want to tell me?'

'I'm sorry,' Hava said. 'I really am. I don't know what happened to Mela. I wasn't there.'

'Mela,' Cohen said. 'You were close?'

'Not that close. I knew her, of course. Everyone at the bank knew Mela.'

'But you handled her account.'

Hava shrugged.

'Is that a crime?' she said.

Cohen watched her. He made her uncomfortable, watching her like this. Like he knew her.

'You're not going home, you know,' he said.

'What?'

'You're not going home again.'

She stared, trying to make him look away. Trying to make him *go* away. Of course she was going home in the morning.

'You could tell me, you know,' Cohen said.

'Tell you what?'

'Tell me the truth. You would feel better. People generally do.'

'Do you?'

'Do I what, Hava?'

'Do you tell the truth, Cohen? Does it make you feel better?'

He just watched her.

'Let's call it a night,' Cohen said. The abruptness of it threw her. He stood up and suddenly she didn't want him to leave. As long as he was there they were just two people talking. She didn't have to think of where she was.

'Can I get you anything?' Cohen said. 'Tea, coffee? Feel free to keep the cigarettes.'

'You're going?' Hava said.

'You need your rest,' Cohen said. 'It's a big day tomorrow.'

'Big day? How? I told you, I'm going home.'

He nodded. 'Of course. Good night, Mrs Nahari.'

He left, and a policewoman came and led her to a cell. A cell! Hava lay down on the bed. It smelled. The whole place was awful. She didn't belong here! How dare they, she thought. How dare they.

51

AVIVA

'I ironed her, I ironed her twice' – *Hava*

She smiled and waved to the photographers on the way to the courtroom. She wore her sunglasses. The policewoman was by her side. Cameras flashed. Journalists shouted questions. One day people would look at old newspaper archives and find her photo, she thought, see the brave woman determined to prove her innocence on the steps of the court.

Inside, the judge presiding. She saw Ehud in the distance. He looked shocked, grim. He must know it was a mistake. Why was she in court? Was there going to be a trial?

In the event it was a let down. It was just some sort of formal process. The police presented a case to the judge. They seemed to know so much. How did they know?

'Mrs Nahari fell into debt and needed money. She and a second person falsified documents to fraudulently withdraw Mrs Malevsky's money from the bank. When Mrs Malevsky discovered the fraud, the suspect and the second person decided to murder her in cold blood—'

She couldn't listen to this. She couldn't bear to be referred to as 'the suspect'.

'But when can I go home?' she said.

'The accused will speak only when spoken to,' the judge said. 'How do you plead?'

'I am innocent!' She laughed at them then, she laughed at them all. She wondered how they knew about a second person. It didn't matter. Aviva was solid. They had a bond of silence. 'I just want to go home to my children.'

'You are detained on suspicion of the murder of Mela Malevsky,' the judge said. He tapped the gavel, and that was that. She stared at him in horror.

'Ehud!' she called. 'Ehud!'

The policewoman escorted her away. Back into the police car, back along the road, back to jail.

'Tell me what happened that night,' Cohen said.

'I told you, I don't know what you're talking about.'

'A confession can go a long way with the judge,' Cohen said.

'I have nothing to confess for.' She'd thought it through by then. 'It was Ehud!' she said.

'What?'

'My husband. He's been cheating on me. He wants a divorce, to keep the kids. This is his doing, Cohen. You have to believe me! He's telling tales about me! He would send me to prison.'

Cohen looked at her through the smoke. She was smoking too much. It was the stress. She needed her Valium. She wondered how the boy and the girl were doing without her. Mummy's gone away for a little bit. She hated Ehud so much right then. It was all his fault.

'Your marriage,' Cohen said. 'It has not been going well?'

'Does anyone's marriage?' Hava said. 'Are you married, Cohen?'

'Me? Yes. Of course.'

'Any kids?'

He smiled fondly.

'Children are a blessing,' he said.

'You love them,' she said.

'More than anything. Of course.'

'You don't look like someone who has kids,' Hava said.

'Well, I do,' Cohen said. 'What *do* I look like to you?'

'I don't know,' Hava said. 'I can't make you out at all.'

'Think of me as a friend,' Cohen suggested. 'Your best and only friend.'

Hava smirked.

'I don't need another friend,' she said.

'No.' He played with some papers in front of him. 'We tapped your phone, you know.'

'What?'

For a moment it didn't register. When it did the horror took her.

'We've been listening to you for months.'

'You can't do that. That's illegal.'

He smiled, like she was telling a joke. 'You think we just pulled you off the street, Hava? We know everything about you. Every movement you made. Every call.'

It still didn't register. Not fully.

'But that means…' she said.

'Yes,' he said, almost kindly. 'We know about Aviva.'

'What… What about Aviva?' Hava said. Struggling to swallow.

'You are very close?'

'She is my friend.'

'Yes,' Cohen said. He looked to the side. Like he was looking elsewhere. Making her follow his gaze, but it was just to the wall. What was he saying? The fear crawled on her then. Where was Aviva?

'You were going to watch *Out of Africa*,' Cohen said.

'I… How dare you,' she said.

'You told her you were scared,' Cohen said. 'You got a phone call about Mela Malevsky.'

'I don't remember that,' Hava said.

Cohen stirred. 'We had a policewoman call you, to see what would happen,' he said. He looked through his papers. 'Did you tell Aviva, "I ironed her, I ironed her twice"?'

'What?'

'Which one of you hit her over the head? Was it you, or was it Aviva?'

'I don't… What? What?'

'Come on, Hava. Playtime's over. Aviva said it was you.'

'What!'

'She says you killed Mela. It was your plan all along, wasn't it?

You drove her out to the sands. You hit her over the head, then you ran her over until she was dead. And then you left her there, like she was garbage.' He looked at her across the desk and his eyes were like the eyes of all the men she'd ever known, cruel and merciless.

'You will go to prison for a very long time,' Cohen said.

'I didn't do it! It was Aviva! Aviva hit her! Aviva said, we had to change the tyres, she knew a place! You don't understand what she's like, people are fooled by her, she seems so innocent, but she is like a snake, she can hold you so hard that you struggle to breathe, that you would do anything she says!'

Her heart beat like she'd run too quickly too fast. The room spun.

'That's not what she says,' Cohen told her.

'She's a liar! A manipulative liar! Cohen, you have to believe me!'

'Then tell me the truth. Convince me, Hava. Let me help you.'

'It was her plan all along,' Hava said. 'She's greedy, she always needs money. It was her idea!'

'Who falsified the documents?' Cohen said.

'She did! She wrote out the authorisation letter for power of account. It was all for her! I gave her the money—'

'Come on, Hava. We know about your debts. How much do you owe?'

'I don't, I—'

'You even had to sell the flat to pay it off,' Cohen said.

'It wasn't like that, I would never… It was her idea, it was all her!'

'Funny,' Cohen said.

'What's funny?' Hava said.

'She's saying it was all you,' Cohen said. 'You stole the money. It was your idea. You hit Mela over the head. You drove over her body. And then you went home to your kids like nothing happened.'

'You have to believe me,' Hava said. 'You have to.'

'I want to believe you, Hava,' Cohen said. 'Here,' he said. He pushed across blank paper, a pen. 'Write it down. Exactly like you told me. Then we'll see.'

She took the pen. Aviva, how could you? Aviva, I trusted you. I loved you. Aviva, you killed poor Mela. I was just along for the ride. It was your idea to steal the money. You're a monster in human form, people are fooled by those thick glasses and that mess of curls. They think you're nothing, when you're everything. She wrote. She signed.

The policewoman walked her back to her cell.

Nights in jail, the hell that was Abu Kabir, the other women filthy, swearing, the junkies shaking from withdrawal, someone crying, someone having sex, the jailers pacing, the food disgusting, her lawyers when she saw them useless, Aviva pinned it all on her, and worse, the police found blood on the back seat of Ehud's car, and a strand of Mela's hair under the car, somehow, some forensic shit, how did they even know it was Mela's?

The next time they took her to court the tears just came. Her hair was a mess. Her hands shook, the fingers yellowed with nicotine. She saw Aviva being led in. She saw Ehud in the galley.

'Ehud!' Hava cried. 'Ehud, she's stitching me up! Ehud!'

Her sister in the gallery too, next to Ehud. She couldn't speak to either of them. The lawyers spoke to the judge. The prosecution spoke to the judge. Aviva sitting separately, saying nothing. Aviva, who she'd loved.

The photographers, when she was led outside, had had enough of her by then. They surrounded Aviva as she was led out, they were mad for Aviva, the Mystery Woman, before her name was released to the press the newspapers were calling her the Woman in Red. Did she wear red that night? It was dark. Mela's blood on the sand, in the dirt. Was that red?

'Sylvie Gold from *This World*,' a journalist said, materialising before her. 'Hava, where did you get the idea to iron the victim? Which of you brought the rolling pin, was it you or was it Aviva?'

'No comment, no comment, no—'

But Sylvie Gold, like the others, lost interest in her, went after Aviva, 'Mrs Granot! Aviva! Aviva!' like she was some kind of a movie star, like she was Grace Kelly. Who did she think she was? Aviva was nothing, a parasite Hava had to endure for years, it was all her fault, all of this was—

Back in the cell, the sounds of the prison all around her, she couldn't bear it, it was hopeless, there was no way out. They had given her back her purse, her Valium, she palmed all the pills, she gobbled them up, she'd kill herself, she drank water, trying to swallow it down, then wrapped the handles of the handbag round her neck and pulled until she collapsed on the mattress.

'You can't commit suicide with Valium,' Cohen said.

'I didn't know that,' Hava said.

'Or by strangling yourself with your handbag, really,' Cohen said.

Hava didn't say anything.

'It won't do you any good, Hava,' Cohen said. 'You want a psychiatric evaluation? You'll get it. But it won't let you off.' He shrugged. 'Worth a try, I suppose,' he said.

'Why are you still here, Cohen?' Hava said. Hating him. Hating that quiet voice and those cold eyes that didn't fool her. She knew what he was just as he knew her. It was as though everything she hated and everything she feared had gathered and crawled inside the flesh of this policeman, Cohen, and a thousand slithering snakes animated him like a golem filled with venom. All the hate and all the fear.

'Making sure,' he told her.

'Making sure of what?'

'Making sure you go to prison, Hava, for the murder of Mela Malevsky.'

'I told you, it wasn't me!'

'It's a little late for that, isn't it?' he said. 'Goodbye, Hava. I have work elsewhere, so I probably won't see you again.'

Back in the cell she found the knife under the pillow. A dull kitchen knife that Uri, the prisoner who cleaned the women's toilets, smuggled in for her. She sawed at her wrists. She'd show them, she thought. She wouldn't give them the fucking satisfaction.

'She has suicidal tendencies, yes,' the psychiatrist said. 'I would recommend putting her under close watch. But she is fit to stand trial.'

'Fuck you!' Hava said. 'I'm sorry, I'm sorry. No. Please. I can't go back to prison. Please! You have to help me!'

The policewoman walked her away.

'Guilty,' the judge said.

Hava scrubbed the pot. She scrubbed and scrubbed. The pot was huge, the kitchen cooked for two hundred women. The pot was black from use and too many bad meals. She thought about the kids. Would the girl be watching *Krovim Krovim* right then? Would the boy be playing football outside? She worried how Ehud would cope but she knew he'd be fine. He was a man, he had his job, had his opinions about the Arabs he was happy to share with the world on TV. He will do fine. She saw Aviva earlier. They never spoke. They passed each other at a distance. Neveh Tirzah, Hava's new home. Most women murdered their husbands, when they could take no more. Not Hava. She scrubbed the pot. The book cart would be along later, she hoped there would be something good to read. There was a crèche in the prison, a little play area with toys for the children. Would they visit her, too? They were too old for toys. They would grow up without her. Forces beyond her control have led her to this point. None of this was her fault. She will get out one day, she thought. She would tell them then. She would tell them none of this was her fault.

PART NINE

NIGHT TRAIN TO CAIRO

1986, Israeli-Occupied Lebanon

52

SUNSTROKE

'We shall have a Hebrew police force
We shall have our very own thieves!'
– Natan Alterman (1935)

5am
The house was in a village only a few kilometres into Lebanon. The cocks were crowing outside. The sun rose gently against the window. Jean paced back and forth in the room, waving the gun, shouting at the informant. Nir kept to one side. He didn't even want to be here.

'You son of a bitch,' Jean said. Boxes were piled everywhere in the room: new VCRs, TVs, cassette players. Thousands of dollars' worth. 'You son of a bitch.'

The informant was named Salim. He stared defiantly at Jean and spat. 'I want more money,' he said.

'More money!' Jean said. Jean was Internal Security. He was a piece of shit, everyone knew that. He was a crook with a badge. He was fired from the prime minister's security detail for fraud and ended up with Unit 504, where they didn't ask too many questions. Salim was his informant, not Nir's. Nir didn't even want to be there. Running agents in Lebanon wasn't his job. Jean was making spare cash smuggling electronics shit across the border. Petty cash. Nir didn't want anything to do with it. 'You son of a bitch,' Jean said.

'Fuck you!' Salim said. 'You don't pay me I'm going to tell them exactly what you fucking do here—'

'You're going to rat me out, you son of a bitch?' Jean said. He was hopped up on coke. There was so much snow falling in Lebanon since the invasion started. The Shi'ite refugees in South America were shipping raw over by the tonne to the new labs set up in the Bekaa. From there it went to Israel and Europe. Coke changed things. Coke, and Lebanon.

'What are you going to do about it, asshole?' Salim said.

Jean didn't say shit. He raised the gun and fired one shot, almost point-blank, hitting Salim between the eyes.

Salim dropped.

'Son of a *bitch*!' Nir yelled. The gunshot hurt his ears.

'Yeah,' Jean said. He stared at the corpse. He did that thing where his eyes went – it wasn't cold, Nir thought. It was just sort of dead. 'Well, are you going to help me load up?'

'I didn't even want to be here,' Nir said. He took the canister from his pocket and did a line of coke. 'Do it yourself, Jean.'

'Fuck you, Nir,' Jean said.

'Yeah,' Nir muttered. He picked up a VCR box and carried out to the truck. He dumped it and went back in.

'Team spirit,' Jean said. Nir ignored him, picked up a TV and staggered out with it. He would have preferred to hit Jean over the head with it. Instead he helped him load up the truck.

'You're going to get done for this petty shit,' Nir told him when they had finished. 'You want to go to prison over a VCR?'

'You know how much money I'm making selling these babies on our side?' Jean said. 'Besides, everyone's doing it.'

Nir just nodded. 'And the guy?' he said.

'Salim? Fuck him,' Jean said. 'Who's going to complain?'

'Well, not him,' Nir muttered. 'I need a coffee,' he said.

'We'll get some at the commissary,' Jean said.

They went back inside.

'You don't want to cover him or something?' Nir said.

Jean looked at him strangely. 'What?' he said.

'Nothing,' Nir said. 'Help me with this, will you?'

They grabbed the remaining container from both ends and lifted it, then carried it through the door like two movers with a kitchen table. They put the drugs in Nir's jeep. He covered them up with tarpaulin.

'See you on the other side,' Jean said. He started the truck and drove off. Nir followed him in the jeep.

5:30am

Nir measured out Elite instant coffee spoons into his cup and filled up water from the samovar. Mashina sang 'Night Train To Cairo' on Army Radio. Five-thirty in the morning and there weren't many people around. He snuck a chocolate wafer out of the tin. Rivka, the cook, didn't like people stealing the wafers. Nir munched on chocolate and drank the coffee. He stared out of the windows. Lebanon, just reach out a hand and touch it.

He wandered out into the corridor. His footsteps in the hall. He went past the interrogation rooms and thought he'd have a peek. He opened the door to the observation room and stepped in quietly.

Beyond, in the next room, Cohen was standing over a guy sat in a chair. The guy had his pants pulled down to his ankles and he was tied up in the chair. Cohen held a straight razor, a new affectation of his. He'd picked it up some place near Beirut and called it his booty of war. Nir couldn't stand Cohen. He couldn't stand any of them. He was alone in the room. He pulled out the canister and did a line of coke, quietly. He watched to see what Cohen was doing.

'Who sent you?' Cohen said.

'Nobody sent me,' the man said. He looked up at Cohen tiredly and Nir saw the fresh bruises on his face. 'I told you already.'

'You crossed the border illegally into Israel,' Cohen said.

'Bullshit,' the man said. 'We weren't anywhere near the border.'

'You were inside the security belt,' Cohen said. 'That's enough.'

'So arrest me and put me in your jail,' the man said. 'You're the illegals here. This is my country, not yours.'

'Lebanon?' Cohen said.

'Palestine,' the man said. 'I told you already.'

'You're a Palestinian,' Cohen said.

'Yes.'

'You are a member of a terrorist organisation.'

'I am nobody,' the man said. Nir thought he couldn't be much more than twenty. But in Lebanon you had as much chance being shot at by a kid. The Christian militias for one loved their child soldiers. So this guy could be anybody, or he could be nobody. It didn't take much to get picked up by the army. Wrong place, wrong time.

'You are a member of the Popular Front for the Liberation of Palestine,' Cohen said. 'You were carrying pamphlets.'

'So arrest me and send me to your illegal jail,' the man said. 'What you are doing is against the law.'

'I am the law,' Cohen said.

'You're just a crook,' the man said. 'You're just a crook with a badge.'

Cohen backhand slapped him. The man's head whipped back. He glared at Cohen.

'Arrest me.'

'Tell me why you were here. Who do you really work for?'

'Nobody!'

'What's your name?' Cohen said.

'Rimawi,' the man said. 'Majdi Rimawi. You have my papers.'

'Papers mean shit,' Cohen said.

'I'm just a guy,' Rimawi said. 'I was visiting my girlfriend. That's not a crime, is it?'

'Terrorism is a crime,' Cohen said.

'If I were going to attack I'd have bombs, maps,' Rimawi said.

'You had a gun,' Cohen said.

'Everybody has a gun!' Rimawi said.

Cohen knelt in front of him. Forced open his legs. He took the straight razor and slid it under the man's testicles. Rimawi sat very still. Nir watched spellbound. He forgot his coffee. There was something about Cohen being Cohen, something in that ruthless, single-minded dedication, that made Nir almost admire him as much as he hated him.

'Tell me,' Cohen whispered.

Rimawi dry-swallowed. 'Or you'll cut off my balls?' he said.

'Or I'll cut off your balls.'

'What are you asking me?' Rimawi said.

Cohen made the razor move, just an inch. Rimawi closed his eyes, only for a moment.

'Who are you working for? The Maliks? The Gemayels? Hezbollah? The Obeyds? Mohammed Biro?'

'Biro?' Rimawi said. 'You ask me about Biro?'

Nir leaned in, suddenly interested. He'd heard about Mohammed Biro. They said he was the largest dealer in Lebanon. But he didn't work with Cohen.

Rimawi saw the sudden interest in Cohen's eyes; he must have. He nodded, very slowly.

'Biro,' Cohen breathed. He looked awkward crouching there, between the other man's legs.

'Maybe we could make a deal,' Rimawi said. 'I can give you Biro. If you would let me go.'

'And how would you know Mohammed Biro, little bird?' Cohen said.

His hand shook. Rimawi closed his eyes in pain.

'Easy,' he said. 'Easy!'

'Tell me,' Cohen said.

'I have a friend who has a friend who knows a guy,' Rimawi said. 'That's all.'

'You *are* PLFP,' Cohen said. He moved the razor, just a little.

'Maybe they want this Biro gone, too,' Rimawi said.

'Maybe they do,' Cohen said. He slid the razor out and stood up.

'Drugs are evil,' Rimawi said.

Cohen smiled a thin smile. 'But you boys run them too.'

Rimawi, too, smiled. He really did have balls, Nir thought.

'Only to fund the Struggle,' Rimawi said.

'The enemy of my enemy,' Cohen said. 'War makes unlikely friends.'

Nir was sure he was quoting someone, but he didn't know who. It was another thing he hated about Cohen.

'Untie me?' Rimawi said.

'Sure,' Cohen said. He cut the ropes. Rimawi rubbed his wrists.

'Let's talk somewhere more private,' Cohen said. He looked at the mirror glass.

'Fuck off, Nir,' he said.

6am

Nir was on his second cup of coffee and an army breakfast. Soldiers coming in from patrol and nightly ambush, drivers in from the security belt, a couple of South Lebanon Army commanders, several drug patrol soldiers, a sole Mossad operative sitting on his own, a table of Internal Security guys in moustaches, Jean sitting with them. Also some pilots, and quartermaster sergeants.

The little guys: drivers, quartermasters. They shipped and stored the product.

The middle guys: border patrol, letting it through.

The big guys: the officers – police, army and security – who made sure everything ran to plan.

The Israeli-Lebanese border: where the magic happened.

An entire machine oiled with ready cash and fuelled by greed and indifference.

No one gave a shit about this war. Not anymore.

So you might as well get paid.

Stuck in it all: Captain Nir Marom, veteran of this fine fuck-up of a war, blackmailed into service of this enterprise by his original commander, General Leider, over a matter Nir really preferred not to recall. Now an aide-de-camp to a bunch of degenerates, first among which, police officer and veteran of the Esther Landes murder investigation back in '74, C—

Cohen came and sat across from him and lit a cigarette.

'You will forget what you saw,' he said.

'What did I see?' Nir said.

'Exactly.'

'You let him go?' Nir said. 'He was PFLP!'

'He was a worm on a hook thrown back to the sea,' Cohen said. He shrugged. 'Maybe it will bring back a fish, and maybe it won't.'

'Drugs,' Nir said, disgusted. 'It's all about the drugs.'

'And yet I don't see you complain,' Cohen said.

'Complain to who?' Nir said, and Cohen smiled.

'Exactly,' he said.

'Why the Popular Front?' Nir said. Curious.

'They're Marxists,' Cohen said. Patient with Nir. Too forthcoming. Cohen wanted Nir, said he was a 'valuable asset'.

'So?' Nir said.

'So they're tight with the Syrians,' Cohen said. 'And the Syrians run drugs worse than anyone.'

'But we're at war with Syria,' Nir said. 'We're at war with the Palestinians.' He thought about it. 'We seem to be at war with a lot of people.'

'We are a small country surrounded by enemies,' Cohen said smoothly. That old line made even Nir smile.

Cohen gave Nir his itinerary. Slid the paper right across the desk. Nir scanned the sheet. Drive here. Go there. Pick up. Drop off. It all looked so bland. It was on official stationary.

An aide-de-camp.

Just a fancy word for bagman.

'Oh, and tonight's orders,' Cohen said. He slid another sheet across. A military memo. *Operation Sunstroke*, Nir saw. Like the Mashina song. A joint action with the drug unit and border patrol.

'Another ambush?' Nir said. He felt depressed.

'Big shipment coming in tonight through Rosh Ha'nikra,' Cohen said. 'It's going to be a big bust. A big win for us. We must stop the flow of drugs into this country.'

'Whose drugs?' Nir said.

Cohen shrugged. 'I expect you will make it back for the operation,' he said.

'Alright,' Nir said. He pushed back his chair. Picked up his tray. The remains of his eggs smeared on the plate. They reminded him unpleasantly of Salim's brains leaking out. Jean spotted him and gave him a thumbs up. Nir ignored him. He dumped the tray and dishes on the washer's conveyor belt.

7am

Easy traffic going south, even the kids usually selling watermelons and figs by the side of the road weren't up yet. A tractor from a nearby kibbutz blocked the road. Nir stuck his head out of the open window, shouted, 'Get the fuck out of the way!'

The kibbutznik ignored him. The John Deere slowed down even more. Nir pressed the horn, laughed, pressed down with his foot and drove the jeep off the shoulder, going fast, coming up on that tractor. He hit the horn again, swerved back onto the road and hit the gas.

'Fuck you,' he said.

He went fast, the suspension tossing him up and down, heard a siren behind him coming off a side road and slowed down. The traffic cops stepped out of their kakamaika patrol car. Nir flashed them his badge. Did anyone still say 'kakamaika'? It was the sort of word his parents' generation might have used. Still, it was a piece of shit patrol car.

'Sorry,' the policeman said when he saw the badge. 'Didn't realise, guy.'

'That's alright,' Nir said. 'As you were, fellows.'

He waved cheerfully as he hit the gas again and sped down the road. He put on the radio. Gali Atari singing, 'I Don't Have Another Country'. Nir dreamed of packing it all in, of getting on a plane to South America. Be like everyone else, put on a backpack, get lost in Uruguay or Peru. Get stoned on the beach somewhere. Climb Macchu Picchu. Do a trek in the Andes. He started to see more traffic, had to slow down. Fuck this, he thought.

8am

He'd stopped for a piss at a petrol station. Now he was somewhere in the Krayot, that maze of featureless social housing blocks that sprouted the other side of Haifa and went on forever: the suburban hellhole of the north. Nir parked the jeep, stared at some kid sitting at the block entrance.

'Army,' Nir said. He showed the kid his gun. The kid spat over the steps.

'So?' the kid said.

'So don't fucking touch it.'

The kid didn't say a thing. He stood up and pressed a buzzer, two short, one long, then sat down again.

'No one's going to touch your jeep,' he said.

Nir went in, the brick in his hand. The door was open. Up three flights of stairs. The hallway smelled of stews and frying. He got to the door and was going to knock but the door opened before he knocked and Tzila stood in the doorway in a robe.

'He's on the balcony,' she said. She didn't look at the brick.

Nir gave her a quick kiss on the cheek. Tzila smiled reluctantly, patted his shoulder and went inside. Nir followed.

'You want a coffee?' Tzila said.

'Sure, thanks.'

'So polite,' she said. She vanished into the kitchen.

'He's on the balcony!' she called.

'Yeah, you said.'

'How do you want your coffee?'

'Hot,' Nir said, and heard her laugh.

The living room was dark, the sofa cushions rumpled, two ashtrays littered with cigarette butts, a set of scales on the table, the smell of weed and frying and unwashed laundry. Nir crossed the room to the open doors and stepped onto the balcony. Itzik sat on a folding chair, his one good leg resting on top of an empty crate and his new prosthetic leg propped against the wall. His stump was naked.

'Hey, man,' Itzik said, with the same genuine, happy smile he always had. 'Pull up a seat. I saw you come in.'

'That kid downstairs working for you?' Nir said.

'Working, eh. He's my sister's boy. You met him before. Ronny. He's a good kid.'

Nir tossed the brick on the table. It was bubble-wrapped and tied with brown tape. He said, 'It's the last one, man. If they knew they'd cut off my balls.'

Thought of that straight razor in Cohen's hand and shuddered.

'Fuck them, man,' Itzik said. 'You can't work for those pushtakim any more. You're a soldier, an officer!'

Nir had to smile. He sat down. 'It's good to see you, Itzik,' he said.

'Yes, well, come anytime,' Itzik said. 'I never see much of you anymore.'

'Work,' Nir said, feeling guilty.

'I'm thinking of going back to school,' Itzik said. 'Study psychology, maybe, or sociology.'

'You'll be great,' Nir said. Remembering the patrol, two years back. The grenade that came out of nowhere. Itzik jumped on it to save the rest of them. And Nir didn't.

'I'm getting a new leg soon,' Itzik said. 'It can bend at the knee and everything.'

'That's great,' Nir said. 'Listen, this is the last package, really.'

'That's cool,' Itzik said. 'I don't even like selling this shit.'

'Just until you get sorted out,' Nir said. 'I mean the money. And they won't miss a brick here and there.'

'A brick is always missed,' Itzik said, and he lost his smile as he looked at Nir. 'You're going to be careful, aren't you?'

'I'm careful.'

'Aha.'

'I hate them, Itzik,' Nir said.

'I know, man.'

Tzila came back with a coffee. Nir drank it without tasting.

'How is it?' Tzila said.

'Hot.'

'Asshole.' But she said it without malice, and Itzik laughed.

'And clean up around here,' Nir said. 'You have brown and weed lying everywhere in the open. The scales—'

'Who's gonna come all the way up here?' Itzik said. 'Only junkies. The police are too lazy, they only raid ground floor flats.'

Nir drank his coffee. He tried not to look at the stump.

'I'll see you, man,' he said, standing. They shook hands, and Itzik beamed again. Tzila walked Nir back to the door, then slipped him the envelope.

He gave her a kiss on the cheek.

'I'll see you next week,' he said.

9am

It was getting hot. The sun was up and the traffic was tight along the coastal road. Nir started to sweat. He pulled into a petrol station outside of Zikhron Ya'akov. Went into the restrooms, found a stall, did a line of coke, then thought fuck it and did another.

When he came out he felt better but he noticed the two guys evidently checking out his jeep. They rode a white Subaru. He gave them a stare but they didn't seem to notice him. One went to the restrooms and the other to the kiosk, so Nir dismissed it.

Past Herzlia he noticed a white Subaru behind him, but then there were a lot of white Subarus. He kept an eye on the rear-view mirror. The white Subaru stayed behind, not turning, not speeding, not falling back. But a lot of people were stuck in the same road, same place. Still. When he got a chance Nir sped up. The white Subaru sped up and followed. Nir slowed down, changed a lane. The white car fell behind but didn't leave his rear-view mirror.

Nothing he could do. He gripped the wheel, took the first right turn, got off the main road. The white car turned behind him, followed. Nir hit the gas, went down pedestrian streets, past a school playground, ran a red light and took a random turn. He took a roundabout route and soon he couldn't see the white car. Maybe he'd lost them. Maybe they hadn't been following him. Maybe.

10am

Ramat Gan. Outside a pleasant house with a garden full of roses. A little wooden sign said 'Sagi'.

Nir slid out of the jeep. He knocked on the door.

A small boy opened it. Nir stared at him in surprise.

'Is your daddy home?' he said.

'He's at work,' the boy said.

A woman inside, calling, 'Avi? Who is it?'

The boy looked at Nir.

'Are you a policeman?' he said.

'Something like that,' Nir said.

'When I grow up I'm going to be a policeman,' the boy, Avi, said.

'Listen, kid,' Nir said. 'Do something else, trust me.'

'What did you want to do when you grew up?' Avi said.

'I wanted to be an astronaut,' Nir said.

The boy gave it some consideration.

'Huh,' he said.

'Give this to your dad, will you?' Nir said. He passed the boy the envelope Cohen gave him and the boy took it.

'Avi? Who's at the door!' the woman called from inside.

The boy stared as Nir went back to his jeep.

'It's nobody, Mum,' he said.

10:35am

'Nirush!'

She jumped on him, wrapped her long arms around his neck and her long legs around his waist and kissed him full on the lips.

'Kippy!' Nir said when she came up for air. 'What are you doing here?'

'Trying out my new outfit,' Kippy said. She let him go and jumped to her feet and twirled around. 'Do you like it?'

Her name was Sarah but everyone called her Kippy, after the talking hedgehog character from *Sumsum Street* that all the kids watched. Kippy Kippod, who was played by a woman under the costume and was strangely sexy for an anthropomorphic animal. Nir stared as Kippy turned. She was dressed like a businesswoman, in a shoulder-pad jacket and smart black shoes. She looked terrific, like a secret agent or somebody's hot secretary.

Benny was sitting at a table against the wall of the warehouse, counting money. He'd barely looked up when Nir came in. Benny had a real boner about Nir, ever since that business in Lebanon. Nir felt bad about leaving him when the shooting started, but what choice did he have? Now he no longer gave a shit. He couldn't stand Benny either.

'You look great,' Nir said to Kippy. 'But why?'

Benny did look up then. 'She's going to Los Angeles,' he said.

'What are you doing in Los Angeles?' Nir said, and Kippy laughed.

'I'm going to Hollywood!' she said.

'Courier,' Benny said. 'You look terrific, Kippy,' he said, distractedly. 'Come on, we need to fit you up with the packages.'

'It's a quick in and out,' Kippy told Nir. 'The money's fantastic.'

'Who do you have in Los Angeles?' Nir asked Benny.

'None of your business,' Benny said.

'Kippy, it's dangerous,' Nir said, but she laughed at him like he knew she would. He'd met her three months back at a party in Tel Aviv. She was from a good home but she liked the bright lights and the excitement. Her last boyfriend went in for a stretch on a double murder. Then she met Nir. He loved her. He pulled her close to him. Smelled the salt on her skin, and a new perfume he didn't recognise. He kissed her hungrily. She leaned into it, grinding against him, then pulled back laughing.

'I'll be back next week,' she said. 'We could go out.'

'Don't let them use you like this,' Nir said in a low voice.

'Use me? I use them,' she said. She leaned back into him. 'We'll go together one day soon, won't we? Permanently, I mean. They say it's always sunny in Los Angeles.'

'It's always sunny in Tel Aviv,' Nir said.

'Tel Aviv is boring,' she said. And that was that.

He watched her and the other girls – a nanny, an air stewardess, a woman in traditional Orthodox Jewish clothes – as they tried on their outfits and strapped the packages. There was so much shit coming in from Lebanon and through Egypt that Benny and his boss were going into wholesale export. Nir wasn't stupid. He knew about Los Angeles. A bunch of low-lives from Bat Yam moved out there back in the late 70s. Now they ran protection, extorting money from local Jewish businesses, and did occasional hits for the local mobs on the side.

'Come on,' Benny said. They unpacked the packages from the jeep and Nir felt relieved. At least he could go back now. The only good thing about the run to Tel Aviv was seeing Kippy.

'You want a coffee?' Benny said.

'No, thanks.'

'You look wired,' Benny said.

'I'm OK.'

'We're light a brick,' Benny said.

Nir shrugged. 'Maybe you made a mistake,' he said. 'Can I go now?'

'What's your rush?'

'Got an operation this evening.'

'Ah, yes,' Benny said. Benny, who was a fucking civilian, knowing about operational briefs. It made Nir mad. But Lebanon got all mixed up. Everyone and no one was giving orders.

'So can I go?'

'Not yet...' Benny said. 'Listen. I need you to do me a quick run.'

'A quick run where?'

'Be'er Sheva. You know our friends in the Negev?'

'Fuck, Benny, you want me to go see the Bedouins? Now?'

'Got a last minute delivery.'

'What is it?'

Benny shrugged. 'What do you care?' he said.

'I have to be back on the other side of the country!'

'Come on,' Benny said. 'It's a small country.'

Nir muttered under his breath as Benny's men loaded crates on his jeep. To them he was just a bagman.

It started off small. Leider, who was his direct commander back then, asking for a favour here and there, small things, but against army code. And Nir did them, and slowly, slowly the asks got bigger until they stopped being asks at all, because by then there was no going back and he was theirs to do with as they wished. God, but he hated them.

Kippy came back and his mood lifted. There was nothing he could do about the Rubensteins and Cohens of this world, just like there was nothing he could do about Lebanon. Life dictated a path and you followed it, and it didn't matter how often you dressed up as an astronaut for Purim, there was still no fucking way you were going to set foot on the moon. So you just got on with it.

'I'll see you next week,' Nir said, when he parted from Kippy after a final kiss. He couldn't even feel the drugs on her. She grinned at him, stuck out her tongue and darted off to join the other couriers.

11:10am

Trying to get out of Tel Aviv in traffic. He thought he spotted a white Subaru again but then it was gone.

11:40am
Past the Ramla intersection at last, the jeep gaining speed.

12:15
He saw a few shops and an Arab restaurant and decided to pull in for something to eat. It was quiet now, with the heat of the day and not too many cars on the road. He was itching to do a line. He parked the jeep with the crates in the back.

A car pulled in behind him but he wasn't paying much attention. Someone bumped into him and Nir started to turn, said, 'Excuse me!' when someone punched him in the gut, quickly and efficiently.

Nir doubled over, gasped for breath. A sack went over his head and then they hit him and everything went dark.

13:05
He could tell the time by his watch. The watch was on his hand. His hand was in his lap. It was tied up with rope to his other hand. He was propped on the back of a pickup truck, facing five men who stared at him like he was a particularly unappetising plate of humous.

'You know who I am?' the man in the centre said. He was dressed in a suit with shiny lapels.

'You're Yehezkel Aslan,' Nir said. His head hurt. They said Aslan murdered his own brother when the brother, Shimon, turned snitch. He was found buried in the dunes back in '83.

'And you're Captain Nir Marom,' Yehezkel Aslan said. 'So now we know each other.'

Nir nodded cautiously. He said, 'Are you going to kill me?'

Aslan said, 'If I wanted you dead you'd be dead already.'

'I figured that. So, what? You're going to torture me? Try to get information?'

'Maybe, sure,' Aslan said. He nodded to his guys. Nir's jeep was parked between the pine trees. He saw the white Subaru and a red Subaru. These guys liked their Japanese cars. Two of Aslan's men went to the jeep and took out one of the crates and brought it out. It was heavy and one of them cursed as it almost slipped, but they put it down carefully on the ground.

'What are you carrying?' Aslan said. 'Do you even know that?'

'Drugs. Money. I don't know.'

'Do you even care?' Aslan said. Which worried Nir more than anything else, that Aslan could see it in him.

Aslan took a crowbar from the back of the pickup and strained at the wood until it opened.

'Son of a bitch,' Nir said.

Inside the crates were M-16s, ammo and grenades.

'You were taking these where?' Aslan said. 'The Bedouins?'

'Son of a bitch,' Nir said.

'Where do you think these will go, Marom? For self-defence? To settle some tribal score? Or do you think they'll end up with the PLO, or Abu Nidal, or the Islamic Brotherhood? Where do you think they'll go? I'm curious. Selling drugs is one thing. Hey, everyone likes to get high and have a good time every now and then. But selling weapons to enemies of the state? By a captain in the army? That's treason.'

Nir stared at the guns and grenades. His mouth moved but he said nothing, and Aslan nodded. Aslan, who seemed to know all about Nir and his business. Aslan, who seemed to read Nir's mind better than Nir knew it himself.

'It's not right,' Aslan said softly.

'No,' Nir said. 'It's not.'

'You're not a part of this world, Nir,' Aslan said. 'You're in it but not of it. I can see it. What are you, a kibbutznik?'

'Was,' Nir said. 'Parents left for the city when I was a kid.'

'It can be hard on a kibbutz,' Aslan said sympathetically. 'No shame in leaving.'

Nir said nothing. His father was born on the kibbutz, his mother was the outsider. She couldn't adjust and eventually they left. His father never really forgave her for taking him away. The kibbutz was all he knew. And the love slowly turned bitter.

'You're from a good home,' Aslan said. It was the sort of expression people used. 'You're a decorated soldier. An officer. You don't need this shit. Shit on your hands. Shit on your face. Eventually, enough shit that you can't tell anymore. I'm not wrong.'

'So, what?' Nir said. 'You want me to work for you?'

'I want you to help me help you,' Aslan said. 'Be my man on the inside. Help me take Rubenstein and those fuckers down.'

'I don't know Rubenstein,' Nir said.

'But he knows you.'

'You don't want to help me,' Nir said. 'You just want to take over the drug routes.'

One of Aslan's men laughed. He was a thin weaselly guy in a damp shirt and with a belt buckle bigger than his fist.

'Help me take them down, and I will set you free,' Aslan said.

Free. The word beat in Nir's brain, following the beat of his pounding blood. Free. Was it even possible to be free? He knew it was a false hope. He looked into Aslan's eyes and saw nothing there, no anger, no compassion. Aslan would as soon make his corpse disappear.

'Not going to the moon,' Nir said quietly.

'What?'

'Nothing. I was just thinking.'

'Think fast.'

'Alright,' Nir said. And there was a great relief in saying it. 'I'll tell you anything you want to know.'

Aslan smiled, a thin-lipped smile that didn't show teeth.

'I want you to do more than that,' he said.

'What do you want me to do?' Nir said.

Aslan said, 'I want you to kill Cohen.'

14:25

He was running out of time and his head still hurt where they'd hit him. Nir drove the jeep across the dirt track to the Bedouin camp. The spotters spotted him. Kids ran. He came to a halt outside Abu Hassan's house.

The camp was semi-permanent and unregistered, like most of the Bedouin places in the Negev. A fire burned outside. Armed men came out, saw Nir, waited. Abu Hassan came out. They shook hands.

'I have to get back,' Nir said.

'What happened to your head?' Abu Hassan said.

Nir said, 'I slipped in the shower.'

The men removed the crates of weapons. Nir said nothing. Abu Hassan passed him a thick envelope. 'Give that to Benny,' he said. Then he slipped a hundred dollar bill into Nir's pocket.

'For you,' he said.

Nir got back in the jeep. Fuck. He was late. It was three o'clock and he had to get across country. It was going to be rush hour by the time he hit Tel Aviv. He cursed. He was so fucked. He couldn't think about the other stuff. He drove fast, using his siren. No one better try and stop him. Cohen gave him that siren. Police issue and all. Nir drove like mad, his hands gripping the wheel.

No time to think, no time at all.

Get back to the base on time.

Go on patrol.

If he gets the chance – shoot Cohen.

15:25
Passing Ramla.

16:45
Stuck, stuck, the roads already busy, people honking, an Egged bus lumbering uselessly, Nir cursing, his head hurt, thinking of Kippy, going off to LAX with heroin strapped to her body, thinking of Itzik with that brick he cut and sold in the Krayot, Itzik who was going to go back to university any day now, who was going to get a leg with a knee that bent. He thought about Benny coming back from Lebanon and wished he'd never come back. He thought of Cohen up by the border, Cohen with a straight razor put to a man's testicles, Cohen quoting the Bible as only a man without faith ever could. And he thought about Aslan, who liked his photos taken for the gossip columns in the newspaper.

And Nir knew he was fucked both ways.

He did a line of coke, right there off the dashboard. A Subaru with a sticker on it from some kibbutz up north passed on his left, a family, the dad driving and the mother fanning herself in the passenger seat, and two sullen small boys in the back fighting.

Nir sweated.

Nir shook.

On the radio that skinny fucker, Yuval Banai, sang 'A Ballad For A Double Agent' with Mashina on drums and electric guitars.

17:55

On the coast road and the sun was setting over the Mediterranean, and a train of car lights snaked across the darkening road.

19:45

Nir pulled into the base with a screech of tyres as two acne-faced privates on the gate ran out with their guns drawn.

'Don't piss yourselves,' Nir said, 'you're not under attack just yet.'

Privates doing guard duty. They were always scared of getting kidnapped. In any attack they'd be the first to go. He remembered doing it himself. Now he drove in and parked the jeep. He felt bone-deep weary. His hands shook and his eyes blurred, and the ground felt like it was still moving under him. He went into the latrines and washed his face in the sink and did two more lines. He stared at himself in the mirror.

Go on an ambush. Arrest or kill some smugglers.

Shoot Cohen if you get the chance.

He nodded to his mirror-self.

'Sir, yes, sir,' he said.

20:00

He grabbed leftover hot food in the commissary. He was fucked if he knew what it was. Some sort of army issue goulash maybe. He forced it down.

'What are you doing here?' Cohen said. 'You were supposed to be at the site.'

'I ran late.'

'So,' Cohen said. 'We'll go up together.'

'You're going on the run yourself?' Nir said, surprised.

'Did not Eleazar serve David, and smite the Philistines until the sword stuck to his hand?' Cohen said. 'So let me serve you.'

Cohen smiled, but Nir had had enough of smiling men.

'Where do you learn all this shit?' he said.

'I take an evening class in Bible Studies,' Cohen said.

'You think you'll ever be a district commander?' Nir said. 'Commissioner, maybe?'

'Never,' Cohen said. 'I know where I belong.'

'And where is that?'

'Serving,' Cohen said, simply.

It was dark. Their lights illuminated the narrow road to the north. It caught the startled eyes of a porcupine. Cohen swerved to avoid it.

'The country,' Cohen said. 'I serve my country.'

Nir didn't even know what to say to that. Cohen drove. It was so quiet.

'I know it hasn't been easy,' Cohen said. He looked torn. Like he wanted to share something with Nir. 'You find the work we do distasteful. So do I. It is not greed that motivates me, Nir, but the need for stability. "A greedy man stirs up dissension, but he who trusts in God will prosper". Proverbs 28. Some things are impossible to stop. War. Drugs. But they can be managed. This is what we do. We hold the line. We keep the peace. Do you understand?'

'No,' Nir said.

'One day, perhaps you will,' Cohen said. He looked like he wanted to say something more but changed his mind.

'Tonight will go smoothly,' he said.

'Yes,' Nir said.

He would wait for the ambush and the confusion to shoot Cohen in the back, he decided.

He had a throw-down gun prepared.

He'll blame it on the smugglers.

They drove in silence. There was no moon. Smugglers didn't like the moon, for obvious reasons.

They reached the hill and parked. A soldier came to escort them. They walked quietly, in camouflage, crouching low. They found shelter behind a rock. The ambush was ready, had been waiting since sundown. No one knew when the breach in the border would happen.

22:00

Nothing. Nir smothered a yawn. He was aware of the soldiers and officers around but he could neither see nor hear them.

23:00

Nothing. Cohen was sitting perfectly relaxed with his hands folded in his lap and his back to the rock, breathing evenly, eyes open.

12:41am

Something moved softly down below. Nir tensed. Cohen unfurled himself like a cat. Complete silence, then something moved again, a stone pushed by a foot, and they could hear footsteps.

An informant gave up the information about the shipment. They had informants everywhere. They knew when the rival drug smugglers were coming and where. They had informers everywhere—

'Don't move! You're surrounded! Put down your weapons and get on the ground!'

The platoon moved, somebody fired a glare, there was confusion down below and then gunfire. Shadows moved in the night, Nir felt the beating of blood in his head, it was all going down, he pulled out the throw-down, they had informants everywhere, they knew about the rival gangs and when they were coming and where—

He turned with the gun in his hand aimed at Cohen. Aimed for the head.

He saw the look in Cohen's eyes as he pressed the trigger.

Pain exploded in Nir's belly. It tore him apart. He fell back, his head smashing against the hard ground. He heard screams, gunshots, the sound of men dying. He screamed too. He was in so much pain.

He tried to grasp the wound. This new hole in his stomach, his chest. His hands were covered in blood. He looked up, helpless. Saw Cohen kneel by his side.

The look in Cohen's eyes. Like the sea at dusk. Cohen had a gun in his hand.

He raised it to fire a second shot. A confirmation kill.

Nir heard the gunshot but he wasn't dead, somehow. Cohen

fell back from him with a look of surprise on his face for once. Cohen, who wasn't surprised very often. There was blood on his chest where some stray bullet got him.

'Man down! Man down!'

Nir heard gunshots below, screams cut short as the soldiers carried out confirmation kills. Cohen sagged beside him.

Nir stared at the stars.

PART TEN

KIPPY

1987, Los Angeles

53

BAGDAD CAFÉ

'They get younger every year' – *Kippy*

'I liked it,' Kippy said.

'It was weird,' Romi said. 'And that German woman.'

'I thought it was good,' Kippy said. 'It was…' She searched for the word. 'Real.'

They came out of the cinema into bright sunlight. California, with its palm trees and its sunlight, was nevertheless nothing like Tel Aviv. Here you could be anything. You could be free, Kippy thought.

'Like Jasmin in *Bagdad Café*,' she said out loud. She often had conversations in her own head these days. Romi, which was short for Romema, only Romema wasn't a name anyone in America could say so she changed it to Romi, looked at her strangely.

'It was a weird movie, that's all I'm saying,' Romi said. 'Do you want to get a coffee?'

'I can't, I'm flying today,' Kippy said.

'Again? You never stop,' Romi said.

'I have to make my nut,' Kippy said, and they both broke out laughing at that weird expression that they'd heard the other day. But Kippy wasn't kidding. She was saving up, or at least trying to, but the money never seemed to stay around for long, and there was always the next party, the next high, and the money just didn't stick somehow. At least she didn't usually have to pay for drinks.

'Kisses to the baby,' she said to Romi. They hugged goodbye and Kippy hopped in a taxi.

'Where to?' the driver said.

She gave him the address in the valley and he made a face but put the meter on. Kippy sat in the back seat and looked out at the road. The driver put the radio on and Whitney Houston sang that she wanted to dance with somebody on KIQQ. As they hit Van Nuys Bono told Whitney he still hadn't found what he was looking for.

'It's another glorious day here in Los Angeles!' the DJ said.

'It sure is,' Kippy said.

'Where you from?' the taxi driver said. He stared at her through the rear-view mirror.

'Culver City,' Kippy said.

They pulled in to a small strip mall off Van Nuys and Kippy peeled off a note to pay the driver. He stared at her roll but didn't say anything, and she waited until he drove off before she went on. She passed the Hatkuma Middle Eastern Foods & Grocery Store and Eli's Electronics – Everything Must Go!, and the Haifa Grill Restaurant where Motti Pilpel was setting up tables, saw her and waved. She waved back and passed the dry cleaners where Shmuel Shmuel sat behind a desk counting pennies, and then she went into the offices of XLS Import-Export Corp., where Shula, Yossef's wife, sat behind a desk.

'Kippy,' she said, without much enthusiasm.

'Hey, Shula.'

'They're in back,' Shula said, and went back to her magazine. She was reading last month's *La'isha*, which anyone making an L.A.–Tel Aviv run was obliged to bring back, along with the newspapers and especially the weekend supplements.

Kippy nodded, went round Shula and to the back room, where Yossef – never Yossi – and Mooshon were stacking up VHS tapes. Yossef had an army of young Israelis, enticed to L.A. after military service. They'd sell the bootleg cassettes in flea markets all over Southern California. Yossef – never Yossi – found the Promised Land of California back in the mid-seventies and it seemed to him a lot better than Bat Yam. He started out small – extortion from the Jewish shop owners, debt collection and that sort of thing – then branched out into selling guns, because the only people who loved Uzis in Los Angeles more than gun shop owners were their customers.

Now business got so big they had ads put out in the newspapers back in Israel, promising green cards and jobs and the American dream to any soldier recently released from national service. If they were any use, Yossef got them a hooker to marry so they were legit.

Kippy worked for Yossef.

Everybody worked for Yossef.

'Good, you're here. There's bad traffic to the airport so you want to get moving pronto.'

'There's always bad traffic to the airport,' Kippy said.

'Take off your clothes,' Yossef said. Mooshon looked up. He was sweet on Kippy.

She stripped. Mooshon brought the wraparound drugs and fitted them on. He was sweaty. Those guys had no class, Kippy thought. But they were effective. She got dressed. Today's outfit was easy, a light dress and a sweater and a raincoat for the destination. She looked good. Mooshon said, 'There's another fifteen kilos in the suitcase.'

'Why not twenty?' Kippy said.

'We don't want to be greedy.'

Yossef looked up. 'Mooshon will take you to the airport. You're OK for the overnight?'

'I'm always OK,' Kippy said.

'Counting on you, buba,' Yossef said. He went back to packing tapes. Kippy followed Mooshon back to the parking lot.

At first there were just the ordinary businesses and the old Jews who paid protection back to Mickey Cohen in the olden days. Then came Yossef and his boys from Bat Yam and they saw a land of plenty. Now they owned the whole strip mall, legit shops laundering the drug money. It was the American dream.

Moosh drove her to LAX. He didn't talk much, which she liked about Moosh. He stared at her in the rear-view mirror, which was something she didn't like about Moosh. What other people didn't like about Moosh was the way he had with them when Yossef decided they owed him money. Moosh had the sort of face people went out of their way to avoid, and the last face a lot of people ended up seeing. The boys never really went into detail when Kippy was around. But she wasn't stupid. She knew what they were doing.

'You know that fucker, Ruvi?' Moosh said. 'The one married to that chick, Romema.'

'Yeah,' Kippy said. 'Why? Romi's a friend of mine.'

'He's being a prick,' Moosh said.

'What does that mean?' Kippy said. But she knew what it meant.

Moosh had a soft spot for Romema. Kippy knew it was meant as a warning, for her to pass along to her friend. But it wasn't her business. She settled back in her seat. It was nothing to do with her, she told herself. She stared out at the moving road.

Moosh didn't say anything else. He had exhausted his conversational range.

Kippy blew Moosh a kiss at LAX and made her way to Departures, ticket at the ready. She really did love travel, which was a part of the charm that surrounded her. She was the last person anyone would stop and, besides, the Americans had shit airport security. It was like they didn't even care.

She waited at the gate with the suitcase, light and made for travel.

'The Delta flight to Salt Lake City is now ready to depart.'

Kippy smiled, walked to the desk, showed her ticket and got onto the plane.

'Good flight?' Little Pinhas said.

'As always.'

What Kippy liked about Salt Lake City was how clean everything was. And the Mormons were always so polite. Little Pinhas had a little electronics shop in East Central. He picked her up from the airport.

'You want something to eat?' he said. He swung off the road to a diner near the airport. Kippy got changed in the bathroom and came out with the stuff for Pinhas in a carry bag he gave her. The rest was in the suitcase in his trunk. Kippy ordered pancakes.

Pinhas drank two cups of coffee one after the other. He was hopping across the table from her. Twitchy little fucker. Kippy tucked into her pancakes. She loved pancakes.

'It's cold,' she said when she finished. She pulled the coat over herself.

'Try living here,' Pinhas said.

'You don't like it?' Kippy said.

'I like it fine,' Pinhas said. 'It's pretty when you leave the city. There are these salt flats? You drive through them sometimes at night, with the full moon shining, it's like… I don't know. Otherworldly.'

'That sounds nice.'

'You don't get that in Israel,' Little Pinhas said.

'There's the Dead Sea,' Kippy said.

'It's not the same.'

Pinhas paid for the meal and left a tip on the table. He drove Kippy back to the airport. He handed her the envelope with the cash and she put it in her handbag.

'See you soon,' Kippy said. She watched him drive off. Then she went in to catch her flight to Miami.

'It's always good to see you, buba,' Eli Siton said. Eli wore a gold Rolex on his wrist and a jacket that was too expensive: it sat awkwardly on his narrow shoulders. Too much tailoring and not enough taste: that was Miami in a nutshell.

'It's good to see you too, sweetheart,' Kippy said. Eli drove a Chrysler. He liked to quote Iacocca on business. He owned a chain of jewellery stores in Miami. Before that he had a fish farm in Colombia. Before that he had another farm in Jamaica. Before that he worked with Oshri and Midget back in Israel where he was big enough to make it on to the original List of Eleven that was in all the papers back then. His brother, another compulsive gambler, was one number ahead of him on the list.

'You should quit those losers in Los Angeles and come work for me,' Eli said. He always told her that. It was night by the time she landed. Eli rolled down the window and a warm breeze blew in. He smoked a cigarette dangling one arm out of the window, flashing the Rolex. 'What's in Los Angeles you can't get right here?'

'The movies,' Kippy said, and Eli laughed a smoker's laugh and said, 'Actors are just playing make-believe all day, what's so interesting about that?'

Eli was the sort of guy who always knew better and told you so. He drove the Chrysler into the club's parking lot. The Anaconda Lounge was as garish as its name. The lighting was too low, the girls too young and the men too old and the food overpriced and the cocktails too sugary. Eli Siton loved it. The problem was that Eli might have been a cheap piece of shit, but he was a cheap piece of shit with good friends in Colombia.

Kippy followed him into the club, past the dance floor and to Eli's private office. He owned the club, of course. Two of his guys stood guard and looked her over without changing expression.

'They get younger every year,' Kippy said.

'Lebanon makes them old quick,' Eli said, ushering her in. 'In Miami I make them young again. You won't believe what pussy and blow will do to a soldier.'

Blow. That was what it came down to. Dope was too bulky and too cheap. Heroin was too junky. But coke only had one source, and coke was what everyone wanted. So Eli, like a hundred other two-bit gangsters, made deals and made himself useful, and he had a pipeline to Cali.

'So?' Eli said.

'So,' Kippy said. She took out the bag she had hidden on herself and tossed it over carelessly. Eli caught it in both hands, face red, and sat down.

'Don't do that,' he said.

Kippy lit a cigarette and watched him. He pulled the string loose and upended the felt bag and let the diamonds out onto the desk. They piled up, catching the light, and Kippy thought how beautiful they were, how their beauty was entirely independent from their function.

Eli fixed a jeweller's glass in his eye and examined the diamonds.

'Good, good,' he said.

'Yossef sends his regards,' Kippy said.

'Yossef is un pendejo,' Eli said.

Kippy stared at him without changing her expression.

'He wants to know when the next shipment's coming.'

'I'll send the boys in a car,' Eli said. 'Usual set up.' He poured the diamonds back into the bag. 'Come on, Kippy. You hungry?'

'Always,' Kippy said.

She sat in the booth with Eli and two of his men and Sandra, who worked for Eli, and Yardena, who was Eli's accountant. They ate empanadas and drank mojitos and listened as the DJ played 'La Bamba', because it was that sort of place. Sandra didn't say anything, and Yardena kept asking Kippy if she brought any newspapers with her from back home, and that she read in *La'isha* that Ofra Haza nearly died in a Cessna airplane crash, and did Kippy hear that Uri Geller was going to fly in a hot-air balloon over England and bend spoons from the skies? And she also read in *Ma'ariv* that Geller healed a mute boy while flying in a helicopter, and what did Kippy think of that? And it said he was invited to Washington to talk to the Select Committee on Intelligence about the Soviet nuclear weapons arsenal.

'You really like Uri Geller, don't you,' Kippy said.

'He's having a busy year,' Yardena said.

Kippy and Yardena and Sandra went to the ladies' room and did lines.

'Where did you meet Eli?' Kippy asked Sandra.

'Fuck Eli,' Sandra said. 'Let's go out properly. We never see you enough, Kippy. When are you moving to Miami?'

'Yes, move here, with us!' Yardena said. She did another line. 'Let's go dancing,' she said. 'Somewhere that's not here.'

Kippy felt the familiar call of the night wash over her, the food and the drinks and the coke lifting her up on a warm scented cloud. They escaped the ladies room and 'La Bamba' and slipped out into the night, laughing as Sandra hailed down a taxi. Then it was off to some place on the beach with music in Spanish and men who swayed like graceful trees in the breeze. In the ladies' bathroom Yardena said, 'Here, take this,' and put a pill in her mouth.

'What is it?' Kippy said.

'Have you heard of Ecstasy?'

They went back to the dance floor. The lights were brighter and softer. Kippy felt so good. She wanted to hug everyone. The music kept her dancing, she had never felt so happy and so free.

'I love you,' she told Yardena.

'I love you too!'

Then it was five in the morning and they were outside looking for a taxi. Kippy kept grinding her teeth for some reason. She slept for three hours, then got a taxi to the airport. Two hours later she was on the plane to L.A.

54

ENRIQUE GONZALES

'I thought everyone in L.A. is in show business' – Enrique

'Good night?'

The man in the window seat beside her wore a light linen jacket that was casually expensive, a gold watch that was casually ostentatious, and a smile that was all white teeth and anything but casual dentistry.

'What?'

'Your pupils,' he said, laughing. 'They're enormous.'

'Oh. I lost my glasses.'

'Of course,' he said, nodding seriously. He had rather lovely eyes, Kippy thought. She still felt a lingering warmth of emotion from the night.

The man stuck out his hand. 'I'm Enrique Gonzales,' he said.

'Sarah Gavrieli,' she said. 'But everyone calls me Kippy.'

'Kippy?' he said.

'Like Kippy Kipod? Never mind,' she said, and he laughed again, and leaned closer, and she could smell his expensive aftershave.

'Where are you from, Kippy Kipod?' the man said.

'Tarzana,' Kippy said, and the man laughed. 'But originally,' he said.

'Israel. You know it?'

'Of course. It is a very beautiful country.'

'You've been?'

'No, but I hope to one day.'

'Where are you from?' Kippy said.

'I am from Panama,' Enrique Rodriguez said. 'You know Panama?'

'I know it's a country,' Kippy said.

'It is very beautiful,' Enrique said.

'I'm sure,' Kippy said. 'What do you do?'

It was the question everyone always asked in Los Angeles. And Enrique Rodriguez wasn't offended.

'I work for a bank,' he said. 'It is very boring.'

'It must pay well,' Kippy said, looking at Enrique's watch.

'You like it? It's a Cartier.'

Kippy shrugged. 'It's nice,' she said.

He laughed. 'You don't even wear a watch,' he said. 'Let me guess, what do you do… You're an actress.'

'No.'

'But I thought everyone in L.A. is in show business.'

'They are,' Kippy said, and Enrique laughed. He laughed so easily, she thought. She'd never met a man who seemed to have so little care in the world. She looked at his even tan and the way his black hair was slicked back just so, and she thought, this is a man who pays attention to the details. So she was a little wary, as much as he was no doubt trying to charm her.

'You're a model.'

'Oh, come on,' Kippy said.

'You look like one.'

He really was putting it on. But she found that she didn't mind.

'No?' he said. 'Then I know. You're an Israeli spy.'

'I can neither confirm nor deny…' Kippy said, and she watched as his lips stretched into that smile again, showing off those perfect white teeth, the tiny wrinkles in the corners of his eyes, that great tan. He leaned closer still.

'So tell me,' he murmured, 'what do you really do?'

'I'm an international drug smuggler,' she told him. He put one hand on her arm. His hand was warm. 'That must be exciting…' he said.

She felt his heat. And she was still buzzing from that pill last night. What did Yardena call it? Ecstasy? Kippy leaned into Enrique. His lips tasted like coffee and berries.

'I don't even know you…' she murmured.

'What do you want to know?'

'What you look like with those pants down,' Kippy said, and this time Enrique really did laugh, and he followed her wordlessly when she got up and straightened her dress and went to the toilet cubicle in the back of the plane.

When the plane touched down at LAX Kippy was pleased to be back on home ground. Sometimes she thought of all her time in Israel as just a dream she'd had. In L.A. it was easy to forget one's past, to become someone new. You could be anything you wanted.

She had been a gawky kid at school, had played the clarinet, was teased by the boys, had few girlfriends. She got good grades, took part in the National Bible Contest in Jerusalem two years in a row. She read a lot of books.

When she turned sixteen she took a job working bar at the Peacock in Tel Aviv. At seventeen she met Bialik, less a poet like his namesake and more a career criminal. With his long hair swept back and that infectious smile she wasn't the only one smitten with him.

Bialik didn't work for anyone but himself, not Rubenstein, not Aslan. At first he mostly robbed banks. Then he got into drugs, and then the drugs got into him. She'd loved him, even when he tried to kill her twice, even when he lost everything but the desire for another shot of Lebanese heroin, even when he went to prison on a stretch for double murder and never came out.

By the time Bialik slipped in the shower on a shiv Kippy didn't have time to sit shiva. What were you supposed to do? She had loved, and loving wasn't wrong, but she had moved on. She had done two years of national service at a miserable secretary desk in the Galilee, but at least she knew how to use a gun. She started a BA in Hebrew Literature at Tel Aviv University, but books no longer excited her.

She still knew the people Bialik knew. And when Benny Pardes offered her the courier job she jumped on it. And when the opportunity came she just stuck around Los Angeles. And now…

She figured she was still finding herself. She wasn't going to be a courier forever.

'I'll see you tonight, babe?' Enrique Gonzales said.

'Don't call me babe. It's Kippy.'

'Alright, Kippy.' That smile again. He reminded her of a big cat. My, what big teeth you have. The better to eat you with, my dear! She shuddered as his fingers brushed the small of her back. Then he was gone with his briefcase, and Kippy put on her sunglasses and stepped outside into the bright Californian day.

There was a lot of construction next door at the nearby terminal. Kippy tried to get a taxi but there was a queue. She checked her watch. A shuttle bus was just pulling in, and Kippy realised the El Al flight from Tel Aviv was due to land. She could go pick up the newspapers from Segev, the Second Officer who was sweet on her. He always brought the weekend supplement and even *La'isha* sometimes. Having the papers from back home was currency better than dollars. She jumped on the shuttle bus.

She briefly remembered Moosh's warning to Romema. But then she dismissed it from her mind.

She wondered idly what Enrique planned for their date later. He was staying at the Waldorf in Beverly Hills. He promised her dinner and dancing. She would just pick up the papers, go drop the cash from Salt Lake at Yossef's place, give Shula the magazine, go home, get a few hours sleep, get dressed and go out again.

Another beautiful, carefree day in beautiful, carefree L.A.

The shuttle bus pulled to the curb. She got out. Checked the board. The flight from Tel Aviv had already landed. She looked out for the crew but didn't see Segev.

Then her eyes alighted on two passengers coming out from the passenger arrivals doors. They carried a suitcase each, and she didn't know the guy on right, but she knew the other man well.

It was Cohen.

55

DRUGS AND MURDER INCORPORATED

'You never say good luck' – *Chaia*

'Cohen!' She threw her arms around him and he looked startled. He winced when she pressed against his shoulder where the bullet hit him. She pulled back.

'I'm sorry,' she said.

'It's nothing,' he said. 'Kippy, what are you doing here!'

'I just came to get the papers,' she told him, smiling. She always had a soft spot for Cohen.

'What papers?' Cohen said. 'The newspapers? Eddie, you kept the newspapers?'

The man beside him frowned. 'I have *Yediot*,' he said. 'You want it? Here.' He rummaged in his carry-on bag and gave them to her. 'Listen, this is not a good time.'

'We're staying at the Howard Johnson downtown,' Cohen said. 'Meet me tonight, we can have dinner.'

'I can't tonight. I have a date. Cohen, what are you *doing* here?'

'Chief Superintendent Raphael? Inspector Cohen? I'm Deputy Chief Reece, this is Detective McKenzie with the LAPD.'

The men shook hands. Kippy stood to one side, bemused.

'How was your flight?' Deputy Chief Reece said.

'It was fine,' Eddie said.

'You want to go to your hotel first? Or we can go past the office, introduce you to the team first. They look forward to meeting you.'

Eddie nodded. 'That would be good for us,' he said. 'Cohen?'

'Yes,' Cohen said. He drew Kippy aside.

'Meet me tomorrow morning, then,' he said. 'Are you still in with that lot?'

'Sort of,' Kippy said.

'Aha,' Cohen said. 'Well, come meet me? You can show me the town. I heard you can get a map to see where all the movie stars live.'

'Sure,' Kippy said. 'We can do that.'

'Aha,' Cohen said. 'Tomorrow, then. Good to see you, Kippy.'

'You, too.'

'Inspector Cohen? Are you ready?' the LAPD man said. He sounded politely impatient.

Cohen turned back to him with a smile, nodded, and the four policemen left together. Kippy stared after them, wondering what it was all about, thinking that whatever it was most likely had to do with Yossef.

'The Salt Lake money,' Kippy said. She tossed the envelope on Yossef's desk. He nodded and put it away into a drawer without looking up. Moosh was in the corner, mixing powder into dime bags.

'And Siton?' Yossef said.

'He said he'll send the usual shipment.'

'That cocksucker,' Yossef said. 'I wish we didn't have to buy from him.'

'You could buy from the Mexicans,' Mooshon mumbled from the corner.

'The Mexicans only work for the Colombians,' Yossef said. 'So what's the fucking point of that?'

Moosh shrugged.

'Mexicans,' Yossef muttered. He raised his head. 'Well, are you still here?'

'I got the newspaper,' Kippy said.

'So?'

'So you won't like it.'

Kippy tossed the paper on the desk.

'What the fuck is this?' Yossef said.

The headline said, *The Israeli Mafia in L.A. – Drugs and Murder Incorporated.*

A small inset had a blurry picture of Yossef.

'Hey, Moosh, look,' Yossef said. 'I'm in the newspaper.'

'It says the LAPD is so concerned with the activities of Israeli criminals in the city that it has requested help from Israeli police.'

'So?' Yossef said. Kippy thought, if anything, he seemed pleased to see himself in the paper.

'So I don't know who the other guy with him was, but I saw Cohen at the airport.'

Yossef mulled it over.

'Cohen has no authority here,' he said. He shrugged. 'Go home, Kippy. Get some sleep. Your eyes look fucked.'

'Wow, thanks,' Kippy said.

'You want a ride?' Mooshon said.

Kippy stared at the two of them and that shitty office. The pirate cassettes and the bags of coke. They were nobodies, but drug money made everybody a somebody.

'Sure,' she said.

'What are you, her driver now?' Yossef said. 'Fine, go, what do I care. I've got a run for you again next week, Kippy.'

'Alright.'

She followed Mooshon to the parking lot and to his shitty Honda.

'You talk to Romi yet?' he said.

She'd forgotten all about the warning.

'I was away, Moosh,' she said.

'Well,' he said. He sat behind the steering wheel and brooded.

'They should make it right,' he said.

'Make what right, Moosh?'

'Stuff,' he said.

Kippy slid into the passenger seat beside him. Moosh was done talking. He looked exhausted from the effort. Kippy turned on the radio. Tiffany sang, 'I Think We're Alone Now'. Kippy sat back and closed her eyes.

'Take me home,' she said.

★★★

The commune was not far from the strip mall. There were between six and eight of them living there at any one time, sharing a large house with a small swimming pool and a white picket fence and some rodents. The neighbours all had identical white picket fences and big cars parked in the driveway and bratty kids who rode bicycles and stared at your tits. Kippy went to the kitchen, flopped on a chair and said to Chaia, 'Pl*eease* make me a coffee.'

'Go to bed, Kippy,' Chaia said without malice. 'You look like shit.'

'I have a date tonight.'

'You have a date every night.'

'Pretty please?'

'Only because I'm making one anyway,' Chaia said. She'd played a corpse on *Hill Street Blues* and had a speaking part on *Starman*. It was only one line but that and some background work got her a SAG card, which Kippy understood was something to do with acting. When Chaia wasn't acting she did some courier work for Yossef, and she was seeing Yoram, who was one of Yossef's new men in town.

'How was Salt Lake?' Chaia said.

Kippy shrugged. 'Same as always.'

'You see Little Pinhas?'

'Yeah.'

'How is he?'

'Still little,' Kippy said.

'He's sweet,' Chaia said. Considering Yoram, her present boyfriend, was the main guy Yossef sent to beat up the Jewish shop owners who wouldn't pay protection, Kippy thought Chaia didn't have the clearest definition of the word. But then what did she know? Little Pinhas always seemed harmless for a coke dealer.

'What are you doing today?' Kippy said.

'I have an audition later. It's for *Matlock*.'

'What's that?'

'Do you even watch TV!' Chaia said, shocked. 'It's about a lawyer who solves crimes.'

'Most lawyers I met worked *for* the criminals,' Kippy said. Chaia shrugged and passed her a coffee.

'Go to sleep, Kippy,' she said. 'I'm taking mine to the pool.'

Chaia sashayed out of the French doors. Kippy watched her go, the high heels and the bikini and that sway.

'Good luck on your audition!' she said.

Not turning her head, Chaia said, 'We say break a leg, you never say good luck.'

'I thought that was just in theatre,' Kippy said, but by then she was talking to herself.

56

SUCH A GANG

'We were four who went to get the meat' – *Pucho*

'I have to go,' Kippy said. She slid out of the bed.

'What time is it?' Enrique said. He didn't sit up. Faint dawn light seeped in through the gaps in the curtains.

'Four, five.'

'Stay.'

'I'm meeting a friend.'

'Do you ever sleep, Kippy Gavrieli?' he said.

Kippy looked around for her clothes. She felt restless. Those hours, end of night but too early for morning: that was when she felt most alert. She did a line of coke off the bedside table, left there from earlier.

'You want some?' she said.

'I want to sleep,' Enrique said. 'With a beautiful woman in my arms.'

'One out of two isn't bad,' Kippy said, and Enrique laughed. He seemed to laugh at all her jokes. He'd taken her out to Spago and then dancing and then the hotel bar for cocktails and then to the room. He seemed fascinated by Israel and the fact Kippy served in the army, and he kept asking about Uzis and Desert Eagles and shit like night vision goggles and unmanned drones, at least until she grabbed his cock under the table and he shut up fast.

'You can buy them in any shop in L.A,' she told him.

'Aha. Hmm. Hmmm… But what if you wanted to buy bulk?'

'Why would a banker need Uzis?' Kippy said.

'In my country,' Enrique said, 'you always need guns.'

They didn't talk about it anymore after that but she sensed the subject would come up again. She figured maybe she could make some money for herself, she just had to figure out the angle. Everyone wanted to sell Uzis, most of all the Israeli military industry, and they weren't that fussy who they sold it to.

'Maybe my friend could help you with that guns thing,' she said, putting on her shoes.

'Yeah? Who's your friend?'

'He's a policeman.'

Enrique laughed. 'Is he a secret policeman?' he said.

'No. Just a regular one.'

'Will I see you again?' Enrique said. 'I'm in town for a few more days.'

'I'll see you,' Kippy said. She blew him a kiss, downed what was left in a glass of champagne and left.

By the time she got to the Howard Johnson the dawn light fell like gold. It couldn't make the city pretty, it couldn't hide the rats in the bins behind the hotel, or the drunk sleeping outside a shuttered taqueria. But it compensated.

When she stepped into the lobby Cohen was already there, sitting in an armchair, reading a book. He didn't see her. She watched him. He seemed older than she'd last seen him. He read with a quiet intensity. He looked up when he heard her footsteps.

'Kippy,' he said.

'What are you reading?' she said.

'Oh, this. *Such A Gang*, by Pucho.'

Kippy laughed. 'But it's old,' she said.

'You read it?'

'It's a boys' book,' Kippy said.

'So you *have* read it,' Cohen said, and she laughed.

'Yeah. It's about that kid Yossinyu who joins the Palmach to fight the British. He dies in the end. Oh, sorry, you're still reading it.'

'It's alright,' Cohen said. 'I read it before. They were a different generation, weren't they. The founders.' He brooded. 'Though it still starts and ends with them stealing a cow from the kibbutz.

"We were four who went to get the meat." It sticks with you, that line. Four, because the fifth one was dead. Maybe they weren't so different from us after all.'

He put the book down on his knees and smiled up at Kippy.

'I couldn't sleep,' he said. 'Jetlag.'

'People like us never sleep at night, Cohen,' Kippy told him. She sat across from him. A Hispanic cleaner dabbed the floors on the far side of the lobby. 'When did I last see you? It wasn't the hospital.'

They'd called her when Nir got shot. She went straight to the emergency room. Cohen was in the same bad ambush. He got a bullet in the shoulder. For a while they didn't think Nir was going to make it. They put him and Cohen in the same room. She sat there a lot, until Nir got better.

'You were never going to be an army widow,' Cohen said.

'No.' Kippy brooded. 'I lost one guy to prison, the other… I don't know where Nir is now. I wasn't going to sit around and wait.'

'You have your own life to live,' Cohen said.

'Yes.'

'It was the funeral! That's the last time I saw you,' Kippy said. 'The one for… what was his name? Fat Mendel.'

'Fat Mendel,' Cohen said. He smiled. 'I remember.'

'Somebody filled up his Peugeot with bullets,' Kippy said.

'That's right,' Cohen said.

'Why were you at the funeral?' Kippy said. She looked at him curiously. 'I never asked.'

'I was the investigating officer. I knew Fat Mendel. He worked for Rubenstein. He was a friendly guy, for a pusher.'

'Did you find out who did it?'

Cohen shrugged again. 'It was Aslan, but we couldn't prove anything. It's still an open case.

'You think you'll still get to pin it on him?' Kippy said, curious.

'I think someone will do to Aslan what Aslan did to Fat Mendel,' Cohen said. 'Guys like these, they don't die in bed, Kippy.'

'And guys like you, Cohen? Do they live happily ever after?'

'I'd like to think so,' Cohen said. 'We're the good guys.' He got up, stretched his legs.

'Want to get breakfast?' he said. 'I always wanted to try those American pancakes like in the movies.'

'I know a place,' Kippy said. 'But don't you have to go to work?'

'Eddie can handle the local cops,' Cohen said. 'I told them I'll sniff around on my own. See if I can find any old informants.'

'Are you calling me old?'

Kippy smiled. Cohen smiled.

'Come on,' Kippy said. 'I'll get you your pancakes.'

Nick's was run by two retired LAPD homicide detectives, but Kippy didn't mind. She liked cops almost as much as she liked crooks, maybe because most of the time she couldn't really tell the difference. They sat on the counter and ordered.

'No pancakes,' the man said, 'but I can do you waffles with blueberries and syrup if that's your poison.'

Cohen agreed without much fuss. Kippy had an orange juice and a bagel and they both had coffee.

'You want bacon with that?' the man said.

Kippy saw Cohen's face and burst out laughing.

'They do things differently in America,' she said.

Cohen dug into his waffles. Kippy drank coffee and nibbled on the bagel.

'So,' she said.

'So,' Cohen said.

'So what do you want to know?'

Cohen chewed a mouthful carefully. He put down the knife and fork.

'Is Yossef still running things?'

'Clearly.'

'The local cops don't mind drugs,' Cohen said. 'But they don't like bodies.'

'You can't have one without the other,' Kippy said.

'He gets the cocaine from where, Miami?'

'That's the place.'

'Old Eli Siton still there?'

'He's connected,' Kippy said.

'So I heard. Friends in Cali. Look, Kippy, I don't really give a shit about all this. This isn't my jurisdiction. You're still running courier for Yossef?'

She nodded.

'Who's the point man with Miami?' Cohen said.

'You're looking at her.'

'Moving up in the world, Kippy Kipod!' he said, and she laughed.

'When did you ever watch *Sumsum Street*, Cohen?'

'I have three children. Another on the way.'

She looked at him, surprised. 'I never knew that.'

'"Be fruitful and multiply, and fill the earth, God said. For I shall bless you and multiply your seed like the stars in the heavens and the sand on the seashore",' Cohen said. 'G—'

'Genesis, yes, I know. And you shouldn't say "seed".'

'What would you like me to say, Kippy Kipod?'

'Stop quoting bullshit at me like you do everyone else and tell me what your plans are. I know you, Cohen. I know you're not here for pancakes.'

'Which is a good thing,' Cohen said. 'Because I didn't get any.'

'You're here to put the lid on Yossef, aren't you.'

Cohen dabbed his lips with a napkin.

'Yossef's a piece of shit,' he said. 'And it might be felt back home that the Bat Yam boys have had their turn in the sun and are proving to be something of a bad investment.'

'Too many headlines?' Kippy said.

'That and the issue with Siton.'

'What's the issue with Siton?'

'He doesn't like sharing his friends.'

'Ah.' Kippy considered. 'But you can't touch him either.'

'No. Too connected – not just the cartel, I mean his family. They go back a long way in Jerusalem. If he goes down it will be in America, not home. But the problem remains. You have to go through him to Cali, and it is felt that a more direct line to Colombia might be beneficial for everyone.'

'Felt by Rubenstein, you mean.'

Cohen shrugged. 'We put him up. We can pull him down. But as long as people want to buy cocaine you won't get rid of people like that. All you can do is make sure they know there is a higher power.'

'And you're the higher power?'

'I just keep the peace, Kippy.'

'And yet we are always at war.'

He inched his head.

Kippy considered.

'There's a guy,' she said. 'Ruvi. He's married to my friend Romema. Maybe you should talk to him.'

She stood, pulled out her roll of notes, peeled one and laid it on the counter.

'My treat,' she said.

Cohen smiled, but it didn't quite reach his eyes.

He followed behind her to the door.

Kippy knew it was a mistake as soon as they walked in. Maybe it was how dark the house was. The blinds were drawn despite the sun outside. Maybe it was the fug of cigarette smoke and weed, and the dirty glasses on the coffee table, or the two Mexicans half asleep in the leather chairs, or the drunk hostile look Ruvi gave Cohen.

'Oh, look at her!' Kippy said. Romi held the baby in her arms. She smiled.

'She's adorable!'

'Do you want to hold her?' Romi said. Kippy took the little girl and cradled her. She was just under a year old, a fat golden thing, a real California baby.

'You want some coffee?' Romi said.

'Had some just now,' Cohen said. 'Thank you.'

'Ruvi! Kippy's here!'

'I can see that,' Ruvi said. He didn't move from the sofa. 'Hey, Kippy.'

'Hey, Ruvi. This is Cohen.'

Still Ruvi didn't stir.

'I know who you are,' he said.

'Then you know why I'm here,' Cohen said.

'You have no authority here, Cohen. Not in Los Angeles.'

'I hear you're having problems,' Cohen said.

'No problems,' Ruvi said. One of the Mexicans stirred. He said something in Spanish. Ruvi shook his head. The two men got up. They shook Ruvi's hand and went past Cohen and Kippy, not saying a word, and left the house.

'I heard you're having a problem with Yossef,' Cohen said.

'No problems,' Ruvi said.

Kippy thought he must be very drunk or very stoned. His eyes were mean. Cohen's were just cold.

'I heard you're fighting Yossef over money.'

'Bullshit,' Ruvi said. 'He's just pissed off I'm going my own way, that's all. But it's a free country here, Cohen. Not like home. A man can be something here.'

'And what are you going to be?' Cohen said, and Ruvi laughed.

'I've got to look after my family,' he said. 'I have responsibilities now.'

'I heard you're going with the Mexicans,' Cohen said. 'Bypassing Siton down in Miami, buying coke direct over the border and straight to L.A.'

'You hear a lot of things,' Ruvi said. He looked accusingly at Kippy, and she shrugged.

'Everyone knows,' she said.

'I thought the Mexicans weren't shit,' Cohen said.

'Yeah, well, amigo,' Ruvi said. 'That's what everyone always thinks. But they'll surprise us all.'

'But they have to buy from the cartels in Colombia,' Cohen said, relentless. Kippy wondered if that was how he always interrogated people. And he wasn't scared of Ruvi, that was for sure. 'So don't you end up paying double?'

'Who is asking this?' Ruvi said. 'You are asking this? Or back home is asking this?'

'Does it matter?' Cohen said, and Kippy saw Ruvi go quiet. Quiet and broody.

'You're not muscling in on this,' Ruvi said. 'This is my business.

Make your own goddamned friends and get the fuck out of my house, Cohen.'

'Alright.'

'Fucking cunt.'

Cohen went still. The baby woke up and cried.

'Give her to me,' Ruvi said. Kippy handed him the baby. He cradled her in his arms.

'Who's a pretty girl?' he said. 'Who's a pretty girl?'

Romi came back with the coffee but stopped.

'You're leaving already?' she said. She looked tired, Kippy thought.

'Another time,' Cohen said.

Kippy shrugged at Romi, followed Cohen out. Felt Ruvi's eyes in the back of her head, like a target.

'Well, that didn't go well,' she said when they were back outside.

Cohen said, 'You think there's something in this Mexican thing?'

'No,' Kippy said. 'Not when the Colombians control everything.'

'I hate coke,' Cohen said. 'And I hate cokeheads. I'll see you, Kippy. I'd better get back to the job. Help the LAPD with their Israeli mob situation.'

'What are you going to tell them?' Kippy said, and Cohen shook his head and muttered, 'Nothing useful.'

57

THE BONAVENTURE

'It's bad for business if you're fighting all the time' – Romi

The next day Kippy went on another run, up to Bakersfield and then to San Jose. Moosh drove her to the airport.

'Did you talk to Romi?' he said.

Kippy just shrugged.

'What's Cohen like?' Moosh asked. 'I never met him.'

'He's just some guy,' Kippy said. She felt tired for some reason, not her usual cheery self.

'Yeah,' Moosh said.

Danny in Bakersfield ran food trucks and sold cocaine but all he wanted to do was talk about oil. In San Jose she got picked up by Gutte, who was called that because he looked a little like Uri Zohar in *Perverts*, and ran real estate, sold cocaine, but only wanted to talk about computers. Then she was finally back in L.A., sitting by the pool, drinking a vodka and orange juice and wondering why she was feeling so melancholic, when the doorbell rang.

'Go see who it is,' she told Chaia.

'You go see who it is,' Chaia said. She was smoking a joint on the inflatable mattress in the pool. So Kippy got up and went to the door, and when she opened it she saw Enrique Rodriguez.

He looked very dapper in an ironed linen suit, and he held flowers, and he was smiling at her in a way that was sort of hungry, and she said, 'What are you doing here?'

'I missed you,' he said, still smiling.

'How did you find me?'

He looked hurt. 'I rang the number you left me. You weren't in but your friend answered. Chaia? Did you know she was in *Airwolf*? I love *Airwolf*.'

'She wasn't in *Airwolf*,' Kippy said. 'She tried out for *Airwolf* but she didn't – did she give you this address?'

'You are very suspicious,' Enrique said. 'May I come in? I brought flowers.'

She stared at him and he was right, she was suspicious. 'I thought we were meeting tomorrow for drinks.'

'Tomorrow, who has time for tomorrow?' Enrique said. 'When tonight is already here? They're roses,' he said.

'They're very nice,' Kippy said.

'Kippy, who is it!' Chaia shouted from the pool.

'Come in,' Kippy said, relenting. She took the flowers. Enrique and his smile followed her in. She put the roses on the table.

'Here, let me,' he said. He busied himself in the kitchen, found a glass vase, filled it with water, put the flowers in and arranged them.

'This is much better,' he said.

'Maybe I should have bought *you* flowers…' Kippy muttered.

'Kippy, who is it!' Chaia shouted from the pool. 'If it's Yoram tell him to fuck off, I'm still not talking to him!'

'It's not Yoram!' Kippy shouted back.

'Why not!' Chaia shouted, outraged. 'Doesn't he love me?'

'I don't fucking know, Chaia,' Kippy said. 'Oh, come on, then, Enrique. You want wine?'

'You have wine?' Enrique said.

Kippy looked around the kitchen.

'Well, no,' she said, and Enrique laughed. Kippy mixed them both vodka and orange juice.

'This is what you drink?' Enrique said.

'This is what Chaia drinks and… Yes, that's what we usually drink.'

Chaia came over from the pool area in her high heel sandals and small bikini, water dripping down her curves. She loomed over Enrique, who stared.

'So this is your mystery friend?' Chaia said.

'Enrique Gonzales,' Enrique said. He took Chaia's hand and kissed it. 'Such a pleasure. I wish to hear more of Ernest Borgnine.'

'He was such a darling,' Chaia said dreamingly.

'You were never in *Airwolf*,' Kippy said.

'I was too, I told you,' Chaia said. 'It was before you got to L.A.'

'You must be a wonderful actress,' Enrique said, saluting her, and Kippy thought he must be a little drunk. That, or he was pretending.

'What do you want to do?' she asked Enrique.

'I don't mind,' he said. 'I just like being with you.'

'Let's order pizza,' Chaia declared. 'I can show you my episode, I have it on VHS.'

She raised her glass. Enrique raised his. Kippy sighed but followed suit and they touched glasses.

'I'll set up the video!' Chaia said. She turned and sashayed to the lounge, giving Enrique something to stare at.

'Maybe put on some clothes first…' Kippy muttered.

Enrique took her hand in his.

'I only have eyes for you,' he said.

By midnight Chaia was snoring on the couch. The ice in the pitcher of drinks on the table had long since melted. Fuzzy static filled the TV screen and the VHS belched out the cassette with a decisive click.

Kippy was a little drunk herself. She watched Enrique's face in the light of the TV. He looked back at her, and the gaiety fell from him a little, and she saw the hard edges of his jaw and that he was not in the least bit drunk.

'What do you really want?' Kippy whispered.

Enrique reached and cupped her chin in his hand. Kippy shivered. She thought, he has rough hands for a banker.

'I want to meet your policeman friend,' Enrique said.

'Why? What is it you want? Who are you really?'

'My name is Enrique Rodriguez,' he said. 'I'm a banker.'

'What kind of a banker needs guns?' Kippy said.

'A banker who works for men who need such guns,' he said, 'and are willing to pay handsomely for them.'

He drew her to him, kissed her on the lips. His hand on the back of her neck now, and she felt the hunger in him, his excitement.

'You will arrange it?' he said.

'Yes,' Kippy whispered. 'Yes...'

His face, bathed in the TV's unearthly light. They made love urgently, quickly, as Chaia snored on the couch.

'Call Romema,' Yossef said. Kippy was back in the back room of XLS Import-Export Corp.

'Why?' she said.

He waved a hand dismissively. 'It's over. I'm not going to war over some money. There is always more money. We'll meet all together, have a few drinks, hash it out. A sulcha.'

'Where?'

'Somewhere nice. I booked us a suite at the Bonaventure downtown.'

Kippy felt sudden relief. It was a classy place. Yossef already moved on, lost interest. 'When can you do another run?'

'When do you need me to?'

'In a few days,' he said. 'Soon as the new shipment from Miami comes.'

'Alright,' she said.

She met Romi for a coffee and they went to the movies. They watched *Three Men and a Baby* and Kippy paid for the popcorn.

'I'm glad Yossef's calling it off,' Romi said. 'It's bad for business if you're fighting all the time.'

They said goodbye until later. Kippy said, 'Kisses to the baby.' She went shopping on Rodeo Drive. The sun shone down, because this was L.A. Kippy wore her sunglasses. Cohen told her the LAPD had these two Yiddish speaking detectives. They were trying to get the Jewish merchants to testify against Yossef. He didn't think it would amount to much, but you never knew. She had the feeling there'd be a couple of shops burned down before the month was out, just as a reminder to the boychiks of who was in charge.

She made it to the Bonaventure with plenty of time. Went up to the room, which was reserved under the name McLaren.

She made herself comfortable. The champagne was already waiting in a bucket of ice when she walked in. Then Romi and Ruvi came in. Ruvi looked fine this time, clear-eyed. He looked happy to put it behind them. Yossef and Moosh came in.

'Well, Kippy, pour us all a drink,' Yossef said.

Kippy turned to the bottle. She saw Moosh in the reflection, raising a gun. She saw Yossef in the reflection, raising a gun. She saw the startled look in Romi's eyes, Ruvi's lips moving, but no words came. She heard the twin *phut*, *phut* of the silenced guns.

Two bullets, two bullet holes, both in the centre of the forehead. She heard Ruvi and Romi drop to the floor.

Kippy didn't turn.

She waited for the bullet, but it didn't come.

'Come on, Kippy,' Yossef said. 'Help us clean up.'

She turned. She saw him put the gun away. He looked down on the bodies.

'Cunt,' Yossef said.

Moosh went out of the room. He came back with a cleaning cart and a black duffel bag. He took out cleavers from the bag. Kippy felt sick. Moosh hefted a cleaver. He nodded to Yossef.

He chopped off Romi's arm.

Kippy was sick in the toilets. When she came back, Romi's head was in a plastic rubbish bag. Moosh and Yossef were covered in gore. They hacked and chopped. Legs, arms. They pushed them into bin bags.

'We'll get rid of them elsewhere,' Moosh told her. He handed her cloth and spray. He and Yossef cut away a part of the carpet where the bodies had bled. They worked methodically, like remodelling men. They replaced the carpet with matching material they had brought with them.

Kippy scrubbed blood. She cleaned the walls. She wiped all surfaces. She felt Moosh's hand on her shoulder and nearly jumped, but didn't.

'There was nothing we could do,' Moosh said.

Kippy just nodded. She cleaned and scrubbed. The room was

spotless. Moosh and Yossef changed. They put on clean clothes. They left the room and took everything with them, the bottle of champagne, the glasses, the cleaning cart, the body parts in bin bags.

They took the service stairs.

Two cars waited for them in the back. Moosh lugged bin-bagged body parts into the hold. Yosef took out a wad of cash and handed it to Kippy. She didn't count but it was a few thousand in there.

'Walk away slowly,' Yosef said. 'Remember you were never here. You did good, Kippy.'

He got into a car and Moosh got into the other and they drove off.

Kippy walked away. She felt drunk. The light was too bright and the noise too loud. No one saw her.

She found a payphone and made a call.

58

EPITAPH

'It's the right thing to do' – Cohen

'You were right to call me,' Cohen said.

They were sitting in a bar in Skid Row. Kippy was on her second martini and Cohen had a beer.

Kippy lit a cigarette. Her hands shook. Cohen lit it for her, cupping his hands around her hand.

'What will happen to them?' Kippy said.

'They'll be arrested,' Cohen said. 'Hopefully jailed. It makes things easier, in the long run. They are not very smart men.'

'I can't testify,' Kippy said. 'They'll kill me.'

'Where are they going to drop the parts?' Cohen said.

'I don't know. Rubbish bins in the valley somewhere.'

'The valley?'

'San Fernando Valley, it's where I...' She shook her head.

'Alright,' Cohen said. 'It doesn't matter.'

'I didn't know,' Kippy said. 'I didn't know.'

Cohen didn't say anything. He sipped his beer.

'What,' Kippy said.

'Nothing.'

'I didn't know!'

He just said nothing.

'Oh my God,' Kippy said. 'The baby.'

She started to cry. Romi and Ruvi's baby. What will happen to her?

'What do you really want, Kippy?' Cohen said. His voice was kind. 'You want out of the life? You want to go home?'

'I don't know.'

'These assholes come and these assholes go,' Cohen said. 'But the operational structure remains intact. Israelis all over the United States, in every major city, with a distribution network that runs and runs. *You* know it. You go through it every other day of the week. I bet you know more about it than Yossef.'

'Me? I'm a woman,' Kippy said.

'The network runs on women,' Cohen said. 'Your friend Romi didn't die because she was a bystander. She was a drug dealer. You're a drug dealer. So what if you're a woman? You can run a business, and you're not afraid of blood.'

'I didn't know,' Kippy said. But her voice sounded plaintive and unconvincing even to herself.

'I'm going to the bathroom,' she said. She left Cohen at the table. In the women's restrooms she stared at herself in the mirror. Who are you, Sarah? She asked herself. It had been easy to drift, to let others make decisions. To just get by, from day to day.

But Cohen was right. She knew who everyone was and they knew her.

Little Pinhas in Salt Lake City, Danny in Bakersfield, Gutte in San Jose, Eli Siton in Miami. And Cohen was right, too, about the women. There was Chava in New York, part of the Jew Crew there, and Shula in L.A. ran most of the business side of Yossef's business. There was Yardena in Miami who did Eli Siton's books. There was Pnina who ran coke to Tel Aviv and heroin back to L.A., the way Kippy used to. They weren't just wives and girlfriends: they were couriers, dealers, accountants, drivers and distributors.

And they knew better than to go kill two people in a fancy hotel room and draw every fucking journalist and LAPD cop's attention.

Why *shouldn't* it be her?

A harder face looked back at her from the mirror. But she liked what she saw.

She went back to the table. Sat across from Cohen. Said, 'I want the baby taken care of.'

'Of course.'

'She must have family,' Kippy said. 'Grandparents.' She remembered Romi mentioning her mother before. 'I want her to go back to Israel. I want a fund set up for her.'

'Yes,' Cohen said.

'I'll testify,' Kippy said.

Cohen nodded.

'Good,' he said. 'It's the right thing to do. But let's wait for them to find the bodies first.'

Kippy went home. She had a drink and a long soak in the tub. She lay on her bed in the dark and listened to the crickets outside. She'd keep Shula, if she wanted to stay. She'd need the work, after all, with a husband in prison. She fell asleep and woke up in the early dawn. The thud of a newspaper hitting the door outside. She went and got it.

Human Remains Found In Dumpster was on page three. The body parts of an unknown man and woman were found in dumpsters in Van Nuys and Sherman Oaks. Police were investigating and appealing for help.

Kippy thought it was short for an epitaph. But maybe that was all anyone got, and sometimes nothing at all.

At least Romi made the papers.

Kippy made coffee, got dressed and made the phone call.

Cohen was waiting in the lobby as Kippy and Enrique came into the Howard Johnson. The two men shook hands. They went and sat in the abandoned lobby.

Enrique lit a cigar. He studied Cohen. Cohen waited him out, until Enrique nodded.

He said, 'My employer needs weapons, and you have weapons. This I know. Uzis, assault rifles, RPGs, specialised equipment like night vision goggles. Is that true?'

Cohen considered. 'What do you need them for?' he said.

'For business.'

'Aha. Well, it's easy to set up. It would need a legitimate export license to someone else, say in Costa Rica or Belize. Antigua, maybe. We ship there, once it's landed you can shift the labels, change the manifesto, where they go next isn't the Israeli government's concern. But, if you don't mind me saying, my country is already doing that in bulk.'

'You supplied the Contras in Nicaragua,' Enrique said.

'I believe so,' Cohen said. He frowned. 'It isn't really my specialty, but I can certainly help. There's also the surplus weaponry from the war in Lebanon. There is a lot of that. Russian-made, a lot of it. Stuff you can't easily trace and can have cheap. But what would you be paying with?'

'Dollars,' Enrique said.

'Who *exactly* do you work for?' Cohen said.

'A man from Medellín,' Enrique said.

Kippy drew air. 'Escobar?' she said.

'No, Gacha.' He saw their faces. 'They call him El Mexicano.'

'You launder money for the Medellín Cartel in Panama?'

Enrique laughed. 'Who doesn't?' he said.

'You knew who I was,' Kippy said. 'In Miami. It wasn't an accident we met on the plane.'

Enrique shrugged. 'That Eli Siton in Miami works with Cali and Cali and Medellín are at war. You must understand that from either of their perspective your country is very small and not important as an export market for cocaine. But you are strong in other ways. Gacha is very interested in you. And so, I am very interested in you.'

'Can he ship cocaine directly through Mexico to L.A.?' Kippy said.

'He has very good friends in Mexico,' Enrique said.

'They will sell to me at the same price Siton gets in Miami?'

'Sell to you?' He looked at her again then and he smiled, but there was real respect behind his eyes this time.

'I am glad I met you, Kippy Gavrieli,' he said.

'Will he?' Kippy said.

'He might,' Enrique said. 'It is good business, so yes. Your people have a reputation and your network in the States is good, which is one of the things I was tasked with checking out. Also, selling to you direct will be a fuck you to the Orejuelas in Cali.'

'Then I am glad we met, Enrique,' Kippy said. 'By chance or not.'

'Do we not make our own chances in life?' Enrique said. 'But I am not yet finished. If we are to work together, El Mexicano has one more request.'

'What is it?' Cohen said.

'Guns are no use in the hands of farmers,' Enrique said. 'Gacha and his friends have many enemies, but their soldiers are untrained. You have the skills and the knowledge. You have the men.'

Kippy and Cohen exchanged glances.

'I'm a bit old to be training soldiers,' Cohen said, and Kippy cracked a smile. But Enrique wasn't smiling this time, for once. She could see he was serious.

'If you will do this you will be friends of Medellín,' Enrique said. 'If you do not, well, we could part here, now, and forget we ever met each other.'

'No, that's fine,' Cohen said. 'I can help you with that. The weapons too.'

'Then we have a deal,' Enrique said.

PART ELEVEN

PUERTO BOYACÁ

1989, Colombia

59

DOWNRIVER

'There is no such thing as Israeli mercenaries' –
Yitzhak Rabin, 1989

There were four of them travelling downriver in the small motorboat, not counting the boy with the AK-47 casually slung over his skinny bare shoulder who piloted the vessel.

It was hot. The Magdalena River was wide. The small town on the right bank was called Puerto Boyacá. Nir had dark patches of sweat under his arms. Teddy Resnick lit a Marlboro from a pack he'd picked up at the duty free before they flew to Bogotá. He didn't offer to share the pack around. Teddy claimed to be ex-Mossad. Nir found it weird that everyone in the Mossad was always called Mike or Bill or Teddy. So maybe Teddy was telling the truth.

They were just a bunch of kibbutzniks. Resnick was married to some girl from Dalia. Ami Fox was from nearby Ramat Ha'shofet. He liked to shoot stray cats for fun. First thing he told Nir, when he'd met him. Lebanon never did a number on him. As far as Nir could tell he was like that from kindergarten.

Then there was Yair, the Colonel. He wasn't smart but he didn't need to be. He was just a guy who climbed the ranks and was good at shooting things and blowing things up. The army gave them a trade and Lebanon gave them a job, and when they left they weren't good for much else but more of the same.

'How far?' Ami said in Spanish.

The boy on the engine shrugged.

'No lejos,' he said.

Nir had jetlag and a hangover. The heat didn't bother him but the humidity did. Small bright boats crossed the river between the banks. People sat on the jetties in Puerto Boyacá and watched them as they passed. Nir wasn't really sure what they were doing there, what this place was. It was a dead-end town in the middle of Colombia. They'd spent a night in Bogotá, then some men came in fancy black jeeps and drove them out to the middle of nowhere. Nir saw Yair in the lobby talking to a man in a military uniform, and he saw an envelope change hands.

It was Benny, of all people, who got him the gig. After the gutshot Nir sort of spiralled. He never told anyone who shot him. It took a long time to recover. He got an honourable discharge but for him, Lebanon was over. The painkillers filled his head with mist. He liked it. It meant less thinking, and for a long time he didn't want to think about anything.

Kippy was there for a while. But then she wasn't. When they finally discharged him from the hospital he didn't know where to go or what to do. He tried to score dope just to numb the nightmares where he dreamed of killing Cohen. But every time he tried, Cohen turned and shot him in the gut.

It was Itzik who pulled him out of it. Itzik, who lost his leg, who used to sell Nir's stolen dope, who actually did what he said he would. He went back to school, studied to become a social worker. He sat Nir down and he told him to get his shit together.

So Nir tried to get his shit together.

The problem was, he was no longer any use to the army and he was no longer any use to the gangsters, and his particular skillset didn't exactly lend itself to an office job. He filled up gas for a while at a petrol station on the coast road, outside Herzliya. That's where Benny ran into him. Filling petrol was a perk job, it was reserved for ex-service guys and you could make a lot on tips. When Benny pulled in he looked surprised to find Nir standing there in overalls, but only for a moment, and Nir thought maybe he wasn't surprised at all. Like Benny knew he was working there. Like this wasn't an accident.

'I'm sorry about what happened,' Benny said. He looked a bit older, Nir though. A bit rounder. 'Listen, buy you a coffee?'

'I'm on for another hour,' Nir said. He filled up the car. Benny paid, then handed him a hundred for a tip.

'I'll see you,' Benny said. 'Unless I don't.'

He drove off and Nir looked at the note and saw the piece of paper that came with it. It had an address for a bar near the cinematheque in Tel Aviv on it, and a time for later that evening.

Nir didn't see Benny again, but he did go into the city and he found Pub Hashoftim on Ibn Gvirol, it had been there for as long as Nir could remember. When he stepped in most of the tables were full and he couldn't see Benny anywhere. Someone tapped him on the shoulder and he turned and saw an older man, straight-backed, with a sort of conman's genial twinkle in his eye. He looked familiar.

'You look a little lost, soldier,' the man said.

'I think I was supposed to meet someone,' Nir said.

'I think maybe you were,' the man said. 'Buy you a drink?'

'You're Colonel Grosse,' Nir said. He recognised him then. 'You headed Counter-Terrorism.'

'I'm retired,' Grosse said. 'And call me Yair. So how about that drink?'

'Sure,' Nir said.

They sat at the bar with a beer and a chaser. 'I heard when you got shot,' Grosse said. 'That was bad business.'

Nir winced. Grosse said, 'Does it hurt?'

'Not anymore. They fixed me up. But sometimes, just thinking about it, you know?'

'Sure,' Grosse said. 'You're fit, though?'

'Fit as anything,' Nir said.

'And what do you do now?'

'I fill up gas.'

'It's a good job,' Grosse said.

'Yeah.'

'You ever want to do anything else?' Grosse said.

'I wanted to travel,' Nir said. 'I wanted to see the world.'

Grosse nodded. 'I can help you do that,' he said.

'What do you do now, Colonel?' Nir said.

'I told you, call me Yair,' Grosse said. 'I run a private security firm. Arrowhead Ltd. It has a license from the Ministry of Defence, and we mostly work contracts overseas. A lot of South America, a lot of Africa.'

'Mercenaries?' Nir said.

'I wouldn't use that word,' Yair Grosse said. 'A lot of what we do is training courses. Sometimes a bit more, but mostly it's not a hard job, and it pays well.'

Nir thought of South America. This wasn't backpacking and sitting on a beach somewhere like he used to dream. But it was something.

'Are you offering me a job?' he said.

'You come recommended,' Grosse said. 'You want to think about it?'

'No,' Nir said. 'I'm in.'

Grosse grinned. 'Good man,' he said. He raised his beer. They touched glasses.

'L'chaim,' Grosse said.

60

DONKEYS

'It doesn't really matter who is fighting who, as long as they're not Jews' – Ami

The motor puttered into life again, then died, and the boy with the AK-47 thumped it a couple of times and then seemed to give up. He shouted to people on the shore.

Nir wasn't sure where they were. Somewhere downriver from Puerto Boyacá, on the left bank. It could have been an island. He saw a farmhouse in the distance behind the trees, and smoke rising, and there were men on the shore with machine guns but they seemed friendly. A couple of them waded into the water with a rope and threw it over. Yair grabbed it and the men on the shore pulled and the boat slowly eased onto the bank.

'Watch where you point that thing,' Ami said to one of the men as he jumped onto dry land.

'Qué?'

'Useless donkeys,' Ami said.

Ami really was an asshole, which was a view shared by most of the mercenaries – sorry, security consultants – who worked for Arrowhead Ltd. But he was very good at his job.

Not that he was wrong about the current clients. The men were young, ill-dressed and badly organised. They were sicarios rather than soldados. They looked like they would kill you and not feel a thing, but they didn't really know much more than how to point a gun and pull the trigger, which any asshole could do.

But then that's what Arrowhead were hired for: take a ragtag crew of teenage killers and, if not exactly turn them into crack commandos, at least provide them with the reasonable basics of tactical warfare.

The first time he took a flight out of Ben Gurion was exciting. Nir had popped a cassette tape of *The Joshua Tree* into his new Walkman, and Bono sang about a place where the streets had no name. Ami and Teddy Resnick sat in the back of the plane smoking. Nir listened to U2 and looked out of the window at the clouds passing far below.

They changed planes and an airline in Paris. The long flight across the Atlantic came next. Ami came by and offered him a handful of pills.

'Take a couple with a drink and it will knock you out until we get there,' he said – a veteran of global crossings. Ami was Yair's number two. Nir took the pills, but that first time he pocketed them. He wanted to be awake to see the landing.

They came out onto hot tarmac in San Salvador. Nir was tired but he was also elated. The air smelled fresh and new, nothing like Tel Aviv. They went through border control and out into Arrivals. Everything seemed new to Nir. The signs in Spanish, the food on display, the girls. Not that he had time to look. A car waited for them outside. They drove out of the city, heading east, until they reached a small town and passed it and came to a valley where two small planes rested in the grass and men with guns were marching in formation.

'Good to see you,' Yair said, clapping Nir on the back. He was already there, looking crisp like a freshly minted note of New Shekels.

'Who are these guys?' Nir said, indicating the marching men.

Ami shook his head disgustedly. 'Contras,' he said. 'They're donkeys.'

A donkey in Ami Fox's terminology was anyone they had to train. The Contras called him El Zorro. He called them donkeys and barked orders at them and taught them how to storm and take a held position, how to improvise an IED and how to use grenade launchers. Not that the Contras really cared all that much. They were from Nicaragua and supposedly fighting Sandinistas, who were also Nicaraguans. It all got a bit confusing.

'It doesn't really matter who is fighting who,' Ami explained to Nir one evening after a day of training. 'As long as they're not Jews.' He looked pleased with himself. 'We just train them and, where possible, sell them the guns.'

One week into the training a small plane came to land and a man came out and Yair took him on a tour of the camp. The man came and sat with the instructors later that evening and had a drink and then another one, sharing the bottle of Wild Turkey around. He was an American.

He said, 'You're doing God's work here.'

In the morning he was gone. In the afternoon another plane arrived and dropped bags. Nir went to have a look but the others stopped him.

He just watched instead. Bags wrapped in masking tape, like the sort of flour bags you got in the store. Hundreds of them. Then in the early evening, not long after the drop, another plane arrived and picked them all up and took them somewhere else.

The gig was three weeks. After three weeks they went back to Israel via Europe. Nir got paid, and for the first time in a long time he felt good, he felt like himself again. He went to the beach and worked out and even asked a girl on a date. The music scene was really starting to kick up in Tel Aviv. There were a lot of new bands, a new sound emerging. He went back to El Salvador a couple more times. Every time there was a new group of Contras recruits and each time the bags of flour would arrive and then vanish. The American never came back again.

From time to time some other Israelis would show up. They all knew Yair. They just dropped by. A couple lived in Colombia and grew flowers or did something in agriculture. One was in Panama as a special advisor for Noriega. A jeweller from Miami came once, Eli Siton. He wore gold and beat them one by one in backgammon. A guy called Bruce who was living in Antigua came. He was some sort of arms dealer. He and Yair talked late into the night about some plans they had. There was a shipment of Kalashnikovs and bazookas and Yugoslavian machine guns that came for the Contras. Nir recognised the weapons. They were captured munitions from the war in Lebanon. Lots of Soviet stuff. Nir wasn't stupid. He figured SIBAT, the security export department of the Israeli Ministry of Defence, were selling the guns to the Contras on behalf of the Americans. The Contras were right-wing and the people they were fighting were some sort of communists and the Americans hated communists. So it worked well for everyone. Nir started seeing a lot of the old Lebanese War weapons around on their gigs, and then new Israeli-made ones, too.

Some of the jobs were closer to home. They ran a course for some of Mobutu's men in a field somewhere in Belgium. In France, they met quietly with Jean-Bédel Bokassa in his exile. He had a handful of men and was still hoping to overthrow the people who overthrew him and become emperor of Central Africa again. Arrowhead took the gig, but when Nir saw the men he didn't think this was going to go anywhere for Bokassa.

Then Chile, training squads for Pincohet. Nir was starting to pick up a little Spanish. He got a taste for empanadas. He tried not to think too much of what it was that they were doing. It was just a job. From time to time arms shipments would be arranged. From time to time a quiet American would show up. The next gig was in Peru, where they trained militias in hunting down Shining Path insurgents. There was always some Israeli already in place, a man with local connections, and another quiet arms deal would be arranged and the next training gig somewhere else. There were Israelis all over Latin America. Nir got used to a few of the faces: Bruce Rappaport and Maurice Sarfati, who were based on Antigua; Marcos Katz, who was based in Mexico; Mike Harari in Panama; Arik Afek in Colombia; the list went on. A guy who was involved in the Iran-Contra Affair back in '86, Amiram Nir, turned up dead in Mexico, the victim of a mysterious plane crash.

'You have to watch those Americans,' Ami muttered when they heard the news. They were somewhere in El Salvador again, drinking beer and oiling their guns.

'Why Americans?' Nir said, startled.

'They blew up his plane,' Ami said, as though it were obvious. 'CIA.'

'Why would they do that?'

Ami didn't say anything. He just shook his head.

Nir didn't really understand the Iran-Contra thing. Hezbollah had been kidnapping Americans in Lebanon on behalf of Iran, in order to extort the American government. The Americans went to the Israelis and a deal was hatched for Israel to sell weapons to Iran in exchange for the release of the hostages. The money from the deal was transferred to Colonel Oliver North, who used it to fund arms shipments to the Contras in Nicaragua. Some of the weapons that went to the Contras were from the Israeli stockpiles seized during the war in Lebanon. Everyone was happy until the newspapers got hold of the story. Then a bunch of people lost their jobs. But the Contras still got their guns.

'It was before your time,' Ami Fox said. So Nir guessed that was that.

He preferred not to ask too many questions. It didn't do, in that line of work. And it made it easier. You did the gigs and you went back home, and he was putting away good money into savings.

He'd keep at it for a few more years, he thought.

61

THE MEXICAN

'Maybe he's a rich farmer' – Teddy

They got settled into the new place. The training camp was on a farm and Puerto Boyacá was really just on the other side of the river somewhere just upstream. There was a herd of cows on a nearby field, and Nir saw men on horses. The recruits themselves were young, slouchy, badly dressed. They had old men's eyes. They were always the same. The man who invited them made an appearance about an hour later. A convoy of cars drove down and passed through the gates and stopped. Nir heard the recruits say, 'El Mexicano, El Mexicano!'

The Mexican stepped out of the car. He had a full round face and a shock of hair under a Panama hat. He wasn't Mexican. He wore a gold watch. He saw Yair and beamed. Yair went over, smiling. The two men shook hands. Yair signalled to Nir. Nir brought over an Uzi. A younger version of the Mexican came out of the car. He was young and overweight and had the same shock of dark hair.

'My boy, Freddie,' the Mexican said. 'He will train with you. You will train him well, Yair?'

'Yes,' Yair said simply. He took the Uzi from Nir and passed it to Freddie.

'A gift,' he said.

The kid laughed. He fingered the weapon.

'Can I try it, Papa?' he said.

'Go have fun, Freddie,' the Mexican said. He looked at Nir.

'This is one of your men?'

'He was a top soldier,' Yair said. 'Wounded in battle.' He made introductions. 'This is Nir. Nir, this is Señor Gacha.'

'A pleasure to meet you,' the Mexican said. He shook Nir's hand. Not far away the kid, Freddie, sprayed bullets against a wooden fence. The young recruits surrounded him, watching with amusement.

'Likewise,' Nir said. The Mexican nodded and turned. Nir was dismissed. He went back to stand with Ami and Teddy Resnick.

'Freddie, you're making too much noise!' Gacha shouted. His son laughed and squeezed a round into the air. Gacha smiled and shook his head. He patted Yair's shoulder.

'Who the hell is this guy?' Nir said.

Ami looked at him, amused.

'You don't know?'

'He doesn't look like a farmer,' Nir said. The people who hired them were, at least on paper, the local association of cattle growers. From what Yair told him before they left they had trouble with communist guerrillas and needed the training. There had been kidnappings.

'Maybe he's a rich farmer,' Teddy Resnick said and laughed.

'The only guy richer than him has a hacienda upriver,' Ami said.

'What?' Nir said.

'You ever hear of Medellín, dickhead?' Ami said.

'The name Pablo Escobar ring any bells?' Teddy Resnick said.

'We're training… who are we training, exactly?' Nir said.

Ami shrugged.

'Who gives a shit,' he said.

And that was that.

Gacha didn't stay long. He and his column of cars drove off but the kid, Freddie, stayed. In the late afternoon Ami sat taking pot shots at cats and Freddie joined him. Nir tried to sleep. He put up a mosquito net and lay under it but he couldn't quite fall asleep, his body was still in the wrong time zone. Teddy was laid flat out, snoring. Nir didn't know where Yair was. Setting things up, probably. Yair didn't sleep. Nir had to give it to him. He looked after his men and he carried out his duties diligently. Nir could smell weed, the smoke drifting on the breeze, then heard Yair shouting angrily. Yair never allowed drugs on the site and as soon as the air cooled down and they all got a little rest they were going to put the fear of God into the recruits, which was the bit Yair enjoyed the most. For three weeks they were his. They lived and died at his command.

Nir couldn't sleep. He plugged in the Walkman earphones. He fast-forwarded through 'Bullet The Blue Sky' and pressed Play again into the mellow sadness of 'Running To Stand Still'.

He tried to think what happened when they got to Bogotá. Yair was talking to some guy in uniform. Nir served long enough to know rank when he saw it. Someone senior in the Colombian military, anyway. It was all above board, what they were doing, or they wouldn't be doing it, he thought. So the ranchers' association had links with the army, that was for sure. He tried to think. The night in Bogotá was a blur. He was too jetlagged and he went to bed early. They were in the hotel bar. Afek turned up at some point, Nir did remember that. Afek always turned up at some point, and he always had a scheme. He was just one of those guys. He liked to talk. This time he was arguing with Yair, in low voices. What was that about? He was warning Yair they were in danger. Yair shook him off. Afek was like a puppy you couldn't get rid of. And Nir went to bed.

Gacha. He didn't look like much. None of the guys they worked for ever looked like much. For all Nir knew the farmers in the Magdalena Valley really did have problems with guerrillas and kidnappings. It was pretty common. Arrowhead had twice provided personal security to wealthy individuals in the region, and once had a strictly off-the-books extraction mission, in Guatemala, and a bunch of people had to get hurt. That was almost like the old days, like playing cowboys and Indians in Lebanon.

'Hola,' a voice said. Nir opened his eyes. Had he slept? How long was he out? He felt groggy. The air was very slightly cooler. The light had faded. A shadow stood in the doorway. He watched her silhouette. She moved forward and flicked on the light and Nir blinked. He watched the woman who stood there with her arms crossed. She had short hair and wore camouflage khakis.

'Who are you?' Nir said.

'I'm your interpreter,' the woman said, in English.

'I don't need a fucking interpreter,' Ami said, in Spanish. He got up and ambled to the door, brushing too close to the woman. 'No offence, sweetheart.'

Teddy Resnick lit a cigarette and watched her through the smoke.

'You'll have to excuse him,' he said, 'he's just a cabrón.'

The woman smiled politely. Teddy got up, stuck out his hand.

'Teddy Resnick,' he said.

'Ana,' the woman said. She shook his hand.

Nir got out from under the mosquito net.

'I'm Nir,' he said. 'Nice to meet you.'

The woman looked at him doubtfully, but then she smiled.

'The Colonel is calling you,' she said.

'Come on, Nir,' Teddy said. 'Time to start the show.'

'Who was that guy Yair was talking to in Bogotá?' Nir said as they went outside.

'Afek? You know him,' Resnick said.

'No, the other guy. The Colombian.'

Resnick stole a look at the interpreter. 'He was DAS,' he said quietly.

'What's that?' Nir said.

'The Colombian security service,' Resnick said.

'Ah.'

'Don't worry, don't worry,' Resnick said. 'We're legit.'

They came to the bank of the river. The men hired by the ranchers' association stood to attention. Yair was already there with Ami. Nir and Teddy went and joined them. They faced the recruits.

'Atten-tion!' Yair screamed.

The sun was setting. Somewhere a parrot cried. Nir smelled fish cooking on an open fire. His stomach growled. The recruits ate earlier. He hadn't. He watched their faces in the fading light.

Ami went past them, one by one, barking orders, telling them to straighten up. Teddy and Nir started distributing weapons: brand-new Galil assault rifles.

'You will learn discipline, you will learn tactical warfare, you will learn these guns and you will follow my orders!' Yair said. 'If you don't, I'll shoot you.'

Ana translated.

Nir saw the recruits nod. Yair spoke a language they understood.

'Drop down and give me twenty,' Yair said.

Ana translated.

Most of them dropped down. One stared sullenly at Yair.

'A la verga,' he said.

'Fuck this,' Ana translated.

Yair lifted his pistol. It was a Desert Eagle, also Israeli made, also brand new.

'I'll count to one,' he said.

Ana started to translate but it took too long. The gunshot was loud and a flock of birds in the trees took to the skies in a dark clouds against the setting sun. The kid Yair shot dropped to the ground. His leg was shot up. He didn't scream but he whimpered. Whoever was still standing dropped to the ground and started doing push ups like their lives depended on it. Freddie Gacha, who was still trying to do just one, looked over and smirked.

'Bloody donkeys,' Ami Fox said. 'Come on, Nir.'

Nir followed him to the kid. They lifted him up and dragged him away, leaving a trail of blood across the dirt. They dumped him under a tree to bleed out or stem it himself.

And so the first day of training began.

62

HIPPOS

'What is this, the fucking seventies?' – *Ami*

The guns were new. Nir didn't have much to do with it. The guns were Yair's deal, Yair's and Rappaport and Sarfati. They were made in Israel and exported legally to Antigua. Nir had a look at the manifest before the guns left Haifa on board a Danish ship. The cargo included four hundred Galil rifles and one hundred mini-Uzis and plenty of ammo. In Antigua the guns were offloaded, put on another ship, and sent to Colombia. Now they were Gacha's, and his men were going to learn how to use them. There were also some RPGs and night vision goggles and other toys.

The training wasn't hard but it was tiring. The recruits were taught basic stuff. How to take over a position. How to shoot from a moving vehicle. How to organise for conflict in an urban environment. How to make and use explosives in an urban environment. They used the farm and a small abandoned village near the farm and simulated various battle scenarios. The men they trained were barely men but they were already killers. They listened and they did what they were told and they got better as the days went on. Nir worked, ate, slept, repeated. Food was cooked by a small army of old women. Ana translated instructions but seldom said much herself. She kept pace with the men and Nir noticed her noticing things, quietly. He asked her where she was from.

'Right here,' she said. 'Puerto Boyacá.'

'And them?' Nir said.

'Them?' Ana said. She looked at the recruits. 'Medellín, mostly. Some from the farms. You notice the rich ones and the poor ones?'

'Do I?' Nir said, startled. 'No?'

'You have the ones from the streets and the ones from the haciendas,' Ana said. 'But they're both bad. You know why you're here?'

'To train them,' Nir said.

'Yes,' Ana said. 'But why?'

'Guerrillas,' Nir said.

'FARC,' Ana said. 'They're communists. The plantation owners and the mining companies and the oil companies like Texas Petroleum, they didn't like the FARC being here. You look around here, a stranger, and you think, what is this place? It is nowhere. But it is the heart of Colombia, Nir. It is rich and it is wild, under the Andes and between Medellín and Bogotá. Some would say FARC fight for justice, for the rights of the workers. And if they have to use violence then who doesn't? But then they all got together, the army and the cartels and the oil people and the farmers, and they made Muerte a Secuestradores. Death To Kidnappers. And they put money into it. Enough to pay for Israeli guns, and Israeli instructors, enough to train a bunch of street thugs and farm boys into a militia. Now they call it ACDEGAM, the farmers' association. But it is the same thing. And that is why you are here.' She looked at him curiously.

'Does it bother you?' she said.

'I am just doing my job,' Nir said.

Ana nodded, very seriously.

'I am, too,' she said.

'You do not approve?' Nir said. 'You have sympathies for—'

'No,' she said, quickly. 'I work.' She shrugged. 'I need a job. My family has been here for generations. I am just… an employee.' She said it sadly.

'You are scared of them?' Nir said.

'Wouldn't you be?' Ana said.

Nir nodded.

'Yes,' he said.

'You should be,' Ana said.

'What do you mean?'

She shrugged.

'No, really,' Nir said. 'Yair's been here before. It's all…' he tried to think of a word. 'Kosher,' he said.

'What's a kosher?' Ana said.

'It's like dietary law,' Nir said.

'What?'

'For Jews.'

'Oh. I still don't understand.'

'I mean it's OK,' Nir said. 'Us being here. It's official.'

'It's official,' Ana said, 'until it isn't.'

'Ana!' Yair bellowed in the distance. 'Come over here!'

Ana smiled.

'I have to go to work,' she said.

'Me, too,' Nir said.

He watched her go to Yair. Then he picked up his Uzi.

A few days went by and it got to Friday. The four Israelis made a Friday night dinner and Teddy Resnick even made chicken soup, and for chollah they used Pandebono someone brought over from a bakery in town. Yair even said the blessing and they dipped the bread in salt and all that. Nir never understood why Israelis always got more religious when they were overseas. Before you knew it they were going to put on yarmulkes and dance a hora.

He figured maybe, outside of Israel, they were just Jews.

The recruits watched them in bemusement. After they finished eating Teddy said, 'What now?' and Ami said, 'Let's go out.'

'You go,' Yair said. 'I'm staying here. And watch yourselves if you go into town. Let's not have a repeat of what happened in Santiago.'

'Santiago,' Ami said. 'This place isn't shit. Come on, Teddy. Nir, you coming?'

'I don't know,' Nir said.

'You're coming,' Ami said. 'And you!' he called to Ana. 'We need an interpreter.'

'You don't need an interpreter to say cerveza,' Nir said.

'So a local guide,' Ami said. 'What's a good place to drink in Puerto Boyacá?' he said to Ana.

Ana shrugged.

'Anywhere that serves beer.'

'See?' Ami said. 'She's invaluable. Come on.'

'Well, how do we get there?' Nir said.

Ami was already halfway to a parked truck. He stopped and turned.

'Oh, yeah,' he said.

They went to the riverbank instead. Several motorboats were moored there and they took one, and Ami ordered one of the recruits to pilot the boat. They pushed across the dark water. Nir could see the lights in the distance, Puerto Boyacá spread across the other side. He felt Ana next to him, pressed shoulder to shoulder. She turned and smiled.

'Do you like to dance?' she said.

'Dance?' Nir said.

She looked at him in amusement.

'Yes,' she said.

'One way to find out,' Nir said.

Her smile widened.

'Alright, then,' she said.

They moored the boat on a jetty. People milled about on the riverfront. They went past a bar and then another. The bars were small, loud. Plastic chairs were set outside. Ana took them to a place called the Tropical. A disco ball swung in the centre of the dance floor, and bodies swayed under the glittering lights. Abba segued into 'Saturday Night Fever'.

'What is this, the fucking seventies?' Ami said. 'I'm going to a proper bar.'

'I'm staying here,' Nir said. Ana danced beside him.

Ami smirked. 'I bet you are,' he said. 'Come on, Teddy. Let's go get drunk like men of our age. Hard and fast.'

'Whatever you say, Ami,' Teddy said. He followed Ami out.

'I thought they'd never leave!' Ana said. She had to shout against the music. Nir smiled.

'Do you want a drink?' he shouted.

'Yes!'

She motioned to the guy behind the bar. He put two shot glasses on the counter and filled them up. They downed them together.

'What the hell *is* that!' Nir shouted. His throat was on fire.

'Aguardiente!' Ana said.

'It's terrible!' Nir said.

'Two more!' Ana said to the barman.

When the music next came it didn't matter that it was a decade too late on a river somewhere in Colombia. Nir abandoned himself to the dark and the glittering fragments of light and the heat and the smoke. He didn't need Hebrew, he didn't need Spanish. He surrendered to the sound. Ana moved beside him, then with him. Who needed language when they had bodies to speak for them?

At last they staggered outside and shared a cigarette, watching the river. It was four o'clock in the morning. Nir thought of kissing Ana. He heard gunfire in the distance, heard a voice on a megaphone, the tread of tires in the dirt. He watched as a convoy of jeeps came driving past, men in camouflage holding guns, a voice on the megaphone intoning in Spanish: 'Están protegidos!' You are protected!

Nir stared up at the man in the lead jeep. Ami and Resnick staggered out of a bar three doors down, each with a girl.

'Carlos!' Ami shouted.

The man turned, saw Ami, smiled and waved.

'Amigo!' he said. 'Shalom!'

'Son of a bitch, Carlos, go to bed!' Ami shouted.

The man squeezed a round of bullets into the air and howled with laughter.

'We must keep what is ours,' he said. 'This town is under my protection!'

Ami shook his head. Carlos and his convoy drove past.

'Send my regards to Jair!' Carlos said.

'Who is that?' Nir said.

Ana stared after the convoy.

'Carlos Castaño Gil,' she said. 'He has his own militia, and he's a friend of Pablo's. It's men like his you train.'

'Sounds like we already did,' Nir said. Ami and Resnick came and joined them.

'That crazy son of a bitch,' Ami said with some affection. 'You know he spent a year in Tel Aviv? He's a donkey.'

They went back to the boat. The kid guarding it was still there, asleep. They woke him up.

'You ever kill anyone, kid?' Resnick asked him, drunk. Ana translated.

The boy stared up at him mutely. He raised three fingers.

'How old are you!' Resnick said. 'What are you, fifteen?'

'Dieciséis,' the kid said.

'Sixteen,' Ana translated.

'Little fucker,' Resnick said. 'No, don't translate that. Come on. Get us back across.'

They squeezed into the boat. Nir and Ana close together, and they shared a look and she smiled. Nir thought of the kiss that wasn't to be. The boat cut across the water, the engine pattering. The night quieted around them. On the bank the bars and discos were illuminated with faint light, and shadows moved sluggishly across the promenade. Carlos Castaño's voice echoed weirdly in the distance, saying, 'You are protected! You are protected!'

Nir's head swam. The strong drink and the late hour converged on him and he was going to be sick into the river. He knelt over the side of the boat.

A dark shadow moved under the water. Nir stared.

The shadow was huge. Nir was sure he was dreaming. The shadow passed under the boat and rose.

A huge monster burst out of the water, mouth open to bite and kill. Its ascent rocked the boat and threatened to capsize it. Nir lost his balance. Ana grabbed him before he fell into the river.

'What the fuck!' Ami screamed.

The creature roared.

It was a hippo.

The boat tried to get away but the hippo was fast, too, and angry somehow. Ami grabbed an Uzi.

'No dispares!' the recruit shouted. 'Escobar, Escobar!' He rose and grabbed the weapon. Ami fired and the bullets went high in a tight burst. The hippo roared again, then sank under the water. Nir grabbed the engine. The boat cruised on.

'What the fuck!' Ami said. He pointed the Uzi at the recruit. The kid spoke fast, in panic.

'It's Escobar's hippo,' Ana translated. 'You can't shoot it.'

'What do you mean Escobar's?'

'From upriver,' Ana said. 'From his zoo. They're always getting out, the hippos.'

'Good night, Ana,' Nir said. He staggered away. Early dawn was just beginning to etch the horizon with faint light. Ami and Resnick smoked on the riverbank, he saw them by the glow of the cigarette tips. From somewhere in the distance over the water he could hear sporadic gunfire.

He went to bed.

63

THE BIRD

'Will they know how I'll suffer, suffer agonies?' –
Chaim Nachman Bialik, 1891

Rocket propelled grenade training.

Combat driving with live fire.

Lunch: grilled fish, beans and plantain.

Obstacle course training.

Supper: grilled fish, beans and plantain.

Sleep.

The mosquitoes buzzed behind the net. Ami snored. Resnick sat up late, reading a poetry collection by Eli Netzer he'd brought from home.

Breakfast: tamales and huevos pericos. Coffee for the instructors. Hot chocolate for the recruits.

Explosives training.

Improvising booby-traps using grenades.

Target practice.

Lunch.

Obstacle course. Drive-by shooting. Dinner.

Sleep.

Breakfast: Freddie Gacha picking on one of the younger recruits. Nobody said anything.

Clearing and securing an occupied target.

Operational planning: access and escape routes in a crowded scenario.

Lunch.

Explosives.

Tracking and tailing a target for elimination.

Supper: steaks and a bottle of wine. Relax with a cigarette. Music: Nir was getting sick of U2. Reading: Resnick finished the Eli Netzer book and said he didn't see what the fuss was about but his wife knew him well, he was from her kibbutz.

Sleep: too hot, and Nir got up and pissed outside under the moon, the mosquitoes biting him.

Breakfast.

Gacha again on a drive-by visit. He spoke quietly with Yair. He took Freddie back with him. No more Gacha. No more Freddie. No more trips across the river, either.

Some light practice with the new Galil rifles.

Lunch.

A telephone call for Yair. He spoke for a short time, came back looking angry.

'What is it, boss?' Ami said.

'Afek says DAS are going to raid us.'

Resnick and Ami exchanged glances.

'Are they, boss?'

'Afek has a big mouth,' Yair said. But he still looked bothered.

'Still. Maybe we should go,' Ami said.

'Maybe we should—'

The sound of something in the skies overhead. Nir looked up with a sense of unreality. The routine shattered. The whoosh-whoosh-whoosh of rotor blades. He saw three helicopters heading their way.

'Son of a bitch!' Ami said.

Yair said, 'Grab the getaway bags. If we get separated try to regroup in Bogotá. If that route's closed make it over the border any way you can. We go now.'

They ran. Nir grabbed the getaway backpack. Yair shouted orders at the recruits. Men grabbed Uzis and Galils. Nir saw soldiers in camouflage coming from the trees. He saw boats on the river. He thought, this is fucked.

They ran.

The recruits opened fire on the approaching soldiers. The

soldiers returned fire. Nir saw Ana – grabbed her – dragged her along. She picked up an Uzi.

'There's a jetty on the other side of the village,' she said.

Yair said, 'I know.'

The recruits were firing with new discipline. They provided cover. Nir ran round the obstacle course, into the abandoned village they used for urban warfare training. He watched out for booby traps. They'd wired it full of live explosives. He fired and caught a soldier in the chest. He watched as another tripped one of the grenades. The explosion tore the soldier apart.

They ran. Into the trees, the noise of battle receding behind them as the recruits and the army engaged in battle. Nir's breath burned in his lungs, his heart beat fast and his hands sweated. They came to the hidden jetty where two boats were moored.

'Get in,' Yair said.

Ami climbed into the boat and Resnick followed when soldiers appeared. They started firing. Nir and Yair fired back.

'Get in!' Yair said.

'You go first!' Nir said. 'I'll cover you.'

Yair didn't argue. He got in the boat. But they were too many, the soldiers. They wouldn't get away, he thought.

Ana put two fingers in her mouth and whistled. Young women and men in camouflage emerged out of the undergrowth. They fired at the soldiers. The soldiers fired back.

'Nir! Come on!'

Nir turned and pain exploded in his leg. He dropped to the ground. He saw Yair in the boat. Yair was going to jump back out and get him under fire. Nir said, 'Go.'

'We don't leave a man behind!' Yair screamed.

'Go!' Ana said. She held the Uzi with easy familiarity. 'We'll cover you.'

'Who are you!' Yair screamed. He tried to jump out to get Nir but a storm of bullets between them threw him back. Nir watched the boat begin to drift out onto the river.

'FARC,' Ana said. She smiled and shot a burst of bullets from the Uzi that hit two of the soldiers unlucky enough to step out of the trees just then. The pain in Nir's leg intensified. He watched the boat with his friends drift off along the bank, going downriver.

'Médica!' Ana shouted. A young woman came running and knelt beside Nir. She looked at him dispassionately and turned him over to look at his leg. When she touched it he screamed. The woman said something.

'You'll live,' Ana translated. The medic worked quickly. She tore Nir's trousers and put a tourniquet on. She bandaged the leg. Nir almost passed out from the pain. The boat with Yair and Ami and Resnick was almost out of sight now. Nir closed his eyes, defeated. He was going to die right here, bleeding on some foreign soil in a place where he didn't even speak the language.

'Mierda,' he said.

'Shit,' Ana translated, then caught herself and laughed. There were dead soldiers on the ground, and the sounds of battle in the distance. Nir heard the helicopters overhead but for a moment no one was shooting at him. More guerrillas appeared. They lifted him onto a makeshift stretcher.

'Where are you… taking me?' Nir said.

'Somewhere safe.'

He closed his eyes. For some reason he thought about Cohen, moving silently through the years, a man for whom, perhaps, the land of Israel was created. Cohen with a gun, and Cohen with a quote, always using other people's words and other people's thoughts. Bialik's 'The Bird', for some reason: 'Sing for me, tell me, dear migrating bird, from your land of distant wonders. Can it be that in that hot and beautiful land there is similar evil and trouble?'

Nir picturing Cohen quoting Bialik; the thought exhausted him. He looked up at the sky and saw a helicopter circling overhead. Somebody in the training camp must have fired the RPG just then. Nir thought, Good work, full marks for paying attention. The helicopter tilted with the explosion. The pilot lost control of the helicopter. It spun in the air. It came crashing into the trees. Nir closed his eyes. The ball of flame lit up the world behind his eyelids. He was conscious the whole time. Of the roar of the explosion and the burst of heat, of the movement of the people carrying him.

The sounds of water, the silence of a boat and paddles, moving softly, moving away, taking him with it to a land of distant wonders.

64

HOME

'It gets cold fast' – Rahim

The FARC camp was like a small kibbutz only somewhere in the jungle. The soldiers were mostly young, dressed in khakis, armed and practical. The camp was camouflaged under the canopy of the trees. Nir thought you could hide a whole city in there and no one would ever find it. He walked with a limp, but he walked. The bullet had gone clean through and he was healing. He didn't see Ana very often.

'Why are you helping me?' he asked her.

'I am not,' she said. 'I am helping the cause.'

'You can get me out of here?' he said.

'Can you pay?'

'I can help train your people.'

She laughed. 'We have our own training,' she said. 'We are an army, Nir. Not a cartel. And we are revolutionaries. We have comrades all around the world.'

'Russia?' Nir said.

Ana shrugged. 'Wherever people fight for freedom and the cause,' she said. 'Cuba, the Basques, the IRA, the Lebanese…'

'What Lebanese?' Nir said.

Ana shrugged. 'They're called Hezbollah, I think. There are a lot of Lebanese in America now, because of their war. Sometimes we cooperate.'

'And the cartels?' Nir said.

'Sometimes we cooperate there, too,' Ana said. 'The cartels

are merely a symptom. It is the political structure that must come down.'

'Why am I not in a cage like them?' Nir said, gesturing to the captives behind their wooden bars. There was a group of them.

'They are valuable.'

'And I am not?'

She sighed. 'You are a pain,' she said. 'You can pay for your freedom?'

'Maybe. I think so. Can you get me out?'

He had ten thousand dollars in his getaway bag, but the FARC took it.

'Can you get us guns like you got Pablo?'

'I told you, I don't know Pablo. We did not work for the cartel. We worked for—'

'Yes, yes,' Ana said. 'The cattle ranchers' association. Does it matter to you?'

The question took him by surprise.

'I suppose it does,' he said. 'I'd like to think the work we do, that I do, it's for a cause. Not for some criminal.'

'Then you're an idiot,' she told him, but she said it kindly. 'I can get you on a plane out of here. To Venezuela, maybe. Can you get us guns?'

Nir shook his head. 'No,' he said. 'I don't think so.'

'That is too bad.'

'So what can I do?' Nir said.

'Think about it,' Ana said. 'A resourceful guy like you can figure something out, I'm sure. Meanwhile, enjoy the hospitality.'

He wasn't in a cage but he was still a prisoner. He sat with the guerrillas for meals and he watched the comings and goings in the camp. A commander came from outside to look him over. He spoke to Ana quietly. Later Ana spoke to Nir.

'Your friends left Colombia,' she said.

'I see.'

'Can they raise money for you?'

'Maybe, but how much?' He shook his head. 'I saw you bring in drugs,' he said.

Drogas. At least he knew that in Spanish.

'It helps fund the revolution,' Ana told him.

'Maybe I can do something,' Nir said.

She looked at him in amusement.

'I figured you might,' she said.

'Can you get me to a phone?'

'Yes.'

She took him into the jungle, across a kilometre of rope, to another hidden section of the base. A communication centre. They had radios and a satellite phone. Nir made the call he wished he wouldn't have to make.

He took a breath.

'It's Nir,' he said.

Ana wasn't there when he left the base. They took him through the forest, blindfolded part of the way, not like he could ever find his way back there or want to. Then to a river, where they put him on a boat, then to a jetty where a car waited. It felt strange being back in a vehicle, back on a road. He saw very few lights. Already Puerto Boyacá seemed like a distant dream. They passed a rusting Texaco sign and turned down a dirt track, nothing but the darkness, and the car drove without lights. They came to a long-abandoned airstrip. Grass grew in the cracks of buildings that had no windows in them. Men came out with guns. The car stopped. Nir was taken out. A small Cessna waited on the runway.

Nir stretched. His leg hurt from sitting too long in the car. He watched men load sealed bags of cocaine onto the plane. He didn't even know who he was with now. Were they FARC? Cartels? The army? He had begun to realise it didn't really matter. Just like he didn't matter. He was just another means to an end.

'You're the cargo?'

The pilot came out from behind a wall, doing up his belt. He reached in a pocket, got out a packet of cigarettes and offered one to Nir.

'Thanks,' Nir said. 'I'm trying to quit.'

The pilot lit up. He puffed smoke into the air. 'What is your name?' he said.

'Mike.'

The pilot laughed.

'CIA?' he said. 'It doesn't matter to me. I'm Rahim.'

They shook hands. Nir watched the coke being loaded. How many kilos was that? Where would it all go?

'Put this on,' Rahim said. He rummaged in the cockpit and threw Nir a short leather jacket.

'It gets cold fast,' Rahim said in explanation.

Nir put the jacket on. They got into the small cockpit. The men watched them from the disused runway with their guns held loosely.

Rahim checked instruments. He started the engine. The small plane coasted and turned. The Cessna gathered speed. It detached from the earth and took to the skies. The plane flew low over dark country. It followed the contours of a river that might have been the Magdalena.

From time to time Nir saw lights down below. They passed villages wreathed in haze. It got cold in the cockpit. Nir shivered and his leg ached from being confined. There was no way to talk with the pilot. The engine thrummed through the cockpit. The stars shone overhead. Nir was lulled into a restless anticipation. He was cargo as much as the coke, his destiny entwined in their twin arrival at their destination. Like the coke, he was disposable. There would always be more cocaine, he thought. But there was only him of all the Nirs.

If he made it through, he didn't think he'd go back to Arrowhead. Yair was a good boss but Nir thought maybe it was time he figured out what he wanted to do. Maybe he'd go back to filling up petrol for a while. Find a woman to like who wasn't involved with drugs for a change. He'd been making a lot of bad choices. Maybe he could back to school, learn a trade. Be a plumber, maybe.

There was good money in plumbing, and almost no one ever shot at you.

The Cessna banked sharply. The plane turned and then began to rise. Nir saw flashes of light down below. The pilot cursed mutely, face frozen in concentration. The plane gathered speed, headed for low-lying clouds.

They were being shot at.

It only lasted a moment. The plane flew higher, the world below disappeared behind thin wisps of clouds. Rahim shot Nir a glance, gave him a thumbs up.

'Does this happen often!' Nir shouted.

'What!'

'Never mind!'

They flew on. The Cessna dipped again. Once again they flew low, silent, Rahim piloting by instruments. Nir fell asleep. When he woke up it was still dark but the quality of the engine changed and ahead in the distance he could see lights burn in two parallel rows, marking a makeshift runway. Nir tensed. Remembered something a pilot told him once, that the only dangerous parts of a flight were the take-off and landing. Rahim was focused. The plane dropped low and glided. It touched the ground with a bump and braked to a halt along the runway. When the engine stopped the sudden silence felt strange. Nir climbed out of the plane and men with guns surrounded him.

He was sick of men with guns.

Rahim spoke Arabic to the men. Maybe they thought Nir couldn't understand. The men offloaded the coke from the plane. Nir waited to one side. He needed a piss.

'Where are we?' he said.

'Venezuela,' Rahim said. 'Come on.'

'Are you really Lebanese?' Nir said.

'Sure. Lots of us here now.'

'I never would have thought,' Nir said.

It wasn't long before the coke was off the plane. The men waited. Rahim lit a cigarette and sighed with pleasure.

'What are we waiting for?' Nir said.

'You're waiting for me.'

Nir turned. Benny came across the grass. He wore a chequered shirt, short-sleeved, open at the chest, like he always did. 'You called me, didn't you?'

'I didn't think you'd come in person.'

'I'm not here for you, Nirushka. It's new business. New business you do in person.'

'Benny,' Rahim said. They shook hands. 'Good to see you again.'

'This it?' Benny said.

'All of it, plus your man there.'

'Let's do this again sometime,' Benny said.

'Whenever you need.'

Benny gestured. Men with guns appeared, local maybe. Then one of Benny's guys from Tel Aviv, Nir didn't remember his name. He carried a briefcase with him. He handed it over. Rahim opened it because, Nir thought, the temptation was always there to open it and see. Even if you didn't really need to, even if most money was anyway just for show, and the reality of it was numbers in wire transactions and anonymous bank accounts.

But there was something about a briefcase full of dollars that everyone liked.

'Thanks,' Rahim said.

'For the cause,' Benny said.

'We'll pass it along to the FARC,' Rahim said. 'We're square.'

'Good.' Benny nodded. His men started taking the coke and loading it onto a truck. How far was it going? Where would it end up? Tel Aviv, maybe. More likely Amsterdam or Marseille. Nir was sick of the whole thing. He was so tired. He just wanted to go home.

'I need a piss,' he said.

'Behind there,' Benny said. 'I need one too.'

Nir didn't look back. He headed behind the small stone building that stood alone by the airstrip. He was tired of airstrips in the middle of nowhere. But he was finally going home. It felt good to piss. He heard Benny come behind him.

'Hey, Benny,' Nir said.

'Yeah?'

'Why did the bullet lose its job?'

'Why are you speaking in English?' Benny said.

'It's for the joke,' Nir said.

'OK, so why *did* the bullet lose its job?' Benny said.

'It got fired.'

Nir finished pissing. He had his back to Benny. He said, 'Hey, Benny. I'm going home.'

'Home,' Benny said.

He touched the barrel of the gun very gently to the back of Nir's head.

'Oh, Benny,' Nir said. 'Oh, Benny. Don't.'

'It was coming, Nir,' Benny said. 'It was coming for a long time.'

The 'pop' was quiet in that night. Benny came back around and he went and washed his hands in a stone basin filled with rainwater.

'Did you finish loading?' he said.

'It's done.'

'Then let's go,' Benny said.

PART TWELVE

UNDER THE PINES

1993, The North

65

CHASING THE STORY

'Some people are stories, and some never get a mention' – Ruth

'Yair!'

'Yair!'

'Colonel Grosse! Do you have a comment about the accusations levelled at you by the Colombian government?'

A warm breeze. The smell of hot oil, car exhaust fumes, cigarettes, jasmine, eucalyptus, sweat. A gaggle of journalists and photographers outside the courthouse.

'Yair! Did you train the men who assassinated Luis Carlos Galán?'

'Hey, Yair! Do you know Pablo Escobar?'

'Yair!'

'Yair!'

'Colonel Grosse!'

Sylvie watched him as he stopped, turned, waited until they all quieted down. He looked, she thought, like he enjoyed attention.

He said, 'I have gone over this a thousand times. The men we trained in Colombia were from the local ranchers' association. I never met Pablo Escobar. I had nothing to do with those political assassinations in Colombia. The people I trained were simple farmers. I do not want to keep reading unsubstantiated rumours and accusations in the media! Everything I and Arrowhead Ltd. did was above board. If you keep printing lies about me or my men I will sue you like I did Ron Ben-Yishai and *Yediot*.'

Sylvie jotted it down in her notebook.

'Can you comment on the murder of your associate, Arik Afek, in Miami two months after he helped you escape from Colombia?'

Grosse shook his head. 'Arik Afek was a lovely guy but he had a big mouth,' he said. 'He didn't help me and I didn't escape, I left the country when my contract was up. I don't know why he was killed, that's a question for the American police. Are we done here?'

'What's next for you, Colonel?' someone shouted. 'Is it true you're now involved in diamond mining in Africa?'

Grosse shrugged. 'No comment,' he said, and with that he turned again and entered the house.

'What do you think, Sylvie?' Gabi said beside her. Gabi worked for *Yediot* now. Sylvie went to work for *Ha'aretz* after *This World* shut.

Sylvie shrugged. She folder her notebook back in her pocket.

'I don't think it's much of a story,' she said.

'Colombia!' Gabi said. 'Drugs, guns, Pablo! If that's not a story, what is?'

'I don't know,' Sylvie said. 'I'm still looking for one.'

'You want to get a coffee?' Gabi said. 'We could catch up—'

'Catch up on what?' Sylvie said. She patted him on the shoulder. 'Good to see you, Gabi.'

She turned and left.

The problem, she reflected, was that the story of Colonel Grosse and his band of little men was a story of the *old* Israel. She couldn't put her finger on it, exactly, but in the past couple of years, at least, she had felt something change. It was like a room that had been shut for too long and then someone opened a window, and a fresh clean air breezed through. She couldn't quite put it into words, couldn't, as yet, define what it was. She couldn't yet tell if it was illusory or real, a new permanent state or a false spring. She was not sure she understood this new generation. When she got into her tiny Fiat and switched on the radio, she didn't know any of these new songs. What did the Top Hat Carriers *mean* when they said the next one in the line was a horse?

Me and me and me and me. This *individuality*. Where had this music *come* from? Two years ago there was nothing like this on the radio. Now it was everywhere.

Carmella Gross Wagner singing about an impressionist painting. The Elders of Safed singing about not being animals but the world. Electric guitar riffs and drums that beat like fists against a door, the musicians young, wild, Dr Casper's Rabbit Show doing a punk version of 'In A Red Dress', the little girl who asked why from the original song interrupted by screaming vocals questioning why she couldn't understand, the whole track a protest and a celebration of youth at once.

What did it *mean*? Sylvie was of an age that she could have been their mother now. Not that she ever had kids, in the end. It just didn't work out. But she didn't understand this new generation, born after the invasion of Lebanon, born into a time where, suddenly, everyone was talking about peace as though it were possible.

Everyone knew there were talks taking place.

Maybe this time it will be for real.

She drove north, listening to Army Radio, Where's The Kid singing about 'Sugar Time' and 'What I'm Going Through' and 'Alice's Tea Party'. New music and a new feeling, that maybe things will work out alright in the end.

But in the meantime Sylvie was chasing stories.

The field, when she finally found it, lay somewhere between Kibbutz Gal'ed and Dalia. She'd covered a story from Dalia three years earlier – one of the members, a young, smiling man who cut the grass, had six years before murdered an Arab attendant at a petrol station nearby, along with a friend. They had done it as revenge, in some weird way, against the murder of a young soldier in the area, Hadas Kadmi, another young woman who died on the coastal road, her death blamed on Arabs this time.

Sylvie had tried to understand what it was like for the young man, to murder someone then go back to everyday life, carrying that secret with him for six long years. The police only found it out when the friend, arrested for another crime, suddenly confessed.

When Sylvie visited the kibbutz no one wanted to talk to her.

'He was always smiling.' That was the only quote she got, off some kid. Well, the man wasn't smiling now, in prison, she supposed.

What was his name? Something Efroni. She remembered the devastated look in his mother's eyes. A sad story. He was led astray by his friend, who was adopted into the kibbutz from a troubled background. Sylvie remembered the Hava Nahari story, a decade past. No one wanted to take responsibility. They always blamed someone else.

But Sylvie had had enough of murder stories. They were common, everyday things. Page three if you were lucky. Page five if it was a woman murdered by her husband, if she made it into the paper at all.

She got off the road, following the dirt track and the sight of parked cars and a TV van, to the wheat field, where kibbutzniks in shorts stood around just to enjoy the excitement. It was a novelty, to have a media event like this.

'So what's the story?' Sylvie said, getting out and stretching her legs. 'Oh, come on,' she said, seeing Gabi was already there. He smiled sheepishly.

'A flying saucer!' Gabi said. 'An honest to God alien landing site. Did you read my series of articles on the topic?'

'Yes, Gabi,' Sylvie said. 'I read your articles.'

She lit a cigarette. This was such a waste of time. There had been a spate of UFO sightings over Haifa in the late eighties. For a time it was all the rage. Like parapsychology and spoon-bending and dowsing for oil and all the rest of it. Chiko and Dicko performing magic tricks on kids' TV. A father and son act. The kid was cute, until he grew up and now he was going on trial for rape and indecent assault. It looked like Dicko was going to prison. No doubt he had someone else to blame.

'A flying saucer,' Sylvie said. She drew smoke into her lungs. It felt good, to smoke under a clear sky, with the smell of fresh hay, of the country.

'See for yourself,' Gabi said.

She followed him through the field and the tall wheat, to a circle formed in the crops. The circle was perfectly round, maybe ten metres across, the wheat flattened underfoot. And she saw that there were two more identical circles formed beside the first one, so that it really did look like some giant spaceship had come and briefly landed here, in this field of wheat, in the middle of the night. Though what it was doing there was anyone's guess.

'It's a bit… eighties, Gabi,' she said.

'It will look great in a picture,' he said.

'Aliens?' Sylvie said.

Gabi shrugged. 'Or a couple of English volunteers who got drunk last night and went out into the fields with a long beam of wood,' he said. 'They make a lot of crop circles like this in England.'

'I wouldn't know,' Sylvie said.

'It's a good story!' Gabi said.

But Sylvie was still looking.

She made notes in her notebook as the expert from Haifa spoke to the journalists. Hadassah Carmeli, with fervent eyes and long dangly earrings that quivered as she spoke. She had made herself visible over the past few years, even attaching herself unofficially to the Haifa Police Force, the person to call when another unidentified object was spotted in the sky.

'The aliens mean us no harm,' she told the press, 'here we have a classic landing site, you can see the impressions made by the visitors' ship as it landed.'

'Was it a flying saucer?' Gabi asked her.

'Yes, yes. Definitely. As you know there are three main types of alien vehicles, the cigar shape or mothership, the flying saucer and the—'

But Sylvie lost interest. She watched the kibbutzniks gawk and point. A tractor pulled up with a cart behind it and kids poured down from the cart to watch the excitement.

But Sylvie couldn't see it. It was an eighties story, destined to fade and be forgotten like all the other sightings. Soon even Hadassah Carmeli will fade out of the public mind.

There was only so far you could take that particular story.

She got back in her car and back on the road, Mikiyagi and the Juvenile Delinquents singing 'Go With Her', and she had a feeling she had missed something, but she didn't know what.

The Tractor's Revenge sang about 'A Game Of Tears' when

Sylvie pulled into the petrol station on the turning to Zikhron Ya'akov. Was that where Efroni murdered the Arab attendant? She filled up the Fiat, then wandered over to the café to get a drink and have a smoke again.

What was it, she thought? The radio in the café still played the old songs, the Southern Command Band singing 'A Dove With An Olive Branch', soft piano and voices in melodic harmony, their hit from a few years back, singing about the hope for peace. Would there really be peace this time? Sylvie thought. A two-state solution, all that stuff?

No more wars, just like in all the songs, 'The Final War', 'The Song Of Peace', 'Flowers In The Gun Barrel', 'When Peace Comes', 'I Was Born For Peace', 'Here Comes Peace', peace, peace, peace, no one sang so much about peace and had so many wars.

It couldn't be that, Sylvie thought, distracted. She was still missing something. Maybe she should go back to Tel Aviv, talk to some of these new bands, try to put her finger on it. A new sound, a new generation who didn't know war, who might now never know it. That sounded like the beginning of a story.

She picked up a copy of *Al Hamishmar*, the kibbutznik newspaper. *On Guard*. What would they call it if there ever was peace? *Not On Guard Anymore*? Not that it was going to last much longer. The paper, like most of the small ones now, was in financial trouble. Sylvie thanked her blessings at least she wasn't working *there*.

The paper only survived by making it compulsory for kibbutz members to subscribe. It was in every kibbutznik's home but not very much elsewhere.

Still. It was a good newspaper.

She leafed through the articles, meandered past the Letters to the Editor, and found herself going through the pages of black-framed death notices when a small announcement caught her eye.

All Invited,
To the annual memorial service for our beloved daughter,
Einav Nevot.

Cruelly taken from us in the year 1976.
Gone but not forgotten.
Two pm in Kibbutz Hadassah cemetery.

Something about the notice, one of a dozen or so on the page, bothered her. Who was Einav Nevot? Why did Sylvie know the name? Why was she cruelly taken?

She went to the public phone and put a token in and dialled the office and was put through to the archives.

'Do we have anything on Einav Nevot?' she said.

It took a few minutes and a handful of tokens before Gerda, the ancient archivist, came back on the line.

'She was one of the girls who was found murdered on the coastal road back in the seventies,' Gerda said.

'What do you mean one of the girls?'

'There were several,' Gerda said. 'Poor things. Always found in the same way, all along the road to Haifa. You don't remember?'

'Vaguely.'

'Raped and murdered? The police put that guy behind bars for one of them, what was his name.'

'Elisha Barnea,' Sylvie said, suddenly remembering. Barnea was even now protesting his innocence in the papers. 'So that's where I know it from. Was anyone ever arrested for Einav Nevot?'

'No,' Gerda said. 'The murderer's still at large.'

Was this her story, finally? Sylvie wondered. She said, 'Gerda, can you find out who the other girls were?'

'What, I have nothing else to do, Sylvie?'

'Please, Gerda.'

She heard Gerda's two-packs-a-day laugh on the other end of the line.

'Call me back in half an hour,' she said.

'Thanks, Gerda.'

She hung up. Bought another coffee and smoked another cigarette outside. Saw Gabi's car pull in. He saw her and suddenly beamed. He was like a puppy. He got out and came over.

'Fancy meeting you here,' he said.

'Are you following me, Gabi?' she said and he laughed.

'The flying saucer lady ran a bit long,' he said. 'I'm heading back to Tel Aviv. You?'

'I have a thing in a minute.'

'Sylvie Gold, Our Correspondent in the North,' Gabi said. 'What's the scoop? A kibbutznik fell off his tractor?'

'There are plenty of stories in the kibbutzim,' Sylvie said.

Gabi shrugged. 'Sure, but you'll never get them. They sweep them under the carpet and no one ever calls the police. It's worse than back in the shtetls.'

'You don't like them?' Sylvie said, surprised.

'Like, don't like, what difference does it make?' Gabi said. 'You might as well squeeze a stone for water. Hey, buy you a coffee?'

'Already had two.'

'Want to get lunch?'

'I can't, I've got to call the desk.'

He looked at her suspiciously. 'What's your angle, Gold? Are you holding out on me?'

'Firstly, Gabi, always. Secondly, I don't know yet.'

'I can see your nose twitching, Sylvie,' he said. 'Like you got a scent.'

'It might be the wrong one.'

'Be like that, then,' he said. 'I'll see you in Tel Aviv.'

He went back to his car and took off and Sylvie went inside to use the phone.

'So nu, Gerda?'

'So nu yourself,' Gerda said. 'You took me down memory lane today, Sylvie.'

A knot formed in Sylvie's stomach. 'How many of them were there?' she said.

'Who can tell for sure? The first might have been Miryam Pinkus, in '66. She was seventeen years old. Then Sarah Lifa or Lipa, in '68. Then in '72, Jacqueline Smith, an English volunteer. Then Esther Landes in '74. That's the one where Elisha Barnea was convicted for the murder.'

'Did it stop then?'

'No, Sylvie. Are you writing this down?'

That knot tightened. A voice in her head saying, this is not the story you want. This is the old Israel, not the new. Her pen pressed into the paper.

'Then Einav Nevot, in '76. Then Leonore Ben-Lulu.'

'My God.'

'Then there was Orly Dubi, in '83,' Gerda said. 'A guy called Haliwa was done for that one. Remember him? They used to call him the Crying Rapist.'

Sylvie did remember. And she remembered Landes, remembered some of the others. It was a fear for every young woman at that time. A fear, she thought, that was still on them, even now. Nothing had changed, after all.

'The last one was Hadas Kadmi, in '84,' Gerda said. 'No conviction. Most of these remain unsolved.'

'Was it over then?' Sylvie said.

'Who can really tell, Sylvie?' Gerda said. 'Some girls went missing but no body was ever found. Some happened in the south, and the victims were shot, not strangled. What do you want me to tell you, bubele? It's an old story. *Davar* did an expose back in '83. *Yediot* ran a story last year. You missed the bus on this one.'

'But no one was caught.'

'Not no one.'

'Thanks, Gerda,' Sylvie said. 'I'm going to be late.'

'Late for what?' Gerda said.

'A memorial service.'

She hung up, got back in her Fiat, her mouth tasting of coffee and cigarettes. This wasn't the story she wanted to tell. She knew that now. It was a story about the past, and she wanted to write about the future. This was a sad story, and she wanted, craved, hope.

She put on the radio. 'And now… The Witches!' Kuttner said. Sylvie listened spellbound as Inbal Perlmuter's throaty voice belted out their hard-rock version of 'Magic On The Sea Of Galilee', the old children's song reinvented and made luminous with bass guitar and drums, and Sylvie was transported into an enchanted world, as though Inbal were telling her a bedtime story, promising it will all be fine in the end, and Sylvie hung on to every bar and every guitar riff.

She found Kibbutz Hadassah after a couple of false turns and drove down the long road to the kibbutz. The gate was open at this time of day and when she rolled down the window and asked a passing teen for the cemetery he pointed her wordlessly to the road that circumnavigated the kibbutz, which was built on a hill. A dog napped in the sun and the whole place felt as quiet as the grave, and she came to the end of the road and a copse of pine trees and saw a small group of people heading to a low metal gate.

Sylvie parked next to a couple of cars already there. She stepped outside and was surprised again by the clear air, the smell of pines, the quiet. She went to the gate and passed through into the small cemetery, where neat rows of graves lay under the trees, blanketed in pine needles.

She followed the voices to the grave.

Einav Nevot, daughter of Kibbutz Hadassah, lay buried in serenity. A candle was lit on the grave and fresh flowers left on the stone. There was only a handful of people there. Sylvie hung back, through the short service, the seventeenth such service since Einav's murder.

At first there must have been hundreds in attendance, Sylvie thought. The whole kibbutz probably came the first year. Then only a few, until almost none were left: the parents, a couple of old friends.

Someone else stood in the shade of the pines. Tall, with a straight back, his face hidden in the shade. Who was that? She listened to the short speeches. The mother seemed frail. A friend from childhood read a poem. Then it was over.

'Hello,' a woman said. 'I'm Ruth.' She looked at Sylvie curiously. 'I'm sorry to ask, but who are you? Hardly anyone comes anymore. Did you know Einav?'

'I didn't, no,' Sylvie said. 'I'm sorry. I saw the notice in the paper and I…' She struggled to articulate what brought her there. 'I'm a journalist,' she said.

'But this happened… Did you think of writing about it?' Ruth said. 'It was so long ago. She died and…' Her eyes welled up. 'It was in the papers for a while and then nobody cared.'

'You were a friend of hers?' Sylvie said.

'Yes. We were together in the commune, in the movement, you know. She just left one evening because our toilets were broken and she needed to go and she said she'd go home and I told her not to go but she wouldn't listen, she never listened, and she must have hitchhiked home and someone picked her up and someone… Did this to her. She was so young. We were so young.'

Sylvie hugged her. A little girl came and pulled on Ruth's arm.

'Mummy, can we go now?'

Ruth pulled away, smiled, wiped away the tears. 'In a moment, Einavy.'

'You named her after your friend,' Sylvie said.

'I wanted to remember her,' Ruth said. 'Well, goodbye. Do you think you will write about it? About her?'

'I wouldn't know what to write,' Sylvie said.

Ruth nodded.

'Some people are stories,' she said. 'And some never get a mention.' She touched Sylvie lightly on the shoulder, then let her daughter pull her away.

Sylvie stayed. It was quiet in the cemetery. She saw the figure under the pine was still there. It lit a match then, and Sylvie saw his face, caught in the glare.

'Cohen?' she said.

He stepped out of the shade.

'Sylvie Gold,' he said. 'It's been a while.'

'What are you doing here?' Sylvie said.

'Cigarette?' he said, offering her the box. Sylvie accepted one. Cohen offered her the match and she lit up and they stood there for a moment in silence and looked at the grave. They were the only ones left, now.

'You knew her?' Sylvie said.

'Only in death. I worked the case, for a while.'

'You couldn't beat a confession out of anyone?'

He tapped ash on the ground. 'You did your homework, then?'

'I know you were on the team that arrested Elisha Barnea.'

'I was only a uniform cop.'

'What does that mean, Cohen?'

'It was not my decision.'

She studied him. His eyes, that were often so hard, were wide open.

'You never bought it, did you,' she said. 'You never thought it was Barnea.'

'This is off the record,' Cohen said, and Sylvie laughed. 'There is no record, Cohen. There is no story anymore.'

'Buy you a coffee?' he said. He looked like so many of her sources had looked over the years. He looked like he just wanted to talk, and when a journalist happened along they could never stop themselves. She thought of someone like Cohen, especially, who must have lived so quietly within himself, who must have kept inside the vault of his mind so many secrets.

And she thought again of this new generation, with its new kind of music. Would they be whole, would they be free? Unburdened of the awful secrets of her generation? Their music didn't speak of freedom, it *was* freedom.

It was an impossibility for her, she realised. And therefore tenfold more for Cohen.

'Sure,' she said. 'Is there a place?'

'Just follow my car.'

They rode out of the kibbutz, passing tanned boys and girls in shorts who sat on the grass, laughing in a way she could not remember how to laugh now.

They left the kibbutz and she followed Cohen until, with a sense of inevitability, they reached the coastal road.

He pulled into a shack on the sea side of the road, a stone's throw from Fureidis. An old Arab man sold olive oil and baked pitas on a fire. Cohen asked him for coffee and after some thought ordered some food for them both. They sat, not awkwardly, as the old man poured them black coffee into the small china cups.

'So,' Sylvie said. 'Barnea.'

'There was a girl in '66,' Cohen said. 'She was my cousin.'

'I'm sorry,' Sylvie said.

'You must have the names of the others, if you are here,' he said.

'I do.'

'Strangled, left on the coast road, usually in the orange groves.

In the trees, anyway. On the beach. Once by the fish ponds in Ma'agan Michael. All hitchhikers. We figured it must have been a driver. He was picking them up. He must have seemed safe, too. Probably a family man. It's why Haliwa never figured for me. He spent most of his time in jail on other rapes and only got out on breaks, and he didn't drive. At least Barnea had a car.'

'So what did you do?' Sylvie said.

'There was a lot of pressure to solve them,' Cohen said, almost defensively. 'When Esther Landes happened… Well, that was the worst of it. It was made clear to us someone had to take the fall. We thought maybe the boyfriend, for a while. But he was an army veteran, a war invalid. Plus, an Ashkenazi. Whereas Barnea…'

Cohen brooded.

'He was a nobody,' Sylvie said.

'His head wasn't right, from the war,' Cohen said. 'But everyone said he was the sort of guy who wouldn't hurt a fly. He did confess, though.'

'You made him confess,' Sylvie said.

Cohen said nothing.

Sylvie said, 'And the murders didn't stop.'

'No,' Cohen said. 'They didn't.'

The old man brought them hot pitas, cool labneh, pickles. He patted Cohen on the shoulder and left.

'You know him?' Sylvie said.

'Knew his kid,' Cohen said, and suddenly smiled. 'He was an ace burglar.'

'What happened to him?' Sylvie said.

'Nothing,' Cohen said. 'He moved to Chicago and has two kids of his own now. He works as a locksmith, I believe.'

Sylvie tore a strip of pita and swiped the labneh.

'Einav Nevot,' she said.

'Yes,' Cohen said.

'She was next?'

'Yes. You have to understand, we had no real basis to assume it was a, what we now call a serial killer. It could be isolated murders. We had to treat them as isolated murders. Try and find a jealous boyfriend, a known sex offender, anything like that. We had to look at money motives. We had to look at everyone, even women. Remember Hava Nahari?'

'I covered the trial,' Sylvie said.

'But each time we'd come up empty. Or they'd say the police beat a confession out of the people responsible, like with the Daphna Carmon case in '86.'

'It was a group of young Arab men,' Sylvie said. 'One of them confessed, then said the police beat him up until he had no choice but to confess to whatever they wanted him to.'

'I'm not saying these things didn't go on,' Cohen said.

'Then what *are* you saying?'

'That we don't know. Maybe we'll never know.'

'You think he stopped? Whoever he is?'

'We had a theory,' Cohen said. 'Me and my old partner, Eddie. He's pretty senior now. But he never forgot Esther Landes, same as me. It was our first big case.'

'What was the theory?'

'We thought it was a tourist,' Cohen said. 'He came to visit around the holidays. Stayed for a couple of weeks at a time, somewhere near Hadera maybe. Drove a rental car. You'd trust a rental car more, wouldn't you? If one stopped for you? We figured he might be French. Somewhere close enough to make these holidays routine for him. He probably spoke Hebrew. Had a good job. It would be easy for him to vanish each time, and the rental went back into the car pool and we'd never have a clue. Not that we had a clue, anyway.'

'Did you look into it?' Sylvie said.

She drank the coffee. It was sweet and bitter at once.

'We tried. The bosses thought it was a waste of time. A year or two would pass, we'd have other cases to deal with. Or there'd be a war. Or a drug murder, those got bad in the eighties. Or just the usual run of the mill. Rapes, regular murders, hit and runs, kidnappings, assault, burglaries. Remember the Bank Ha'poalim heist in '84? A million and a half in dollars, it was a fortune.' Cohen smiled. 'That kept us busy for a while.'

She could sense he was leading to something. A man with a weight on his conscience, as they said.

'So what did you do? With the tourist angle?' Sylvie said.

'Nothing.'

'Come on, Cohen.'

'I can tell you a story,' he said. 'But it's just a story, Sylvie Gold.'

'I like stories.'

He shrugged.

'Let's say there were these two cops,' he said. 'They kept their ears open. They had some people at the rental agencies they could lean on. Who'd feed them stuff. Same in Border Control. And these two cops, they'd check hotels in the area. Especially around the holidays, whenever they could. Nothing ever came of it. But one day maybe they got lucky. A routine report came through, about a girl who said she got a lift from a guy who tried to drag her somewhere. She jumped out of the vehicle and managed to escape. The desk sergeant was liable to dismiss it. She wasn't the most stable of people. An institution kid, you know. And she couldn't remember shit about the guy, other than that the car was white and she thought maybe he had a French accent. But somehow the report landed on one of the cops' desks, and he showed it to the other. Maybe they were feeling kind of pissed off, at the time. For all kinds of unconnected reasons. And they did some extracurricular detective work and they found a guy who fit the profile. A French tourist, quite well-to-do, came over twice a year for the holidays. He was renting a place not far from here, actually. In the story, anyway. And maybe the two cops watched him. They saw him go for long drives, back and forth, along the coast road.'

'It doesn't add up to much,' Sylvie said.

'No,' Cohen said, and he lit a cigarette and again offered her one, but she shook her head. 'No, it doesn't.'

'So what did you – what did they do?' Sylvie said.

'It's just a story,' Cohen said. 'It's not real.'

'In the story, I mean,' Sylvie said.

A seagull cried in the distance. The sun was low on the horizon now. The air turned cooler. Cohen said, 'Maybe they went and paid him a visit. Showed him their badges, but they were in civilian clothes of course. "Come with us, please," they said. "We have some questions to ask you." And he came along, especially when they pointed their guns at him.'

'God, Cohen,' Sylvie said.

'They drove him to Tantura,' Cohen said, and she wasn't even sure he was seeing her. 'To the spot where all those years ago they found Esther Landes on the beach.'

'God, Cohen,' Sylvie said.

'Then they asked him if he did it. And he said no. No, he had no idea what they were asking him. Why had they taken him? He could pay them to let him go. It was dark, and it was quiet there, on the sand. They'd brought shovels.'

Sylvie felt sick.

'"Please," he said. "Please." Do you think that's what she said, too, when it happened to her? To all of them? "Please, don't."' Cohen blew smoke.

'They gave him a shovel and asked him to dig,' he said.

'Cohen, don't. I don't want to hear it anymore.'

'It's just a story.'

A seagull cried in the distance. Sylvie turned the empty coffee cup between her fingers. This wasn't the story she wanted, she thought. This wasn't a story anyone wanted.

'What happened?' she said, despite herself.

'The man dug a hole. Then the two policemen gave him one last chance. If he confessed they'd take him away from there, they said. To a court and a judge. All they wanted was just to know the truth. Did he do it? Did he kill all those women, in all those years? The man was crying. "Yes," he said, "yes." He did it. Please, will you arrest him?'

'Then you shot him,' Sylvie whispered.

'The people in the story?' Cohen said. 'I guess maybe they did.'

'God, Cohen.'

He smiled suddenly. 'It's just a story, Sylvie,' he said. 'If you go out to Tantura now and dig then what, you think you'd find a skeleton?'

'I think there are other ways to get rid of a body,' Sylvie said.

'Maybe there are,' Cohen said. 'And maybe the two cops slept better at night after they did what they did.'

'What if they didn't, though?' Sylvie said. She felt tears come to her eyes unbidden. 'What if they thought that, as long as they lived, they'd never know if they were right that night, or if they just murdered—'

'I think they'd sleep fine,' Cohen said. He got up abruptly, stretched his long legs, tossed twenty shekels on the table.

'If you ever tell anyone else this story,' he said, 'I will kill you.'

Sylvie watched him leave.

The old man came over. He took the money and started to clear the table.

'Why are you crying?' he said. 'Is something wrong?'

Sylvie shook her head. 'Just an allergy,' she said.

'Yes,' he said, 'my granddaughter has that too.'

Sylvie went back to her car and pointed it in the direction of Tel Aviv and gunned the accelerator. She played the radio in full volume all the way home, electric guitars blaring notes that dribbled out of the open window and onto the road as Corinne Allal sang 'There Are No Horses Who Speak Hebrew' and Where's The Kid sang 'Her Sadness' and Dr Casper's Rabbit Show sang about the little girl in the red dress who asked why?

But no one had an answer.

PART THIRTEEN

HIGH ROLLERS AND HAPPY PILLS

1994, Tel Aviv – Elyakim

66

FIST OF ECSTASY

'Exta, exta. Dance, dance' – Shai Goldin

Avi popped The Witches' new album into the Walkman and the first bars of 'Until The Next Pleasure' blared out of his headphones. His hair was down to his shoulders and he wanted to grow it longer. Having long hair was a prerequisite for being a rocker, at least until he turned eighteen and joined the army. They shaved your head when you joined.

His knees went up and down as he pedalled the bicycle up the hill. Inbal Perlmuter sang about pleasures Avi couldn't even begin to imagine, though he did his best to. He had a huge crush on Inbal.

Lior's little sister, Natasha, answered the door when he knocked. She was dressed like a princess, in a pink dress, and she beamed up at Avi with her braces.

'Hey, Avi,' she said, 'do you want to hear a joke?'

'Alright,' Avi said.

'The teacher told us to write an essay on the topic, "There Is Only One Mum". So I wrote that Mum asked me to get two tomatoes for salad and I went to the fridge and then I said, "There is only one, Mum!"

She burst out laughing, snorting so hard that snot shot out. Avi smiled.

From inside Lior shouted, 'Tasha, leave him the fuck alone!'

The Goldin boys sat in the living room. The oldest, Shai, was sprawled in the armchair. Lior and Yair sat on the sofa. *Star Trek* was on TV with the volume down low.

They all looked up when Avi came in.

Yair grunted. Shai stared. Lior smiled, waved for Avi to sit down.

Avi perched on the edge of a hard-backed chair.

'What's going on?' he said.

'We got plans,' Lior said.

'What sort of plans?' Avi said.

'Plans to make money,' Lior said.

Shai kept staring at Avi. He'd just come back from a year backpacking in Asia. He wore tie-dye pantaloons and his already-thinning hair was gathered back in a sweat band. He had a look in his eyes that was somewhere between menacing and lost. Of all the Goldin kids he was considered the brightest, had even planned on studying mathematics before he was ensnared by the lure of Thailand and Goa.

Avi was only there because Lior said he was alright. The other two brothers preferred to keep family business in the family.

'So? Nu?' Avi said.

Lior grinned and held his fist out to Avi. He opened it slowly over the table, and Avi watched a rain of pink pills fall gently onto the glass surface.

'Ecstasy,' Lior said.

'What's that?' Avi said.

'Exta, exta,' Shai said impatiently. 'Dance, dance.'

'What?'

'You'll see,' Lior said, still grinning. He put a pill in his mouth. 'Come on,' he said.

Avi approached with some trepidation. Shai and Yair took a pill each, and Shai smiled for the first time since Avi came in.

Once again all three stared at him.

Avi picked up a pill and looked at it dubiously.

'Where did you get it?' he said.

'What are you, a shtinker?' Shai said.

Lior said, 'Chill, man. Avi's like family.'

'But he's not,' Shai said.

Avi put the pill in his mouth. It didn't taste like much.

'Now what?' he said.

Lior shrugged, and Avi realised he'd never done it before either.

Shai went to the sound system and popped a tape in. A thudding bass filled the room. Shai turned the volume up high.

'What is that!' Avi shouted over the music.

'Techno, techno!' Shai said.

He started dancing, his long arms flopping by his side. Little Natasha burst into the room.

'Techno, techno!' she shouted happily. She started to dance like Shai.

'What the fuck, Lior?' Avi said.

Lior shrugged, looking uncertain. 'I don't know,' he said.

'Do you feel anything?' Avi said.

'No. You?'

'No.'

Shai opened the doors to the yard. The music blared out. He started to dance under the washing lines.

Avi took Shai's place on the sofa. He and Lior watched Captain Kirk battle a salt monster on an alien planet. Avi wasn't sure what was going on. He wasn't sure how long the episode was. The lights of the television started to sparkle. His body twitched with the beat of the bass.

He stared at the starship on the screen. It was sort of amazing.

'Whoa,' he said.

Yair started to dance. He joined Shai outside. Avi felt a sudden warmth spread through him.

'I love you, man,' he told Lior.

'Dude, I love you,' Lior said. 'Brothers forever.'

'Brothers,' Avi said and giggled.

The music swept them then. It suddenly made sense. The noise resolved into intricate patterns, like colours in a kaleidoscope.

How had he not noticed it before? He followed Lior outside.

It rained and Avi started to flail, arms going everywhere, the raindrops touching his face like kisses.

He didn't know how long they danced.

Gradually, the euphoria faded. The music lost some of its perceived meaning, until it became just a thud of bass again. Avi looked at his watch and was shocked to see three hours had passed.

They spent the rest of the afternoon inside, playing on the Goldins' Nintendo. Avi gradually felt normal again, though he kept grinding his teeth.

'So what do you do with them?' Avi said. 'The pills?'

'Nature parties,' Lior said.

'What's that?' Avi said.

'They do them out in the forests or wherever,' Lior said. 'People come from all over. We could sell them there. We just need the money to buy more pills. To buy bulk.'

'So where do we get the money?' Avi said. 'Rob a bank?'

'Not a bank, no…' Lior said, and he started laughing excitedly.

Yair shot him a warning look. He stared at Avi, a lit cigarette dangling from his lips, so loosely that it was in danger of falling on his T-shirt.

'We're going to rob a poker game,' he said.

67

THE BIG GAME

'Players and muscles' – Lior Goldin

Avi and Lior lurked across from the Dan Panorama Hotel.

'I don't see the point,' Avi complained.

Lior took a sip of soft drink they got at the Burger Ranch.

'What do you care?' he said. 'You got something better to do? Just keep an eye out for players and muscles.'

'I guess,' Avi said.

Avi bit into his burger. An old woman went past with her very small dog. The dog barked at Avi and then pooped on the floor. The old lady glared at Avi and walked on with her dog.

'Hey, giveret!' Lior called. 'Pick up your dog shit!'

'Fuck you!' the old woman said, without looking back.

Avi laughed. Then he spotted someone going towards the hotel.

'Hey,' he said, 'isn't that Tuvia Tzafir?'

'What, the comedian?' Lior said.

'Do you know another one?' Avi said.

'I can't tell,' Lior said, 'he's wearing a baseball cap and glasses.'

'Only so you won't recognise him,' Avi said.

He took out the piece of paper Yair gave them and crossed off the name.

'Looks like the right place, then,' he said.

It was Yair who came up with the plan. Yair played poker at the Alhambra in Jaffa most days, the only club that never moved around, some heavy-hitters bankrolled it and kept the cops away. Yair had his ears open, and from time to time he'd get a tip about a moving game, some of them big, some of them small.

But only one game was the Big Game, for the real high rollers, and eventually Yair got a lead on where it was.

The game took place every week in a suite at the Dan Panorama Hotel on the promenade. But Yair didn't know when or in what room. So this was the third day Avi and Lior hung around in the sun outside, hoping to spot someone from the list of known players, which included a couple of Orthodox singers famous in the religious community, a Knesset member, an army general, a few businessmen and entertainers like Tuvia Tzafir, even a mathematician from the Weizmann Institute.

A black car pulled to a stop in front of the hotel and two bulky men in dark suits came out. They went into the hotel and didn't come back again.

The muscle.

Lior called Shai from a phone box and let him know. Then he and Avi went into the hotel and stood around in the lobby.

Before too long they saw an Orthodox man with dark sunglasses come in looking sort of furtive. One of the musicians on the list. He went to the lifts. They got in with him and stayed on until he got off on the third floor.

Avi held the doors from closing. Lior stuck his head out, then nodded once the man got some distance from them.

It was some real Erich Kästner *Emil And The Detectives* shit.

They followed the Orthodox man and saw him vanish into a room at the end of a corridor after knocking three times in a pattern.

'Did you get that?' Lior said.

'I think so,' Avi said.

He tapped on the wall, three times.

'No, it was like this,' Lior said, tapping his own version.

Avi frowned. 'No, it was my thing,' he said. 'I think.'

They waited around a while but no one else came. They went back down to the lobby and called Shai again and told him.

'What does he say?' Avi said.

'Tonight,' Lior said.

Avi felt excitement build inside him. 'What do we do now?' he said.

'We watch,' Lior said. 'We wait.'

Avi just nodded. Then he said, 'But we can't do it with Tuvia Tzafir there. He's, like, famous.'

'Then we wait till he leaves,' Lior said. 'Who gives a shit. Come on.'

'Hey, Lior,' Avi said. 'Did you like that exta stuff?'

Lior shrugged.

'It was alright,' he said.

'Yeah,' Avi said. 'It was a little weird.'

'You don't have to take it,' Lior said. 'You just have to sell it.'

'Right. Lior?'

'Yeah?'

'Who runs the Big Game?'

'How the fuck should I know? You saw who plays in it. It's all civilians.'

'I'm not talking about the players. I'm talking about the owners.'

'Will you relax? They won't even know what hit them. How do you think you get to be big, Avi? You have to be willing to take on anyone, big or small.'

'OK, Lior.'

'Come on, fucko. Hey, is that Dudu Topaz?'

'No fucking way,' Avi said.

'No, really, look, it's him.'

'You think he's here for the game?'

'Why, you want to ask him for an autograph?'

They bickered like that, and nobody paid them any attention.

'Good job, Lior. You too,' Yair said to Avi.

Avi was touched. Yair never said nice things.

They were outside on the promenade. It was late evening and quieter now.

'What's the security like?' Shai said.

'At least two men inside,' Avi said. 'Probably armed.'

'How many players left?'

'We're not sure how many we spotted,' Avi said. 'We saw five from the list go in, and three of them left looking pissed off so I guess they left their money on the table.'

'Where we want it,' Shai said. 'Let's wait. Yair, you want a burger?'

'I want a burger,' Yair said.

'We already had burgers,' Lior said.

'Then have a pizza,' Yair said.

'Alright,' Lior said.

They went and got pizza and burgers. Avi sat with them and felt a part of the gang.

It was nice to be a part of something.

At one o'clock they went back to watch. At two o'clock they saw another man from the list leave. The member of the Knesset.

'Alright,' Yair said.

'Alright,' Shai said.

Avi went into the hotel alone. It was late and the place was almost deserted and he explained to the sleepy security guard he was just there to pick up his mother, who cleaned on the late shift. Once inside he went through the Staff Only doors and found the exit to the bins in the back and let the Goldins in.

They went up the service lift to the third floor. They walked softly down the corridor. They stopped outside the room.

Yair and Shai took positions on either side, flat against the wall.

Avi knocked, three times in a pattern.

The door opened.

A big man looked down on Avi.

He said, 'What the fuck are you—'

Yair and Shai came round at the same time. They pressed their guns to the man's stomach.

'Shh,' Yair said.

They pushed the man into the room. When they entered Avi saw five players around the table, chips and cash in the middle.

Yair moved fast and he hit the second guard over the head before the man had a chance to shoot. The guard collapsed on the carpet.

'You know whose game this is?' the first guard said.

'Shut the fuck up,' Shai said. He made the guard sit down and Lior tied his hands with rope.

Shai tossed Avi his backpack.

Avi went round the table, collecting money.

'Everybody, take out your wallets,' Shai said. 'Place them on the table, slowly. No one needs to be a hero.'

'You don't know who you're fucking with,' one of the players said. The general.

Avi collected wallets, watches, cash. He shoved them into the backpack.

'OK?' Shai said.

'OK,' Avi said.

'Step out and I will shoot you,' Shai said. He had his gun trained on the door all the way down the corridor, but nobody came out.

For all Avi knew they just went right back to playing.

Small Baruch waited for them in a car on the promenade. They squeezed in and took off fast.

'Yeah!' Yair said.

Then they all started to laugh at once, hollering and whooping as they made their way out of Tel Aviv, back to the safety of the Goldins' house.

68

PARTY PEOPLE

'Trance is freedom' – *Shai Goldin*

Of course there was nothing in the papers. No one was going to report the robbery of an illegal poker game. That night they counted their loot on the table in the Goldins' living room, amazed and excited at what they got.

'Just this watch is worth, like, ten thousand shekels!' Yair said, and they all stared, because it was an unimaginable amount. Avi didn't know what to expect, but not this: not over a hundred thousand in cash.

They were rich.

Shai gave Small Baruch a cool five thousand for driving the getaway car. He gave Lior and Avi three hundred shekels each – 'Pocket money, you deserve it,' he said.

The rest was going on the exta venture.

Shai, who knew all these people from back in Goa, drove with Avi and Lior to Tel Aviv. They went into a place called Krembo Records on Sheinkin.

The shop was dark, lit with luminous tubes and ultraviolet lamps that made trippy paintings glow eerie colours on the walls. A deep thrumming bass made Avi's teeth ache. He checked out a bunch of flyers stuck to a board.

Give Trance A Chance, one said.

Amp for sale, said another. *Used, good-condition. Ask for Gil.*

Another offered the services of *DJ Razz, Trance, Techno, Goa Sound, All Styles, Friends and Family Rates.*

Avi didn't really know what any of it meant. There were more offers for sale, speakers, turntables. Nothing about the next trance party.

Shai had a quiet conversation with the guy behind the counter. The guy passed him something, furtively. Then Shai came back and gave them the nod, and they followed him out to bright sunshine.

'So?' Lior said.

Back in the car Shai showed them the flyer. It was tiny, the size of a matchbox. All it had on was a date two days away and an address for a petrol station somewhere up north.

'It's in a petrol station?' Lior said.

'No, idiot,' Shai said. 'You only get the location when you get to the station.'

'What is this, the Mossad?' Avi said.

'Listen, fucko,' Shai said. 'Trance is *freedom*. You two don't have a clue. What's that shit you listen to, Avi? Mashina?'

'Yeah?' Avi said.

'Trance is like…' Shai said. 'It doesn't need *words*. It's not about thinking, it's about *being*.'

'Being what?' Avi said.

'Being an asshole,' Lior said, and they both smirked.

'Shut the fuck up,' Shai said. 'It's about *not* being a part of anything, it's about being away from everything. So that's why you *don't* want the police or the security services or nosy neighbours or *anyone* to know where you are. Because it's all about the *music*.'

'And the drugs,' Lior said.

'And the drugs,' Shai said. He started the engine.

'Give Trance A Chance,' Avi said solemnly, and then he and Lior burst out laughing.

Two days later they were in the car again heading north. By evening they found the petrol station, near Elyakim. A girl in shorts gave them directions to the party. They drove in the dark through the woods. A toilet roll hanging from a branch marked a turning. Soon they could see lights ahead. Music boomed out of giant speakers.

The beat filled the car, merged with the bumps of the tyres on the dirt track, with Yair's fingers tapping on the seat, with Shai's cough. Other cars were already there. In fact, Avi only then realised there were three other cars behind *them*, that they had inadvertently become the head of a convoy.

A DJ table was set up in the distance with lights flashing. Cars were parked haphazardly between the trees. Out in the open space people were dancing, and a girl twirled fire on two ropes.

A makeshift bar was set up to one side. No one paid the Goldins and Avi any attention.

Everyone danced separately, but they all danced together, somehow.

Shai dropped a bag of pills into Avi's hands, another into Lior's.

'We're going to check it out,' he said. 'You two sell as many as you can. Two hundred for one, or make it three hundred if they buy two. Get it? Got it? Good.'

Avi was tempted to take one of the pills. Surrender to the music, be free like those others, loose-limbed and swaying in the moonlight. Pretending they were back on Koh Phangan or the beaches of Goa, places Avi only saw in his imagination. They were all pretending they were elsewhere.

Or maybe this was how things were always going to be from now on. For all Avi knew he wouldn't even have to join the army. Rabin and Arafat on the White House lawn, Bill Clinton beaming beside them.

A new peace. A new Israel.

A land of prosperity and happiness for all.

'You want exta? Exta?' Avi said.

A gangly long-haired man in his twenties stopped dancing and blinked.

'How much?' he said.

'Two hundred,' Avi said.

'Two hundred!' the man said.

Two girls were watching and now came over.

'You have ecstasy?' one of the girls said in English.

'Yes, yes,' Avi said, 'Where are you from?'

'Denmark,' the girl said. 'And you?'

'From right here,' Avi said. The two girls looked at him in amusement.

'How much?' the first one said.

'You're cute,' the second one said.

Avi blushed and hoped no one could see it in the dark.

'Two hundred each,' he said, 'but for you, two for three hundred.'

'He *is* cute,' the first girl said.

They rummaged in their shoulder bags.

'Here.'

'Yeah, I'll take two,' the Israeli guy said. 'Hey,' he said to the girls, 'Wanna take them together? Hey, Ofer!' He waved to a guy who stopped dancing and came over. 'This kid's got exta.'

Avi watched in some bemusement as the four of them took a pill each and then wandered over to the dance area. He looked at the money in his hands.

He suddenly had six hundred shekels, and all for four tiny pills.

Maybe he could meet a girl here. He was suddenly popular. People kept coming up to him. Before he knew it he had two thousand shekels. He wondered how Lior was doing.

The dancers were everywhere now, dancing between rocks, under trees, with each other, alone. A bonfire burned in the middle of the improvised dance floor and people danced around it, and the beat just beat on.

A girl with dreadlocks came over to Avi. She swayed from side to side.

'Give me two,' she said.

'Three hundred shekels,' Avi said.

The girl rummaged in her purse. She brought out crumpled bills. She leaned in to Avi. He smelled her breath, alcohol and cigarettes. Her hot lips closed on his. She stuck her tongue down his throat, pressed close. Avi felt painfully erect just then. The girl pulled back.

'Better make it two hundred,' she said. 'I'm short.'

Avi gave her the pills and she smiled, ran her fingers down his jaw and turned back, popping both pills at once. Avi stared after her longingly.

He adjusted his trousers. Just then two guys he didn't know found him. They pushed him into the trees. His feet crunched pine cones.

'You the fucker selling pills?' the first guy said. He grabbed Avi by the shirt.

'This is *our* party, you little shit,' the second one said.

'You prick.'

'You fuck.'

'You sell pills only if *we* say you can sell pills,' the first one said.

'It's nothing personal,' the second one said. 'But how do we know you're even selling real MDMA and not some cut up shit?'

'Horse tranquiliser,' the first one said.

'Who the fuck are you?' Avi said, with more courage than he felt.

'I'm Dor,' the first one said, like it was supposed to mean something.

'So what's he?' Avi said.

'I'm Gadi,' the second one said. 'This is our party, man. We figured maybe someone will try to take us over eventually but you're what, fifteen? Sixteen? You're just a putz.'

'A klumnik,' Dor said.

'Dog shit on the grass,' Gadi said.

'A fart,' Dor said, and made a fanning motion. 'Poof, you're gone.'

Avi stared at them and tensed for a fight. He said, 'Maybe.'

'Maybe what, fucko?'

'Maybe I'm nothing,' Avi said. 'But *they're* not.'

Dor turned and Yair hit him in the face.

Avi kicked Gadi in the balls.

Yair saw, grinned, said, 'Nice one.' He hit Dor again.

Shai and Lior materialised behind him. They pushed Dor and Gadi deeper into the trees. Nobody noticed. Or maybe they noticed but nobody cared.

The Goldins propped the two party organisers against a tree. They stood over them in the dark. The bonfire burned in the distance. Avi thought longingly about the girl with the dreadlocks. He was going to think about her for *days*.

'You broke my nose,' Dor said. His face was covered in blood.

'I'll make it short,' Shai said. 'We want to take over your parties.'

'They're just parties, man,' Gadi said. 'They're for a good time. We're not, like… You know.'

'Criminals?' Shai said. He made to slap Gadi and Gadi flinched. Shai laughed and patted him gently.

'You've got it all wrong,' he said. 'We don't want to fuck it up for you guys. We want to *invest*.'

'What do you mean, invest?' Dor said.

'This party's great,' Shai said. 'But it could be so much better. Your sound system is shit. The bar looks like it belongs in a moshavnik's bar mitzvah. And people are desperate for drugs.'

'Well, they're hard to get,' Gadi said. 'I mean, you have to be like, you know.'

'Criminals?'

'I didn't mean—'

'What do you mean the sound system is shit!' Dor said. 'Do you know what it takes to lug all the equipment here? Speakers, amp, DJ set, generator? Do you know what it takes just to scout locations? Find somewhere hidden away, make sure you don't get Bedouins or soldiers in basic training or kids on a school hike go through? This isn't a *hobby*, man! This is a calling!'

'But we can help,' Shai said. 'We can help make it *better*. New sound, a proper bar – good drugs. And security. If you're with us, no one will mess with you.'

'But no one *was* messing with us!'

Gadi nudged Dor.

'We always figured it was a matter of time, though,' he said quietly.

'How much are we talking about, here?' Dor said, capitulating very quickly. 'Like, percentage wise.'

'We'll give you twenty per cent,' Shai said.

'Twenty! It's *our* party!' Dor said.

'Twenty of a lot is better than a hundred per cent of nothing,' Shai said.

'He's right, man,' Gadi said.

'And new music,' Shai said. 'Goa Trance, not this shit your DJ's playing.'

'You know Goa?' Dor said.

'I *lived* Goa,' Shai said.

'Hey, did we meet at all?' Dor said. 'When were you there? Do you know Raj?'

'Raj from the jewellery store?' Shai said.

'No, from the juice stall,' Dor said.

'Juice Stall Raj!' Shai said. 'Shit, man! I got half my hash from him!'

'No way!' Dor said. 'Hey, did you ever meet the German guy who always got stoned by the Coconut?'

'He never left his hammock!' Shai said.

He and Dor burst out laughing, and Dor wiped snot and blood off his face.

'I guess you're alright,' he said. 'I'm Dor. This is Gadi.'

'I'm Shai,' Shai said. 'This is Yair. That's my brother Lior and his friend Avi.'

'Minors, nice,' Gadi said. 'Smart. If they get caught selling it's no big deal. Hey, what's your phone number? Let's set up a meet when we're all back in town, yeah?'

Shai helped Gadi and Dor up. 'No hard feelings, right?' he said. 'Here.'

He opened his hand. It had four pills in it.

'It's still a party, right!' Gadi said. 'Very cool, man. Very cool.'

'L'chaim,' Shai said. The four of them touched pills and laughed, then popped them.

'What about us!' Lior said.

'Shut the fuck up, Lior, and go sell the rest of it.'

The four men wandered off back to the party.

'Fuckers,' Lior said. 'One day I will be boss and then they'll see.'

'I made out with a girl,' Avi blurted.

Lior looked at him pityingly. 'Mazal tov,' he said. 'Come on. Let's sell this shit.'

69

THE DEBT COLLECTOR

'We grow up too fast in this country' – Benny

Avi was pretty tired on the way back to Tel Aviv. He looked for the girl with the dreadlocks but didn't see her again. Lior snored on the seat beside him. It was near dawn.

The cars had pulled out one by one at the end of the party. Shai and Yair talked with their new business partners, going over logistics, the equipment, scouting the next location. Now they were both mellow in the front, on a happy comedown from the pills. They even popped an Arik Einstein cassette into the tape player, and were now badly harmonising 'Drive Slowly'. It was old people's shit.

The had made twenty thousand shekels, easy. That was for just over a hundred pills, give or take the discounts.

Yair and Shai were talking expansion. In a year they'd control distribution at any nature party going, but the next step was going to be the clubs. Not clubs like the Logos or the Roxanne. There were clubs for techno and trance, out in the industrial areas, old soundproofed warehouses, a lot of Russians. Shai figured they could make millions.

Avi was happy with the five hundred they gave him.

That, and the kiss from the girl in dreadlocks. That one had been free.

He stared out of the window as the street lamps flashed past. Soon more houses appeared, then more. The great metropolitan area of Gush Dan, Greater Tel Aviv: the suburbs.

They stopped at last outside the Goldins' house. They went out quietly but not too quietly. They were all happy with how the night went.

'Don't wake Natasha,' Shai said.

'Sir, yes, sir,' Lior said, and Avi smiled.

Shai opened the door. It was dark inside. They tiptoed in so as not to wake Natasha.

Someone switched on the light.

Three men sat in the living room and watched them.

Avi heard movement behind them. More men, holding guns. They removed Yair and Shai's weapons and pushed them on the floor.

They pushed Avi and Lior on the floor too. They knelt.

No one said a fucking word. The man in the armchair got up. He walked up and down, studying them without any particular expression.

He said, 'I never thought you'd be so dumb.'

'Natasha—' Yair said.

'Your little sister? She is fine,' the man said.

'And Ima—'

'Your mother is locked up in the bathroom upstairs. Behave, and they don't have to get hurt.'

No one said anything. The man nodded.

He said, 'Do you know who I am?'

Avi looked at him. He knew his face from the papers.

He said, 'You're Aryeh Rubenstein.'

No one said anything else.

Rubenstein said, 'That's right. Now, what I don't understand is, why did you lot think you could rob my poker game?'

'*Your* poker game?' Avi said.

Yair said, through closed teeth, 'Shut up, Avi!'

'Yes, my poker game,' the man said. 'Whose game did you think it was?'

Shai said, 'We didn't know, I swear. I swear to you, we didn't know!'

'Does it matter?' Rubenstein said. The other two men sat on the sofa. They hadn't said a word yet. They shook their heads.

No, they wordlessly said. That didn't matter. That didn't matter at all.

'We can pay it back,' Shai said.

'Yes, we can pay it all back!' Yair said. 'We didn't even spend it all, we just needed the money to buy—' he subsided abruptly into silence.

'Buy drugs,' Rubenstein said. 'Yes?'

'Yes...' Yair said.

'*My* drugs,' Rubenstein said. He kicked Yair abruptly in the face. The sound of the *crunch* was awful in the small, closed room. Yair whimpered, blood running down his chin.

'How dumb can you *be*?' Rubenstein said, 'to pay me with my own money?'

'We didn't know we were buying from you!' Shai said. 'It was just some guy I know in Bat Yam!'

'*My* guy,' Rubenstein said. '*My* drugs. They're all my drugs.'

Avi stared at the men on the sofa. They looked at him, then turned their gaze on the others. They looked like the Biblical prophets of wrath, about to pass judgement on the people of Israel and finding them wanting.

'We didn't know,' Shai said.

'We can pay you back!' Yair said. 'We have plans, we just made twenty thousand shekels tonight, you can have it!'

'Twenty thousand?' Rubenstein said. 'Doing what?'

'Trance parties,' Shai said desperately.

Rubenstein looked to the men on the sofa. One of them shook his head.

'Chicken shit stuff,' he said.

'It's not chicken shit!' Shai said. 'It's the future. Are you stupid? Exta is a *party* drug. It has to go to the *parties*. We can sell in the clubs, we can sell in the parties, we *are* the scene, man!'

'Twenty thousand? Tonight?'

'That was just the start. We could clear a hundred grand easy, plus make money on the bar. Factor in the clubs and we could make a million a month easy.'

'You'll have added costs, though,' the man on the sofa said. 'Equipment, DJ, bartender salaries, transportation. Bribing the cops. Cutting in the club owners. Hiring more people to distribute. And so on.'

'Who are you?' Shai said.

'I'm Benny,' the man said.

'And who's he?' Shai said, nodding to the other man on the sofa.

'He's none of your fucking business,' Benny said.

'"Let the boys rise and play before us",' the other man said. 'Samuel, 2:14.' He looked disinterested.

'We can make it work,' Shai said. Avi just wished he would shut the fuck up. Avi just wanted to get out of there alive. Avi wished they'd dropped him off at home *before* they went back to their house.

The man on the sofa, Benny, looked at him again, like he could read that in Avi's face. Was it Avi's imagination, or did Benny give him a tiny nod?

'It could work,' Benny said, and Avi almost sagged in relief.

'I still have to punish you,' Rubenstein said. 'You understand.'

'We can pay—'

'You *will* pay. You will work for me. But this is not about money. It's about reputation. Which I am sure you understand. So. You. You're the oldest? Shai?'

'Yes, but—'

Two of Rubenstein's men grabbed Shai from behind and picked him up.

Rubenstein lifted the gun. He fired twice.

Shai screamed.

Avi watched horrified as Shai collapsed to the floor. Rubenstein had shot his knees.

'No!' Yair screamed, and a man hit him from behind with a pistol. He fell face down and didn't get up.

Lior stayed alone of the brothers. He didn't move, just stared at Rubenstein, his face barely twitching. Avi never saw so much hatred in one look. There were muted screams coming from upstairs. Natasha and the mother.

'You, the Sagi kid,' Benny said. 'We'll drop you off home. Get up.'

Avi pushed himself upright, stumbled. His legs fell asleep while he was kneeling.

'Lior,' he said. 'What do you—'

'It's cool, Avi,' Lior said, still not turning his head, not looking at him at all. 'You go now.'

And Avi thought of Lior, saying, *One day I will be boss and then they'll see*. He shuddered.

He just wanted to go home and sleep forever.

'Come on, kid,' Benny said. He had his hand on the back of Avi's neck and pushed him to the door. The men streamed out of the house into the silent street.

Avi thought about Shai, and whether he'll live, and whether he'll ever walk again. He thought about Natasha upstairs. He was so tired, and he felt sad.

He wanted to cry, but boys didn't cry.

Benny bundled him into the back of a black car and got in with him. One of his men drove.

Benny said, 'I knew your father.'

Avi was startled but tried not to show it.

'Why,' he said, 'he arrest you or something?'

Benny smiled. 'Or something,' he said. 'He was a hard man, Chief Inspector Sagi. What's a kid like you doing hanging around with these assholes?'

'They're my friends,' Avi said.

'They are not your friends,' Benny said. 'If you don't realise that you're dumber than I thought. And I don't think you're dumb.'

Avi just shrugged.

'Listen, kid,' Benny said. 'You join the army in what, a couple of years?'

'Yeah,' Avi said.

'You could do great things,' Benny said. 'Don't waste your time with punks. I don't want you involved with them anymore.'

'What are you, my father?' Avi said.

'That I am not,' Benny said. 'But then your father's not around to tell you better, is he?'

The silent road went past. A postman walked eerily alone distributing mail from door to door.

'And do what?' Avi said.

'Be a kid a little while longer,' Benny said. 'We grow up too fast in this country.'

Avi didn't answer. His house was coming up. The car slowed down.

'If you need anything,' Benny said, 'come see me instead. What do you say, Avi?'

'What you did back there...' Avi said, and didn't finish the thought.

'It had to be done,' Benny said. 'You know that.'

'I guess,' Avi said.

'You guess, or you know?'

'I know,' Avi said.

The car stopped. Avi got out. He breathed in fresh morning air. He smelled of campfire smoke and sweat and fear.

He turned to look at Benny, sitting there in the back of the car.

'Thanks,' Avi said. 'I guess.'

Benny smiled.

'I'll see you, Avi Sagi,' he said.

PART FOURTEEN

CAVIAR

1994, Allenby to King Saul

70

ORDINARY PEOPLE

'There are fish you can eat and there are fish who eat you' – Alexei

11pm

'Good night, Ofra.'

His wife pointedly ignored him. Her lips were pressed. Earlier they shouted. Now it was wordless between them. Benny sat alone in the living room. Ofra switched off the light at the wall and went upstairs, leaving him in the dark.

'Fuck you, too,' Benny muttered when she was safely out of earshot.

It was one of those periods when they just couldn't seem to get along, no matter what they did. At least they still shouted at each other. The worst was the weeks of silence, the polite brushing past one another in the kitchen, the fixed smiles for the kids. Not that the kids were stupid. Yoni was out every night and wouldn't say where he was, and Michal was acting out at school. And the little one, Maya, was needy, wanting to sleep in their bed every night.

At least Sigali was doing well, she was in the Negev, studying for a psychology degree. Benny wished he'd seen more of her, but she only came home every other weekend.

Benny sat in the dark. He didn't mind. The television flickered on a black-and-white film, some sort of Western. Benny sat in the armchair and watched men on horses shoot each other. He could go to the club, he thought. But he was a man in his forties with kids and a wife. He wasn't going to be like Yehezkel Aslan, who used to party every night with models and singers, at least until someone filled him up with bullets outside a fish restaurant last year with his girlfriend next to him. Aslan had five kids, for crying out loud. He had no business being out all night.

Aslan and Rubenstein hated each other for years. It was the casino flights that really put the nail to it, though. Flying gamblers to Turkey, which Aslan controlled until Rubenstein decided to take it from him. Plus, Rubenstein just hated that fuck. Which had to count for something. The point being, Benny wasn't like that, he was a family man, he wasn't going to go out now in the middle of the night and pretend he was something he wasn't, when he was just a middle-aged guy with a potbelly and thinning hair, and if he did get laid outside the home he did it discreetly, Ofra was pissed off with him enough as it was.

He waited for Yoni but of course Yoni didn't come home. Benny dozed. On the screen, a man in a white hat rode down the main street of a town that only had one street. He shot from the hip and men in black hats died.

Benny rooted for the good guy to win. He thought he was a good guy, too. He was a white hat guy. He was just providing for his family. He loved the kids. And when he put his ring on Ofra's finger at their wedding and said, 'By this ring you are consecrated to me as my wife according to the laws of Moses and Israel,' Benny fucking *meant* it.

He sighed. He wanted to light a cigarette but Ofra didn't like him smoking in the house. He'd just have to ride it out until it passed and then the clouds would break, suddenly, and they'd be good again for a time. For now he was happy to take the sofa.

5am

He must have slept. When he woke up the television was tuned to the test card that meant broadcasting was over, and faint dawn scratched at the window. Benny's mouth tasted bitter. Something woke him, but what?

Something scratching at the door. Goddamn it, Benny thought. He got up and yanked the door open and Yoni fell in.

He reeked of booze.

'Get up,' Benny said. Yoni just lay there on the carpet, grinning up at him goofily.

'Get up! No, don't you dare, Yoni! Don't you d—'

But it was too late, and his eldest, his pride and joy, threw up all over the carpet and almost on Benny's feet only he jumped out of the way first.

'Goddamn it, Yoni!' he said.

'What is it?' he heard Ofra's voice up the stairs. He turned, saw her coming down, hair mussed from sleep.

'Oh, Yonile! What happened!'

'What do you think happened,' Benny said. 'Just look at him.'

'I remember when you used to come home like this,' Ofra said.

'I was never like this,' Benny said, disgusted.

'Come on, Yonile,' Ofra said. She knelt by her teenage son and tried to pull him up.

'He's just a kid,' she said.

'He's going to the army in a few months,' Benny said.

'Yes,' Ofra said. 'But he's still just a kid. Help me get him up.'

Benny did. He always did what Ofra told him. Together they carried Yoni upstairs to his room. The boy collapsed on the bed. Ofra tucked him in, like he was still a child. Benny stood and glared at his son. The clock on the bedside table said it was five in the morning.

Ofra said, 'I'm going back to bed.'

At the door she turned, her face softer, and he was struck by the lines in her face, and her grey hair, and how much he loved her still.

'Are you coming?' she said.

Benny said, 'In a minute. I'll clean up downstairs first,' and Ofra smiled and left him there. Benny sat on the bed and stroked Yoni's hair. The kid was snoring.

Benny kissed his sleeping son's forehead. Then he went out and closed the door softly and went downstairs and scrubbed his son's puke off the carpet.

Then, at last, he went back to bed, which really *was* much more comfortable than the sofa, and it was still warm.

6:30am

An hour and a half later he was woken from deep sleep when Maya climbed into the bed between them. Benny grunted, turned on his side and buried his head under a pillow as Maya sat up, already perfectly perky and awake, and started singing an Aviv Geffen song.

'I hate Aviv Geffen!' Benny mumbled into the sheets. He didn't say it loud: Maya would be furious with him if he did.

'Aviv says…' Maya said, then launched into the latest digest of what Aviv was saying, or thinking, or singing. Aviv Geffen dressed outlandishly; he wore makeup; he sang about children flying in the air and reaching for the moonlight; and Maya loved him devoutly.

Finally Maya got tired of talking about Aviv, or at least of not getting an adult response.

'Aba, get up!' she said. 'Get up! Get up!'

Benny pretended to still be asleep, though of course it was impossible. Then he roared like a lion and sprang up, and Maya laughed as he started to tickle her.

'Aba stop! Aba!' Maya wriggled, giggling. 'I'm hungry, Aba! Breakfast!'

'Yes, your ladyship,' Benny said. Ofra was already up. He could hear her in the kitchen, moving pots and pans. Benny got up, knocked on Michal's door.

'Time to get up!'

'Go away, Aba!'

'School!'

'I'm not going to school! I'm never going to school!'

'Get up, Michali!'

'Five minutes!' Michal shouted from inside. 'And don't you dare come in!'

'Five minutes!' Benny shouted back. He knew in five minutes he'd have to go wake her up again. But he could smell the coffee now so he followed the smell to the kitchen and Ofra offered him a cup.

'Thanks, love,' he said.

She touched his arm lightly and, just like that, their fight was over and they were good again.

Benny drank his coffee. Ofra turned on the radio. The news were all about peace talks between Prime Minister Rabin and King Abdullah of Jordan. Benny thought about the possibilities in an open border but he didn't think it mattered. The Arab families he and Rubenstein dealt with had their own channels into the Jordanian drug market. After the news, Galgalatz played Aviv Geffen and Benny groaned.

That nasal voice singing, 'Should I Be In Love With You?' and Maya made a sad face and pretended to hold a microphone as she sang along with relish.

'Michali, school!' Benny shouted up the stairs.

'Five minutes!'

'Now, Michali!'

'Aba, nu!'

He heard something fall on the floor upstairs and smiled. At least she was up.

'You'll drop them at school?' he said to Ofra.

'Sure. You'll talk to Yoni? Tonight?' she said.

'I don't know what to say to him.'

'You're his father. You should say something.'

Benny rubbed his temples. He wanted a cigarette.

'I'll try,' he said.

'Are you home tonight?'

'I don't know, love.'

He kissed her lightly on the lips, kissed Maya, shouted, 'School, Michali!' – 'I *know*!' – and left the house.

He lit a cigarette when he was in the car, rolled down the window, put on the radio but was chased on the airwaves by Aviv Geffen again. What did the kids *see* in that guy? A north Tel Aviv, dad's famous, piano lessons, all-the-opportunities, vanilla kid? Never did the army and even Benny did the army, even if he didn't serve combat.

He just didn't *get* these Moonlight Kids, as they called themselves. And the fact Maya had posters of Aviv on her walls and kept asking Ofra to take her to one of his shows, it irked Benny. What was that Aviv Geffen song where in the middle of it he just screamed 'Our generation is fucked!'? He found himself humming it now. That was the worst part. After a while, whether he wanted it to or not, the songs just filtered into his mind and took over. Like every generation wasn't fucked in its own unique way.

9:30am

The café-bakery on Allenby had been there for as long as Benny could recall. They made cremeschnitte and schillerlocken just like back in Austria. Not that Benny had anything to do with Austria, his family hadn't come within three thousand kilometres of the Austro-Hungarian Empire as far as he was aware. But he liked the pastries.

Besides, no one there was a cop or a criminal. It was just old guys doing their crossword puzzles and old ladies taking the dog for a walk, and the proprietress, Giveret Bergmann, always gave Benny a vanilla crescent with his cappuccino. Benny took his regular table at the back, facing the door. He lit a cigarette and Mrs Bergmann brought his coffee.

When he finally popped the crescent in his mouth it was as sweet and flaky as always, so soft that he thought he could just inhale it. Ofra told him off for eating sweets. Hitting his forties had really started to spread his weight around, and most of it on to his belly. That and his smoking, Ofra had quit a couple of years ago, now she used a thigh master and did step aerobics and spinning, whatever that was. But Benny figured all in all he was happy as he was.

He was going to read the paper and maybe have a cremeschnitte when the door opened and a heavyset man came in. He came in from the sun outside so Benny couldn't make his face out clearly but there was something familiar about him and something dangerous, and Benny reached covertly for his gun under the table. Then the man took another step inside, and then another, and spotted Benny, and he smiled.

Benny recognised him then, though he couldn't believe it. He got up, pushing the table with his knees, and took a step and stopped.

'*Alexei*?' he said.

The man smiled again and extended his hand for a shake.

'You remember,' he said in English.

'How could I forget?' Benny took his hand, then on an impulse hugged him. Alexei Ivanovich, that was the crazy Russian's name.

'It is good to see you too, Benny,' Alexei said. 'I am glad you got out of Lebanon.'

'Thanks to you,' Benny said. He looked at him closely. 'KGB?'

Alexei laughed. 'Didn't you hear?' he said. 'There is no more Soviet Union.'

'I mean, before. When they came to rescue you… I wondered.'

Alexei shrugged. 'Does it matter? This is a new age, my friend. An age of peace and prosperity for all. Didn't you know?'

'So I keep hearing,' Benny said. 'Come, sit. You want a coffee?'

'Da,' Alexei said. He motioned to Mrs Bergmann and began to talk rapidly in German. Mrs Bergmann was charmed. She offered up a volley of rapid German in return. Alexei countered and Mrs Bergmann laughed delightedly and hit him on the shoulder.

When she came back she had two more coffees and an assortment of pastries which she placed on the table. She pointed at Benny and said something in German and then both she and Alexei laughed.

'She says you like her baking,' Alexei translated.

'I do like her baking,' Benny said, maybe a little more resentful now, and Mrs Bergmann withdrew. It was hard to be resentful with a mouthful of strudel, though.

'How did you know where to find me?' Benny said. 'What are you doing here? What happened after I last saw you? I thought about you sometimes, Alexei. I even tried to find out what happened to you, but it's not like anyone could tell me where to find the KGB's last man in Beirut.'

'Oh, I was never in Beirut that much,' Alexei said. 'And there is no KGB anymore, not by that name, anyway. I'm just a Foreign Service man with a pension, Benny. But a Russian pension isn't worth much these days. So I got a new job now. It pays a lot better. Enough for pastries.' He smiled and bit into a schillerlocken.

'This is very good,' he said, his lips covered in cream.

Benny narrowed his eyes and sipped his coffee and lit his third cigarette of the day. He played with the lighter on the table.

'I am going to guess running into you now isn't exactly a coincidence,' he said. 'And that this isn't a social call.'

'It seems pretty sociable to me,' Alexei said. 'But I appreciate your directness. Israelis have much to recommend them in that area. Other people might see it as rudeness, but I like it.'

'No bullshit,' Benny said.

'No bullshit,' Alexei said. 'Yes.' He wiped his lips with a napkin from the dispenser. 'My new employer is Yevgeni Nahumovich.'

Benny sat back.

'The billionaire,' he said.

'The billionaire,' Alexei said. 'Da.' He smiled.

'You smile a lot more these days,' Benny said.

'Life is good,' Alexei said. 'For you too, I hear. Business is good?'

'Business is good,' Benny said.

'So smile. Have a cake.'

'I think I'm done with cakes for now,' Benny said. 'So what does Yevgneni Nahumovich want with me?'

'With you?' Alexei said. 'Nothing. He doesn't even know who you are.'

Benny waited.

Alexei pushed the plate away and had a sip of coffee. 'Mr Nahumovich owns several new office buildings near the Diamond Bourse,' he said. 'Very nice places. Mr Nahumovich likes to invest in real estate. He had just bought himself a villa in Netanya, for the family. He wants the children to learn Hebrew, become Israeli. Mr Nahumovich is a very good Jew.'

'Only his grandfather on his father's side was Jewish, wasn't he?' Benny said. He read the papers like everyone else.

'That may be so,' Alexei said. 'But that still entitles him to an Israeli passport. And Mr Nahumovich is keen to integrate. Now, those office blocks. It appears there is an outfit running protection in the financial district, and that said outfit has been making demands of Mr Nahumovich's management company. I believe windows were broken, and a car was set on fire when they would not pay. That sort of thing.'

'Aha,' Benny said.

Alexei shrugged. 'The problem went up the ladder. Mr Nahumovich asked me to look into the matter. So I did.'

'Aha.'

'Imagine my surprise when I came across an old friend, Benny.'

'I am trying to.'

Alexei grinned. 'It *is* good to see you,' he said.

'Does Mr Nahumovich not wish to pay?' Benny said.

'Mr Nahumovich has more important things to do,' Alexei said. 'Which is why *I'm* here, asking you to drop it.'

Benny sighed. He stabbed out his cigarette. 'You know, my kids,' he said, 'My boy is going to the army soon. Now he goes out and gets drunk with his friends every night. You have kids, Alexei?'

'One, back in Russia,' Alexei said. 'A girl. She is studying engineering in Moscow now.'

'My girl, she just turned teenager,' Benny said. 'Sleeps all day. Wears black. Has a nose ring. A nose ring, Alexei!'

'Kids are not easy,' Alexei said.

'No one gets so rich so quickly being clean,' Benny said. 'Not me, not you, least of all Yevgeni Nahumovich. So what's the deal?'

'It's a fair question,' Alexei said. 'Like his fellow oligarch émigrés, Mr Nahumovich sees Israel as a place of shelter. It is liberal, international, with lenient tax laws and excellent banks, and with a particularly lax attitude to cross-border money transfers, which is convenient for the international businessman. In short, whatever Mr Nahumovich may or may not do elsewhere, he intends to make Israel his *home*. And one's home is a place to be kept kosher.'

'So no protection money.'

'Come on, Benny. There are fish you can eat and there are fish who eat you. Consider it a favour.'

'Sure,' Benny said.

Not like he was going to go to war with a guy who could buy presidents. Benny was realistic about his place in the world.

'Bol'shoy spasibo, my friend,' Alexei said.

'Don't mention it. Though I will have to explain to my boss why he's going to be short the money.'

'Ah,' Alexei said. 'You just did me a favour. Maybe I could do you one in return.'

'I'm all ears, Alexei,' Benny said.

'You know, Benny, in Russia we always had the Vory,' Alexei said. 'Though they call themselves the Mafiya now, I think because of too many American movies. They were the subversive elements in society. Ones who did not adhere to the rule of law. Even in in the Soviet Union, where to be caught was to be executed or sent to Siberia. Still, they existed. Because they provided services even people in the Central Committee sometimes needed.'

'Thank you for explaining crime to me, Alexei,' Benny said, and Alexei laughed.

'What do you need?' Benny said. 'Dope? Girls?'

'Mr Nahumovich is having a party,' Alexei said. 'For important people. He has just donated a lot of money to a hospital. Or maybe he bought the hospital. It doesn't matter. After the party, maybe some of the guests would like a smaller, more intimate gathering.'

'I understand,' Benny did.

'You deal with a lot of politicians, Benny?'

Benny shrugged. 'Sometimes,' he said. 'Not directly.'

'Of course.'

'It's as you said,' Benny said. 'There are things people need.'

Just then his telephone rang. Benny struggled with the Pelephone on his belt, and when he answered the line was crackly until he remembered to extend the antenna all the way. Then he heard Ofra, sounding upset, and Benny's first thought was that maybe something bad happened, that someone took a run at his family, even though everything was copacetic now, ever since Rubenstein took out Aslan and Rabin shook Arafat's hand on the White House lawn, but then he heard Ofra mention Michal, and school, and Benny said, 'Slow down, Ofra, what happened?'

12:30pm

'Michal hit another child,' the principal, Mrs Lipshitz, said, her lips tight with disapproval. Benny and Ofra sat in her office. Benny chewed on a mint, then, with a sharp elbow from his wife, swallowed it.

'What happened, exactly?' Benny said.

Mrs Lipshitz turned her cold blue eyes on him. 'She hit another child,' she said, enunciating clearly, as though Benny were slow. 'To be precise, Mr Pardes, she pulled the other girl's hair in clumps and scratched her face until she drew blood. You will be lucky if the other parents don't press charges.'

'No one is pressing charges,' Benny said. 'I want an explanation. I send my daughter to your school expecting she will be looked after.'

'You send your child to this school because that is the law, Mr Pardes,' the principal said. 'This is still a nation of law.'

'What… what will happen to her now?' Ofra said.

'Suspension,' Mrs Lipshitz said. 'And we will consider what happens next. I had hoped to avoid expulsion—'

'Expulsion!' Benny said.

'Yes, Mr Pardes. You did not come to the last parents evening, I believe?'

'I had a business trip,' Benny said.

'Yes,' Mrs Lipshitz said, with more disapproval. 'Business. Well, as I explained to your wife at the time, Michal's grades have been suffering lately, as has her behaviour. She is rude and surly, does not listen to her teachers, and does not interact well with the other children. There have been smaller incidents, but today is the straw that broke the camel's back, as we say.'

Mrs Lipshitz did not look like she liked camels. Or straw. The walls of her office were decorated with her diplomas. A certificate from the Oranim Teachers College, an M.Ed from Levinsky, a special commendation from the Ministry of Education, another from Wizo.

A picture of Yitzhak Rabin looked down from the walls. He looked a lot more fun than Mrs Lipshitz.

'She's been a little difficult at home,' Benny said, 'but it's just normal teenager stuff. How long, suspension?'

'Like I said, Mr Pardes. Until we can decide if she is ready to come back to school. Or… not.'

'I am not taking her out of school!' Benny shouted.

'Don't raise your voice at me, Mr Pardes,' Mrs Lipshitz said. '"If you sow in tears you shall reap in joy". Psalms 126:5.'

'What?' Benny said. The quote reminded him unpleasantly of Cohen, who had a habit of wielding Bible quotes like other men used guns.

He took a deep breath. 'I want to hear from Michal herself what happened,' he said.

'Indeed,' Mrs Lipshitz said. She pressed a button on the phone on her desk. 'Orna, will you ask Michal to come in, please? Thank you.'

She looked up at Benny and Ofra.

'She will come in now,' she said.

Benny said, 'Thank you.'

The door opened. Michal came in. She stood defiant and angry, that's what Benny thought at first. Then he saw the way his daughter held herself, the pride and the worry. He wanted to get up and hug her. He wanted to tell her everything will be alright.

Mrs Lipshitz said, 'Well, Michal? Explain your actions.'

'I have nothing to explain.'

'You hit the other girl,' Mrs Lipshitz said.

'She was—!' Michal said, and then stopped.

'Yes, Michal?' Mrs Lipshitz said.

'She was saying stuff,' Michal said. 'I got angry.'

'You scratched her face!' Mrs Lipshitz said. 'She is going to need stitches!'

'Good!' Michal said.

'Michal!' Ofra said, shocked.

'What did she say to you, Michali?' Benny said. His daughter stood mute, her arms crossed.

'What did she say, Michali?' Benny demanded, and this time there was a dangerous edge to his voice, and even Mrs Lipshitz, with all her diplomas, took notice and seemed for just a moment to grow a little bit smaller in her chair.

'Nothing,' Michal muttered.

'Tell me,' Benny said.

'She called you a criminal!' Michal shouted. 'She said we were criminals. That you were a gangster, a drug dealer and a… a murderer. I told her to keep her fucking mouth shut but she wouldn't so I… I told her what I thought.'

'With your fists!' Mrs Lipshitz said in disgust.

'She listened, didn't she?' Michal smirked. She turned to her parents.

'We're not criminals,' she said, 'we're good people. Ordinary people. I stood up for us, Dad. That's all.'

'We do not tolerate violence in this school,' Mrs Lipshitz said. Her eyes were on Benny, not Michal, and he realised his fists were closed and he was breathing heavily.

He opened his fingers. He settled his breath. He said, 'I understand, Mrs Lipshitz.'

Mrs Lipshitz lifted a pen. 'We will discuss this at the next board meeting,' she said. 'And will let you know our decision.'

'Yes,' Benny said. He stood up.

'Come on, Ofra,' he said. 'Come on, Michali. Let's go home.'

1pm

He didn't say much on the drive home. None of them did.

'What's going to happen to me, Dad?' Michal said. He could see she was holding back tears. 'Am I going to have to leave school?'

'I don't know, motek,' Benny said.

He dropped them off at home.

'You'll fix this, Benyamin,' Ofra said quietly, leaning into the open window once Michal went inside.

'What do you want me to do, Ofra!' Benny said. 'They're kids. Michali will just have to go back and apologise and hope they let her go back to school.'

'You think you're so strong,' Ofra said. 'But you're nothing.'

She left Benny there. He stared at the wheel. When he hit it in frustration the horn sounded and a pigeon, startled, took to the air.

He hit the gas. There were people you could fuck over and there were people who fucked you. What was he going to do, send Amos to beat up a teenage girl?

He drove to the Central Bus Station. The new building only opened last year. Benny ran some protection there, or tried to, but the building was huge and most of the shops remained empty. The ones that opened were kind of shit. Benny parked on Fein. The area was rapidly going downhill. He saw someone shooting up in the alley near Bentovich Books. Benny kicked him until the junkie, mumbling to himself, shuffled away.

Benny went into No. 1. As far as brothels went this wasn't the worst, and it was busy even at this time of day. He saw Marina, the madame, who came over and gave him a brief hug and a peck on the cheek.

'Want a cup of tea?' she said.

She didn't do coffee. Only tea, with lemon and imported sugar cubes, like they still did back in St Petersburg or wherever. Benny had a general rule of not accepting food or drinks in a whorehouse, so he politely declined.

'So what brings you here, Benny?' Marina said. Benny could hear moaning through the thin walls. The whole place was divided into cubicles over three floors. The smell of cum and disinfectant made him want to gag. 'Money's not due until Friday.'

'I need some girls for a party,' Benny said. 'Do you have any new ones?'

'I have this Arab girl fresh from the village,' Marina said. 'Poor thing, you know the type. A bit rebellious, left home, taxi driver I know brought her to me. Told her I helped girls like her. Wasn't wrong, either. At least now she has a trade.'

'No Arabs,' Benny said.

Marina considered.

'Big party?' she said.

'Maybe. I don't know.'

'I have a couple of Ukrainian girls just off the cargo containers in Cairo,' Marina said.

'Clean?'

'So far.'

'Keep them on hand for me?' Benny said.

'For when?'

'Tonight.'

'They have to work, Benny.'

'If I don't call you, I'll make sure you still get paid.'

Marina shrugged. 'Tov, nu,' she said.

Her accent was so thick you could dunk it in borscht.

Benny said goodbye and walked out as a guy in a towel stumbled out of one of the rooms, hairy chest and pot-belly protruding.

Benny nodded politely.

'Minister,' he said.

The air outside was fresh in comparison to the inside, only bus fumes and grill smoke and cigarettes and piss, the usual Tel Aviv air.

2pm

The offices of VIP Escorts were on the second floor of an office building just off Dizengoff.

Sarah, the receptionist, smiled when she saw Benny.

'Coffee?' she said.

'Please.'

'Shai's just coming back from lunch.'

'I don't pay him to have lunch,' Benny muttered. But Shai did a good enough job. He kept the girls happy and the clients happy and he was discreet. So Benny had his coffee. Sarah read *La'isha*, with beauty queen Jana Khodirker on the cover. Another Russian import, one Benny didn't mind. The Russians were like any other wave of immigration, they had their own ways but sooner or later they would melt into the melting pot and become just another facet of Israeli; whatever that meant these days.

Shai came in and Benny said, 'Charlie!'

Shai made a pained face and said, 'You know I'm not called that anymore.'

'Changing your name doesn't make you any more Ashkenazi,' Benny said, and Shai said, 'Mizrahi, Ashkenazi, black, white, it doesn't mean shit anymore, Benny. When are you going to get your head around it? It's a new age, man. It's going to be the twenty-first century soon. You ever hear of the Internet, Benny? It's going to make everyone the same, anywhere in the world. No more Arabs and Jews, no more wars. Soon Rabin will make peace and then you'll see, in a few years you could drive from here straight through Jordan and Iran and all the way to China if you wanted to. Imagine that, Benny!'

'Are you high?' Benny said, and Shai grinned and said, 'Only on life, my friend.'

'I need girls for tonight,' Benny said. 'Big party.'

'Of course, of course. We're here to serve. What time tonight? Let me check the books. Sarah! Who do we have on the roster tonight?'

'Avigail, Lily, Galit, Rotem, Polina, Irina, Natasha M., Natasha P., Maria, Lucia, Elena and Venus.'

'Book them all,' Benny said, 'and draft in a couple more if you can.'

'Sure, I'll just make a call,' Shai said. 'What's the occasion?'

'I don't know,' Benny said. 'Some Russian billionaire.'

3pm

He stopped at a falafel stand on the way home, ate standing up, getting humous on his shirt.

4:15pm

All the kids were home when he got in. Yoni sat on the sofa with Maya, watching some kids' programming on TV.

'Hey, Dad,' he said. He had the decency to look sheepish. 'Sorry about last night.'

Maya jumped up and ran to Benny. She gave him a hug.

'Daddy!'

'Motek,' Benny said. Michal came in from the kitchen then, carrying a sandwich.

'Hey, Dad,' she said.

She sat in the armchair near the sofa and started to eat.

Ofra came down the stairs. 'I spoke to Mrs Lipshitz,' she said.

'Oh?' Benny said cautiously.

'Michal will apologise. Properly. And we will make a donation to the school. Mrs Lipshitz says the teachers' lounge needs a new refrigerator, and a coffee machine. Like a fancy one, an espresso maker.'

'An espresso maker!' Benny said. 'What's wrong with instant?'

Ofra ignored him.

'They'll let Michali come back next week. So all she gets is a few days' suspension.'

'I'll take care of it,' Benny said.

Ofra's eyes softened.

'Are you staying home?' she said.

'I can't stop, love,' Benny said. 'I just came by to pick up some stuff. Do I have a suit?'

'A suit?' Ofra said.

'Yeah.'

'Like a wedding suit?'

'Do I wear suits for weddings?' Benny said.

'Not usually, no.'

'But I have one, right?'

Ofra sighed.

'Are you going to a wedding, then?' she said.

'No,' Benny said. 'A fundraiser.'

'What do you have to do with a fundraiser?' Ofra said.

'Nothing.' For a moment Benny felt resentment he tried to tamper down. 'I'm just the hired help.'

'Well, we'd better find you a suit, anyway,' Ofra said.

He followed her upstairs, where she looked through the wardrobe and laid clothes on the bed. Benny stripped, conscious of his belly and his pale flabby flesh. He put on trousers and Ofra said, 'You have to pull them high, over your waist.'

Benny did, feeling ridiculous. He put on a shirt and felt a little better.

'You need a belt,' Ofra said. 'And tuck in your shirt, it tucks in, with a suit.'

'What am I, an ambassador?' Benny said. But he did as she said, and when he put on the jacket he had to admit he actually didn't look bad.

'Very handsome,' Ofra said. 'Now you need shoes.'

She made him put on black shiny shoes, and finally a tie. Benny couldn't remember the last time he wore a tie. He admired himself in the mirror. He looked like a respectable businessman, maybe not very successful but an honest one.

Ofra adjusted his tie.

'Don't come back too late,' she said.

Benny said, 'I'll try.'

7:30pm

Aviv Geffen sang about the children of the moonlight on the radio as Benny drove to the Tel Aviv Museum of Art. He felt self-conscious going there. Black government cars – Volvo, everyone in the government drove in a Volvo – came to stop by the entrance, drivers letting off their various charges. Benny parked on the street. He went to the service entrance, mentioned Alexei's name and was let in.

'You came,' Alexei said.

Benny had tracked him down to a painting by Nachum Gutman.

'You invited me.'

'I wasn't sure you'd want to be seen.'

'I don't want to be seen with *them*,' Benny said, and Alexei laughed.

'The politicians are the real crooks, and so on?' he said.

'Something like that,' Benny said. 'I had a long day.'

He didn't have anything to be ashamed of. He wasn't in prison, he wasn't accused of anything. He was just a man who provided for his family. He stood with Alexei and they watched all the important people come in.

Shlomo Artzi and his band set up in the corner. Waiters circled with glasses of champagne and trays of caviar on blini. Benny remembered in the old days when all they had to eat at home were tinned sardines, how you'd sometimes open the fish and find the eggs inside. He'd hated the sight and smell and everything about it. But his father always made them eat the eggs.

It was hard to believe this was Israel now, with all the men in suits and ties and the smell of new money everywhere. Drinking champagne and eating caviar.

'Where is your boss?' Benny said.

Alexei pointed.

Someone not very impressive in the distance, greeting guests. Benny felt a little disappointed and didn't even know why. Nahumovich was too remote for him. Like a mountain or a cliff-face, what happens when so much dirty money accumulates until it has nowhere else to go and it becomes clean and buys a hospital, a football club, and the politicians.

It was nothing to Benny. Benny still lived in the streets, with the dirt and the noise. Benny still used the service entrance.

'Where is your boss?' Alexei said.

'America.'

'Ah, yes,' Alexei said. 'America. I would like to visit one day. It seems strange. We were at war for so long. Then came Gorbachev and glasnost and somehow communism didn't seem that important anymore. I hope we don't come to regret it.'

'What's the use of regrets?' Benny said. 'You can't change the things that happened.'

They stood and looked at the guests. Olmert, the current Mayor of Jerusalem. Olmert liked money the way flies liked shit. Moshe Katsav, a smug man in a suit who, whispered stories said, liked to force himself on the women who worked under him. Genghis, the former general and current member of the Knesset: both crooked *and* a rapist, like winning the full prize at the Purim parade. On and on they came: Benizri, Deri, Ramon, Mordechai, Flatto-Sharon, Gonen Segev.

There was a young Russian, Avigdor Lieberman, now a political operator. Alexei was watching him with a strange smile, like he knew him quite well. Benny filed that information away.

And there was Lieberman's boss, Benyamin Netanyahu, whose brother was a war hero. Died in the raid on Entebbe. Netanyahu had just come back from a gig as the Israeli ambassador to the UN. But he had his eye on a bigger political career. He was going to need a lot of money for that.

More and more they came. The thieves and the rapists, and didn't Bialik write, or was it Ben Gurion, 'We shall only have a true state when we have our own Hebrew thief, our own Hebrew whore, our own Hebrew murderer?' And so it came to be, Benny thought. So it came to be. But maybe it will all be different now.

Just then Shlomo Artzi started singing 'Moon', and the assembled dignitaries turned, drinks in hand, to watch. Benny thought he'd had enough. He came, he saw, he was left disappointed.

It was just a bunch of men in suits but then, the world was run by men in suits these days.

10:30pm

He stopped by the villa to make sure the girls had arrived ahead of time and with them the discreet supply of pharmaceuticals. They were good girls. They were good drugs. Benny didn't stick around for the important politicians to arrive.

As he left the museum Alexei slipped him a thick envelope with cash.

It made Benny feel like a pimp.

'Remember, my friend,' Alexei said. 'There are men who serve you, and there are men you serve.'

12:00am

When he came home Yoni was asleep on the sofa, the TV light flickering on his face, black and white, black and white. Benny covered him in a blanket, kissed his forehead, switched off the TV where cowboys chased Indians across a desolate land.

He removed his shoes and went upstairs in socks. Michal's door was closed and all was quiet. When Benny got to bed he found that Maya had climbed in with them again and now lay stretched across the sheets, snoring peacefully, and Ofra was on the far edge. Benny removed the uncomfortable suit in the dark. It didn't fit him, he decided, to wear a jacket and a tie. He was just a working man.

He pushed Maya gently until he could get into bed. His daughter turned, wrapped her small arms around his neck and nestled into his chest, and he could feel her breathing.

Benny closed his eyes and drifted into sleep, for once content.

PART FIFTEEN

ARAD '95

1995, The Negev Desert

71

ROCK THE NINETIES

'And I don't belong to the children crying in the Square' – *Lior Tirosh, Remnants of God*

17 July, 1995: Day

Avi hefted his backpack at the entrance to the Central Bus Station. He had a change of clothes, a toothbrush and toothpaste, a deodorant and a light sleeping bag. He had a couple hundred shekels in his Velcro wallet and a bus ticket for the Egged bus to Arad.

Inside the cavernous depths of the station he was momentarily lost. A man sold pirate tapes from a blanket on the floor in between two stores, and a portable tape player blasted out Zohar Argov. A row of mannequins wearing last year's clothes stared at Avi with blank faces.

A girl in jean shorts and Biblical sandals went up the escalators with a backpack, and Avi stared after her, noticing the others heading the same way. He followed, up to the upper level, away from the stores to where passengers waited for the buses. Kids his own age milled about or sat on the floor, and more than one played an acoustic guitar to pass the time. Avi had to study the piano but he was never much good at it, and he always wished he'd learned to play the guitar instead so he could impress girls. He would have liked to be in a rock band. Not like the Elders of Safed but maybe like Mashina. He could be the vocalist, like Yuval Banai in Mashina. The band was breaking up. They were going to perform their last ever concert in Arad. Avi was going to go if he could. If he could get a ticket. He had the programme for the festival in his pocket. The Tractor's Revenge and the Friends of Natasha. Aviv Geffen and Ofra Haza. Something for everyone. For just one week this small town in the desert was going to become the beating heart of music for the entire country.

A small country surrounded by enemies, the Cameri Quintet joked on TV, but after Oslo and that handshake in the White House with Arafat, Rabin went and signed a peace accord with Jordan, and suddenly the list of enemies was shrinking. Unless you listened to the right-wing demonstrations and the settlers and Netanyahu and those people who burned effigies of Rabin and called him a traitor, at least. Not that Avi paid much attention to any of that. All Avi really knew was that he was going to the desert, he was going to see Mashina's last concert if it was the last thing he did, and he was desperate to kiss a girl. He tried not to think about the last time that happened.

The girl in the jean shorts and the Biblical sandals stood with two girlfriends near the falafel stand. She looked his way and said something to her friends and laughed, and Avi blushed and looked down at the festival programme, where he had circled half a dozen shows he was hoping to catch.

For one glorious week he could be anything he wanted, because no one knew who he was. His mother let him go but then, everyone's mothers let them go. Avi was on his own, he didn't hang much with the Goldins anymore, not since that thing with the exta, and he just focused on his studies and exercise, because he would need both to get into a good combat unit, he wanted to go to Matkal or Flotilla 13, something elite anyway, not like Golani or something. But right then none of that mattered, the only thing that did was the trip to Arad, and right now, for some reason, the look from the girl in the jean shorts and the Biblical sandals that made her out as a kibbutznik because who the hell else wore Biblical sandals?

He looked up and saw that, improbably, the girl was coming towards him and her two friends were watching with barely concealed amusement. The girl came close and she said, 'Excuse me, do you know when the next bus to Arad goes?'

'Yes,' Avi said, 'I mean, no, I mean...' He gestured to the gate, where a bus was just pulling in beyond the glass doors. 'I think this is it,' he said.

'I'm Inbal,' the girl said, and this time *she* was blushing, and Avi could see her two friends looking over at them and laughing, and he said, 'I'm Avi,' and then, for something to say, dumbly, 'Are you going to Arad?'

'Well, *yes*,' Inbal said, and then they both laughed because it *was* so dumb.

'Are you going to see Mashina?' Avi said.

'I really want to, but I don't have a ticket. You?'

'I don't have one.'

'They're so great?' Inbal said. She reminded him a little of Inbal Perlmuter from The Witches. The Witches played Arad the year before but they weren't there this year. 'Do you really think it's their last ever show?'

'Inbal, come *on*!' He heard her friends call. The bus driver climbed down from the bus and a conductor had wandered over with a ticket puncher in his hand.

'I have to go,' Inbal said.

'Oh,' Avi said. 'Well, it was nice to, like...'

'Are you coming?' she said.

'To? Oh, right,' Avi said, because of course they were both going the same way, and he blushed again.

'Then come on!' Inbal said. And she took his hand so naturally that it didn't even feel weird, just like it was always supposed to be like this, and he ran alongside her for the bus as the gates opened, both their backpacks bumping up and down, up and down as they ran.

There was a scramble for the bus and the driver stood smoking a cigarette and the conductor was saying, 'Tickets only! Tickets only!' Avi stashed his backpack in the cargo hold alongside Inbal's, and when they finally made it onto the bus it was already packed, and the other two kibbutznik girls got a seat together near the front so he and Inbal ended up sharing the one remaining seat right at the back, over the wheels and near the engine. The driver finished his cigarette and climbed into his seat and shut the door, and merciful aircon began to blow cool air as the bus pulled out of the station slowly.

'Your friends seem nice,' Avi said, for something to say.

'They dared me to talk to you,' Inbal said. He was conscious of her closeness, her side pressing into his. He thought it was a long drive to Arad.

'Why did you?' he said.

She shrugged. 'I don't know. You looked so lost.'

'I wasn't, I mean…'

She laughed.

'And cute,' she said.

'Lost and cute,' Avi said. 'That's what I was going for.'

'Right!' Inbal said. 'Now it all makes sense.'

The bus meanwhile lumbered through the city. It was amazing how quickly Tel Aviv disappeared. Soon just the road and hills with pine trees, and dusty cars that passed the bus on the way to elsewhere. Here and there a gas station, a clump of houses, a field of dried wheat. Avi learned that Inbal came from a kibbutz up north. A Young Watchers kibbutz, which must have meant something really important to her, but Avi didn't really understand the difference with what some other kibbutzim were. Her class was called Neurim, Youth, apparently on the kibbutz all the classes had names, not numbers. She didn't live with her parents but in the regional communal school, which she called the Mossad, the Institute. Avi thought of his kibbutz cousins, realised he hadn't seen them in years and could no longer recall what they looked like.

'And you never lived with your parents?' he said. She shook her head.

'We see them between four and eight in their room,' she said. A room was what kibbutzniks called their house. 'Then we always go back to the dormitories.'

He didn't understand half the things she said. She found him equally exotic.

'And your dad was a police officer?' she said, wide-eyed.

'Yeah,' Avi said. He didn't want to talk about the stroke and then the final moments. He wanted to remember his dad the way he was, strong, confident, loving. His dad always made him laugh when Avi was a child. Everyone else saw the tough police officer. Avi just saw his dad.

'I'm going to join the police after the army,' he told Inbal.

'Where are you going in the army?' she said.

'I don't know yet. But combat.'

'Maybe soon there won't be any wars,' she said.

'Maybe,' Avi said.

'I'm going to be in an army band,' Inbal said. 'Then I'm going to move to Tel Aviv. I'm going to work in a café but only for a few months and then I'll be discovered. I'm going to sign a record deal and I'll do two albums here and then a third in London, in Abbey Road. Then I'm going to tour Europe and America, until I get a gold record. Then I—'

'You have it all figured out,' Avi said, laughing.

'You have to,' Inbal said, and she looked very serious. 'You have to think about the future.'

Then she couldn't hold it any longer and burst out laughing. 'Your *face*!' she said.

'You sounded just like a teacher!' Avi said.

'My mum's a teacher,' Inbal said. 'She teaches arts and crafts on the kibbutz.'

'I bet she's pretty,' Avi said on impulse, then wished the ground would swallow him up.

'Why?' Inbal said.

'Because you are.'

She was still beside him. He felt her closeness, her warmth. He was so acutely aware of her breathing. The backs of their hands touched. He felt her hand move. She held his hand. They didn't say anything. The bus lumbered on in silence.

When the desert began it did so abruptly. One moment there were hills and trees and shade and birds. Then there was sand, and the sun beat down like a man with a belt punishing the landscape.

'Look!' Inbal said, pointing. 'Camels!'

Two camels sat sleeping by the side of the road, Bedouin

tents visible in the distance behind them. The bus didn't stop, the driver indifferent to camels, and the road, which had sloped down sharply from the mountains, now straightened as the Negev stretched away from them on all sides.

They were now the only moving dot in the landscape. It felt as though they weren't moving at all. The engine thrummed and shook the seat, the aircon blasted tepid air, across the aisles kids like them talked and laughed and sang and fell in love.

Then a small patch of colour appeared in that desolate land, and as the bus made its slow way across Avi saw other cars, and red and blue and green balloons, and roadside signs advertising upcoming shows by David Broza and Yehudit Ravitz and of course Mashina, and he saw patches of grass watered with criss-crossing lines of drip irrigation.

The Arad Festival Welcomes You! a sign said. *Rock the Nineties*! In moments they had breached the tiny town, a blink-and-you'll-miss it green in all the yellow. The bus moved slowly, the street ahead crowded with teens, stalls, police, vehicles. When it came at last to a stop the passengers inside awoke from the lethargy of the journey and once again there was a scramble for the doors. When Avi stepped outside the dry heat squeezed itself around him.

He found his bag and put it on his back. Inbal stood with her two friends from the kibbutz. They were discussing something, he couldn't hear what. None of the girls looked in his direction. He felt momentarily alone, abandoned, before remembering he had set off here on his own, and didn't need anyone, but it still hurt.

Then Inbal called out to him and his heart lifted suddenly. He went to them.

'We're going to find a place to camp,' she said. 'Are you coming?'

'I mean, sure,' Avi said. 'I was going to, anyway.'

'You ever sleep outdoors, Towny?' one of the other girls said. But she was smiling when she said it.

'I'm Tami, this is Roni,' she said.

'Tami and Roni, got it,' Avi said.

He followed a step behind them There was no more hand holding with Inbal. But Avi didn't have time to think about that. He took it all in instead. There were thousands of teens wandering around. Music blared from speakers everywhere. Stalls sold hot dogs and corn. Women from the Black Hebrews wove teenage girls' hair into plaits. A TV journalist stood sweating in the heat with a camera pointed at him. A juggler juggled balls. Avi went past a stand selling mad hatter hats and a stand selling cheap sunglasses and a stand selling glow sticks. He hurried after the girls.

'There you are,' Inbal said. And just like that she took his hand in hers again. Avi saw her friends watch and smirk. But he ignored them. He held Inbal's hand because it felt like the most natural thing in the world to hold hands. And together they walked through the makeshift parade. Avi saw a wall covered in torn posters and someone had spray-painted *Death To Arabs* on it. A skinny guy mixed flour and water in a bucket. He dipped a roller in the homemade glue and passed it over the wall, and then plastered a poster for his band over the graffiti.

'You think this is a notice board?' a man eating a tuna and egg sandwich said, leaning out of a doorway, a little hostile.

The skinny guy pointed at the wall. 'Does this look clean and tidy?' he said. He had a thick Russian accent.

'At least stick a naked woman on there or something,' the guy with the sandwich said. 'Give us something to look at.'

The skinny guy stuck a cigarette between his lips and shrugged. 'No budget,' he said.

He admired his handiwork and lit the cigarette, then noticed Avi staring. 'Five-thirty this afternoon on the green,' he said. 'You should come.'

'What sort of music is it?' Avi said.

'Ambient Hardcore Jazz-Trash,' the skinny guy said.

A second guy, who was carrying the bucket, ambled over.

'It's more experimental funk metal, you know?' he said.

'You guys Russian?' Avi said.

'And you're what, Columbo?' the skinny guy said.

'Come on, Avi,' Inbal said, pulling him after her. 'We need to find a place to sleep.'

'I kind of want to see those guys later,' Avi said.

'We've got tickets for Aviv Geffen later,' Tami said.

'I *love* Aviv Geffen,' Roni said.

'He really articulates the voice of our generation,' Tami said, and nodded, and Avi thought she must have heard someone say that on TV.

'Yeah?' Avi said. 'What's that?'

'What's what?' Tami said.

'What does he articulate?' Avi said.

'The voice,' Roni said, repeating Tami, slowly, like Avi was dense. 'Of our generation.'

'But what is that?' Avi said.

'Don't be an asshole,' Tami said.

Inbal hid a laugh.

'Are you going to Aviv Geffen?' Avi said.

'Of course. Do you have a ticket?' Inbal said.

'No. I have The Tractor's Revenge later,' Avi said. 'But,' he added, 'I could try to swap it. I mean, I don't mind Aviv Geffen, I like "It's Only The Moonlight".'

'Aviv is the best,' Roni said.

'The best,' Avi said. Inbal gave him a sideways glance, trying not to laugh.

'Don't try so hard,' she said. She came close when she said it, he could feel her breath on his cheek. He felt a flutter of excitement in his belly.

'How *am* I doing?' he said, also speaking softly. Their heads were touching, like it was the most normal thing in the world.

'You're doing alright.'

She suddenly darted and gave him a quick kiss on the cheek, then pulled away before he had the time to process. Avi smiled goofily.

An Orthodox man in black heavy clothing and a wide-brimmed felt hat, despite the heat, held his own impromptu stall nearby and spotted Avi.

'You!' he said. 'You put on tefillin? Come do it now, it's a mitzvah.'

He was a Chabadnik, they always stood in public places trying to get people to do it. The man held the leather straps of the tefillin in his hand and a Bible in his other.

'I'm alright,' Avi said.

'Listen,' the man said, 'If I gave you twenty-four shekels, would you give me back two?'

'Well, sure,' Avi said, wary of the question but falling into it all the same. 'Even more, I guess.'

'So doesn't God give you twenty-four hours every day, to live and to breathe?' the man said.

'Alright, yes,' Avi said.

'So would you not give him back just two? One prayer in the morning, one in the evening, is that too much to ask?'

'I guess not,' Avi said.

'Come put these on,' the man said.

Avi went sheepishly.

'When's the last time you put on tefillin?' the man said, 'your bar mitzvah?'

'I guess.'

The man helped him with practice born of long experience, looping the leather on his arm and forehead.

'Repeat after me,' he said. 'Baruch ata adonai…'

Avi escaped with some relief when it was over. The girls from the kibbutz looked at him strangely.

'What?' he said, defensive.

'Guess you're a Towny,' Tamar said, like that explained everything. Which, maybe for her, it did.

'I think it's cute,' Inbal said, and the other girls snorted.

'You just can't say no to those guys,' Avi said. 'I mean… Besides, what's the harm?'

'Don't mind them,' Inbal said, and she put her arm through his. 'Come on, we've got to find a place.'

They walked slowly through the thronging market. The air was so hot and so dry and the sun beat down and the dust settled. A Red Magen David ambulance stood to one side and the paramedics looked bored and offered cold water to the teens walking past, and signs said to beware of heatstroke. A guy in tie-dye pants and dreadlocks spun plates. Under a marquee that said *Story Teller* a man with white hair and white cotton clothes sat cross-legged in front of a group of children, reading from a book. Parents stood watching or sat with their children.

Avi was conscious of Inbal moving beside him, of her arm through his. They came to a grassy area already filled with teens with sleeping bags sitting in groups everywhere. A few trees were planted for shade and Roni and Tami made for this one spot that remained miraculously free. They dropped their bags on the ground with relief and sat down, and Tami opened an army-issued olive-green water canteen and drank, tipping the water directly into her throat without the mouth of the canteen touching her lips. Avi watched, impressed.

'She herds the sheep back home,' Inbal said, explaining.

They put down their bags and sat in the shade. Somewhere nearby a girl with an acoustic guitar played Mashina's 'Goodbye Youth, Hello Love' and Avi thought of Baruch Goldstein, the doctor who murdered twenty-nine Palestinians as they prayed in the Cave of the Patriarchs the previous year. Mashina had written the song the day after the event and referenced it in the lyrics. The girl strummed the strings. Avi hummed along with the song.

Inbal stretched out on the grass, in the shade. She looked at Avi. They knew nothing about each other, he thought. But it didn't matter. He lay on his back on the grass next to her. He could see the clear blue sky through the branches overhead. He felt Inbal's hair on his skin. He turned and looked into her eyes. She looked back, smiling. He thought of the sign that welcomed them into the town.

'Rock the Nineties,' he said.

'The nineties…' Inbal said. She didn't smile now. She looked almost worried. Avi forgot the music, the noise of the carnival going on just out of sight. He looked into Inbal's eyes. He half-turned on his side. So did she. They were so close, almost touching. Inbal closed her eyes. Her face closed on his. Their noses touched.

He kissed her.

Or did she kiss him? He didn't know. Their lips touched lightly, softly. Her lips moved like she was speaking without sound. She put her hand around him and ran it over his scalp and he shivered, and was embarrassed by how hard he suddenly became.

Their kiss lengthened, their lips pressed harder. He felt her tongue dart for just a moment into his mouth and felt a current run through him. He didn't want the moment to end.

Then he heard Tami say, 'Gross!' and Roni said, 'Get a *room*!' and he and Inbal parted from each other, and he was so aware of her breathing and the way her breasts moved under the T-shirt, and of his own painful erection. He lay on his stomach to hide it.

Inbal's hand stayed on his head. She ran her fingers through his short hair.

'I really want to see Mashina,' she said dreamily.

17 July, 1995: Night

As evening fell the heat abated slightly. They abandoned their packs and sleeping bags under the tree and went in search of food. Tami got her hair braided and Roni spent ten shekels at a funfair shooting gallery and won a teddy bear.

Avi and Inbal walked hand in hand. There was no need to talk between them. Once, Avi stopped, thinking about everything that's happened to him, and he said, 'I'm not what you think I am, you know.'

Inbal stopped too. She looked at him very seriously then, and she said, 'I'm not what you think I am, either.'

He didn't know what she meant, but he knew that she meant it. They kissed again then, under some balloons, this time going further, their bodies intertwined, first her tongue and then his darting and meeting, and he stroked the back of her head and felt her press against him, almost rubbing.

Maybe they didn't need words, Avi thought. Maybe this was all that needed to be, right there, right then.

Arad '95, with the sun setting over the desert and Aviv Geffen setting up on stage, somewhere out of sight. Maybe they really were just a fucked-up generation.

He walked her to the concert. A guy was selling tickets in front of the gate.

'One ticket, two hundred!' he said when Avi asked.

'I don't have it,' Avi said.

'Bad luck,' the guy said.

Avi turned to Inbal. 'I'm sorry,' he said.

'What for?'

'I'll wait for you,' Avi said.

'I'll meet you back at the tree, after,' she said. The girls turned to go into the enclosure. Avi stood watching them, wishing he was going in.

Just before they went inside Tami turned back. She went to Avi. He thought she was going to give him her ticket, maybe.

'I don't know you,' Tami said. 'And you seem like a nice enough guy. A bit lost, maybe. But harmless. But I don't know that, so I'm only going to tell you once. We look after each other where we're from, and whatever cute thing Inbal's got going with you is cool, but don't fuck her over or you'll be sorry. You get it?'

'I get it,' Avi said, though it took him a second, he was a little taken aback.

'She's been through a lot,' Tami said. And then she turned back and went in and Avi didn't see them.

He was alone again, but it was nice to be alone. The streetlights had switched on and the festive air continued, and he was free. He didn't know what Tami meant about Inbal. But maybe that was why he and Inbal had that connection, somehow. They'd both been through some stuff.

He could hear Aviv over the walls. He wasn't alone standing there, a lot of people who didn't have tickets came to listen outside the concert.

He would see Inbal later. His heart beat faster at the thought. He walked without aim, just being somebody who had no name in a place that wasn't his home, under a sky that belonged to no one. He bought candy floss from a stand and picked strands of sugar and stuffed them in his mouth. He felt so awake and so alive. He saw the Russian guy from earlier, the one who hung the poster. He was on a makeshift stage on the grass, writhing and singing into a microphone, drums and screaming guitars around him.

'Death to Arabs!' the guy screamed. 'Death to Jews!'

The small crowd around him turned ugly.

'Death… to… God!' the guy screamed.

A punk with a Mohawk haircut jumped on stage. He hit the singer, who staggered back but held on to his guitar. The Mohawk's friends went for the band. The band went for the punks. Bored security guards who milled about took a moment longer before wading into the fray. The singer had blood pouring from his shaved head, and the blood mingled with the Soviet red sickle he had drawn on his scalp with a marker.

It was nothing to Avi. He turned away from the violence. In the night around him more couples hooked up, bodies entwined under the stars, and groups of teens roamed in packs, and the air felt different then, more potent, filled with a dangerous promise. Avi saw three dark shapes conducting a transaction. He thought it was a ticket scalper and went closer but then saw money change hands and then pills. One of the shadows lifted its head and saw him.

'Avi!'

It was Lior Goldin.

'Lior,' Avi said cautiously. 'What are you guys doing here?'

'Working,' Lior said. 'Nu, nu, you got what you wanted, no? Fuck off,' he said to the teen who'd just concluded the transaction with him. The guy, in a striped T-shirt and a beanie hat, nodded slowly and turned with equal slowness and started shambling away to a group of his friends who were waiting for him.

Lior grinned.

'Avile!' he said. 'So, nu? You've become a Moonlight Kid?'

It had to be the Goldins, Avi thought with a sinking heart. Just when he was feeling free for the first time.

'No,' he said. 'I just…' He didn't finish the sentence. Yair stood next to Lior. He looked up at Avi and grunted.

'You want to help us out?' Lior said. 'We're cleaning up, Avi. Be like old times.'

'We can't,' Avi said, 'what if Rubenstein—'

'Do you see fucking Rubenstein?' Lior said. He looked from side to side theatrically. 'We're going to get that fucker one day. In the meantime, you want to make some money or not?'

'Sure,' Avi said. Lior wasn't someone he liked to say no to. 'What are we doing?'

'We're doing this,' Lior said. He opened his palm. Three fat pills, a little smudged with his sweat.

'Exta?' Avi said.

'Sure,' Lior said, but he was grinning, 'something like that. One hundred shekels a pop.'

'That's cheap,' Avi said.

'They're bringing in so much now,' Lior said. 'Supply and demand, you know? We don't really sell like this anymore, we pass it on to other crews, only me and Yair figured we'd come up, check out the music, find some chicks, you know?'

'Sure,' Avi said.

'You get laid yet?' Lior said.

'Working on it,' Avi mumbled.

'Come on, dopey!' Lior said. 'We need you for muscle, not charm. Where are we meeting Shemesh, Yair?'

'City centre,' Yair said.

'Like this shithole even has a centre,' Lior said. 'Here,' he said. He passed Avi a pill. 'Take that. It won't kick in for another hour.'

'I don't know,' Avi said.

'Take it,' Lior said.

So Avi took it.

He didn't like arguing with Lior, either.

He followed the Goldins as they pushed through the crowds. Avi had his ticket for The Tractor's Revenge. But now that he'd met the Goldins he was stuck with them. Maybe he could still make it. It would be nice to have some money, anyway. He didn't have much, not since Rubenstein put an end to Avi's involvement with the Goldins. He had an after-school job offloading crates for the local greengrocer. But that didn't pay very much.

The pill was bitter when he swallowed it. He trudged after the Goldins. They came to a narrow street that had fewer people going through it. Not much there but large industrial bins on both sides of the street, and all overflowing with rubbish from the festival. Avi saw broken sunglasses and expended glow sticks, cigarette butts and crumpled packs, empty Coca Cola bottles, a torn bra, two broken sandals, food wrappers with half eaten hot dogs stained with mustard. Rats the size of kittens scuttled in and out of the bins.

They waited.

'What are we doing here?' Avi said, half whispering.

'Selling this,' Lior said, hefting his school kid backpack in one arm. It had a faded Transformer on it.

Three figures appeared on the far end of the alleyway. A whistle cut through the noise, and Lior stuck two fingers in his mouth and blew a whistle back.

Yair reached for a plank of wood on the floor. Grunted at Avi to do the same.

'Are we expecting trouble?' Avi said. He picked up a plank. It was part of a broken barrier fence like they used for the concerts.

'No trouble,' Lior said. 'No trouble unless there's trouble.'

Avi felt his heart beat fast. His mouth was dry. The shadows coagulated. The giant rats slithered in the rubbish. A rat stood on its hind legs on ledge of the metal bin and looked at Avi with bright curious eyes. It's not so bad here, it seemed to say. It's not so bad here down with the rats.

Avi blinked, the rat vanished. The night went still like a black-and-white photograph. Three figures came slowly along the alley. Avi whispered, 'What did you *give* me?'

'It's a new thing,' Lior said, distracted. 'They make it in a lab in America or somewhere.'

'It's designer,' Yair said. They walked to meet the others and stopped in the middle of the alley.

'You got the drugs?' the guy on the other side said. He was a short fat guy and wore a yarmulke crooked. He was maybe seventeen.

'You got the money?' Lior said.

'What is this, my first minyan?'

'Come on Shemesh, I didn't come here to fuck about, I just came to fuck,' Lior said, and Shemesh grinned.

'Then fuck away, my friend, my town's yours to party in.'

He tossed Lior a brown gym bag. Lior passed it to Avi. Avi opened it. Saw the money. Nodded.

'It's kosher,' Shemesh said. 'So nu?'

Lior tossed him the Transformers school bag. Shemesh opened it, looked impressed and closed it.

'You want some?' he said. 'Before you go?'

'Already took some,' Lior said, and Shemesh grinned.

'Till next time, then, boychiks,' he said.

'See you, Shemesh.'

But Avi's insides were roiling. The air was too still and the night too full of silence. The street lamp at one end of the alley flickered and went out. A rat scuttled past on Avi's left and vanished. A sudden gust of wind came out of nowhere, blowing cigarette butts and discarded concert flyers across the paving.

'I don't like this,' Avi said.

'What's not to like?' Lior said, but then the street lamp at the other end of the alley went out. Now it was dark. Now Avi was scared. Now Avi heard footsteps, running.

'Stop right where you are!' somebody screamed. 'Police, stop right where you are!'

'Like fuck!' Shemesh said. And he pulled out a gun.

'He's got a gun!' Avi shouted.

The approaching shadows on both sides of the alley slowed down.

'We've got guns, too!'

'Everybody gets a gun!' Shemesh screamed. He lifted his in the air and fired. It made a loud popping sound and then another and another: it was a cap gun.

Shemesh roared with laughter. Avi thought he must have already been high.

'Shemesh, get on the ground!' the police voice said.

'You won't take me alive, coppers!' Then Shemesh tossed something else at the cops and they fell back. When it exploded, thick smoke came pouring out: somehow, Shemesh had got hold of a real smoke grenade.

'Run!'

Avi moved blindly. His eyes stung. He was conscious of Lior and Yair somewhere to his right, of cops moving in the smoke, nightsticks raised; heard Shemesh grunt as he was hit, heard the big guy fall. His two teenage associates jumped the cops. Avi just wanted to get out of there. He burst through the shield of bodies and the smoke and ran, he just ran, and only when he couldn't go anymore and his lungs burned too hard did he stop.

He didn't know where he was.

He didn't see Lior.

He threw up on the ground, hands on his knees, the remains of his falafel lunch and his hot dog dinner and a Coke running down his chin and onto the dirt.

Somewhere in the distance, snatches of music, and for just one moment ten thousand voices or more rose together in song, and they must have been the audience in the Aviv Geffen concert, and one of those voices was Inbal's, calling to him, singing 'Growing Lost'. Avi threw up until he had nothing left inside him. Then he staggered in place, blinking, and realised he still had the bag with the money.

He started to laugh. Tiny lights danced at the edge of his vision. Where *was* everyone? Why was it dark, why was he alone? The crowd in the distance sang about love and Avi whispered, 'I love you, I do,' as though something had been suddenly decided. He felt better now, so much better. He started making out the things around him. Unmoving shapes. What were they? An angel with its wings outstretched. A ballerina frozen in mid-dance. A dozen butterflies as large as fists suspended in flight around a flower as tall as a child.

Where *was* he?

Somewhere beyond the dark the festival continued and music played. Here in this garden of statues the music died and the light did not penetrate. He picked his way carefully across the silent figures.

Two trees stood in the heart of that garden and he went to them. They were laden with fruit. He did not know what fruit these were or who had planted the trees. He wanted to clear the foul taste in his mouth and so unthinkingly reached for one of the trees.

A coiled thing on the branch moved and two bright eyes opened and a forked tongue hissed at him. Avi jumped back. The snake slithered on the branch.

'I wouldn't do that,' it said. 'If I were you. One gives you life and the other knowledge, and you're too young to need either one just yet.'

'You're a snake,' Avi said.

'No shit,' the snake said.

They regarded each other uncertainly.

'I think you're tripping,' the snake said at last.

'I think you must be right,' Avi said.

He looked longingly at the fruit. It looked so tempting, just sitting there.

'Are you really here?' he asked the snake.

But of course there was no one there.

He wasn't sure, later, how long he'd sat there. At some point he thought he saw his father, walking through smoke. A man in the old police uniform, with insignia on his chest, and a large black moustache and lively eyes.

Something had caught in Avi's heart and squeezed.

'Aba?' he said. 'Aba!'

The man in the smoke looked this way and that, as though searching for the source of the sound.

'Listen, Cohen,' he said. 'I told you not to bother me again. What?' He cocked his head, listening. 'All we do is hold the line,' he said. 'Watch out for my boy if I am gone.'

He turned to somewhere unseen and began walking away, growing smaller. Avi stared as Inspector Sagi vanished from sight.

'Aba, wait!' he cried. 'Aba!'

The smoke thickened around him.

'They never stick around for very long, you know,' the snake said.

'The dead?' Avi said.

'Fathers.'

He heard the snake hiss laughter, then it was gone again.

When the smoke in his mind began to clear, Avi found himself sitting with his back to an old fence. The statues were all around him. He heard a gate open and close. A man came through, and he brought forth a flaming sword and swished it this way and that, though in another part of Avi's mind he knew it was just a flashlight. In that light Avi saw an old Great Priest of Israel, a

Cohen, with a face weather-worn but formidable still. The man saw him.

'There you are,' he said. 'I was looking for you. You took something you shouldn't have.'

Avi's voice caught and the wise old priest reached down to him with his arm extended. Avi tried to take his hand but the wise old priest reached instead for the brown gym bag and took it.

The man sat on a rock and opened the bag. He rifled through money.

'You did good,' he said. 'I'll take that.'

'But the Goldins,' Avi said.

'I'll sort those little fuckers out,' the man said. He looked at Avi thoughtfully. Avi had seen him before, he realised. He was the third man on the sofa the night Shai Goldin had his legs broken by Rubenstein.

'"Cursed is the land for you",' the Cohen said, '"in sadness shall you feed upon it all of your days. And thistles and thorns it shall grow for you".'

'Genesis,' Avi mumbled. 'God, speaking to Adam.' He looked up at the wise old priest.

'Are you real?' he said.

The man considered the question carefully.

'In every time and in every place,' he said, 'there must be someone to speak for the soul of their nation.' He stared into his hands. 'You're just having a bad trip,' he said. 'It will wear off soon. I'll see you, Avi.'

The priest vanished into the dark. Avi was left alone.

A snake slithered nearby.

'I prefer Where's The Kid to the Elders Of Safed,' it said conversationally.

'I think most people do,' Avi said.

The snake stared at him with its bright eyes.

'If you just keep sitting here,' it said, 'how are you ever going to get the girl?'

Avi blinked. The snake vanished.

Inbal!

He could no longer hear the Aviv Geffen concert, had not heard it in hours. How long had he been there? Avi looked around him, and saw that where he stood was just a small park filled with some local artist's metal sculptures. The thing he had taken for a snake was a rubber hose connected to a tap.

He looked, but the bag with the money was gone.

He got up to his feet. His mouth was dry. He opened the gate and ran outside. Sound and light came back, the crowds thinner but the stalls still open. It was only a short run back to the green. Avi looked for the tree, trying to make out features in the relative dark.

'Inbal!' he said.

'Avi!' she clung to him. Her cheek was wet against his. He realised with surprise she had been crying.

'What happened?' he said.

'Our stuff got stolen,' Tami said, behind him.

'We came out of the concert,' Inbal said, 'and there were these awful guys and they kept calling to me, to us, and we tried to ignore them and then, and then…' She held on to him tightly, her arms around his neck. 'We ran and found a policeman and then they went away. But when we got here all our stuff was gone. Yours too.'

'It's OK,' Avi said. He stroked the low of her back. He felt so protective just then. He wanted to hold her in his arms forever and make sure nothing bad ever happened to her from now on. He also realised he was extremely hard again.

'It's just stuff,' he said.

'But what are we going to do?' Inbal said.

'We'll sleep under the stars,' Avi said, and it must have been ridiculous, the way he said it, because Inbal started to laugh. She laughed into his neck, snorting in a way that took him by surprise, and then she raised her head to him and kissed him, fiercely, on the lips.

18 July, 1995: Day

Dawn found them entwined each in the other's arms. They lay together into the small hours of the night, talking softly and kissing and feeling each other's closeness. At last they dozed off, together, then a great big sleep came and washed over Avi.

When he opened his eyes only a few hours must have passed but he felt good, refreshed.

The sun peered down through the branches. Inbal stirred, smiled, snuggled into him.

'Good morning,' Avi said tenderly.

'Good morning…'

Tami and Roni lay nearby. Avi saw with some surprise they were also each in the other's arms.

'Tami snores,' he said.

Inbal laughed. 'She does,' she said. 'The three of us shared a room together since kindergarten. I always tried to fall asleep before she did.'

'You sleep three in a room?' Avi said.

'Four,' Inbal said. 'But we're older now so we get one room between two of us.'

'Who do you share with?' Avi said.

'Relax!' Inbal said. 'It's a girl called Einat, she likes horses and poetry books and she has an older boyfriend who drives a tractor.'

'That's a big thing, right? Driving a tractor?' Avi said.

'Huge,' Inbal said. 'Don't laugh! If you have a tractor license on the kibbutz you're like… You're everything. Oh! Did you get to see The Tractor's Revenge last night?'

'No,' Avi said.

'How come? And where were you, anyway?'

'I met some friends from back home,' Avi said. He didn't want to talk about it. Already the night before was fading in his mind. There had been a… snake? And thick smoke, and a priestly man who took the Goldins' money. This much at least he didn't dream.

'We need to find a bathroom,' he said. 'And some toothpaste.'

Inbal kissed him, her tongue darting into his mouth. She pulled back laughing when Avi enthusiastically responded.

'You're right,' she said. 'We need toothpaste.'

They left Tami and Roni to sleep and went in search of a sink.

There were mobile bathrooms set up and taps outside. Inbal bummed a tube of toothpaste off a girl and she and Avi washed their hands and faces and brushed their teeth with their fingers and some paste.

'This is romantic,' Inbal said.

They laughed. Inbal gave the toothpaste back and they walked off, hand in hand, searching for breakfast. The eighteenth of July, 1995. The height of summer. It was such a normal day.

They passed a faded election poster on the wall outside a barber shop. Yitzhak Rabin, his face peeling off. *Israel Waits For Rabin*, the poster said. Avi stared.

Somewhere in Oslo, teams of Israelis and Palestinians were negotiating lasting peace. Rabin was all but ready to sign later in the autumn, just like he made peace with Jordan the year before. Who would have thought Rabin of all people would be the one to make peace. Rabin, who was the head of the army that occupied the West Bank and Gaza and the Golan Heights. Rabin, who was prime minister when the settlements began to expand across the territories. Rabin who kept a foreign bank account stuffed with dollars, Rabin who was always rumoured to be a drunk, Rabin who headed the Security Ministry during the Intifada, who ordered mass imprisonment and houses destroyed and said to break the Arabs' hands and legs, a comment some of the soldiers took literally.

Avi knew all this, vaguely. Mr Moritz from the grocery store where he worked after school always ranted about Rabin.

'Someone should put a bullet to him,' he said.

And yet it was Rabin making peace. It was Rabin promising Avi and Inbal and all the Moonlight Kids a new and different future.

Go figure, Avi thought.

'What are you staring at?' Inbal said.

Avi shook his head.

'Nothing,' he said.

They got milky coffee and cheese sandwiches at the market, and saw Merav Michaeli from Galgalatz in a short sleeveless black top leave the radio booth and get herself a coffee. She came right up close and Inbal elbowed Avi. He never met anyone famous before either.

'Merav, are you going to the Mashina show tonight?' Inbal said.

Michaeli turned, stirrer in hand.

'Are you kidding?' she said. 'Their last ever show? I have to go, just to say I've been there.'

Inbal and Avi took their coffees. They sat in the shade of a palm tree and listened to a street musician belting out Mashina covers and talked about the future each of them wanted to have, and which was just ahead and out of sight.

18 July, 1995: Night

There was a different air to the night. A wild mood had taken hold of them. Avi and Inbal went to the Mashina concert. Thin metal walls enclosed the makeshift arena. Security guards stood in front of the only gates, allowing people in through narrow fenced-in columns. Avi could hear the music from inside. Tipex warming up the crowd. Mashina haven't even arrived yet.

There were thousands of them trying to get into the concert. A sea of people, and Avi held Inbal's hand tightly in his own. From time to time a police officer tried in vain to push back the crowds, but there was too much crowd and barely any police.

'Get back!' someone shouted through a megaphone. 'Get back!'

'We're here to see Mashina!' someone screamed from the crowd.

Someone pushed Avi and he stumbled. Bodies pressed all around him.

'I think we should get out,' he said to Inbal. She held on to his hand. They were near the metal walls. They could hear Tipex inside. There was no way to the gates. Avi tried to push against the bodies behind them. Realised there was no way back.

The human tide carried them with it. The man on the megaphone gave up shouting. The speakers inside belted out Kobi Oz's voice. Avi didn't even like Tipex. He wasn't here for Tipex. No one was here for Tipex. He looked up at the walls. They were topped with barbed wire. *Why* were they topped with barbed wire? He knew it was to stop people from trying to get into the concert without paying, but still – it suddenly seemed like a really bad idea.

They lost Tami and Roni somewhere in the crowd. Inbal was pressed against him, her hand sweaty in his. The mood felt ugly.

He didn't know any of the kids around him. There were so many. He tried to look over their heads, to find a way out, but all he could see was a sea of children, a sea of children with no end in sight.

He pressed against the thin metal walls. The metal was hot. He held Inbal in his arms. He could feel her heart beat fast against his skin. She felt hot to the touch.

'I don't want to see Mashina anymore,' Inbal said. 'I just want to go home.'

'We'll go home,' Avi said. The bodies pressed against them, pushing him against the wall.

'Watch it!' he shouted.

But no one could hear him or, if they could, they could do nothing to help. The pressure built. Avi's face pressed against the wall, the weight of all the people behind them pushing, pushing…

He felt the wall *move*.

Inbal screamed.

It was so hot and the bodies pressed and pressed against them, some kid with dyed blue hair and a girl in a *Peace Now* T-shirt, and some guy with a nose ring, pushed Avi and Inbal, pushing, pushing—

The wall, with a groan of metal, toppled and took them down with it.

'Avi!' Inbal screamed. 'Avi!'

The thin wall fell and they fell down with it. The barbed wire came down. There were people on the other side. Avi and Inbal slipped down the metal, slid towards the wires. He saw the concert, suddenly and all at once. Thousands of teens packed tight into the enclosure, the stage impossibly small in the distance, Kobi Oz's tinny voice coming out of the speakers.

He heard screams.

The press of bodies came behind them. Avi tried to rise and couldn't. People fell on him, pushed against him, a herd in panic trying to escape in every direction. He felt Inbal slip away. A foot landed on his head, a leg kicked him in the ribs, more footsteps came, more bodies piling, he held on to Inbal's hand for dear life but their grip was weakening, the coils of barbed wire were suddenly *there*, his hand caught, he screamed in the pain, he heard

Inbal's shriek as it caught in her hair. He tried to pull her, they had to get up, but the bodies that pressed on them came from all sides, those trying to get in, those trying to get out.

Everything after that was cut to shreds in Avi's mind. Ambulance lights, flashing. The cry of a siren somewhere in the distance. Pain, blood. Someone came on stage and cut the music.

'Why are you still singing? There are kids getting hurt out there!'

He was buried under a sea and the sea was moving, relentless, and could not be parted. He lost consciousness for a while. When he opened his eyes the lights hurt. There was no more music. There were still thousands of people there, just standing now, confused. No one knew what to do. Avi crawled, looking for Inbal.

There were medics somewhere. Police. But they were far away. He saw someone on the ground nearby. Inbal. He crawled to her. She lay on her back. Her eyes were closed. Her clothes were torn and she had lost a shoe and there was barbed wire woven in her hair.

He thought his leg was broken. He pulled himself across the ground to her.

'Medic!' Avi screamed. 'Medic!'

'They're coming,' he heard someone say. There were kids on the ground everywhere. Some didn't move. He pulled himself to Inbal. Put his head on her chest and felt a tiny breath, and he started to cry then.

'Medic!' Avi screamed. 'Medic!'

'They're coming,' he heard someone say.

There was no more music. He closed his eyes. He listened to her faint, faint breath.

Goodbye youth, hello love, Mashina sang, but only in his head. He felt hands turning him, someone said, 'They're still alive.'

He blinked. Blurry faces above him.

Felt them try to move him but he held on, he held on to Inbal.

'Calm down,' he heard someone say. 'It's going to be alright.'

He felt a touch of something cold and sharp on his arm.

Avi went slack.
They took Inbal. He didn't see her.
They put him on a stretcher.
He swore he could see the Mashina tour bus going past.
Avi closed his eyes. The voices sang, but only in his mind.
Rock the nineties, rock the nineties, rock the nineties.

PART SIXTEEN

'THREE SHOTS FROM A VERY CLOSE RANGE'

1995, Kings of Israel Square

72

ESKIMO LIMON

'Do you want to cry?' – Yair

They were in the Goldin house to watch Eskimo Limon on Channel 2. Shai in the wheelchair chain-smoking cigarettes. Avi with his barbed wire scars. His broken leg had healed since the summer. Yair and Lior shelling sunflower seeds.

Even little Natasha sat with them.

In the movie, three guys stole empty bottles from the corner shop. Then they went inside to get the deposit on the bottles back from the shopkeeper. A pretty girl came in. She wanted to buy half a loaf of bread but the shopkeeper only sold whole loaves. The main guy said he also needed half a loaf of bread, so the shopkeeper cut the pretty girl a half-loaf and the main guy ran after her to try and chat her up.

Avi was sort of getting into the movie at that point. It was not a good movie. But it pulled you in.

Then the movie cut off.

A panicked newsreader appeared.

'Ofer, talk to me on the earpiece, please,' he said. 'Ofer, talk to me on the earpiece.'

He turned to someone else off screen. 'Tell Ofer to talk to me on the earpiece,' he said.

He cut off, and was replaced with strange promo animation of a transformer robot. The robot fired bolts of energy from its gun.

When the newsreader reappeared he looked even more uncomfortable in his suit.

'Good evening,' he said, 'we have a special news report, following an assassination attempt, about an hour ago, on the life of Prime Minister Yitzhak Rabin—'

He vanished from the screen but continued to talk. Images flashed of Rabin, smiling, shaking hands on stage, a huge crowd of people assembled in the Kings of Israel Square in Tel Aviv. Blue and white balloons, the crowd singing, 'A Song For Peace'—

'Talk to the microphone, Guy,' someone said off screen, 'into the microphone.'

Rabin with his wife, Rabin smiling.

'He was hit with three shots, he has been rushed to hospital, his condition is not known to us, not known to us—'

They all just stared at the screen.

A cloud of police officers pushing the suspect to the wall.

'The suspect in the middle there, in a blue shirt—'

'How many shots?' someone off screen said.

'Three shots, from a very close range, Mr Rabin collapsed, witnesses say—'

Natasha started to cry.

'The mass demonstration for peace which called for a stop to violence, to say No To Violence—'

Confused police officers in the car park.

The phone rang in the room. No one answered it. Avi felt numb.

Shai said, 'He's dead.'

The phone rang and rang.

'How do you know?' Avi said.

Shai said, 'He's dead, Avi.'

The television cut to a reporter in the hospital.

'Mr Rabin is on the operating table—'

'Dead,' Shai Goldin said; and no one argued with him.

Avi wasn't sure who suggested going there. Natasha had fallen asleep on the sofa, her face smudged with tears. Shai's ashtray overflowed with half-smoked cigarettes. Avi's throat felt raw from the smoke.

They got in the car. Yair drove. They drove into Tel Aviv and saw a city in shock. People walked around in a daze. Police were out in numbers. They parked their car and walked the rest of the way. Avi didn't know what they would find. He didn't expect the crying teenagers and the candles.

They filled the square. Blue and white balloons drifted over piles of rubbish, discarded flags, banners for Labour and Peace Now. Posters for Aviv Geffen, who had played the stage earlier. The kids sat around in groups, crying. Avi didn't know where they all came from. Maybe, like him and the Goldins, they just all got up and came there on impulse.

Remembrance candles burned on the ground. The girls mostly sat. The boys stood, as though guarding them from some awful, invisible enemy. Police officers walked aimlessly, looking as lost as the teens.

'So what do you want to do?' Yair said. 'Do you want to cry?'

'I want to make someone cry,' Lior said.

'Yeah,' Avi said.

Yair smiled.

'Then let's find someone,' he said.

They walked in the night. Dawn was not yet on the horizon. The city that never slept waited, anxious. They saw an Orthodox Jew in black clothing walk hurriedly down a side street.

'Let's get him,' Lior said.

They went after him. Saw a group coming their way, the man in black caught between them. He turned down an alley and vanished.

'What you fuckers looking at?' a guy from the other group said.

'Looking at you, ya manyak,' Lior said.

Avi gripped the metal bar he'd picked up in the square. He felt an ugly rush of glee.

'Yeah?' the other guy said. 'What are you going to do about it?'

Avi didn't even know who they were. They could have been anybody.

It really didn't matter anymore.

'We're going to do this,' he said.

He raised the metal bar. He took a run and a swing at the guy from the other gang. The bar hit true. The other kid fell to his knees, blood gushing down the side of his head.

Avi laughed.

'We'll fuck you up!' he screamed. 'We'll fuck you up!'

Then they were on him, fists and kicks. Then Lior was by his side, the knuckledusters he bought from the mall on his hands. He smashed a guy's face in. Someone broke a bottle on Lior's head. Yair waded in, not speaking, grunting, using only his fists.

Avi lost the metal bar, picked up a brick.

He watched for just a moment from the side. They were just kids, just taking it out on each other. But they weren't going to stay kids anymore. He lifted the brick.

He went charging back into the fight, screaming wild joy.

PART SEVENTEEN

ROOM 816

2001, Jerusalem

73

UNFINISHED BUSINESS

'They have their ways, as we have ours' – *Cohen*

The call came at seven in the morning.

Sylvie was already up. The passing years saw her wake earlier, the sleep she had was filled with the uneasy dead. She'd started with a gossip column. Sometimes she wished she'd stayed. She remembered the shelling of Beirut and being groped by ministers and politicians, the dead girls on the old coast road and the murder of Mela Malevsky, the Tel Aviv Strangler and reporting on the gang wars of the nineties. She remembered Arik sparking off the second Intifada. Remembered Rabin with those bullets in his back. The dead kids in Arad, the day the music died. Billionaires and mercenaries, whores and wars. Sometimes she wished she could scrub it all clean.

All the stories that she wrote were so specific, of their time, their place. They were uniquely Israeli. And only later, when she looked at the yellowing clippings, did she see they could have happened anywhere.

'The Hyatt,' Cohen said. She knew it was him on the line. 'But you'd have to come now.'

She was already dressed. She had waited for some kind of call. The second Intifada, the daily news cycle, dead kids in Gaza and suicide bombs in Tel Aviv and Mir breaking down in the atmosphere as it fell down from orbit.

She took her notebook. She went out.

'What is it?' she'd asked Cohen.

He said, 'Old, unfinished business.'

There were police cars parked outside the hotel. She showed her ID and was allowed inside.

Police comforted an elderly woman in the dining room. Sylvie knew her face. Cohen came to meet Sylvie. A medical team departing. Someone in civilian clothes who must have been Internal Security cupped a cigarette under a No Smoking sign.

They came to room 816.

The door was ajar. More police outside, the medical examiner. Cohen nodded. Sylvie followed him in.

Zrubavel 'Genghis' Ha'navi lay on the floor. It was hard to tell it was him at first. One bullet hit his jaw. The other penetrated the skull and entered the brain. Genghis lay prone. He looked peaceful in death.

'Who did it?' Sylvie said.

She wanted to look away, but couldn't.

She had hated Genghis for so many years, for what he did, for what he stood for.

He'd never be convicted for the rapes now. For trying to kill her. For his organised crime links. For those Bedouins he murdered. For intimidating journalists. For the incitement, the racism, for who knew what more that would never be revealed now. He was dead now, and his crimes would be forgotten and forgiven, and he would be memorialised and celebrated as a great general and politician. They would name bridges in his honour.

She should have been happy, or angry, or *something*.

But now he was dead she realised she felt nothing at all.

'The Popular Front,' Cohen said. 'We think.'

'How?'

'They knew where he was staying,' Cohen said. 'We think they booked a room using a false ID. Then they waited overnight. Genghis went down for breakfast early with his wife this morning.'

'He didn't have security?' Sylvie said.

'He didn't believe in it,' Cohen said. 'As I said, he had breakfast with his wife, then took the lift up to the eighth floor alone. At that point we think they came out and shot him in the corridor. He stumbled into the room and they finished the job.'

'Why did you call me?' Sylvie said.

'I thought you should see it,' Cohen said.

'Did you catch them?' Sylvie said. 'The assassins?'

'Yes. They're being interrogated.'

'How would they know where he was? How would they have his room number?'

And she thought of the phone call of the day before, when Cohen told her to come up to Jerusalem. Almost like he knew.

Cohen shrugged.

'They have their ways,' he said. 'As we have ours.'

'Why the Popular Front?' Sylvie said.

Cohen said, 'You know, I arrested one of them once. It was a long time ago. During Lebanon, some time. He was just a small fish then, so I let him go. Guy called Rimawi. Guess he's not such a small fish anymore.'

Sylvie felt sick.

'You arrested him?'

'He was part of the assassination team. Maybe the leader.'

'Funny, that,' Sylvie said.

Cohen shrugged again.

'These things happen,' he said.

Sylvie looked at the corpse. The Minister for Tourism. Palestinians had never assassinated a minister before. There'd be military reprisals. The usual. Then the whole cycle of violence would start again.

Not that it ever stopped.

Sometimes she got so tired of it all.

Someone stuck their head in through the door.

'Cohen, the reporters are outside.'

'Already?' Cohen said. 'You better take him out the back.'

Sylvie stole one last glance at the corpse. She felt nothing but sadness now. Who for, she didn't even know.

'Like the trash,' she said.

'Yes,' Cohen said. 'Just like the trash.'

PART EIGHTEEN

DEATH IN CANCÚN

2008, Mexico

74

INDEPENDENCE DAY

'Fashioning a new nation demands sacrifice' – *Cohen*

The sun shone and the sea was warm and palm trees shook gently in the breeze. Avi sat on a lounger by the pool and drank mezcal. He was getting a nice buzz going.

Girls in bikinis walked on the beach. American college kids, down to party. When Avi first arrived in Cancún he was dazzled by it all, the carefree way the American tourists who thronged the beaches had about them. You could tell an American by the way they walked. Like they owned the place. Like they owned everything. There were cops in Cancún just like there were cops everywhere. But they were there to make sure everything was clean, and they didn't give two shits for Israelis unless they dropped bodies, which Avi tried not to do anymore.

The sun was strong. He'd been working on his tan. Later he'd get up, pick up some lunch from the stalls outside. Take a nap in the apartment, maybe. When he first got here he'd wanted to party every night, just celebrate being free, being alive. It wore on him after a while. Now he was just as happy catching anything in English on the TV.

'Order me another drink, Avi,' Astrid said, slightly slurring her words.

'I'll order you a burger,' Avi said. Cancún catered to Americans. You could always get a burger.

'I don't *want* a burger,' Astrid said, with that slow dedication of a drunk attending to their words. 'I *want* another drink.'

Avi signalled to the waiter. He'd tipped him to know what he wanted in advance. The waiter vanished and returned with another margarita for the lady.

'Was that so hard?' Astrid said. She lay face down on her lounger and didn't look up. The waiter placed the salt-rimmed glass on the floor beside her.

'Gracias, Alejandro,' Astrid murmured.

Avi met Astrid a couple of months back at a party in the city, off the tourist strip. The party was held by an associate of Avi's, Doña Lucía, an ex-policewoman who recruited former army and police officers and started her own Cártel de Cancún because, as she told Avi one time, 'Why should the criminals get all the money?'

Astrid was there with some Swedish trafficker. The Swedish trafficker's body was found by the side of a road a few weeks later, the result of some unavoidable dispute, but that didn't seem to faze Astrid. Nothing much did.

'He was just a banker, really, you see,' she told Avi, shortly after they first hooked up. She shrugged. 'But he was good looking.'

The Swedes were there to buy drugs. So were the Bulgarians, the Russians, the Dutch, the English, the Lebanese, the Israelis. Cancún welcomed everyone. It had welcomed Avi when he fled there. After the arrest in Israel he had agreed to turn state evidence. When they released him home he hopped a plane in Ben Gurion on a false passport and didn't look back. There was nothing to go back to, anyway. He was wanted for criminal association and for murder, for one thing. Benny had him shoot a guy called Ofer Gafni while Gafni was in hospital. Gafni was a low-level enforcer for a crew from up north. Avi never even figured out why Benny wanted him gone but Benny wanted him gone so Avi did the job. Avi had easy access to the room on account of being a policeman, and it *was* an easy job, all in all, but he'd missed a camera so that was that.

And Rubenstein, who survived almost four decades at the top and every hit somebody put on him, was finally done in by the Americans, of all people. Their Department of Justice indicted him for conspiracy to distribute ecstasy and he was extradited to the US to wear an orange prison jumpsuit.

From a distance it all looked so petty. With a couple more shots of mezcal and a fresh cigarette he could almost be nostalgic for it. Over there it went on as it always did. They built a giant wall along the West Bank, and another one to close Gaza in.

There was a second, shorter war in Lebanon.

Ninette won the first season of *A Star Is Born* and became a huge star. Avi liked her songs. No one listened to those old rock bands anymore, the ones Avi used to like, but he didn't really miss them. Mashina reformed and went back to performing, but no one cared by that point. They were just old men singing old songs on stage.

Cancún was alright. You could even get a taste of home. Somehow, you could get kubbeh everywhere from the street vendors, deep-fried balls of meat in crust, just like Lior's mum used to make them. And the other week he and Lior even went to Shabbat dinner in Chabad House, where the Rebbetzin made chicken soup with kneidlach, just like it should be.

His phone rang. Avi reached for the mobile, took another shot of mezcal, answered.

'Yeah?'

'Are you coming tonight?' Lior said.

Lior followed Avi into exile about a year back. He kept insisting it was temporary. The prosecution had a state witness against Lior for murder, so he left the country for a while and came to Cancún. He was going to go back just as soon as the witness vanished. Avi had no doubt the witness was, sooner or later, going to disappear. Meanwhile he was stuck with Lior.

They shared an apartment in the complex together. Lior had his own thing going in Cancún. He made friends with guys from Los Zetas in the Gulf Cartel and still ran his business back home and in Europe. With Rubenstein in prison there were opportunities for expansion. And cocaine was back on the menu in a big way. So Lior did alright.

'I don't know,' Avi said. 'I don't know that I feel like it.'

'Come on, Avi,' Lior said. 'It's Independence Day! Everyone's going to be there. Dudu Topaz is even coming to perform, they flew him over specially.'

Independence Day. The local Israelis all got together, rabbis and gangsters, tourists and restaurant keepers. They hired a venue and decked it out in blue and white flags. They tried to get Ninette but only got Dudu Topaz. There'd be cotton candy and falafel.

Avi couldn't imagine anything worse.

'Maybe,' he said.

'Pussy,' Lior said. He hung up.

In truth, they barely saw each other these days. The flat was spacious and their times erratic. And Avi spent more and more time with Astrid at her place.

She was fast asleep now, and snoring. Astrid took to siestas while Avi had never liked them, back in Israel had had detested that time between two and four where the shops closed and the adults came out and shouted at you if you played ball outside.

'Fuck it,' Avi said. That last shot of mezcal did the job and he felt light-headed and ready to do something other than sit by the fucking pool.

'I'm going, Astrid,' he said.

'Mmmf,' Astrid said.

She farted gently. Avi got up, got changed and left. He told the taxi driver outside to take him to Doña Lucía's place.

Like the police, most of the taxi drivers worked for Doña Lucía. Beyond the tourist strip the city became just another town, housing blocks holding the residents who worked as cleaners and waiters and drivers for the Americans. The Americans loved drugs so everyone sold them drugs, and just about every cartel had a presence in the city, which kept the local police ineptly busy, what with all the dead bodies that kept popping up.

Doña Lucía had the backing of Sinaloa, though, so she wasn't going to take any shit from the Gulf or anyone else. In a short time she'd made this her town. The driver pulled right up to her mansion. Armed men stood on guard. They patted Avi down, then let him in.

'Avi,' Doña Lucía said. She was having a sandwich in the kitchen. 'You want some?'

'I'm good, thanks.'

'Eat,' Doña Lucía said. So Avi picked at the food.

'I've got everything set up for tomorrow with the Irish,' Avi said.

'Good, good.'

'And the Nigerians want an answer,' Avi said.

Doña Lucía made a face.

'They're good guys,' Avi said.

He mostly made a living nowadays being a go-between. It was an arrangement that worked for everyone. Avi liked being useful.

'Fine,' Doña Lucía said, 'you arrange it, then.'

'Alright.'

'Listen, Avi,' Doña Lucía said.

'Yeah?'

She came closer, put her hand on his shoulder.

'You look after yourself, OK?'

'OK,' Avi said, taken aback.

Doña Lucía nodded.

'And go easy on the booze,' she said.

When he left one of Doña Lucía's men passed him an envelope with his fee from the last deal. Avi thought maybe he'd take Astrid out, somewhere fancy, not too touristy, not too local. Somewhere with tablecloths and a view and wine that came from a wine menu. Somewhere that didn't serve hamburgers, anyway.

He had a vague sense of unease after seeing Doña Lucía. People didn't tell you to look after yourself unless they meant you needed to. He got another taxi, to the other side of town, to a small garage that mostly fixed broken scooters. Avi had bought the place a year or so back when the garage was going out of business. Miguel, the manager, looked pleased to see him.

'Coffee, Avi?' he said.

'Thanks, Miguel.'

There was a safe in the office. Avi had it installed when he first took over the place. He waited for Miguel to leave. He opened the safe.

It wasn't smart to be a foreigner with a gun in Mexico. Which is why Avi kept the Glock in the safe. He took it out now, made sure it was loaded.

'Thanks for the coffee, Miguel.'

'See you, Avi.'

He got another taxi. He felt better with the gun. He'd bring it back if it amounted to nothing. There was a black SUV behind the taxi. Avi watched it in the rear-view mirror. He said, 'Take a left here.'

The driver obeyed. The black car swung left behind them.

'Take a right.'

The black SUV continued on the road and vanished. Avi felt the tension in his stomach release, just a little. It was nothing. It was probably nothing.

He got back to the strip without incident. In the bright sunlight and the familiar comfort of the tourist stretch he felt foolish. He had a good thing going here.

His phone rang.

'Yes, Lior?'

'You coming tonight?'

Being exiles together made them sort of friends again. Avi never asked about Natasha. Last he heard she'd released a single and was going on a reality show. Everybody had to make a living.

'Maybe.'

'I'll save you a seat.'

Lior hung up. Lior was like this, married to his phone. If he wasn't running business back home or in Amsterdam or wherever he was phoning Avi five times a day.

When he got back to the complex Astrid was gone from the pool. Avi took the lift upstairs. The apartment felt cool after the heat outside. He stripped and showered, knocked back mezcal. He lay down naked on the bed and slept.

When he woke it was early evening and the apartment felt less empty than deserted. Avi put on boxer shorts, sat on the side of the bed and flicked through channels on the television. News in Spanish, a telenovela, CNN. No news from back home. He switched on the television, reached for his laptop, let his arm drop.

The telephone rang.

It was the landline phone plugged in at the wall, not the mobile. It rang a few times until Avi picked it up.

'Hello?' he said.

'Avi.'

He knew the voice immediately, almost intimately.

'Cohen,' he said.

'How have you been?' Cohen said.

Avi could hear sounds in the background, on the phone. People talking, the sound of explosions.

'What's that noise?' he said.

'Fireworks,' Cohen said. 'It's Independence Day.'

'What do you want, Cohen? How did you get my number?'

'You were a good soldier, Avi,' Cohen said. 'I wanted you to know that. I wanted you to know it wasn't your fault. Fashioning a new nation demands sacrifice. That's all.'

'How is your granddaughter?' Avi said. Hating himself. Hating Cohen.

'She is very well,' Cohen said. 'Thank you.'

Avi thought he heard the door open softly. He turned to look but the apartment was quiet. He looked out at the sunset. It was so beautiful here, in Cancun.

He felt the gun press against his head. He didn't move.

'Why, Cohen?' he said.

'It was coming, Avi,' Cohen said. 'It was coming for a long time.'

Avi closed his eyes.

The gun went *pop, pop*.

Then silence.

Someone replaced the receiver gently back on the phone.

Cohen looked out at the fireworks through the window. He placed the receiver gently back on the phone. The family had decorated the walls with flags and balloons, and there were birthday cards from the grandkids on the table. He still preferred to celebrate the Hebrew date, not the Latin one every year.

There was cake on the table. He remembered a time when there was no cake on his birthday, and now there was cake.

The sky above Tel Aviv burst with coloured lights as rockets shot into the air all over the city.

'Granddad, I'm scared!' Elinor said. She ran to him and jumped onto his lap.

Cohen held her in a hug.

'Don't be scared,' he said. 'This is a celebration.'

He held her on his lap and together they watched the fireworks. She was warm and alive in his arms, his granddaughter: and he marvelled at how perfect she was in every way, the flesh of his flesh, the blood of his blood.

'I love this country,' Cohen said.